Sign up for our newsletter to hear about new and upcoming releases.

www.ylva-publishing.com

OTHER BOOKS BY
A.L. BROOKS

Miles Apart
Dark Horse
The Club

Up on the Roof

A.L. Brooks

ACKNOWLEDGEMENTS

First, as always, a massive thank you to the lovely publishing team at Ylva—Astrid, Daniela, and Andrea for their tireless work; Lee for an awesome editing experience; and Amanda and Paulette for copy-editing and proofreading (and dealing admirably with the Britishisms!).

Thanks to Glendon for the great cover. I know we went back and forth a few times but I love the result.

To my fabulous beta readers—Katja, Erin, Tara, and Sarah—you women rock! You made me work hard at this one, but I think we all agree it was worth it.

A huge thank you to the British Indians and Pakistanis I interviewed about their reality of being second-generation LBGTQ people in Britain. It was heart-breaking to realise that the stereotypical rejection by traditional, first-generation parents was, unfortunately, still far too true for so many of you. I wish it weren't so, but I'm glad that some of you have, at least, seen a softening in your parents' stance in relation to your sexuality/gender since you first came out to them. Let's hope that time will see yet more progress on that.

And lastly, to my partner, Tanja, thank you for your continual support and love in your role as my number one fan.

DEDICATION

To all the LGBTQ people let down by their birth families—I hope you have a chosen family to give you the love you deserve.

CHAPTER 1

THUNK!

Lena whipped her head round, and her book tumbled out of her hands to the floor. Both cats bolted out of their beds and shot under the small table in front of where the fireplace used to be, their tails and backs arching.

That was definitely the sound of something large hitting her front door. Lena's heart pounded as fear crept through her. Was she being burgled? It was eleven o'clock on a Saturday morning—could burglars be that bold? Before she could move from her chair, she heard another thump, then… laughing?

"Up your end."

"Up yours, bitch."

Both voices were female, and loud, and tinged with mirth.

A third almighty thump on her door and more laughter.

"Shift it, you great lump."

"Shut up, I'm doing the best I can."

Curious now rather than alarmed, Lena stood, walked slowly across the room and down the narrow, curved staircase that led to her front door. Her heart was still racing, despite the laughter coming from the other side of the door. She pressed her eye up to the peephole. The fish-eye view revealed the backside of a woman bent over the end of a sofa. Extending her gaze beyond this alluring sight, Lena spotted another woman on the other end of the sofa. Both women were snorting with laughter as they attempted to manoeuvre the sofa around the small landing at the top of the communal staircase.

Like most Victorian conversions in London, the building that housed Lena's flat was far from regular in its layout. On opening the front door of the building, visitors were met with stairs and, to one side, the door to a ground-floor flat. At the top of the stairs, which curved in a sharp bend two-thirds of the way up, was a landing area that had the doors to Lena's flat and her neighbour's. But, due to a quirky design of the converted building, when Lena opened her front door, she was greeted with another flight of steps to her loft flat. So while she had a front door on the same level as her neighbour, she lived a level higher than them. And that front door was currently being battered by each move the women made with the sofa.

While the noise and disturbance was irritating, Lena tried to take some comfort from the fact that the clumsy sofa-turning attempts meant someone was finally moving in to the flat below. It had been empty for a couple of months, and although not one to seek the company of others that often, there had always been comfort in knowing someone was down there, especially at night.

Satisfied she was not under attack, she turned to make her way back up the narrow stairs to her living space, when a quite different sound caused her to freeze and sent her irritation rocketing.

Screech!

It was the unmistakeable sound of something sharp scraping across her front door.

A sound that was followed by a gasp from one of the women outside her door, and a loud, "*Oh, shit.*"

Lena turned back, breathing deeply in a vain attempt to control her agitation, and pulled open the door.

Facing her, wearing horrified expressions, were the two women, the sofa wedged between them. Lena's gaze followed theirs to the deep scratch gouged across a span of about twelve inches of the door. The flakes of paint it had carved out were already dropping silently to the floor like snowflakes.

Lena stared at the door for a moment, words refusing to form in her brain despite the anger that was churning in her stomach. She lifted her gaze to meet that of the woman nearest her. She was tall and solid-looking—a big-boned girl, as Dorothy from the ground-floor flat would say. She had blonde hair tied up in a long ponytail and pale, almost translucent skin. Her extraordinary blue eyes were wide with fear. She was dressed in a T-shirt and jeans, the shirt covered in swirls of colour in geometric designs that Lena was sure would give her a headache if she looked at it for more than a few moments. Holding the jeans up was a studded belt that was clearly the offender responsible for the damage to the door.

Lena's gaze dropped momentarily to the belt then back up again.

"I'm so sorry," the blonde whispered. "I got pressed against the door, and when I tried to sort of slide away from it—"

Lena held up a hand.

"We'll pay for it!" the woman said quickly, and looked at her companion, who was nodding vigorously.

This one was equally as tall as her partner in crime, but skinny, with short-cropped hair and deep brown skin, a few shades darker than Lena's own. She was wearing a black T-shirt and jeans, and they highlighted the trim body and almost flat chest, which Lena only noticed because of the words "You're next" emblazoned across the front of the T-shirt.

Exhaling slowly, Lena brought her gaze back to meet the blonde woman's eyes.

"Yes, you will." Lena's voice was clipped, each word snapped out with precision.

"Sorry," the blonde said. "Not the best way to be introduced, but—" she twisted around, balanced the sofa on one thigh, and stuck out a hand "—I'm Megan, your new neighbour. And this is Jen."

Lena swallowed. She didn't like to touch people, strangers. You never knew where their hands had been. Inwardly grimacing, because she knew shaking hands was the polite thing to do, she quickly clasped Megan's warm hand and shook it for a few seconds. The handshake was firm, and Lena only just avoided blushing at the sight of well-formed biceps in Megan's arm that flexed with each movement of their joined hands.

"Lena," she said, averting her gaze from Megan's mesmerising eyes.

"And I promise I'll pay for that to be fixed. It's not much damage so it shouldn't be too difficult to sort out." Megan gestured at Lena's front door as their hands parted.

Lena bristled at Megan's oh-so-casual brushing off of the horrendous scar that now marred her front door. Fighting every one of the instincts that made her want to wipe her hand on her jeans following their handshake, Lena forced a smile, if only to avoid this confrontation getting any more uncomfortable than it already was.

"I will get some quotes and be in contact," she said, turning back to enter her flat.

"Um, sorry, could I ask a favour?"

Lena sighed and looked back at Megan over her shoulder, raising her eyebrows in question.

"Well, um, it's just…I think this whole manoeuvre would be a lot easier if you could leave your door open for a minute. It'll give us a bit more room to swing in, if you see what I mean."

Lena glared at her. "If you cause any more damage—"

"We won't! I promise. We'll be really careful, won't we, Jen?" Megan looked meaningfully at her friend, who nodded vigorously again.

Then, one-handed, Megan began unbuckling her belt.

"What are you doing?" Lena asked, her eyes nearly popping out of her head at the sight of the rather attractive woman pulling her belt out from the loops that contained it.

Megan smiled. "Just being careful." She threw the belt gently on the sofa in front of Jen, who shook her head, laughing.

"At least those hips of yours are big enough for the job," Jen said. "Unlike my own." She gestured at her significantly thinner body, and Megan grinned.

Lena's cheeks blazed as she dared to glance down at the enticing strip of abdomen that was revealed now that Megan's belt-less trousers had settled down onto her hips. The view was even more distracting after Megan turned round—the top of what looked like some very lacy underwear was clearly on display when Megan bent slightly to juggle her end of the sofa.

Lena blinked rapidly and stepped backwards into her flat. She hopped up the first couple of steps and perched on the edge of the third, quietly watching the two women as they—carefully—moved the sofa around the turn, making the most of Lena's open doorway to give them a bit more wriggle room. She winced at every move they made but had to admit they were being solicitous. This time.

Finally, they had the sofa lengthwise down the passageway, and Megan glanced through the doorway at Lena.

"Thanks. All done. Really sorry again—let me know when you've got the quotes and I'll get that sorted for you."

"Thank you," Lena said stiffly, and without another word closed the door. She inhaled a deep breath, her mind a swirl of confusing thoughts about the two women she had met. She glanced down at her hands to find them shaking slightly and remembered the handshake. Barely holding back a yelp, she sprinted up the remaining steps and rushed into the bathroom.

After washing and rinsing her hands three times—once more than usual because who knew what else Megan had touched while she moved her possessions in—Lena finally relaxed for the first time since the drama had started. She made herself a fresh cup of Earl Grey tea and returned to her book. The cats had snuck onto the sofa in her absence, trying their luck again, and she shooed them off. They glared at her before slinking off to their beds in the corner of the room.

After brushing their hair off the sofa, she pulled her inhaler from her pocket and took a quick puff. As she sat down, she sighed heavily. The interruption to her day had unsettled her but if she returned to her routine quickly, everything should be okay. Routine was important. Without it, life was too…messy. And Lena didn't do messy.

Megan stared at the closed door, then turned to look at Jen.

"Wow," Jen mouthed.

Megan merely nodded. The entire incident with Lena had unsettled her in ways she couldn't quite interpret. At least, not when she had a sofa to move, a sofa that was getting heavier each minute they weren't actually moving it.

"Come on." She grunted as she shifted its weight in her arms. "Let's get this thing in there."

Jen nodded and Megan moved backwards, shuffling along the tight space of the passageway and wincing as the sofa brushed solidly against the walls.

"It's okay," Jen said quickly. "No marks."

"Thank God for that."

Finally, they were through Megan's new front door and into the flat. The space was open-plan, with a large lounge, a small kitchen in one corner, the bathroom next to that, and two doors on one side of the lounge that led to the bedrooms. It was by far the biggest place Megan had ever lived in, and she was excited about having the extra space. Her last home had been a cramped studio so moving into so large a flat, even if the rent did push her funds a little, felt like heaven.

After dumping the sofa unceremoniously in the rough area Megan needed it, both she and Jen arched their backs and let out loud groans.

"At least we got the worst bit done first," Jen said, rubbing at the small of her back and looking around the room.

"Definitely," Megan agreed. "Boxes are going to be a piece of cake after that." She flexed her arms, working out the slight ache in her biceps. One advantage of being a fitness instructor was that she'd never needed any professional help in moving home. With Jen's equally impressive strength, honed from years of working in a bar and lugging barrels of beer around in the cellar, they made a formidable team.

"This is a great-size room." Jen wandered over to the front window to glance down at the street below.

"Want the tour before we head back down to the van?"

Smiling, Jen nodded. "Totally. Show me your palace."

Megan snorted. "Hardly that, Jen. But yeah," she said, before Jen could jump in, "I know, it's bigger than your place."

"Just a bit!" Jen laughed.

Megan was glad Jen kept her response light—Jen's place was tiny and more than a little tatty around the edges. She knew Jen was envious of Megan's move, and also that Jen had been subtly angling to take up residence as a tenant in the spare room. Something that Megan had equally as subtly been pushing back on. The whole idea of getting the bigger place was to have some space, and she didn't need another person, even her closest friend, invading that.

The tour took a few minutes, as they not only checked out each empty room but discussed Megan's plans for furnishing each space.

"And, of course," Jen said, as they walked back into the lounge, "you know you have a hot neighbour too. Couldn't be better really." She grinned.

Megan shook her head. "Trust you to spot that in the middle of that embarrassment."

She had to be honest with herself though—she'd also noticed Lena's subtle beauty, despite the iciness of their meeting. Deep brown eyes with eyelashes that went on forever, and a cute face, golden brown in colour, which hinted at an Indian heritage. Her dark hair was shoulder-length and had been half pinned up at the back, leaving tantalising wisps to drape over her ears and brush her cheeks.

Megan had only dared the briefest of glances at Lena's body, but it looked proportioned in all the ways that set Megan's heart racing: full breasts, even fuller hips and thighs, and Lena's height was a good few inches shorter than Megan's five feet nine. Megan was a sucker for a smaller woman—someone she could enfold in her embrace, their head tucked under her chin.

"Are you seriously trying to tell me you didn't notice her hotness?"

Megan cursed her pale skin as the blush rampaged across her cheeks. "No," she muttered. "Of course I did. I am laughing, though, because, as usual, your libido took more notice of events, no matter what the hell else was going on."

Jen laughed. "And yours too, I'm guessing."

Megan's blush deepened as she remembered in vivid detail what Lena looked like. Cursing under her breath, she poked Jen in the arm as her friend laughed even louder.

"Yeah, okay. She's very attractive. But come on, chances are she's straight. And maybe a little uptight based on how she was with us. So, let's ignore the eye candy and get on with unpacking that van, yeah?"

"All right, Megs. Whatever you say." Jen moved past Megan towards the front door. "But I wouldn't be so sure about her being straight," she said, smiling. "I'm pretty sure she plays for our team—her eyes were all over me."

Yes, they were. As usual, the hot ones are always more interested in you than me.

When she'd first become friends with Jen, it had been hard to take that everywhere they went, women flocked to Jen's side, and Megan felt like a background extra in a Hollywood blockbuster. She didn't exactly have an abundance of self-confidence, and Jen's dazzling personality and—some might say—arrogance around women only dented that more. But gradually, over time, their deepening friendship allowed Megan to open up a little about her feelings, and Jen, to her credit, tried very hard to remember to take them into account. Mostly.

Sometimes, however, she couldn't help herself, and not for the first time Megan wished she had even an ounce of Jen's confidence and self-belief.

Trying to shut out the image of the beautiful woman who lived upstairs, and who apparently only had eyes for Jen, Megan let out a breath and followed her friend out to the hallway.

CHAPTER 2

LENA UNLOCKED THE HEAVY FRONT door and pushed it open. The hallway light flicked on, triggered by the motion sensor the landlord had finally agreed to install the year before. As usual, Mr Jarvis had done so with some reluctance, never one to spend any money on the building if he could possibly avoid it. Numerous letters from Lena and Dorothy, the tenant in the ground-floor flat, had finally done the trick though. Until that point, the light source in the main hallway was a single naked bulb that could only be switched on from halfway up the staircase, a ridiculous position that caused many bumps and bruises after dark.

She collected her mail from the neat pile it formed on the shelf beneath the window. For all her faults—and there were many, in Lena's opinion—this little daily task that Dorothy had taken upon herself was much appreciated. Dorothy was retired and seemed to take a disproportionate amount of joy in being able to take in the mail each day and sort it on behalf of each of them.

After tiredly plodding back up the stairs, Lena grimaced—again—when her scarred front door came into view. It had been a long week and she still hadn't found time to phone around for some quotes. Her job had been exhausting—quarter-end for an accounting team always was, but this one had been especially trying with a new forecast due and demands for better numbers coming in two or three times a day from their head office.

She felt grateful as she stepped into her flat and locked the door behind her. As she switched on the overhead light, she frowned; there was that little damp patch on the carpet again, on the fourth step up. Gazing upwards, Lena squinted against the brightness of the light fitting to try to see past it to the darkened skylight above. She was sure that's where the leak was, but she'd yet to find it. While she loved the skylight, loved the patterns of light it sent dancing down her narrow stairs on a bright day, lately it was annoying her greatly by leaving this same patch after every rainstorm. Ruefully she accepted that she'd have to borrow a step ladder to have a proper look—and only one person in the building had a step ladder. Dorothy.

She inhaled sharply. That could wait for another day. While Lena had learnt to be courageous in the past few years—coming out as lesbian in an Indian family wasn't for the faint-hearted, after all—there were some situations she still shied away from. And dealing with Dorothy was usually on that list. No, what she needed right now was some soup to warm her up on this icy cold October night and her book to escape into.

The mewling of the cats greeted her as she reached the top of the stairs, and her mood darkened. Irritating little beasts. Another thing she needed to deal with and hadn't found the time to do so. Her last two text messages to Chris had gone unanswered. She frowned, staring down at their rotund faces. Their pitiful cries, pitched to tug at a heart that cared, did nothing but raise her ire once more at the fact that they were even living in her flat. She stomped over to the kitchen, slung some food in their bowls, and topped up their water, all the while swerving away from their attempts to wrap their slinky bodies around her legs.

It wasn't their fault, she knew that. But Chris wasn't here and they were, so they got the brunt of her unhappiness about the situation. The black one, Midnight, glanced up at her as she side-stepped him once more, and she sighed. He really was quite beautiful. She bent down slowly and used the tip of one finger to scratch a gentle back-and-forth path in the centre of his head. His purr made her smile, in spite of herself, and when Snow, the white one, approached, clearly feeling left out of the love fest, Lena demurred and scratched her too. She indulged them—and herself—for a few minutes before rapidly straightening and heading for the bathroom to wash her hands.

After stripping out of her suit in the bedroom, she sighed blissfully as she slipped into her baggiest, comfiest pyjama bottoms and her Hogwarts hoodie. She finished off her slouchy outfit with the big fluffy socks her sister Madhu had given her for her birthday last year, smiling as she pulled them on. Though they were a little tattered around the edges, she cherished them, not only for the comfort they gave to her tired feet, but for always

9

making her think of Madhu whenever she wore them. After hanging up her suit, and ensuring the trousers lined up dead centre of the hanger, the crease razor-sharp, she took a puff on her inhaler and headed for the kitchen.

With hot, spicy parsnip soup and a bread roll balanced on her tray, she snuggled down into the sofa and picked up her book with one hand, her spoon with the other. She pushed the cats away with her feet when they made their usual evening attempt to sit with her on the sofa and ignored them as they huffed off to their beds. Carefully eating mouthfuls of soup as she read, she immersed herself back into the story of Drew and Annie and their oh-so-sweet romance. She'd read this one a few times before, but when she was stressed, as she had been recently, she returned to it like a comfort blanket, guaranteed to make her feel better.

In between chapters, she cleared her tray and quickly washed up her bowl and spoon. Dirty dishes could not be left out for even a few hours in Lena's abode—cleanliness was everything. After wiping down the counters with antibacterial spray and dropping the remaining crumbs into the bin under the sink, she took a look around, satisfied that all was as it should be. She topped up her tea and returned to the sofa, tucking her legs up so that her feet were nestled securely under her buttocks. It was nearly nine o'clock, and she had to be in bed by ten thirty in order to get her required eight hours sleep. Contentment imbued her as she faced the remaining ninety minutes of her evening tucked up with the book. It wasn't much, not compared to what she had this time last year with Chris, but it was enough.

Mostly, said a quiet voice in the back of her mind.

Megan shoved open the front door and rushed through it as quickly as she could to get in out of the cold. She slammed the door behind her and stamped her wet boots on the mat before heading to the stairs. She'd just placed her left foot on the first step when a sharp voice rang through the hallway, making her stumble and wobble between the floor behind her and the step before her.

"Young lady!"

Megan grabbed at the bannister to right herself, then turned, slowly, to meet the piercing gaze of a short, rotund woman whom she guessed to be somewhere in her sixties if the grey hairs that edged her temples were anything to go by. Huge round glasses dominated her black face, her eyes wide behind them, magnified by the thick lenses to comic proportions. Megan only just held back a giggle under the withering stare of those eyes.

"Yes?" she asked, keeping her tone respectful.

"I've held my tongue until today, thinking the Lord would help you to see the error of your ways in His own time. But as that clearly isn't the case, which by-the-by has me in fear for your soul, poor child, you leave me no choice but to address the issue in my own way."

"I'm…sorry, what?" Megan had no idea what this woman was talking about, and anyone spouting religious talk always made her nervous. Aunty Jean had a lot to answer for.

The woman's arm shot out with surprising alacrity, and she pointed a finger at the front door behind Megan.

"The slamming of the door, girl! Shaking this house, rattling my windows until I fear they're going to fall from their frames. I'm praying to my Lord Jesus every time, praying this won't be the day the roof comes tumbling down around my ears." The woman was quivering, her hands now placed on her chest, held together in prayerful aspect.

Megan swallowed. "I'm so sorry. I-I didn't realise I was doing it."

The woman huffed, her frown easing a little. "Well, now you do. Let that be the end of it." With that, she turned away and walked through what Megan assumed was the doorway to her own ground-floor flat. The door closed with a soft click, and Megan exhaled.

The main front door opened behind her, and she turned to see Lena step through and shut it carefully. Lena started as she saw Megan halted with one foot on the first step, and she tilted her head.

"Are you okay?" Her voice was tight, her eyes narrowed; clearly the scratched-door incident had not been forgotten. Or forgiven.

Megan shook her head, pointing at the door of the ground-floor flat. "Who…who is that?" she asked.

The smirk that painted Lena's face held no warmth.

"That is Dorothy. What did you do?"

"Um, slammed the door. One time too many, apparently."

Lena's eyes rolled and she crossed her arms in front of her. "Great. Just great. Well, I hope you didn't have any plans for some peace and quiet tonight."

"What?" Megan was getting more confused by the minute. What the hell was going on in this house?

"How angry was she?" Lena walked across the hall to scoop up her mail and motioned impatiently for Megan to continue climbing the stairs, Lena following two steps behind.

"Well, pretty angry, I guess," Megan said, over her shoulder, looking down at Lena and trying hard not to stare at how…glorious Lena looked with an angry scowl on her face.

"Did she quote the Lord?"

"Yes, actually. How did you—"

Lena's sigh was audible. "Then there will definitely be no peace for us tonight. Thanks very much."

With that, she turned her key in her lock, pushed open her door, and disappeared.

Megan stood next to the closed door and slapped her own cheek. Nope, definitely awake. What on Earth was—

The organ music was loud. Unbelievably loud. Megan hadn't had a religious upbringing, despite Aunty Jean's best attempts, but even she could recognise "Onward, Christian Soldiers" when it was blasted at that volume. The glass in the window of the main hallway was vibrating softly in its frame as a result. The floor beneath her feet was trembling, giving her a realistic impression of what it would be like to stand in an earthquake zone. In a daze, she walked along the passageway to her door and unlocked it.

The sound was even worse inside her flat; clearly her main room was above wherever the source of the music was situated. Singing was now audible too, and part of her brain had to be honest enough to register that Dorothy, if it was she who was singing, had a remarkably good voice. A loud voice, but good nonetheless.

Shaking her head, still not quite understanding the sequence of events that had unfolded since she'd first arrived back in Jackson Road fifteen minutes previously, Megan walked through to her sparse bedroom. She'd still only got as far as purchasing a bed but had plans to meet her father with his van at IKEA on Saturday to obtain wardrobes and a few more bits for the living room. Renting an unfurnished flat had added to her list of expenses, but actually she didn't mind—it was fun buying all of her own things and getting exactly what she wanted. And despite the less-than-stellar start with her neighbours, she liked where she was living. The high ceilings and original features of all the rooms in her flat made it seem even more spacious. As did the lack of furniture, and although she still needed some essentials, she didn't want to overfill her new home.

"Abide with Me" was playing when she walked back into the kitchen to start making some dinner. How long, she wondered, did the live and unwanted concert go on?

CHAPTER 3

"FORTY MINUTES?" MEGAN'S MUM SPLUTTERED. "That's outrageous!" She sat down on the sofa, tutting.

"You know what, it wasn't that bad in the end." Megan laughed. "I mean, I was cooking for most of that time so by the time I was ready to sit down and watch some TV, she'd finished."

"And does she do this every night?" Her dad was grinning.

"Not so far. Just that one night. I think it was my punishment, or something."

"She's a fucking nutter," Jimmy said.

"Language!" Her mother reached across the sofa to slap Jimmy's bicep. He barely flinched—like Megan, Jimmy, her youngest brother, was a fitness instructor, and his arms bulged with muscles that were as solid as wood.

"All done!" Callum's voice floated out to them from the spare bedroom. He was her oldest brother, with four years separating them. Callum was a builder by trade and had insisted on being the one to put together all the flat-pack furniture from IKEA she'd bought the day before. Helping him was Daniel, two years older than Megan, and not generally known for being interested in physical labour. Callum's bribe of twenty quid and a couple of pints later down at their local seemed to have worked wonders on his attitude.

They appeared in the doorway to the spare room, and Callum beckoned Megan over. She leapt up from the sofa, crashed her shins against the box of books that was serving as a temporary coffee table, and groaned as three mugs of tea shot sideways and catapulted onto the floor. Callum snorted, her father following suit swiftly afterwards. Jimmy caught Megan's eye and gave her a sympathetic smile.

"I'll get it," her mum said, holding up her hands and laughing.

"Sorry, Mum." Megan sighed.

Her mother laughed louder. "It's good to see some things never change." She walked off to the kitchen area and returned with a wet cloth, and a dustpan and brush.

Megan's clumsiness was the stuff of legend in the Palmer family. Some classic incidents from the past were regularly trotted out at major social events, earning Megan guffaws from anyone within earshot and endless teasing. While the retellings always amused everyone else, Megan merely smiled politely, writhing internally with embarrassment at having her infamous fault be the centre of attention.

Once the spillage had been dealt with, and Megan had hugged her mum in thanks, the whole family followed her to inspect the results of the brothers' labour.

Megan beamed. It looked exactly how she'd envisioned. A foldout sofa bed was centred on the wall opposite the window, and a large desk took up the other half of the room. She'd tried to make the best use of the space possible for multiple purposes. While she didn't want to give Jen the impression that she could move in, she did want her to stay over now and again, especially when Megan started throwing parties. Equally, she wanted a space for her desk and computer without them intruding on the main room, which she wanted to keep as her lazy lounging-around area. It was already filling up nicely with big floor cushions, the bookshelves the brothers had assembled earlier, and the big media unit on the longest wall.

"Nice work, my brothers." She clapped each of them on the back, laughing as Daniel winced. While she, Jimmy, and Callum were all big-boned and solid like their dad, Daniel favoured their mother and was considerably slighter. He never took well to any of their hearty greetings and gestures.

"Right, that calls for beer," she said, and laughed as her entire family cheered. That was the last of the construction finished—earlier that afternoon they'd all helped put together the wardrobes in her room, and arrange the table, chairs, bookcases, and media unit in the main room. Now all she had to do was unpack the rest of the boxes and she was done.

She pulled cold lagers out of the fridge for all of them, and they swigged from the bottles, her mother included. For as long as Megan could remember, her mother had disdained washing up and was happy to cut any corners she could to avoid it. Using glasses to drink beer was a complete waste of time as far as Rosie Palmer was concerned.

Megan smiled as she looked around at her family. Her dad was talking to Callum, the pair of them looking like peas in a pod, even down to their thinning hair. Both well over six feet tall, with broad shoulders, they dominated any room they occupied. Her dad's beer belly was expanding faster these days, and she knew her mum had been nagging him about it.

She glanced over at her mum, who was rearranging cushions on the sofa. A foot shorter than her husband, and slim of figure, the contrast between her parents couldn't be greater. However, her mum was no diminutive pushover, despite what people might take from their appearances—she definitely wore the trousers in that relationship, ruling her household with a sharp tongue and a vicious flick of a tea towel when things got out of hand.

Jimmy and Daniel were rummaging around on the floor trying to set up the TV connections. Megan smiled. Daniel would be in his element. Anything electronic or gadgety and he was your man. He'd always been the quietest of the family, ensconcing himself in the room he'd shared with Jimmy as a kid, tinkering with who knew what on the desk that served as his electronics testing ground. She chuckled as Daniel smacked Jimmy's meaty hands away from a couple of cables. Jimmy may have been built like the proverbial brick shithouse, but Daniel wasn't intimidated by him. Although nearly four years younger than Daniel, Jimmy had come to the more timid Daniel's rescue a couple of times through their school years, and while that meant Daniel had a certain kind of hero worship for his younger brother, he also wouldn't let him get away with anything. Jimmy grinned at his older brother and swigged from his beer.

"Hey, Lumpy!" Megan's dad grabbed her attention with her old nickname, the name she despised but had never managed to talk her family out of using. She scowled and they all chuckled, which only irritated her more.

"What?" She tried hard not to snap, but it was difficult.

"How about some music?" Her dad was smiling widely.

Mentally shrugging away her annoyance, Megan flicked the speakers on and connected her iPod, then scrolled to a mix she'd put together for a party earlier this year. While it was only her family here, and still the middle of a Sunday afternoon, she was up for adding a little party atmosphere to the day. She and her family had always been good at that, spinning any event into an excuse for a good laugh and some drinking. When she spotted Callum nodding his head to the beat, she turned up the volume slightly and smiled when he grinned at her, knowing they were on exactly the same wavelength.

Lena slammed her book down on the sofa. She took back everything she'd said about being happy there was now someone in the flat below hers. This was the third time in the last two weeks that Megan had played her music loud enough to disturb Lena, and she'd had enough. So what if it was a Saturday night, a night when most people might anticipate a measure of frivolity? It was all about manners—or in this case, the lack of.

Without spending another moment thinking it through, she marched across the room to the stairs and stomped down them. After unlocking the door, she walked quickly down the passageway to Megan's front door and knocked rapidly.

She waited.

And waited.

She knocked again, louder this time, her knuckles smarting at the energy she put into the action.

After a few moments, the music reduced in volume and the door swung open. Expecting to be faced with Megan, Lena prepared to launch into her complaint but stopped short when she realised it was the other woman—Jen, she vaguely remembered—staring at her, a wide grin on her face.

"Well, hello again," Jen said, running her hand over her very short-cropped hair in what Lena had to begrudgingly admit was an extremely sexy gesture. "How lovely to see you." Jen smiled widely.

Lena bristled. Was this woman actually trying to flirt with her? Now?

"Where's Megan?" Lena snapped.

Jen's eyes lost a little of their sparkle, and she took half a step back. "Um, somewhere inside. Want to come in?" She gestured behind her, and Lena glanced into the low-lit flat to see a room full of people, all swinging and swaying to the music and knocking back drinks like there was no tomorrow.

"Please get her," Lena said through gritted teeth. As if she'd want to step into…whatever it was they were doing.

Jen shrugged and her smile faded. "All right, whatever you want. Be right back."

Lena watched her walk away and fidgeted on the worn carpet of the hallway. She was suddenly, excruciatingly aware of how she was dressed compared to the people she could see in the room beyond. They in their sparkly tops and tight jeans, and she in her pyjamas and, she glanced down—*oh, no*—floppy-eared bunny slippers. Maybe she should go now, before Megan appeared. Maybe facing her tomorrow, in the cold light of day, would be a better idea. She took a step backwards, forgetting that the awkward shape of the slippers—with the big ball of a tail on each foot—always inhibited any reverse movement, and in the next moment found herself on her backside. Before she could scrabble to her feet, Megan appeared in the open doorway. Eyes wide, rushing forward to help Lena to her feet, the drink she was carrying in her hand sloshed over the rim of its glass and in a graceful arc, made a beeline for Lena. It was as if it happened in slow motion, and yet there was no time for Lena to dodge it; in the next moment, she was wearing a significant quantity of something orange. And cold.

"Oh, shit!" Megan flushed and quickly deposited the now empty glass at her feet. "Oh, Lena, I'm *so* sorry."

Lena stared up at Megan. Vaguely, she noted Megan was wearing a bright purple T-shirt with the words "Bite me" stencilled on it in silver letters. Megan's long hair, almost white it was so blonde, draped over her shoulders in a way that Lena found inexplicably alluring. She wondered how soft it was. It looked like it would be incredibly silky to the touch, if she ran it through her fingers and—

Her chest was cold. Very cold. She plucked at the front of her pyjama top, her cheeks flaming as she realised where her thoughts were going and how they had completely made her forget the predicament she was in. She was also acutely aware that she was still flat on her backside with her legs akimbo, her now very wet pyjama top clinging in places that would leave little to anyone's imagination. She wanted to sob from the embarrassment.

Ignoring Megan's outstretched hand of help, she hauled herself back to her feet under her own power, pulling the soggy pyjama top away from her as much as she could. She took a deep breath, emptying her mind of everything except her annoyance.

"You okay?" Megan asked, her smile tentative, her face only a shade lighter than beetroot. "I'm so, so sorry," she repeated. "Can I get you a towel?" She made to take a step back but Lena held up a hand.

"I'm…fine," Lena lied, wishing her own blush would fade as rapidly as it had appeared. "I'll deal with this—" she gestured to her wet chest, then blushed again "—when I get back inside. I only came down to ask you to turn the music down."

Megan's eyes widened again. "Oh, God, sorry. I didn't think. Have we woken you up?"

Lena snorted, her eyebrows lifting. "It's only nine. I wasn't in bed."

"Oh," Megan said, pointing to Lena's pyjamas. "I guess I assumed…"

"Well, yes. Whatever." Why couldn't she stop blushing? "I was trying to read and your music is too loud. I read. In the evenings. And you are disturbing that."

Megan held up her hands. "Again, I'm sorry. I'm not making a very good impression on you, am I? Since I moved in, I mean."

Lena closed her eyes momentarily. "It's…well, I guess we just have to get used to each other. The situation, I mean. You living here." She stopped talking. Why couldn't she string a sentence together? Yes, Megan's pale eyes were ridiculously distracting, but she was angry at Megan for disrupting her evening, her routine, and for throwing a glass of whatever it was all over her. She needed to focus only on that. "Anyway, the music. Turn it down. Please."

Before Megan could respond Lena turned, carefully making sure she didn't trip over the extended ears of her slippers, and walked back towards her flat, keeping her clammy pyjama top away from her skin as best she could.

"Will do," Megan called. "And if you need the pyjamas to be dry-cleaned, please give me the bill so I can pay for it."

"I'm sure that won't be necessary," Lena snapped over her shoulder.

"Okay." There was a pause. "By the way—nice slippers."

Lena's cheeks flamed red again as she pushed open her front door.

CHAPTER 4

"Stop ignoring me, Leelawati."

MADHU'S VOICE CARRIED MORE THAN a hint of frustration. The voicemail was the third Lena's sister had left in as many days, and Lena sighed as she deleted it. She couldn't avoid her forever; Madhu was a force of nature once something had wound her up enough. From the sounds of it—especially as she was using Lena's full birth name—she'd now reached that point. Knowing it was better to get it over with, Lena scrolled to Madhu's number in her list of missed calls.

"Alive then?" The greeting from her younger sister was acerbic.

"Madhu, please."

There was a loud exhalation. "Sorry." A pause. "How are you?"

Lena settled back into her sofa. "I'm okay," she said quickly, then, before Madhu could follow up, "How's Jay? And the baby?"

Madhu chuckled. "Jay is fine. Working all hours, of course. The baby is kicking way too good, and I can tell you, that is not nearly as much fun as Mum led me to believe."

Just that single sentence stirred up a host of emotions in Lena, and she swallowed hard before responding.

"Is she helping you?"

Madhu sighed. "Yes and no. She means well, but... Ugh, it's all such old-fashioned advice. And I've lost count of how many aunties have been on the phone since she spread the news, all with their own top tips for a healthy pregnancy and baby. And don't even get me started on the suggestions for names." She groaned. "But I know it's coming from a good place, so I bite my tongue and let them chatter on while I ship orders."

It was good Madhu was still sounding happy about being her own boss selling cosmetics and henna supplies on eBay. Lena felt a stab of envy at her being able to work from home with the blessing of her husband, Jay. Now, with the baby on the way, it made even more sense for her to be working from home. The downside, clearly, was Jay having to pull extra shifts at the bank's call centre to bring in whatever additional money they needed with their first child on the way. Lena could picture Madhu surrounded by her stock in the small spare bedroom and wondered what would happen to it all once the room became the nursery.

"Business good?" she asked.

"Not too bad at the moment. The summer was crazy, with wedding season and holidays."

"I can imagine."

"So, seriously, Lena, how are you?" Madhu was nothing if not tenacious.

"Like I said, I'm okay."

"Okay doesn't sound that good."

"I'm fine."

"Fine isn't much of an improvement."

"Oh, Madhu, please!"

"Lena, it's only because I care. I-I worry about you. On your own."

"Ugh, now you sound like Mum."

"How dare you?" Madhu sounded horrified, and Lena snorted. Madhu started giggling, and suddenly the tension was gone.

"Madhu, I am okay. Yes, I am on my own but that is my choice. My work keeps me busy and…well, everything else will happen when the universe is ready for me."

Madhu sighed. "I take it you still have the cats? Has that woman arranged anything about—"

"No." Lena cut her off, noting that it had taken her sister only three minutes to launch into her monthly rant about the cats, Chris, and Lena's situation in general.

Lena closed her eyes momentarily, willing her voice to come out evenly as she said, "No, and I know I have to get this sorted out, but it's been very busy at work. I will do it."

Her sister snorted.

"I will!"

21

"Lena, the woman *cheated* on you, moved out with no warning, left you with *her* cats, which you are *allergic* to, and you've done nothing about it in six months. When exactly *are* you going to do something about it?"

Lena knew Madhu didn't mean to sound so harsh. She knew her sister was only speaking from a place of love and concern, but she really wished she'd shut up.

"Madhu, I will do it. This is my battle to fight, so let me fight it."

"But—"

"Enough!"

There was a strained silence. Then, "Sorry." Madhu's voice was small.

Lena accepted the apology graciously.

After a moment, Madhu spoke again. "Lena, I really don't want to sound like Mum, but I don't like the idea of you being on your own. I know you don't go out much, and you bury yourself in your work and those books, but—"

"I know. Madhu, I-I don't want to be on my own forever. I don't. I just need some time. Chris was—"

"Chris was a cheating cow," Madhu interjected.

"Well, yes. Yes, she was."

"Has it put you off? You know, being lesbian. I mean, she was your first real girlfriend."

Lena smiled. "It doesn't quite work that way." She chuckled. As supportive as Madhu had been when Lena finally took the plunge to come out to her family four years ago, she still seemed to think it was some kind of choice that Lena had made. As if Lena could have controlled it, somehow, and should therefore be able to switch it on or off at will. As if the intensity of those feelings was ever something Lena could have ignored...

"So," Madhu said after a few quiet moments. "How's work?"

Lena spoke about her job and the progress she felt she was making in the role. She'd been there a little over eight months now—changing jobs had, unfortunately, coincided with her discovery that her girlfriend of nearly two years had been cheating on her for the previous two months. Lena was still amazed she'd managed to keep the job given how hopeless she'd felt in those first few weeks as she dealt with both situations.

The break-up with Chris had been...ugly. Chris had obviously been frustrated at Lena's career focus, and the additional hours she'd been putting in to add a corporate tax qualification to her accountancy background. However, rather than talk to Lena about it, and negotiating for more of Lena's attention, she'd gone looking elsewhere. And yet still come home to their place every night after each of her...liaisons...with that woman. Belinda the diamond dealer. Chris had apparently met her at a work function her company was hosting in Hatton Garden. Lena still flushed with embarrassment at not realising what was going on. She'd only found out when Chris sent her a text that was clearly meant for Belinda. The fight that night had been short and nasty; by the time it was over, Lena had the flat to herself and all evidence of Chris had gone.

Except for the cats, of course.

"Oh, and someone finally moved into the flat below."

"Yeah? Have you met them? Man or woman?"

"Woman. Megan." Saying her name conjured up—surprisingly—not irritation at all the problems around her moving in, but an image of those pale blue eyes. Lena shook it off. "She's... Well, she's noisy. And clumsy. She damaged my front door on the day she moved in. And she has lots of loud parties."

Madhu chuckled. "Oh, no. This is not going to go well, is it? I know how you love your peace, and no disruption to your little routines."

Lena bristled. Her routines were her friends. Dependable. Reliable. Comforting. Her family had teased her endlessly as a child, and her peers at school had thought her more than a little odd. Lena simply liked things done a certain way, preferably at about the same time every day, and ideally with no interruptions. What was wrong with that? Yes, Chris had scoffed at her too, at Lena's obsession with order and cleanliness. The fact that Chris had deliberately tried to goad Lena about it in the last few months they were together should have set alarm bells ringing, but Lena had been oblivious.

"Madhu, you make it sound like there's something wrong with me," she said, petulance colouring her tone. "I just like things done my way."

"I know, I know," Madhu soothed. "So, want to come up and visit?"

From one thorny subject to another, thought Lena, sighing. Her sister was on a roll tonight. "Let me get the cat situation sorted out, and then we'll see."

They said their good-byes, and Lena set to work laying out the ingredients for her lunch. The vegetables for the Thai curry were laid out in the order in which she'd need to use them—they had been scrubbed clean minutes after being brought home from the supermarket and only needed a rinse now. The chopping board was set squarely in the middle of the counter, and the knife she would use for chopping sat alongside it within easy reach. The can of coconut milk she placed next to the hob, with the can opener in front of it, and the pan she would use was given a quick wipe down and set upon the biggest ring. She was reaching for the pack of rice in the storage cupboard when a gentle knock sounded at her door.

After quickly wiping her hands, she motioned the cats away as she walked down the stairs. The spy hole revealed a wide-eyed Dorothy a few paces away from the front door. Lena smiled to herself. That could only mean one thing.

She swung the door open and said, "How big, and where?"

Dorothy wrung her hands together. "Oh, Lena, thank you! As big as my hand and in my bath."

Lena smiled and moved past Dorothy to the stairs. "I'll shout when it's safe to come back," she said, and trotted down the stairs.

She pushed Dorothy's front door open and walked confidently to the kitchen to grab a glass from the cupboard, and a piece of junk mail from the pile Dorothy always accumulated on the table. She breathed in the enticing aroma of whatever it was that Dorothy was cooking today. She'd have to ask and see if she could get the recipe…

The bathroom was at the back of the flat and was small, like her own, but brightly lit from the south-facing window above the bath. And that light was all she needed to see the beast that had interrupted Dorothy's day. As she'd suspected, the spider wasn't nearly as big as Dorothy's hand, but she knew that Dorothy's arachnophobia would always exaggerate her nemesis.

"Well, you certainly picked the wrong day to come indoors, didn't you?" she murmured as she placed the glass over the spider and scooped it up by placing the piece of paper underneath. She walked it out of the flat and to the main front door, which she opened with one hand while the other kept the glass and paper firmly attached to each other. The spider was given its freedom in the hedgerow that separated their building from the one next door, and within moments Lena was placing the glass in the sink in Dorothy's kitchen and the paper in her recycling bin by the back door.

"All clear," she called up the stairs as she pulled Dorothy's front door partially closed behind her, not wanting the older woman's heat to escape too much on this cold day.

"Oh, bless you, Lena," Dorothy said as they passed on the stairs. "You are an angel sent from the Lord above. I know not why He sends me these trials, but I thank Him for sending me you."

Lena blushed. "Any time, Dorothy, you know that." She smiled to herself as she let herself back into her flat. Another rescue mission complete—for both the spider and Dorothy.

CHAPTER 5

LENA SLOTTED HER KEY IN the lock and paused. She looked down at the pristine new panel in her door and gave a contented sigh. It had taken her two weeks to organise, but the repair had been completed three days previously, and it still gave her a happy little glow every time she looked at it. The man Megan's brother had recommended had done a good job; you would never know the incident had happened. The whole door had been repainted to suit the new panel, and the glossy whiteness of it shone in the bright light of the communal hallway. And Megan had been true to her word, paying for the whole thing.

Lena had to admit she had been pleasantly surprised; she'd assumed Megan had been saying only what Lena wanted to hear when offering to pay for the damage. That she'd come through with the money, and in cash, the same day Lena presented her with the bill had led Lena to up her respect level for her noisy and clumsy neighbour.

Finally, she turned the key and stepped into her flat. Midnight and Snow were on the bottom step, staring silently up at her. It unnerved her every time they did it; something about their eyes was particularly creepy, as if they were busy plotting her undoing. She knew the relationship she had with them was strained, given the circumstances, but at least she hadn't thrown them out. They could be a tad more grateful about things, instead of stalking her at every opportunity.

She pushed past them after hanging up her coat and sighed as they crept behind her up the steps, their sinuous bodies sliding alongside her legs. After feeding and watering them, she set about the most disgusting task involved in looking after her adopted charges: cleaning out the litter tray. For someone such as Lena, for whom cleanliness definitely came above godliness, this was a task she only just survived. And it didn't matter that she had done it every day for six months; nothing would ever make her get used to it. As she wrapped dusty poo in sheets of newspaper brought home especially for the task, she cursed Chris for the millionth time for putting her in this position. And cursed her own weakness for allowing Chris to do so.

"But honey, I love my little kittens. And I know you're allergic, but they always say that the more you're exposed to it, the more you get used to it. So I think it will be fine. Please, honey."

The last two words had been delivered in a sweet, coddling tone that Chris had perfected in twisting Lena around her little finger, and Lena had capitulated. To be fair, she *had* thought she might build up some immunity to the kittens once they were in her flat 24/7 and so had semi-willingly gone along with Chris's plan to bring them with her when she moved in.

Unfortunately, over two years later there was no sign of that immunity ever kicking in. She had a prescription on repeat at the local pharmacy for her inhaler, and taking an anti-histamine tablet had become part of her daily ritual at breakfast time. Luckily, she had managed to keep the cats out of the bedroom since Chris had moved out, and after some heavy-duty carpet cleaning and vacuuming, it was one room that was relatively allergy-free.

She finished dealing with the litter tray and sat back on her haunches to watch the cats eat. They really were gorgeous, but they had to go. She couldn't do this anymore. If that troll girlfriend of Chris's didn't like cats, that was Chris's problem, not Lena's.

It was time for an ultimatum.

Megan bounded up the communal stairs with the first two bags of supplies and dumped them outside her front door. She was excited—today she started painting the bathroom. The landlord had given her carte blanche to do what she wanted with each room. In fact, he seemed not to care at all what she did and how, which had rung a small alarm bell in the back of her mind about what sort of landlord she'd got now. Excitement won over her doubts and she'd shrugged them off. Then she'd wangled herself a Saturday off at very short notice and had got herself up nice and early to get on with the decorating. She'd thought she'd have to put it off another couple of months until she could save up for the things she'd need, as her credit card had taken quite a hit at IKEA recently. However, Callum had called her the day before to tell her about a job he'd finished and all the gear he had left over.

"Honestly, sis, it's cool. The guy's already paid for the paint and laughed at me when I asked if he wanted to keep what was left. So I'm only going to take it down the tip unless you want it."

"And it's okay to use in bathrooms?"

"Yeah, totally. It's a kind of cool blue colour. Any good to you?"

Anything had to be better than the shitty brown colour that currently adorned her bathroom's walls, she'd thought, and gratefully accepted Callum's offer of two tins of paint.

She hopped back down the stairs for the tins themselves. Though they'd both inexplicably been opened, each of them was at least half full, so she probably had just enough to do the whole room. It would take at least two coats to bury the brown, possibly three.

She was musing on this calculation as she turned the corner at the top of the stairs. The bellowing of the organ from the ground-floor flat made her jump out of her skin and before she could stop it, the tin of paint in her left hand escaped her grip and sailed across the landing. It only took one point six seconds for its momentum to come to a halt.

Against Lena's front door.

The newly repaired front door that, until one point six seconds ago, was a shiny polar white.

Thanks to the lid of the paint tin popping open on impact with the wood, the door was now bipolar; white at the top, cool blue at the bottom.

Megan stared at the carnage in horror, her mind numb, her heart racing.

Oh. My. God.

"*All things bright and beautiful,*" came Dorothy's strident voice from somewhere below. "*All creatures great and small.*"

Megan closed her eyes, hoping against hope that when she re-opened them, everything would be bright and beautiful again, and not blue.

No such luck. She stared at the pool of paint congealing on the carpet right outside Lena's front door, willing her brain to come up with something, *anything*, to rescue this situation. She tried to console herself with the thought that this one really wasn't her fault. This one wasn't down to her clumsiness. Not really. But something told her Lena wouldn't see it that way.

The sound of the lock being turned from inside Lena's flat jolted Megan's stomach down to her knees and back again. The warning she tried to formulate died on her lips as the door was pulled sharply open and the still-wet blue paint that had previously been descending the door changed trajectory. Splatters of it flung themselves, lemming-like, at the wall opposite, and onto Lena's clothes, and down onto her shoes.

Lena stared at Megan, then down at herself, then at the door, then back up again to Megan.

"I-I can explain," Megan began, only to be cut short by Lena's fierce glare and raised hand.

"This...you...*argh!*" The scream was shockingly loud from someone as relatively small as Lena, and it rocked Megan back on her heels, nearly sending her tumbling back down the stairs behind her.

Below them, the singing and organ-playing stopped, and a few moments later, Dorothy's front door opened.

"What in the Lord's name is going on up there?" she cried.

Megan glanced down at her over the bannister.

"S-sorry, Dorothy. Just a-a little accident. Nothing for you to worry about."

"Used to be so quiet in this house," Dorothy muttered, as Megan watched her turn back to her flat. "Nothing the same since she moved in. Lord help me." The door slammed shut.

Megan closed her eyes and breathed out. *Please let this be a bad dream. Please let me wake up.*

"Well?" Lena's voice couldn't have been icier if she'd have been standing in the middle of Antarctica.

Megan raised both hands, the right still clutching tightly at the other tin of paint. "I swear, I will fix this. I am so, so sorry. I didn't realise the lid—"

Lena raised her hand again. "I. Don't. Care." She stared at Megan, and Megan's heart lurched when she saw the shimmer of tears in Lena's eyes.

She stepped forward. "God, Lena, I'm so—"

"Don't," Lena whispered, stepping back. "Please...don't." Without another word, she shut the door to her flat.

"Jen, stop laughing. It really wasn't funny." Megan closed her eyes, gripping her phone tightly against her ear, willing her temper not to flare. It was rare for it to do so; generally, Megan was considered the happiest, go-luckiest person on the planet, but the memory of Lena's tear-filled eyes cut deep, and Jen's amusement at the situation pained Megan.

"Oh, come *on*, Megs. How can you say that?" Jen snorted. "I mean, it's priceless! Just when the door gets fixed from the scratch, it gets redecorated again, and—"

"Enough!" Megan snapped. She heard Jen's sharp gasp but refused to apologise. "I mean it, Jen. I know we've laughed about my mishaps over the years, but no one's ever really got hurt by them. This one…this time I really upset someone, and that kills me."

There was a short silence. Then, "I'm sorry." Jen's voice was quiet.

"I know everyone thinks it's hilarious that I'm so clumsy at home when I'm so co-ordinated at work. But you know what? It's losing its charm. The more it happens lately, the more embarrassed I am. I feel like this big lumbering idiot—"

"Oh, hey," Jen interrupted, "you're not that at all. You get a bit…over-excited, sometimes, and rush into things. No one thinks you're an idiot. Promise."

"Well," Megan mumbled, "I think I am."

"Okay, I think we need to get some drinks inside you and chill you out. What do you say?"

Despite the pinkness in her face, Megan smiled. "I could get behind that plan," she said, shaking her shoulders to try to loosen her mood.

"All right! So, what time are you working to tonight?"

Megan walked over to her desk and flicked open the calendar on her PC. "Um, last client will be gone at eight thirty."

"Cool. So, come straight to the bar after work, yes?"

"I'll try. The boss has been after me to fill in some paperwork I keep forgetting. If I can avoid her, I'll be with you by nine."

"Which boss? The BDSM high-heels boss, or the other one?"

Megan chuckled. "The BDSM one."

Jen whistled. "Hmm, one day you are going to have to introduce me to her. You know that, right? It's what best friends are for, you know."

Megan laughed, and realised her glum mood of earlier had departed. Funny how that often happened when she talked to Jen.

"We'll see," she said. "Anyway, got to go. See you tonight."

"Cool. Laters."

Jen hung up, and Megan tucked her phone into her pocket before going on the hunt for her favourite sneakers. She remembered kicking them off as she came home but not really watching where they landed. She stepped over the pile of dirty towels thrown in the corner of the bedroom—she had to remember to wash them at the weekend—and through into the living room.

Shifting a pile of books and newspapers from beside the sofa she stepped around the furniture and found the sneakers lying haphazardly in the middle of the rug, an empty coffee mug and the scrunched-up wrapper of a protein bar beside them. Picking the litter and mug up and mentally noting that some housework might be in order at the weekend too, she deposited them in the kitchen, then pulled on her sneakers and packed her bag for the day. She had a full day of private clients rather than classes, and time in between appointments to get a decent workout in for herself, so she crammed her gear into her bag and headed to the door with a spring in her step.

The health club was busy when she walked in. Tuesdays always were, she'd noticed. Most people couldn't be bothered on a Monday, when they were all mellow or knackered from their weekends, but the guilt of weekend over-indulgence set in on Tuesday and the hordes appeared. The spin class was crammed, and she could hear Jason bellowing out his commands as he pushed everyone that little bit harder than they wanted to go. The circuit class was also in full swing, and she paused for a moment to admire Kimberly at work. Completely unattainable Kimberly, but she was still worth a look. Kimberly caught her watching and waved, which sent an instant flush across Megan's cheeks. That Kimberly knew of Megan's crush really didn't help matters. Still, at least she was cool about it, which a lot of straight women wouldn't be.

Megan walked to the changing room and threw her stuff in a locker. She had two client sessions over the traditional office lunch break time of twelve to two, then she'd be able to get her own body in action. She grabbed her brush and ran it though her long locks, then swept them back and up into a ponytail. She'd flirted occasionally with the idea of cutting it all off given how many times a week she got sweaty and had to wash it. But she'd always shied away from that big decision—she had enough comments about her 'manly shape' without adding short hair to the mix. She smiled as she remembered the look of fear on her mother's face when Megan had finally plucked up courage to come out to her.

"Does…does that mean you're going to cut your hair off and be one of those…butches?" her mum had asked, a tremor in her voice.

"Mum, butch isn't just about the haircut," she said gently. "But no, I'm not going to cut my hair off."

Her mum had sighed with relief, and that was that—Megan was out and her mum was happy.

As she departed the changing room, she heard heels clicking down the corridor behind her and sighed inwardly. That could only be Alisha. The BDSM high-heels boss, as Jen had dubbed her, all based on the initial description Megan had given her when she first started working at the club. Tall, slim, big-breasted, and always decked out in a tight skirt, tight blouse, and high heels—while she wasn't actually Megan's type, Alisha still gave Megan's stomach a little flutter every time they spoke. She had a sensuality about her that was hard to ignore.

"Megan," she called, her velvety voice just audible over the piped bass-heavy music.

Megan turned to face her. "Hi, Alisha."

Alisha smiled, her full lips glistening with a plum-coloured lipstick that looked fantastic against her brown skin. Megan blinked rapidly to pull her gaze from that inviting mouth.

"I still need those feedback forms you promised me," Alisha said.

The hint of admonishment in her tone made Megan squirm, as if she were a teenager being told off by the headmistress. *You wish, pervert.*

"Yeah, sorry. Um, if I promise to get them to you first thing, will that be okay? Only I've got a thing to get to this evening and—"

"First thing?"

Megan swallowed. "Definitely."

"I'll be waiting. Don't let me down." Alisha's grin was almost feral, and Megan's body made it very clear it liked it—the heat that travelled through her limbs to a specific point between her legs was intense. She shuffled her feet to ease the sudden ache between her thighs. Was it her, or was it suddenly very hot in the corridor?

"Never," she squeaked, and pivoted on her heels before trotting down the corridor to the main workout room. Clients. Time to focus on clients.

CHAPTER 6

LENA GLARED AT HER HALF-BLUE door as she reached the top of the communal stairs. Although Megan had profusely apologised on Sunday—when Lena had finally consented to open the door to Megan's repeated knocking—the mere sight of the re-damaged door made her heart sink. As for the ruined patch of carpet in front of it…

She used to love living in this building and in her flat in particular. Now, with Chris gone, the issue of the cats still unresolved, and her great bumbling bear of a neighbour, life at 7 Jackson Road had lost its appeal. At the same time, she didn't want to move. Moving involved change, and Lena struggled so hard with change.

She let herself into the flat, trying not to look at the door again, and hung up her coat on the hook on the back of it. As she turned back to the stairs, she noticed the damp patch again. It had rained pretty heavily the night before and all morning, and they were forecasting a series of storms over the next week or so. She looked at her watch: seven p.m. Way too late to be bothering Dorothy for her ladder. Maybe she could do it on Saturday morning, before Dorothy headed off to church organ practice.

She sighed. Dealing with Dorothy since the blue-door incident hadn't been easy either. After Lena's animalistic scream of pure frustration at what Megan had done—a sound Lena would never have imagined she was capable of making—Dorothy had marched up the communal stairs and demanded to know what in the Lord's name was going on these days. Through the tears that she was trying valiantly to hold back, Lena had briefly explained, pointed to the door, and exhaled gratefully when all Dorothy did was huff and stomp back down the stairs. But on Monday Dorothy had ignored Lena's "good morning" when they met in the hallway as Lena left for work, and that level of impoliteness wasn't Dorothy's style at all. Too tired to deal with it, Lena had merely left the house without another word and tried very hard to put all thoughts of home out of her head as she'd trotted off to work.

The trouble was, she mused, as she side-stepped the damp patch and met the cats at the top of her winding staircase, that her home was her sanctuary. She didn't want to put thoughts of it out of her head. Coming home to it every night, especially since she'd got the place back to herself, and immediately immersing herself into her evening routine of dinner, cleaning, reading, and sleeping, kept her steady.

Kept her from acknowledging that she was lonely.

She looked down at Midnight and Snow, who sat at her feet, their big eyes staring up at her. Somehow, today, they didn't look scary. Just…cute. She bent down and gave each of them a few quick strokes on their cheeks, smiling involuntarily at the purrs her touches elicited. She'd rung Chris earlier that day and left a voicemail demanding she come and get the cats or Lena was going to ship them off to Battersea Dogs and Cats Home.

"I wouldn't really do it," she whispered to the felines, who gave her blank gazes. "Just so you know. You're a pain for me, but it's not your fault."

Suddenly realising she was talking to two cats, Lena straightened and shook her head. She needed to escape into one of her books, something that would take her far away from her reality.

She finished climbing the stairs and headed for the kitchen to, first, wash her hands, and second, feed the cats. And third, wash her hands again. When she'd done that, she made her way through her spotless and tidy living room to her equally clean and tidy bedroom. Not an item was out of place in the top floor flat at 7 Jackson Road. Even the books on the two large bookcases were aligned so that their spines were perfectly straight. And alphabetised by author, obviously. The sofa had its cushions plumped every day before being covered with the dust sheet that prevented cat hair from smothering the sofa itself. The two cat beds were cleaned with a handheld vacuum cleaner every evening, and every photo or memento on the large windowsill was dusted twice a week. In the bedroom, no clothes were left lying around, everything either hung up, put away, or in the laundry basket. The bed was re-made, hotel style, every morning before she left for work, and the en-suite shower was wiped down immediately after her morning ablutions.

Lena knew it was not normal behaviour for most people, but she had always been this way. So for her, this *was* normal. She couldn't change, nor did she want to.

The phone rang as she was eating the last of her noodles. She glanced at the caller display and sighed, even as her heart rate increased.

"Hello, Chris."

"Hey, Lena." Chris sounded nervous, and a subtle thrill coursed through Lena; for once, she felt the powerful one in their interaction. "I got your message," Chris continued, when Lena said nothing.

"Yes?"

"Yeah. So. Um. The thing is—"

"No! No more excuses Chris. I mean it," Lena said, with an apologetic glance towards the two cats. "Come and get them or they go to the Home."

There was a short silence. "Lena, I... Wow, I'm astonished you would use my cats as a pawn in this."

Lena bristled and took a couple of deep breaths before responding. "That kind of pathetic emotional blackmail doesn't work either. They are your cats. Your problem. Not mine." It was tempting to plead, to try to appeal to Chris's better side, but Lena knew that would get her nowhere. It hadn't done for six months, and that wouldn't change now. Firmness and strength was required, so she gritted her teeth and ploughed on. "You have until Saturday morning. If you haven't appeared by ten a.m. I'm going to Battersea. Clear?"

She heard Chris exhale. "I'll be there Friday evening after work," she said meekly, and hung up.

Lena placed her phone beside her on the sofa, her hand shaking as she did so. She held up both hands, the tremors they were exhibiting making her eyes widen. Her stomach clenched, and she took a few more deep breaths. She hadn't known she had it in her, to be that forceful.

It felt...wonderful. Scary, but wonderful.

At a little after eight on Friday evening, the door buzzer rang and Lena jumped, despite knowing to expect it. The one thing she hadn't thought through since their phone call on Wednesday was that she would have to face Chris again. It was only the second time they'd seen each other since Chris had moved out six months ago. About a month after she'd left, Chris had called up asking if she could see the cats, and Lena had let her come to the flat for a morning. It had been awkward to the point of distressing, and Lena had given up after thirty minutes, retreating to her bedroom with a book while Chris fussed over the cats. Lena had thought that visit would have encouraged Chris to do something about the cat situation, but it wasn't to be. Belinda was clearly holding out against them going to her place, where Chris was now living, and Chris clearly cared more for Belinda than she did her cats.

Lena walked slowly to the intercom to let Chris in, then just as slowly walked down the spiral stairs to her front door. As she opened it, she became aware of two voices outside the door, and her anger flared.

She flung the door open and took in the sight of the two women before her. Chris, her short dark hair ruffled in that just-got-out-of-bed look she'd always favoured, was shuffling on a spot a few feet from the door. She looked different, and it took Lena a while to realise it was because she was wearing make-up, something she'd never done while she was with Lena. Lena's inner bitch wasn't quite sure the look suited Chris. At all. But her attention was drawn more to the tall woman standing slightly behind Chris, who Lena could only assume was Belinda. She was gorgeous, of course, with shoulder-length blonde hair, piercing blue eyes, and legs that didn't stop. She was everything Lena wasn't, and the contrast between them couldn't have been more painful to see.

Lena's hackles rose.

"Who is this?" she said, by way of greeting. She took a little pleasure at seeing Chris wince.

"Hi, Lena. This…is Belinda. She's come to—"

"No. She waits outside. She's not coming into my home." Lena's voice shook, but it wasn't quiet.

Chris took a small step backwards, and Lena marvelled at the impact this strong version of herself could have on her ex. Somewhere deep inside, she wondered how different things might have been between them if she'd stood up for herself a little more when they were together.

"Er, okay. Fair enough," Chris said, absently scratching at the back of her neck. Behind her, Belinda tutted, but when Lena turned her glare on her, she also took a step backwards.

"I'll wait...outside," Belinda said, and in the next moment spun round and practically sprinted down the stairs. As she slammed the main door behind her, Lena winced. Was Dorothy home? Would she make a—

Her question was answered instantly. Dorothy's front door opened and she called out, "Stop slamming that door!"

Lena sighed and stepped past Chris to look over the bannister. Dorothy spotted her and glared up at her.

"Sorry, Dorothy. It won't happen again."

Chris moved to look over the bannister too. "Yeah, sorry, Dorothy."

Dorothy's glare switched focus to Chris. "You?" she said, and Lena was stunned at the level of venom in that one word. "What, pray tell, are *you* doing back here?"

Chris flinched. "I'm...I'm just getting the cats."

Dorothy huffed. "And about time too," she snapped. She turned her gaze back to Lena, and her tone softened as she said, "Do you need any help?"

Lena was so taken aback by Dorothy's demeanour, to both herself and Chris, she struggled to find words. Eventually, she managed to squeak out, "No, it's all good. Thank you."

"Well, you let me know if you do. I am home all evening," she said, staring intensely back at Chris. She pointed at her and said, "I'll pray for you, young lady." And then she was gone, her door closing loudly behind her.

Chris chuckled, but it was nervous and lacked warmth. Lena, on the other hand, was glowing. Who knew Dorothy could be so...amazing?

She turned to Chris. "Come on. Let's get this over with." She didn't wait for a response but walked back into the flat and up the stairs.

It took Chris three trips to ferry all the cats' equipment and toys down to Belinda on the front doorstep, then she came back up one last time for the cats themselves. Instead of cages, which they hated, she'd fashioned a couple of slings that were going to wrap around her body with a cat in each. They'd used the system before for taking the cats to the vet, and it seemed to work.

Lena stood in the middle of the living room and watched as Chris coaxed the cats over to where she sat on the sofa. The poor suckers probably thought they were finally going to be able to snuggle on the sofa, thought

Lena. Suddenly, sadness washed over her. The cats were going. As much as they'd caused her ill health and irritation ever since they'd moved in, now that they were going she realised, that in a way, she was going to miss them. They'd been two personalities she'd come home to every night—two living, breathing creatures that had, despite her attitude towards them, always been happy to see her. Mainly, she guessed, because she fed them. But perhaps, possibly, because they loved her. The tears that pricked at her eyes were embarrassing, and she brushed them away.

In a matter of minutes, Chris had both cats wrapped in the slings and one over each shoulder. The cats looked bemused, rather than panicked, and Lena was grateful. She didn't wish them any ill or stress.

Haltingly, she stepped across the room to within a pace of Chris and tentatively reached out a hand. She scratched each cat on its forehead a couple of times and smiled as they reached up for more.

"Right," Chris said, and cleared her throat. "All done."

Lena nodded and stepped back. There was nothing she needed to say that hadn't already been said.

"Thanks for looking after them all this time."

Lena snorted. Like she'd had any choice.

Chris flinched. "Yeah, well," she said, walking towards the stairs. "I'll…I'll be going now."

Lena nodded again. "Please shut the door on your way out." If she sounded cold, she didn't care—after what Chris had done, there was no way she could feel warmth towards her.

A few moments later, the door shut and she had the place to herself again. She breathed out a couple of times, then glanced at her watch. Excellent timing—she had the rest of the evening to get things moved around ready for the carpet cleaning company she'd organised to come in first thing Saturday to do a deep clean of the place. For the first time in over two years, her flat was going to be cat-hair free.

Perfect.

CHAPTER 7

Hi Lena, just to let you know, my brother will be able to replace your door next week. Please let me know what day works best for you. Weekends are okay if that's easier. And I'm having another party tonight, Saturday. You're invited and I'd really like it if you came down to join us, but if nothing else, I wanted to warn you about the noise. Megan

LENA FOUND THE NOTE SLIPPED under her door when she got back from doing her groceries. The carpet cleaning firm had been and gone and done an excellent job. She could swear she was breathing easier already. The only unsettling incident of the morning was spotting a dark—possibly damp—patch on the wall near where the old chimney must have been. The patch was new, she was sure of that—but then, she'd been more than a little stressed lately so it could have been there for a while… Either way, she'd have to do something about it. Contact the landlord, presumably.

She sighed and looked at the note clutched in her hand, a range of emotions swirling through her. On the one hand, it was pleasing that Megan had warned her of the party and organised the new door that quickly. It obviously paid to have a brother who was a builder. But at the same time, a few hours' notice wasn't much for the party. If she'd known more in advance, she could have made plans to be elsewhere.

She closed her eyes and sighed again. Who was she kidding? Where else would she go? Since arriving in London nearly four years ago, determined to set her life on a different course from the one her parents had mapped out for her, she'd struggled to make friends. Sure, she got on okay with some of the people she worked with and occasionally joined them for drinks after work. But friends outside work had been hard to come by. She'd only met Chris through a seminar they'd both attended—Chris was also an accountant—and once involved with her, Lena had thought that was all she needed to be happy.

Now, of course, she realised the folly of that way of thinking. Especially as she'd lost all the people she called friends back in Bolton. It wasn't only her parents who'd had an issue with her announcement about her sexuality. It was amazing how quickly people she thought she knew quite well had disappeared from view after she told them. All except Madhu, of course, who truly loved Lena unconditionally.

Knowing there was nothing she could do about it now, she braced herself for an evening of noise and exuberance that would disturb her reading. Again.

It didn't take long to start—she could hear Megan's first guests arriving around seven o'clock, and grimly she snuggled farther down under the blanket on the sofa, her legs pulled up underneath her, her hands gripping her paperback. The volume of the music got louder, as did the screams and shouts. She vaguely wondered what Dorothy made of it all—had Megan warned her too? Did Dorothy have other places she could be to avoid being disturbed? Lena wouldn't be surprised if that were true. Dorothy seemed to play a pivotal role in her church and probably had many friends as a result.

At nine, she was startled by a firm knock on her front door. She waited, thinking perhaps one of Megan's guests had got the wrong door, despite each door being labelled with a letter to distinguish it from her neighbours. She was C, Megan was B.

The knock came again, slightly louder.

Sighing, she unwrapped herself from the blanket, pulled her hoodie tighter around her body, and trotted down the stairs. She looked through the peephole, and her eyes widened. It was Megan.

After unlocking the door, she inched it open, staring at Megan, who was bouncing on the spot with a huge grin on her face.

"Hey, Lena!" Megan said, expansively, and instinctively Lena knew Megan was already rather drunk.

"Hello," Lena said cautiously.

"How are you?"

Lena gave a slow nod. "Fine. What can I do for you, Megan?" What on Earth was Megan doing on her doorstep when her own party was blaring only metres away?

"I was… Well, the thing is." Megan shuffled from side to side, her cheeks flaring. "Well, I wondered if you'd like to come to the party. I know we must be disturbing you, so I thought…well, I thought maybe if you joined in, it might be nicer for you."

Lena stared at her. Megan's size made her intimidating in so many ways, but here she was, nervously stumbling her way through a personal invite to her party and looking…bashful. It seemed incongruous, and—Lena had to admit—endearing.

"I…I'm not sure that's a good idea," Lena said automatically, even as one part of her brain questioned why. Why not go to a party? Why not have some fun on a Saturday night, for once?

"Aw, really? Come on," Megan wheedled. "It'll be fun."

"Um, thanks. Really. It's…" Lena paused, wondering how much to admit, and in the next instant saying it anyway, "I don't do that well around strangers," she said quietly.

Megan cocked her head. "But I'm not a stranger," she said, grinning from ear-to-ear.

In spite of herself, in spite of everything Megan had done wrong since she moved in, Lena smiled.

"No, you're not. Really, it's nice of you to ask, but…I can't." It was too much, too soon. The thought of being surrounded by a lot of merry people who all knew each other, with the music that loud and the alcohol clearly flowing—it was too daunting. Maybe another time…

Megan's smile faded, and she shoved her hands into her jeans pockets. She looked down and back up again, exhaling as she did so. "Okay, fair enough. See you around," she said and turned back to her own flat.

Lena slowly shut her door and leaned against it. It was the right decision. It was.

And, three hours later, when her floor was vibrating from the thump of the music and her ears were ringing from the constant screaming that punctuated every track, she knew it was. She'd have hated that level of… frivolity. She'd have felt like an outsider, the wallflower nobody talked to. The weirdo everyone left alone.

Yes, not going had definitely been the right decision.

So why did she feel so hollow inside?

"Oh, my God, how much tequila did we get through?" Megan threw another empty bottle into the recycling crate and glared at Jen, who was slouched on the over-sized sofa. Jen could barely open her eyes and winced as Megan spoke.

"Please, I beg you. Not so loud." Jen's voice only just made it above a whisper.

"I'm talking normally," Megan said, wincing as her own head pounded at her words. "But maybe quieter would be good," she said, dropping her level down.

Jen gave a soft chuckle. "Trust me, you weren't complaining about the tequila last night when that hot chick was licking salt off your abs."

Megan groaned, rubbing the area where the hot chick's tongue had been. Yeah, that had been a highlight, all right. Until later when grains of salt started appearing in places they had no right to be.

"Who was she anyway?" Jen asked.

"No idea. I thought you knew her?"

Jen laughed, shaking her head. "Nope. But I sure would like to."

Megan couldn't actually agree. As much as she loved throwing parties, a party woman like that wasn't someone she would think to pursue. She'd done that before, a couple of times, and had been disappointed in the experience. Going drinking every night and dancing until the small hours had got very boring, very quickly. She'd soon also realised that both of those women she'd dated weren't interested in anything serious, only when and where the next party was. While she didn't want anything as serious as she'd had with Julie—at least, not yet—she wanted something more than the frivolous shallowness those women had offered.

She shook her head as she moved around the kitchen tidying up. Best not to let thoughts of Julie get into her sore head—it was bad enough remembering her when she was sober and lucid. A hangover would surely make the memories feel ten times worse.

Ten minutes later, Megan finished piling empty bottles and cans in the recycling crate and dumped it by the front door. She turned to survey the flat. It looked like a bomb had hit it. There were empty pizza boxes strewn all over the living room, items of clothing that she was sure weren't hers or Jen's draped over the floor cushions and sofa, and her media centre was covered in empty CD cases and what looked like peanuts. She walked over. Yep, peanuts. She had no idea how they had got there.

She stood with her hands on her hips, wondering if she had the energy right now to deal with this. It took only a nanosecond to decide that no, she really didn't.

"Want to get some brunch?" she asked Jen, who smiled widely.

Later—much later, after a long brunch with Jen that involved a couple of hairs of the dog—Megan finally began sorting through the crap from the night before. She'd already had two calls from people claiming items of clothing, and those had been set aside for collection Monday evening. The rest of the clothing had been folded up and stacked in a corner. The rubbish had been taken down to the bins outside, Megan being very careful not to disturb Dorothy, as there was no way Megan could deal with her and a hangover at the same time. She'd heard no sound from Lena upstairs, and her heart sank a little again at the thought of the beautiful but oh-so-shy woman who lived above her.

Lena was a mystery to Megan. On the outside, she always came across as irritable and snappy. But there was something in her eyes, something that said there was a whole different person on the inside, itching to get out. That was why she'd tried to get her to join the party. She'd thought it would be good for Lena to cut loose. But she'd been shut tight again, turning Megan down with what seemed ease. Only…it had been there, again. In her eyes. A kind of haunted desire to break free.

Megan shook her head. Not her problem. She wasn't exactly Lena's favourite person at the moment, after all the nightmares she'd caused her.

So why couldn't Megan stop thinking about that golden-brown skin and those amazing brown eyes with their luxurious lashes?

"Argh!" Her cry was muted because her head still couldn't take full volume, but it was loaded with the frustration she felt at the situation her own stumbles had created with Lena.

She flopped onto the sofa and switched on the TV. The BBC News channel was on, and she'd happened across the weather forecast for the week ahead.

"…and it's going to be a fierce one, that much we can tell you." The forecaster pointed at the map of Britain behind her. "We're going to see very high winds, and lashings of rain, leading to localised flooding in many areas. There are amber warnings in place in many areas of the UK, and red alerts on most of the eastern coastline. And those of you in the cities, especially London, don't think this one will pass you by." The forecaster clicked her remote, and the map changed to a more detailed representation of southern England. "As you can see, London and all major towns in the south-east are directly in the path of this storm, and the Met Office are urging everyone to be prepared."

Megan muted the TV and gazed at her windows. She assumed they were weather-proof enough for a storm of the magnitude the forecaster had been talking about. She stood up and walked over to them. A few rattles of the old sashes, and suddenly she wasn't so sure. Some things seemed awfully loose, and there was definitely a wicked draft coming from one corner where the sash didn't quite fit as it should. She found some thick tape and patched the hole as best she could for now. When the storm was over, she'd get Callum to take a look, see what he could do.

Lena battled her way up Jackson Road, her hair whipping in the wet wind, her face running with cold rain. She'd given up on her umbrella the minute she left the Tube station as the thing had almost got ripped from her hands. The wind was fierce, and every now and then it would shoot her sideways as she lifted a foot off the ground to take a step forwards. There had been reports on the news of trees and walls down all over London, so she had at least been prepared for this staggered method of getting home. This was the tail end of the storm that had started a little before dawn—the first blasts of wind against her windows had woken her with a start, and she'd never fully got back to sleep afterwards. In the end, she'd given up and arrived at her desk an hour earlier than normal, simply because it was easier to get on with the day than try to sleep around the noise.

Thankful that Jackson Road was only a five-minute walk from the Tube, she grunted in relief when number seven came into view. She opened the small, black metal gate and wedged it tightly shut behind her after she'd passed through—the last thing any of them needed was that swinging and clanging in the wind all night. She walked quickly up the path and breathed for a moment in the relative shelter offered by the brick archway over the front step. Lena slotted her key into the lock, pushed open the main front door, and walked into a storm of a different kind.

"...all afternoon! I am very tired of having this conversation with you, young lady."

Lena shut the front door behind her and stared at the confrontation in front of her. Dorothy was standing at the bottom of the stairs, waving a finger at Megan, who was two steps up the communal staircase and looking like she'd rather be anywhere but here.

"But Dorothy, I've been out all day. I've only just got home." Megan's voice was strained.

"What's going on?" Lena asked, shaking water off her coat onto the mat below her.

Dorothy spun round. "Banging and crashing around! This afternoon!" Her eyes were wide, her finger still pointing at Megan. "Ever since she moved in, it's been nothing but noise, Lord help me."

Lena stared at Megan, who said, her voice a whisper, "I swear, I only just got home. I don't know what she means."

Lena cocked her head and looked back at Dorothy. "What sort of noise was it?"

Dorothy threw her arms up. "Banging! And crashing!"

Lena held her hands out in a placating gesture and took a deep breath. "Okay, Dorothy. Wait..." She paused, as a sudden thought pitched into her brain. What if...what if the noise was burglars? In either Megan's or—she gasped—her flat?

"What?" asked Megan and Dorothy simultaneously.

"What if...it's burglars?" Lena managed to squeeze the words out before she clapped a hand over her mouth in fright.

Dorothy gasped and clutched at her chest. Megan's eyes widened, but in the next instant she stood up even taller and squared her shoulders.

"Dorothy, please go inside your flat and be ready to call the police if I shout, okay?"

Dorothy stared at her, but the strength of command in Megan's voice was clearly not something even she could resist. Lena watched as, without another word, Dorothy slowly turned and walked to her own front door,

46

hovering inside her flat, her wide eyes staring at Megan with something close to…respect.

Lena turned to Megan. "Wh-what are you going to do?"

Megan smiled grimly. "I'm going to find out what's going on." She turned away, but Lena rushed after her, grabbed her arm, and pulled her back round. Absently, Lena noted how strong that arm was.

"What?" Megan asked, frowning.

"But…but isn't it dangerous?" Lena's voice wobbled as her fear at what Megan would find—and what might happen to Megan if she did find someone up there—rushed through her in a cold wave.

Megan smiled and gently prised Lena's hand off her forearm. "Don't worry. I know how to look after myself."

Lena took in the confident woman standing in front of her and didn't doubt it for a moment. "Okay," she said quietly, and stepped back down to ground level.

Megan nodded and turned back to continue walking up the stairs.

Ignoring the small flutter of panic that was churning in her lower belly, Megan strode up the stairs, flexing her fingers into fists and out again. She was strong, and although she had learnt a few martial arts moves from various fitness instructors she'd worked with over the years, she was actually completely winging it right now. It had seemed like the right thing to do—project confidence and strength to keep both Lena and Dorothy from sliding into full-blown panic mode. But now she was nearing the top of the stairs and wishing her gut reaction had been something different.

Like, call the bloody police and hide in Dorothy's flat until they got here.

However, here she was, resolutely marching up the stairs to meet who knew what fate.

She turned the corner of the stairs, her gaze darting left to her own front door, which looked intact, then right to Lena's, which also looked intact. She pondered that for a moment. Either the burglars, if that's who it was, had keys and had calmly let themselves in and shut the door behind them, or they'd got in through a window. She snorted softly to herself. *Yeah, right, Megs.* How would they do that without a ladder?

Relaxing slightly as her instinct told her the problem probably wasn't burglars, she walked first to her own front door and pressed her ear against it. It wasn't easy to focus, as the wind was still rattling the large window over the stairs in the main hallway now and then. But in between gusts, she concentrated on listening for any sound coming from within her flat.

Nothing.

Another minute.

Still nothing.

She straightened and pulled her keys from her bag. Leaning over the bannister to her left, she met Lena's worried gaze.

"No sound from my place and both doors are intact. I don't think it's burglars," she whispered.

"Then why are you whispering?" Lena whispered back.

Megan blushed. "Sorry," she said, in a normal tone. "Let me go into my flat and check around, then we'll do yours, okay?"

Lena nodded.

It took less than two minutes to confirm that all was well in her own flat, with absolutely no sign of disturbance. She walked back out to the narrow hallway between hers and Lena's flats and leaned over the bannister again.

"Do you want to come up?" She saw Lena's eyes widen. "Or do you want to give me your keys and I'll do a quick check first?"

Lena nodded furiously, even as she blushed.

"Hey," Megan said softly. "Don't be embarrassed. It's okay to be afraid."

Lena's blush deepened as she walked up enough of the stairs to hand Megan her keys over the bannister. She turned back away before Megan could say anything else, and she decided now was not the time to push Lena.

She unlocked Lena's door, wincing as her gaze automatically went to the blue coating on the bottom half of it, and pushed it open.

The first thing she noticed was the cold. The next was the smell—damp and musty and earthy, almost smoky. Baffled, she slowly climbed the staircase, but she had only made it about four steps up when water dripping on her head made her look upwards and gasp. Where there used to be a window—she could see the frame barely hanging on from one corner—there was now a gaping hole. Underneath it, a rafter, pitted and marked with age, lay at an unnatural angle with another huge hole in the roof above where it had fallen from, through which Megan could see the stormy sky. Her gaze dropped downwards and now her brain registered the broken tiles and dusty debris scattered across the top of the winding stairs.

She closed her eyes for a moment. Poor Lena. Her stomach clenched at the thought of having to show Lena what had happened, and she wanted to put that off for as long as possible. She needed to know how bad this was before she let Lena up here. It crossed her mind that it might not be safe, so she took a moment to listen, to hear if there were any sounds of things still falling or disintegrating. All she could hear was the storm raging overhead, and the only things that fell were raindrops on her upturned face.

Cautiously, making sure that each foot was securely placed before moving the next, she crept up the staircase. She turned the few steps at the top, which opened up her view to the main room of Lena's flat, an open-plan living room and kitchen much like her own, only smaller. Megan stopped dead on the last step, and her heart lurched again for poor Lena.

The flat looked like a bomb had been dropped on it. Across part of the living room another roof beam lay in pieces, and scattered over it, in a pattern that gave away where they came from, were broken, dusty, and blackened bricks.

It could only be the chimney.

Or, she corrected herself, part of it—there wasn't quite enough damage for it to have been the full stack itself. Although the damage was horrendous as it was nonetheless. Above all the mess was another enormous hole in the roof, currently letting in rain all over the remains of Lena's possessions, which must have tumbled on impact with the falling chimney. Books, for the most part, it seemed, flattened under tiles and bricks, and getting wetter by the minute; some were already pulp. The far end of the beam that had crashed through the ceiling had also smashed into Lena's kitchen worktop, and, as Megan gingerly stepped further into the room, she could see the remains of a microwave and kettle on the floor. The sofa, which had clearly once been a sort of apricot shade, was now mostly dirty grey, and she couldn't begin to hazard a guess at what colour the rug in front of it must have been.

Shit.

Almost on autopilot, she pulled her phone from her pocket.

"Hey, sis," Callum's voice boomed. "What's up?"

"Bro, I need you. Right now."

49

CHAPTER 8

WHAT WAS TAKING SO LONG? Lena paced the hallway in front of the main door, nibbling at her fingernails and huffing out choppy breaths. What was Megan doing up there?

"Calm yourself, Lena."

Lena snapped her head up. She'd forgotten Dorothy was still there. The older woman had crept up on her with surprising stealth. She was staring at Lena, her hands clasped together in front of her rotund belly, a warm smile stretching her mouth wide.

"She'll tell us when she's ready." Dorothy reached out to pat Lena on the shoulder. "She knows what she's doing, that one. Bless her." She closed her eyes. "Bless her," she repeated in a whisper.

"I-I know." Lena's voice shook, but she couldn't seem to stop it. She was…afraid. Afraid of what had happened to her flat, and—more surprisingly—afraid that something would happen to Megan. She wasn't sure she liked Megan. The woman had, after all, made Lena's life a misery since she moved in last month. But that didn't mean Lena wanted any harm to come to her. That's all it was. Simply natural concern from one human being to another. She twitched at the thought. It wasn't that, not precisely.

Dorothy's hand on Lena's shoulder squeezed, bringing Lena's attention back to what she realised was a warm and friendly face, still split by a wide smile. "Have faith, Lena," Dorothy said. "He will protect Megan, and all of us."

Lena wasn't so sure about that, but she let it slide. Dorothy had never particularly preached to Lena since they'd become neighbours, and she was grateful for that. She could let Dorothy have these occasional moments.

The sound of Megan walking across the landing above them pulled Lena's attention back to the staircase, and she gazed up it as Megan rounded the turn at the top.

Lena didn't know what Megan did for a living, but she hoped it wasn't anything where she had to give bad news out often, because she completely lacked a poker face. That something dreadful had happened was written all over her features, and Lena's hands flew to her own face before Megan even said a word.

"What is it?" Dorothy asked what Lena couldn't.

"Lena, I'm so sorry," Megan began, slowly descending the stairs. "It's… it's the storm. It's…the chimney's come down."

Dorothy gasped and clutched at Lena's shoulder again. "Be strong, child," she murmured. "He works in mysterious ways. There is always a reason."

Lena barely heard her above the rushing sound in her ears. The chimney? What did Megan mean exactly?

"Wh-what?" It was the only word Lena could manage; her brain was spinning at a hundred miles an hour, and no single thought could sit still long enough for her to focus on it.

Megan had reached ground level, and she shuffled on the spot although her gaze never left Lena's face. "Part of the chimney stack has come down… into your living room."

Lena gasped and swayed. Only Dorothy's hand on her shoulder kept her upright.

"It's brought down two rafters, and some kind of window that was in your roof."

"Skylight," Lena murmured, wondering why she felt the need to grammatically correct Megan at this exact moment.

"Right. Skylight." Megan rubbed at her chin with one hand. "Well, it's…shit—" Dorothy tutted and Megan winced "—it's a bit of a mess up there."

Lena wondered why the hallway had suddenly gone all blurry. Was she back out in the rain?

"Oh, child, don't cry." Dorothy's voice seemed to come from far away; Lena could barely hear it. Cry? What did Dorothy mean? Then she felt the dampness on her cheeks, and on her chin, and the sob that escaped her throat sounded awfully loud. The next thing she knew she was pulled into an extremely soft and expansive bosom and rocked gently, while her sobs got louder and more painful, but there was no way she could stop them.

"The tarps will keep the worst out, for sure, and the boys have done a good job of pinning it all down." Callum was wiping at his face with a tea towel while Megan made him a cup of tea. "But it needs to get looked at soon. I'm not a surveyor, but even I can see that chimney stack's been disintegrating for years. It needs stabilising and rebuilding, and the whole roof needs to be replaced coz it's probably been weakened in so many places over the years, thanks to the chimney. You got a landlord, right?"

Megan nodded, handing him the tea.

"Thanks, sis." He took a sip and sighed appreciatively. "Well, then she needs to get him on the case, pronto. Like I said, it seems okay up there for now, but you never know. And if we get another storm…" He met Megan's concerned stare and shrugged. "I don't know. It's a mess all right."

Megan sighed and rubbed her hands over her face, her tiredness threatening to swamp her. It was gone eleven. Callum and his boys had been amazing, dropping everything they had planned for the evening and arriving in a sequence of cars and vans that had made it look like a raid was taking place when they'd all screeched to a halt outside the building. They'd leapt into action the minute she let them in, hauling huge sheets of tarpaulin and ladders up into Lena's flat, propping up the downed rafters or putting supports in place where chunks were missing, and generally being extraordinarily efficient and chirpy. In turn, she'd ordered in a stack of pizzas and made endless cups of tea to keep them happy.

Now it was just Callum left, and she couldn't begin to express her gratitude to her brother. His behaviour wasn't surprising though—if there was one thing their parents had instilled in them from a very early age, it was the need to be there for each other, no matter what.

"Callum, I—"

He raised a hand before she could get any further. "No need. You're family, and family always comes first."

Except Lena wasn't family, and Callum had done it anyway, simply because it affected someone Megan knew in the place where she lived.

She closed the distance across the kitchen to her brother and pulled him into a rough hug. He patted her awkwardly on the back. "S'all right, Megs. No worries."

"Thank you," she said, pulling back to gaze at him. "You're the best."

Callum blushed. Actually blushed, which Megan didn't think she'd ever seen happen in her whole life. Not knowing quite what to say to him in that moment, she turned away and made a pretence of clearing up the tea things.

Callum cleared his throat. "How's she doing?" he asked quietly.

Megan turned back to him, sighing. "She's a mess."

They both looked towards the sofa, where Lena was wrapped up in a bundle of blankets, sleeping. It hadn't taken Megan nearly as much persuasion as she thought to get Lena to stay the night. Lena was in shock, of that there was no doubt, and her resistance was minimal. It was tomorrow Megan wasn't looking forward to—Lena was going to wake up in a strange place with none of her things and all hell would probably break loose.

But still, that was tomorrow. Tonight, now, Megan needed to get to bed. Her own adrenalin rush had worn off long ago, and she ached for the comfort of her duvet.

"Right." Callum drained the last of his tea. "I'd better get off. Karen'll be wondering where I am."

"Sure. Say hi to her and the kids for me."

Callum grinned and nodded, and Megan walked him to the front door. After closing it quietly behind him so as not to disturb Lena, she walked over to gaze down at the sleeping woman. She hadn't meant for Lena to fall asleep on the sofa—she had a perfectly serviceable spare bedroom after all. But Lena had suddenly collapsed there, a while after Callum's team had finished the main work. Megan had walked into the room to find Lena snoring gently, her head twisted at an odd angle, with a line of drool slowly inching its way down her chin. Laughing softly to herself, Megan had gently pushed and pulled Lena into a horizontal position. She'd removed her shoes, found some blankets from the spare room, and tucked her in.

Megan sighed. She and Lena had had their differences, for sure. But no one deserved this shit to happen to them. She just hoped Lena could get herself sorted out with somewhere else to live soon.

Lena was conflicted. While it did feel comforting, in a way, to have Megan right behind her as she made her way up the stairs in her wrecked flat, at the same time she'd rather Megan didn't witness the tears that kept falling. She'd rather keep her despair to herself, thank you very much. But Megan had insisted, citing concerns over how stable everything was—or wasn't—and Lena had been too tired to argue. She had also been amazed that Megan had excused herself from work for the day, citing an "emergency" so that she could be here for Lena, who had also taken a day out from her own job to deal with this…nightmare.

She'd slept fitfully. Not because Megan's sofa was uncomfortable—far from it, in fact. But she wasn't in her own place, her own bed, with her own neat space surrounding her. Instead she was wrapped up in blankets that might or might not have been clean, in a flat that was distinctly less than tidy compared to her own. She'd shuddered at the piles of pizza boxes left strewn around the living room after the builders had left, even though she'd simultaneously been grateful for all they'd done. She'd flinched when she'd had to use the bathroom and seen pale blonde hairs *everywhere*—on the floor, on the counter top, in the sink. Deep down she knew Megan wasn't that messy, not really. But all of it, the strangeness of being in someone else's place, the things not left where Lena would have left them, it all conspired to leave her unsettled and deeply uncomfortable.

And now she had to face the reality of what Megan had briefly described to her yesterday, and the sight of her carpet covered in dirt all the way up the stairs was already causing her breathing to quicken and her pulse to race. She could tell from what little Megan had said that Callum's team had cleared away a lot of the debris—no tiles lay scattered across the stairs, for example. But the dirt was there, and possibly even worse after being trampled into the carpet by those many pairs of booted feet last night.

She heaved in a huge breath as she reached the top of the stairs and saw the carnage that awaited her. Fighting back more tears, she made herself walk into the room, across the squishy damp carpet, as far as was safe to do so. She could see where Callum's team had erected supports and steered clear of those, placing herself near the kitchen area, which seemed to have avoided the worst of the damage. Except for the enormous crack down the middle of the worktop, of course. The broken rafter that had caused that had been cleared away, but the scar told its story.

"You okay?" Megan's voice was quiet behind her. Lena looked around and noted Megan had stayed at the top of the stairs, giving Lena some space.

Lena shrugged. "Not really." She looked back into the room, and a sob caught in her throat. Piled up on a square piece of tarpaulin were the remains of her books. Her beloved books, now a mash of wet and damaged paper with barely a single one left unscathed. She trembled as she stepped closer to the pile. Was anything retrievable? She knelt on the edge of the tarp before the stack, and all hope left her. For some, the titles could still be read on the spines, but the pages were crinkled and glued together. For others, even the spines couldn't be read, the water damage was so great.

"Given what Dorothy said, once she'd calmed down, we think it happened around three o'clock. Which means they sat in the rain for four hours, nearly five, before Callum could cover them up. I'm so sorry." Megan did sound genuinely sad for Lena, and it helped. A little.

Shaking her head, Lena turned away, trying to get the image of that sodden pile out of her head. Her gaze fell on her floppy-eared bunny slippers, wrecked almost beyond recognition. She wanted to cry. "What... what about the bedroom?" she asked, even though she was scared to hear the answer.

"It's not so bad in there. Your bed has a little damage, like on the duvet, but I think your wardrobe and chest of drawers are intact, so your clothes should be okay."

It was something, at least. Deciding the living area was too depressing to look at, Lena walked to the bedroom. A quick glance round told her Megan was right: the damage here was nowhere near as bad as the main room. Avoiding looking directly at the bed, where out of the corner of her eye she could see a swathe of dirt across the duvet, she opened the wardrobe and found clean, undamaged clothes. Her stress level dissipated a notch.

"Do you want some help packing?" Megan was in the doorway, pointing to the open wardrobe.

There was no way a stranger was touching her clothes. Lena bit back a snippy retort, acknowledging Megan was only trying to be friendly, and shook her head.

"It's okay. I can do it." Lena reached up to the top of the wardrobe, then realised with a sigh of irritation that she couldn't reach the suitcases she'd stored up there, and her short ladder steps were buried somewhere in the mess that was her kitchen. She closed her eyes for a moment, then said, "Please could you get these down for me."

Megan, to her credit, said nothing and simply walked into the room, pulled down both suitcases, then left the room just as quietly.

"Thank you," Lena belatedly said after her.

"I'll be just out here," Megan called. "Let me know if you need anything. And take your time."

"Oh, no!" Madhu's voice in Lena's ear was a balm. After the stress of everything she'd had to deal with today, being able to spill it all out to the one person who got her was an enormous relief. "Oh, Lena, I am *so* sorry to hear that. What are you going to do? Are you okay? Were you hurt?"

Lena smiled at the barrage of questions and realised it was probably the first smile she'd managed since Sunday, two days ago. "I'm okay. I wasn't home when it happened." She shuddered as she pondered the implications of that. Imagine if she'd been sitting on her sofa reading when that destruction rained down? Would she still even be alive?

"Well, at least there's that," Madhu said. "But…what now?"

Lena sighed and shifted position on the sofa. It was still only the day after the storm, but it felt like she'd been at Megan's for days. Megan had retreated to the spare room to catch up on e-mails—and to give Lena some privacy for her phone call—but Lena was very much aware that she was invading Megan's space.

"I have no idea," Lena said, her voice small. "We called the landlord last night, to report the damage. Now we have to wait for his insurance assessor to come round and see what they say. I can't live there, that much is obvious. I assume his insurance will pay for me to live somewhere until it's done. But that's going to take some time to sort out. And…"

"And?"

Lena closed her eyes, and her voice dropped to a whisper. "It will probably be somewhere awful, Madhu, and you know I don't like change anyway."

"I know." Madhu's voice was equally quiet. "But I don't know what else you can do. I mean, I'd offer you our spare room but—"

"Oh, Madhu, of course not. I mean, how would that work? I can't commute from Bolton every day, and anyway, you really don't have the room, especially not with the baby on the way."

"I know. I just don't like to think of you with nowhere to go."

Lena swallowed. "I know. And it could be months, Megan's brother said, before my place is fit to live in again."

"Months?" Madhu squeaked.

"I know." Lena passed a hand tiredly over her forehead. "I don't know what to do."

"Could you get a hotel for a few nights? Just something really cheap? Or ask someone at work if they can put you up for a while?"

"I-I guess I could ask around, see if anyone has a spare room." The thought nauseated her. It was unsettling enough not having her own space, but to share with someone she barely knew, and learn a whole new routine, a new commute? The shivers that ran down her spine chilled her.

"Hey." Madhu's exclamation broke into Lena's maudlin thoughts. "What about those cousins, remember? The ones Mum doesn't really talk to anymore." Madhu giggled. "Probably means you'd like them."

Lena snorted, then laughed, and it felt good. "I can't remember where they live, can you?"

"I've got this idea it was way out east London somewhere. I'll try to find out. Maybe Dad will tell me. There's no way I'm asking her."

They talked for a few minutes longer before Madhu had to hang up. "I'm sorry, Lena. It's my stupid bladder. I've got to go."

Lena laughed. "I understand."

"Call me later. I'm sure Megan won't mind you staying with her a couple of days until we can get you sorted out, so I'll get that info about the cousins as soon as I can, okay?"

After she ended the call, Lena tapped the phone against her chin. She supposed it would be okay to stay here for a couple of days, but if Madhu couldn't come through with the info on the cousins, or if they didn't have room, or didn't even live in London anymore—

She closed her eyes in exasperation. This was…impossible. For the tenth time that day, tears threatened, but she didn't have the energy to let them fall. She was so tired of crying and feeling sorry for herself, but she had no idea how to change that.

CHAPTER 9

"WHAT DID THE ASSESSOR SAY?" Megan asked as she shrugged out of her coat. She'd had to go back to work today, but Lena had taken one more day off work to meet the assessor. She'd felt odd being alone in Megan's home and in fact had gone out for a long walk during the morning to try to ease her discomfort. It didn't help much at all—her whole life felt completely disjointed. She'd spent last night in Megan's spare room, her suitcases and few other belongings rescued from the nightmare above them placed as neatly as she could in the small room. Sleep had been difficult; there were new noises to get used to, a bed that wasn't as comfortable as her own, a different detergent smell on the bed clothes. All of it sent her anxiety levels rocketing and left her looking quite the worse for wear come morning.

Megan had tip-toed around her over breakfast, and although Lena was grateful, she couldn't bring herself to say so, or engage in any kind of conversation. She was unravelling at the seams. Madhu had texted her a couple of times, however, and that had helped a little.

Now, the simple question from Megan set Lena's heart pounding again, and her hands fidgeted with the mini iPad she held in her lap. Megan sat down beside her on the sofa.

"It... He told me what happens now, and how long it's all likely to take." The anger bubbled up, and the next words spat out of her mouth. "And he also told me that our landlord only paid for the basic policy they offer. So although they have declared the flat uninhabitable, which relieves me of paying rent, the policy doesn't pay an allowance for me to be re-housed while the repairs are going on. So I have to find somewhere else, and unless I want to pay significantly more than I was paying upstairs, I can only afford to get something like this at short notice." She thrust the iPad in Megan's direction.

Megan leaned over to look at what was displayed on the screen.

"Ew," she said immediately.

"Yes," Lena snapped. "Exactly."

Megan sat back, her eyes wide. "Wh-what are you going to do?"

Lena sighed and sunk back into the sofa alongside Megan. Snarling at Megan didn't help anybody. She breathed in and out a couple of times to get her heart rate down.

"I'm sorry for being short with you," she said quietly. "This whole scenario is very stressful for me."

Megan waved her apology off. "Of course," she said. "Anyone would react the same way."

Lena offered a weak smile. "I don't actually know what I'm going to do. To start with, I need to call my sister back. There are some distant cousins somewhere in east London who could possibly put me up. If that doesn't work out, I'll ask around at work tomorrow. I'll be out of your way soon. And I am very grateful for what you've done for me."

Megan's smile was warm. "Hey, you're welcome. I was happy to help. It was awful what happened to your flat. I'd hate to go through something like that. I think you're doing pretty well, actually."

"Thank you." Lena straightened her shoulders. She really did need to stop wallowing now and get on with sorting this out. The quicker she did it, the quicker she could get some kind of routine back. "Okay, I am going to call my sister." She stood and walked off to the spare room.

Megan sipped her beer and looked at the door to the spare room for about the tenth time in as many minutes. Lena had been in there a long time considering she only had one call to make. Maybe she just needed some space. Some quiet time. Although she'd been on her own all day, so surely she'd had enough quiet time already?

Stop worrying. She's a grown-up. If she wants to talk, she will.

But…when Megan had first come home, Lena had looked completely distraught, sitting rigidly on the sofa, her cheeks slightly flushed. Megan couldn't help worrying about her. She'd figured out pretty quickly in the last forty-eight hours that Lena was an anxious person, to say the least. Megan thought that was probably her normal behaviour, so having to deal with the roof disaster could only have been making it a hundred times worse. She hoped Lena's sister could come through for her. Funny, she'd never mentioned her parents in all of this...

Megan chugged some more of her beer, then began chopping ingredients for a quick stir-fry. She'd make enough for two, in case Lena was hungry, and—

The sound of a throat clearing behind her had her turning quickly.

Lena's expression was downcast, but at the same time her mouth was set in a firm line.

"No luck?" Megan asked, pretty sure she already knew the answer.

Lena shook her head, her gaze darting away. She motioned towards the pile of vegetables on the counter. "Can I help?"

Megan stared at Lena for a few moments. If Lena didn't want to talk about it, she had to respect that. But she was dying to know what her sister had said.

Lena frowned, and Megan snapped out of her thoughts.

"Sure," she said, pulling another chopping knife from the block. "I'm making a stir-fry if you'd like to join me?"

"Thank you," Lena said quietly, and Megan knew she wasn't only talking about dinner.

"You're welcome."

They ate quickly and silently, the TV news on in the background. When they'd finished, Lena insisted on clearing up. She clearly wanted to keep busy, and Megan was happy to let her—clearing up was one of her least favourite tasks. From the happy humming sounds Lena made as she worked, Megan guessed it was the complete opposite for her guest. She surreptitiously watched Lena as she methodically wiped down every countertop, even the ones they hadn't gone anywhere near during the preparation of the meal. Monica from *Friends* sprang to mind, and Megan only just held back a snort of laughter.

"Having fun?" she asked.

Lena whirled round, the cloth clutched tightly in her hand. "What?" Her eyes had narrowed in a look that frightened Megan a little bit. Well, okay, more than a little.

"I-I wondered if you were enjoying yourself. You were humming and—"

"Look, I like cleaning, okay? It's no big deal." Lena's face had scrunched into a frown so deep Megan feared it would leave permanent marks. "Just… leave me alone." Lena turned back, folded up the cloth, and placed it neatly on the draining board, and before Megan could think to respond, Lena marched off to the bathroom.

Megan sat on the sofa in a daze. What the hell had just happened?

Lena pressed her face into the towel and exhaled a long breath. What had she done? She'd ripped Megan's head off for no reason whatsoever. Here, now, in the cool bathroom with her face damp from where she'd washed it, her temperature had eased off to a level that felt under control. But back there, in the kitchen, she'd literally seen red when Megan made that joke about her being so happy cleaning. It had taken Lena right back to all the times Chris had teased her, only Chris's teasing had *hurt*—needle-sharp words that had dug away at Lena's sense of self until her anxiety made her nauseous.

Megan wasn't doing that. Lena knew this, and yet she'd still snapped at her in an almost automatic reaction. She pulled the towel away from her now-dry face and dared to look at herself in the mirror. Her eyes, amazingly, hadn't lost their shine—she'd always been complimented on her eyes, the irises a brown that almost glowed it was so intense. Her hair looked a mess, she couldn't deny that. It needed a wash, and a deep condition, something to remove the tangles from where she'd been running her fingers through it over the last two days. Her skin had also lost its glow, but given how badly she was sleeping, that also made sense. She looked years older than thirty-two, and the thought only added to her depression.

She turned away from the mirror and hung the towel up. Maybe she should call it a night, see if she could get a long sleep before she returned to work tomorrow. She had to go back, if only to start asking around about possible places to stay. She shuddered; it was the last thing she wanted to do, but life had served up this mess to her and she had to get on with it.

Bracing herself, she unlocked the bathroom door and stepped back into the living room.

Megan was on the sofa, drinking from a bottle of beer and watching TV. Lena walked over to stand by the arm of the sofa.

"Megan," she said, her relief swamping her as Megan deigned to turn and face her. "I am so sorry for snapping at you yet again just then."

Megan nodded, but her eyes were dim, and Lena couldn't begin to explain to herself why that sight tugged so sharply at her belly.

"I get it," Megan said, shrugging. "You're going through a really stressful time."

"Yes, that's true, but that's no reason to take it out on you, especially when you have been so generous and…wonderful about letting me stay here and getting your brother to help out."

Megan shrugged again and made to turn back to the TV.

"Wait, please," Lena pleaded. She saw Megan exhale before she turned back to face Lena. "I want to thank you, again, for letting me stay here. I'm sorry I can't tell you when I'll get out of your way. I really hoped the cousin idea would work out but it appears they want nothing to do with me, despite us having common ground in being ostracised by my mother." The admission came without warning, and Lena blinked rapidly as she realised what she'd said.

Megan's eyes widened, and she shifted slightly in her seat to face Lena more easily.

"I'm…I'm sorry to hear that," Megan replied.

Lena wondered how hard it was for her not to ask for more info. Her respect for Megan grew when no questions were immediately forthcoming.

"Yes, well, it's…it's a long story." Lena sighed. "Anyway, tomorrow I will go back to work and ask around there to see if anyone has a spare room I could use for the next few months."

"Are you close to the people you work with?"

Lena shrugged and laughed softly. "Not really. But if I offer them the money I would normally pay as rent, maybe someone would be willing." She looked away from Megan's gaze, those astonishingly beautiful eyes distracting her again. "So, I wanted to apologise, and thank you, and to say that I'm going to have an early night. Goodnight."

She walked quickly away, but as she reached the door to the spare room, Megan called out, "Lena, wait. Please."

She turned back to find those pale blue eyes staring intently at her.

"You know, I was thinking," Megan said, getting up off the sofa and taking a few steps towards Lena, her hands tucking into the pockets of her sweatpants. "Maybe you should stay here. Until your place is fixed. However long you need." Megan's face was flushed but her voice was firm. "I've got a spare room, and I could, you know, rent that to you. You wouldn't have to change your commute and all that. You'd be on site to monitor all the repairs. And I'd get a bit of money to help me out for a little while—I kind of maxed out my credit card buying all the furniture so God knows I could do with the cash." She grinned.

Lena swallowed. Was she—? "Are you *serious*?" Lena's voice came out significantly squeakier than she'd hoped. "I mean," she said, clearing her throat, "you really wouldn't mind?"

Megan shrugged. "Like I said, it seems the easiest answer. I know we haven't exactly—"

Lena held up a hand. "Wait," she said. "Just…give me a moment."

She closed her eyes. Could it work? They definitely had got off on the wrong foot from the minute they'd met. Megan was awfully untidy. And noisy. And too…exuberant. But they worked different hours from each other, so wouldn't necessarily see each other *that* often. And maybe Lena could spend the weekends in Bolton with Madhu, to have a break. Although that would bring its own challenges for her borderline-OCD nature, given how small and packed with…stuff Madhu's place was. Megan's place was big enough, she supposed. The spare room was a little small, but maybe with a bit of shuffling Megan's brother could help get her wardrobe down there, and—

She opened her eyes. "Yes. Please." Lena's stare was as wide as Megan's as her words blurted out. "I mean, can we at least try?"

Megan smiled.

CHAPTER 10

"You did what?" Megan's mum's voice was awfully loud down the phone, and she winced. "I thought the whole point of getting somewhere bigger was to have some space to yourself? And now you've let a virtual stranger move in. A woman, I might add, who hated your guts until very recently. Possibly still does, despite all the help you've given her this week. Oh, Megan…"

"Mum, I couldn't help it. She looked so sad, and there's obviously some issue with her family, and—"

"Oh, why am I not surprised. Don't tell me, she turned some gorgeous puppy eyes on you and you were a goner." There was laughter in her voice.

"No, it wasn't like that! I just… She needed a friend. So before I even knew what I was doing, the offer was out there."

"Sweetheart," her mum said, softening her voice, "you're not interested in this woman, are you? I mean, after everything you've told us about her, I'm worried she's another Julie, and—"

"No, Mum, I promise. That's not it. I genuinely wanted to help out someone who was in a bit of a mess. And trust me, Lena is not a Julie, whatever else she is."

Her mum sighed, and Megan silently appreciated all that the sound meant. When Julie, Megan's only really serious relationship in her life, had finally pushed the last of Megan's buttons with her neediness, her demands for all of Megan's time, and her mind-boggling mood swings, Megan's mum had been the one to comfort her and give her a bed for a few nights while she completed the break-up. It hadn't been pretty, and Megan had resorted to taking her brothers to the flat she'd shared with Julie for nearly two years to make sure she got the last of her stuff out without a fight. Julie hadn't wanted to let Megan go, and Megan shuddered at the memories of extricating herself from that soul-sucking relationship.

"So, dare I ask, what does Jen think of all this, eh?"

Megan winced again. "Yeah," she said, scratching at the back of her neck, "that didn't go down so well." That was the understatement of the decade; Jen had actually hung up on her for the first time in the twelve years they'd been friends. Megan had tried to explain how it was only temporary, and nothing to do with how hot Lena was—Jen's main assumption—but Jen had been hurt nonetheless. Megan could understand, but at the same time, if she had to do it all over again, she would. Lena had no one, and that was just...wrong.

"I swear, you'd give the shirt off your back to anyone who needed it, wouldn't you?"

Megan sighed. "Mum, didn't you and Dad always drum into us that we should always be there for people in need?"

Her mum laughed softly. "Yeah, yeah, throw my own wisdom back at me, why don't you."

They finished their call a few minutes later, and Megan slouched back on the sofa after she'd hung up. Her mum was right—Megan *would* offer someone the shirt off her back. It was the way she'd been brought up, and the harsh realities of adulthood hadn't lessened her generous nature. Making that spontaneous offer to Lena had seemed so very right, in the moment. Sure, a day later, she was starting to question it a little bit, but they'd get used to each other.

Wouldn't they?

She glanced around at her pristinely tidy living room and sighed. When she'd got home from work the night before, at around nine, Lena had already been home for two hours and it showed. The rooms they now shared were spotlessly clean and rearranged, and she'd caught a sheepish Lena in the process of wiping down the kitchen surfaces again. Megan had silently walked past her to the bathroom and felt like reaching for her sunglasses when she'd switched on the overhead light. She didn't know it was possible for a bathroom suite to sparkle so brightly.

Now she was scared to put a thing out of place, and that feeling was unnerving her. She wasn't a slob, not by a long shot, but she liked to relax in her own home, throw the odd jacket over a chair, or kick off her sneakers wherever she happened to park her arse. Gazing around the supremely organised room, she felt like an interloper in her own space.

Grinning, she picked up the pile of magazines stacked neatly in one corner of the coffee table and flopped them back down on its surface. As expected, they fanned out and shuffled themselves into a haphazard arrangement that made her feel infinitely—though childishly, she could admit—better.

She glanced at her watch: just after ten. She wasn't due into the club until eleven thirty and was already showered. Maybe some Netflix to pass the time. The remote control was barely in her hand when her doorbell buzzed.

"It's me." Jen's voice was muffled by the intercom but unmistakable.

Swallowing hard, Megan buzzed her in, and moments later an embarrassed-looking Jen stood in the doorway to the flat.

"All right?" she said, shuffling from one foot to the other.

"All right," Megan replied, standing to one side to leave the way free for Jen to stroll in.

"Took a chance you'd be on a later shift. Was just passing. You know." Jen was looking around the flat as she spoke, her eyebrows rising slowly. "Shit," she said, turning back to Megan, "what happened in here?"

Megan blushed and shut the door before walking across the room to stand beside Jen, also gazing around at their surroundings. "Lena. She likes to clean."

"No shit." Jen whistled. "It's making my eyes hurt."

Megan snorted. "Then don't go anywhere near the bathroom."

Jen turned to her, her eyes wide. Then, suddenly, they were both laughing loudly, and everything was good again.

"Put the kettle on, I need a brew." Jen flopped onto the sofa.

"Yes, Your Highness." Megan made them both a tea and joined Jen on the sofa. After a couple of sips of the steaming hot liquid, she said, "I never meant to hurt you."

Jen held up one hand. "Forget it, I was being a brat. Of course you're going to offer her a room while her place gets sorted. Makes total sense."

Megan smiled. "Cool."

"So what's the latest?"

Megan put her tea down on the table. "Still waiting for the insurance company to gather quotes. I tried to get Callum's company on their list but no chance—they've got a handful of companies they always use, and it has to be one of those. Would have been sweet if Callum did it, because then we'd know it would get done pretty quick. Now we're stuck waiting for all their boxes to be ticked and all that crap."

Jen exhaled. "That sucks. And how's Lena doing? Have you seen her naked yet?"

Megan slapped Jen's thigh. "Shut up, gutter brain."

Jen snorted.

"She's…okay. She doesn't talk much. Other than catching her in the act of turning this place into a photo spread for *Hello!* magazine last night, she's kept to her room so far. We sort of crossed paths in the morning, and that's going to take some juggling around bathroom time, because it seems she likes routine. It's only been two mornings, I know, but she's got up at exactly the same time on both of them. And I mean, *exactly*—I was awake both times and it was like seven a.m. on the dot."

"Creepy."

"Kind of."

"How much of her stuff did she manage to rescue?"

Megan sighed, remembering Lena's sad little face when she'd dragged her two suitcases into the spare room. "Just her clothes and bathroom stuff, really. Pretty much everything in the living room was ruined after four hours exposed to that storm." She shrugged. "I offered to go back up there and see what I could retrieve, but she told me not to bother. She seems really upset about her books. I mean, her own contents insurance will pay for replacements, but that's all going to take time." She glanced sideways at Jen. "I'm still wondering if it's worth trying to get up there and see if any of the books survived."

"I've always wondered what a caved-in roof would look like," Jen said, rubbing her chin with her thumb.

Their eyes met, and they both snorted.

"Come on," Megan said, "I've got the keys."

Two minutes later they were standing in the wreckage of Lena's living room, rubbing their arms against the cold. While the tarps that Callum's team had put in place over the gaping holes were keeping any rain out, nothing could be done about the temperature.

"Bloody hell." Jen's eyes were wide. "This isn't remotely funny, is it?"

Megan shook her head. "I can't imagine coming home to find this."

"Me neither. Fuck."

Megan walked gingerly over to the pile of books. She knelt on the edge of the plastic they sat on, and started carefully lifting one book from on top of another. Some peeled reluctantly apart with squelching sounds, but most refused to let go of their partner at all. By the time she'd reached the bottom of the pile, she'd determined that literally only two books out of about one hundred in front of her were retrievable. She stood up with those two in her hand.

"That's all?" Jen was leaning on the kitchen counter, her hands in her pockets.

Megan nodded, walking over to stand next to her. She held the books up for Jen to see the slightly wrinkled covers.

"Whoa," Jen said, grinning, "what have we here?" Both covers displayed air-brushed photos of two women embracing. In one, the women were clothed—one seemed to be a doctor, her partner a cop—and in the other, they were semi-naked, arms and legs wrapped around each other, lips about to meet in a kiss.

Jen laughed. "What was that you were saying about Lena being straight?"

Megan couldn't quite decipher why there was such a warm glow spreading through her body, given how cold the room was.

Lena stared at the books propped against the door to 'her' room. Irritation warred with warm gratitude within her mind. She'd specifically told Megan not to go up to her wrecked flat and sift around in the ruins, but she'd done it anyway. She bent down and picked up the two books, holding them almost reverently in her hand. Megan had disobeyed her, but here Lena now stood with two of her beloved books in her hand, and her eyes moistened at the sight. How truly…thoughtful of Megan this gesture was. Lena was almost glad Megan wasn't home yet; she'd need some time to compose herself before she thanked her.

As she stared at the covers of the books, a new thought shot into her brain. Oh dear. Lena had just been outed to Megan. Would that be an issue? While it was easy to stereotype and assume Jen was gay, Lena wasn't at all sure about Megan. Not going anywhere or seeing anyone meant Lena had never developed one of those gaydars she'd read about. She sighed. *I hope this isn't going to make things awkward between us.* Should she say anything? Or simply know that Megan now knew and leave it at that?

Deciding the latter was probably the best course of action, she stepped quickly into the bedroom and changed out of her work clothes. She pulled on an ordinary pair of socks with a sigh and reached for a second pair almost immediately, knowing the extra layer would be necessary. Since her bunny slippers were ruined, the only extra-warm socks she had were the ones from Madhu, and they were currently drying on the airer out in the living room from when she'd done her washing the night before. Another thing she'd need to purchase as a result of the roof incident, especially as the nights were only getting colder this early in November.

Padding out to the living room, she made a beeline for the kitchen area to heat up some soup, switching on the TV en route. The volume blared out, sending her jumping sideways. She scrabbled frantically for the remote on the coffee table, finally locating the volume controls and lowering the sound pounding through the speakers. Megan had a surround-sound setup which was impressive but way more than Lena was used to operating with. She glared at the screen; some sort of music channel, with half-clad teenagers gyrating on a scaffolded platform. This was what Megan watched in her downtime? Lena rolled her eyes. Gross.

She flicked through the channels until she found a home improvement program and smiled happily as she left that on in the background for company while she set about heating up her soup and buttering a large roll to have with it.

Once she'd eaten, washed up, and cleared away the evidence of her time in the kitchen, she switched off the TV and returned to her room. She didn't feel comfortable in the living room. Everything there was Megan's, and she couldn't shake off the feeling that she was intruding. Reading in her room would suffice, and although it was in a bedroom rather than her own living room, it was some semblance of her regular routine, and as such was helping to allay some of her anxiety over the events of the week.

She'd found it fairly easy to adjust both her morning and evening routines to suit her new surroundings, and she'd been pleasantly surprised by that. Credit for that had to go to Megan, Lena acknowledged. Her new flatmate had been so generous and supportive, especially given how much they'd clashed up until last weekend. Megan's very nature had made an awful situation far more bearable. Although, she had looked more than a little affronted when she'd come home the night before and observed what Lena had been up to. Lena hadn't meant to offend, and she couldn't really understand why Megan was. What sort of person would complain about coming home and finding their home cleaned so beautifully? Lena had been proud of her achievements and not at all impressed that no thanks had been forthcoming. Megan had been positively cold, in fact.

She looked down at the book in her hand, one of the two Megan had rescued from the flat. It made no sense—why do something this nice when the night before she'd appeared so annoyed? She shook her head. Megan was a mystery to her, and would probably always remain so.

Shifting her position on the bed, she grunted. The mattress on this sofa bed was awful. There was no other word for it. She'd woken up stiff and sore that morning, and the thought of spending even one more night on it filled her with dread. She looked left and right. It was a decent-sized sofa bed, wider than some she'd seen. Wide enough for a proper mattress? She scrambled off the bed and went back out to the kitchen. After rummaging through all the drawers and storage baskets under the counters, finally she located the tape measure she was hoping to find. Two minutes later, she was tapping the measure against her chin, deep in thought. It would just about fit, but it was getting it downstairs that would be the difficult part. Unless she had help, of course.

"So, here's a question." Jen's expression was unreadable, which immediately put Megan on high alert.

"Okay," she said, dragging the word out slowly.

Jen rearranged a couple of the mats on the bar, her gaze drifting away. "Well, I was wondering." She looked up finally and met Megan's eyes. "How would you feel if I asked Lena out?"

Megan's eyes widened. "What's it got to do with me?" she asked, even as her insides churned with what she couldn't deny was jealousy. Which was crazy because there was no way Lena would be interested in someone like Megan.

Jen shrugged. "Just making sure I wouldn't be, you know, invading any territory."

Megan schooled her features into a relaxed, unconcerned look. It took far more work than she would have expected. "Of course not. Go for it."

Jen beamed. "Cool."

But later, as Megan strode home from the Tube station, her chin tucked down into the collar of her jacket, it didn't feel cool at all. It felt anything but. What if Lena said yes? Would that mean she and Jen would be hanging out at Megan's place? Would Megan have to watch them get all gooey with each other? The thought made her nauseous. She'd been trying to deny that she found Lena attractive ever since the storm had thrown them together, but she knew she was fooling herself. Despite Lena's less-than-warm demeanour, Megan found her physically attractive, at least. And, sometimes, there'd been glimpses of something much softer, more approachable in Lena. Although, there *was* that freaky stuff about the cleaning that had rattled Megan so much the night before...

She entered the flat a few minutes later in a deep funk, throwing her jacket over the back of the sofa before heading to the fridge for a beer. She'd had one earlier in the bar with Jen but suddenly needed the buzz she'd get from another.

The sound of Lena's bedroom door opening had her taking a deep breath before turning to face her new flatmate. Who had no right to look so adorable in that Hogwarts hoodie and soft cotton pyjama bottoms. Mentally sighing, Megan plastered a smile on her face.

"Hey, Lena, you okay?"

Lena gave her a weak smile as she walked over. "I am, thank you. How was your day?"

Megan shrugged and took another sip of beer before answering; Lena's luminous eyes were throwing her concentration to the wind. "Good, thanks. Clients all day, which I like."

Lena nodded and shuffled from one foot to the other. "I wanted to thank you for the books. That was very thoughtful of you." There was a slight huskiness to her voice.

Megan blushed slightly. "Hey, you're welcome. I know you said not to go up there, but you really seemed to be missing your books, so..."

Lena nodded again. "I was. I-I love reading. It's one of the most important things to me. So, I admit I was at first a little irritated that you'd gone up there, but when I realised why, I... Well, it was a lovely thing to do. Thank you."

Megan's blush deepened. "Any time," she said, gulping at her beer in an attempt to deflect from her reddening face but only succeeding in over-tipping the bottle and pouring beer down her chin and onto her chest.

"Shit!" She leapt backwards from the sudden cold on her shirt and slammed the bottle down on the counter. Where it promptly frothed up its contents all over the counter and onto the floor below. "Shit!" she cried, even louder, closing her eyes as her cheeks burned even brighter.

"I'll get it," Lena said quietly, and Megan opened her eyes to see her reaching for the tea towel that hung by the fridge.

"No! Hey, it's my mess, I'll clean it up." Megan reached for the tea towel but Lena pulled it back.

"It's fine. You clean yourself up—" she smirked, the first time Megan had seen her do so "—and I'll take care of this part."

Giving in, Megan nodded and rushed to the bathroom. She ripped off the wet shirt and quickly wiped at her chest with a damp facecloth. After rubbing her skin dry, she stood stock still as realisation dawned. Having removed the shirt, she was now clad only in jeans and a bra. Which meant she had to walk across to her bedroom like that. In front of Lena. Well, there was nothing she could do about that now—there was no way she was putting a beer-soaked shirt back on. Squaring her shoulders, she opened the bathroom door, and as nonchalantly as she could, walked out to the living room.

Lena tried not to stare. She really did. But Megan strolling casually across the living room with all that body on display had her mouth dry and her heart thumping rather loudly. Chris's skinny ribs and bony arms had always slightly bothered Lena in ways she tried not to delve too deeply into. Megan's bigger, bulkier form affected Lena in such contrasting ways that she almost laughed out loud.

Fearing Megan would catch her staring, she dragged her gaze away from the sight of all that skin and flustered her way through the rest of the cleaning-up job. When she was satisfied the counters had been cleaned sufficiently with antibacterial spray and the now-dirty tea towel was scrunched up ready for the laundry basket, she exhaled a slow breath and made her way to the sofa. She needed to regroup so that she could ask her big favour of Megan. She only hoped the beer-spilling incident hadn't soured Megan's mood.

Megan returned five minutes later, her skin now covered by a bright blue, long-sleeved top. The colour only emphasised Megan's amazing eyes even more, and Lena had to force herself not to stare. What the heck was wrong with her?

Taking a deep breath, she said, "Megan, I wondered if I could ask a favour?"

Megan perched on the arm of the sofa furthest away from Lena. "Sure, what's up?"

"Well, the mattress on the sofa bed is too uncomfortable. I measured up and I am pretty sure my regular double from upstairs would fit in its place. I can't carry it down by myself, so I was hoping you could help me?"

She saw something flicker across Megan's face and her eyes tighten. "Right, I see."

Megan's voice lacked its usual warmth, and Lena tilted her head. "Okay?"

Megan stood up. "Sure. You want to do it now?"

"That would be perfect, thank you."

"Right." Megan walked to the door without another word, and Lena stared after her. Why was she being so abrupt? Shaking her head in mystification, Lena trotted after her.

CHAPTER 11

MEGAN ATE HER TOAST AGGRESSIVELY the next morning, noting that she wouldn't have known it was possible to aggressively eat toast until now. It took a lot to get her this wound up. She knew some people in the past had considered her a bit of a doormat, easily stomped over by other people's needs and attitudes. Megan had always considered herself easy-going, refusing to stoop to other people's level, and letting it all slide off her like water off a duck's back.

But Lena Shah was riling Megan up in ways she didn't know how to deal with.

There was something about the way Lena delivered her words, such as her complaint about the mattress the night before, that was so…rude. There were so many better ways she could have approached that conversation with Megan that would have softened the blow. Megan got it, she really did—sofa bed mattresses were notorious for being okay for one or two nights but not longer term. But given that Megan had taken Lena, a virtual stranger, into her home for an indefinite period of time, she could have at least prefaced her words with an "I'm really sorry, but…" And it had hurt even more after Lena's thanks for the books—just when Megan thought things were softening, back Lena came with the sharpness.

Moving the mattress had been fairly easy in the end, between the pair of them. And Lena had been right: it just about squeezed into the space available, and her glee *had* been kind of cute to witness. But then she'd metaphorically slammed the door in Megan's face moments later, wishing her a curt goodnight, and Megan had been left standing in the living room with her blood boiling in ways that were totally foreign to her.

Her phone buzzed beside her with a text message from Jen.

Hey, you home tonight? Got a rare Saturday night off, thought we could hang

Megan smiled. Yeah, hanging with Jen might be what she needed to put the smile back on her face. She checked her calendar app then flicked back to messaging.

Should be home by eight. Bring beer

Jen returned a smiley face, and Megan felt lighter simply from that brief exchange. To hell with Lena.

"Megan?" Alisha's voice came from within the office as Megan walked by. She backtracked and stuck her head round the door. Alisha sat primly upright on her chair, swivelled round from her desk to face Megan, who tried very hard not to look at the expanse of leg on display. Alisha's short skirt was made to look even skimpier by the way it had obviously ridden up while she sat. Megan swallowed hard before speaking.

"Hi, Alisha, what's up?"

"Do you have a minute, please?" Alisha's usual clipped tone was softer, and a hint of a smile chased across her full lips.

"Just about. Got a client due in five minutes. Can I check if they're on the floor already and let them know where I am?"

Alisha nodded and Megan trotted down the corridor to the main room. She glanced over to the floor area where free workouts took place; no sign of Geoffrey. She walked quickly back to the office and shut the door behind her when Alisha motioned her to do so.

"Thank you," Alisha said, smiling again. She'd never been this nice in all the time Megan had been working there. It was unnerving.

Megan sat in the spare chair and crossed one ankle over her knee. "What's up?" she repeated, glad when her voice came out strong and clear, betraying nothing of her inner nervousness at being up close and personal with Alisha like this.

Alisha crossed her legs at the ankles, and Megan willed her eyes not to look at the red patent stilettos that graced Alisha's feet. It never ceased to amaze her that Alisha would wear something so impractical when the rest of them were stomping around the club in sports shoes. However, Megan wasn't complaining—as much as Alisha wasn't really Megan's type, she was a sucker for high heels.

"It's a little bit of good news, actually. As you know, we introduced an employee of the month award a few months back, voted on by way of feedback forms from the clients. As you know, this award is open to full-time employees and contractors such as yourself. I'm happy to say that you are October's winner."

Megan gaped. "Seriously?"

Alisha chuckled, and the husky sound did strange things to Megan's spine, making it seem as if it was melting. "Completely. I'll present your award at the staff meeting on Monday, but I wanted to tell you in advance. I always like to do that to make sure the winner will actually turn up to the staff meeting." She smiled ruefully, and Megan grinned.

"Wow, this is cool." Megan couldn't remember ever winning anything.

"It is indeed. So, see you at the meeting?"

"Definitely!" Megan stood up and made for the door. The soft and incredibly warm touch of Alisha's hand on her forearm stopped her, and she turned to face her, her heart suddenly racing in her chest.

"Well done, Megan. You deserve it," Alisha said. She was so close to Megan she could practically count each eyelash that framed Alisha's rich brown eyes.

"Th-thank you," she said.

Alisha's smile told Megan she knew *exactly* what effect she was having on Megan, and her hand squeezed Megan's arm slightly before letting it go.

"See you Monday." She spun on her delicious heels to return to her desk.

Megan fumbled with the door handle and yanked it open, shooting out into the corridor like the cork from a champagne bottle. She only just avoided colliding with Kimberley, who laughed and waved as she strode by.

Megan slumped for a moment against the wall.

Alisha had flirted with her in the most overt way yet. Was she seriously interested in Megan? And if so, how did Megan tell her it wasn't reciprocated? Because it wasn't, despite the sexy heels. Alisha, quite frankly, scared the crap out of Megan, and she wasn't remotely interested in her. Oh sure, on the surface she could appreciate that Alisha was hot, but when Megan thought about being with someone, she thought about a woman who was less intimidating, with more curves, and golden-brown skin that looked like it would be as soft as candy floss...

She stood upright. Okay, that was...ridiculous. She was mad at Lena, remember? Not attracted to her. No.

She blinked rapidly and headed into the main room.

"So, is she home?" Jen nodded towards Lena's room, her smile wide, and Megan flinched. She'd forgotten Jen's plan.

"Er, yeah, I think so."

Jen took a swig of her beer. "She likely to appear or is she in bed already?"

Megan shrugged. "Her normal routine is to stay in there until about ten fifteen, then she cleans her teeth, pours herself a big glass of water, and heads off to bed."

Jen's eyebrows rose. "How do you know so much about her routine already?"

The blush was quick to heat Megan's cheeks. How the hell did she know? Her subconscious had clearly been working overtime. Which was bizarre; she and Lena had only spent five nights living together, and the first one of those was the night of the storm, which didn't count as routine at all.

"I'm just going on what happened last night." The lie didn't come easily—Megan hated lying to anyone.

Jen's expression turned quizzical. "But I thought you said you moved the mattress last night?"

"Well, yeah." Megan was getting more uncomfortable by the second. "But then after that, she stayed in her room until ten fifteen."

"Right," Jen said, looking sceptical, but thankfully dropped the subject with her next words. "Well, I'll have to stay here until at least ten fifteen then," she said, chuckling.

Megan dragged a smile from somewhere and hoped it looked genuine.

Jen started talking about some crazy customer they'd had in the bar the night before, and Megan let the story push all other thoughts away—

especially the thoughts that involved Jen and Lena together. That image really didn't fit well in her mind's eye.

Lena's appearance in the living room at precisely ten fifteen had Jen smirking and Megan blushing again.

"Hey, Lena," Jen said, in her most sultry of tones.

Lena stopped like a deer caught in the headlights, halfway across the space between her room and the bathroom. Her eyes wide, and her hands twitching at the hem of her Hogwarts hoodie, she stammered, "Oh, er, hello. Jen."

Jen stood and walked round the back of the sofa to lean against it. Megan swallowed the last of her beer, stood rapidly to attempt to escape to the kitchen, and crashed her shin into the coffee table.

"Oh, sh—sugar," she blurted, grabbing at her throbbing shin, giving it a furious rub. She heard Jen guffaw behind her, then a loud "tut" from Lena. Great, now she'd pissed off Lena again.

"Quiet," Lena hissed. "She could have hurt herself."

Wait, what? Megan whipped her head round just in time to see Lena glare at Jen, and Jen's face drop.

"S-sorry," Jen said, shuffling on the spot. "Hey, Megs, you okay?"

Megan stared at the pair of them. "Er, yeah. Fine." She spun round and walked—carefully—to the kitchen to deposit her empty beer bottle.

"So, Lena," she heard Jen say, "I was wondering if you'd be interested in getting a drink with me sometime."

Megan risked a glance over her shoulder. Lena was staring at Jen as if she'd grown two heads, and Jen's usual confident stance was wilting under the pressure.

"No, thank you," Lena said tightly. She turned away from Jen and continued her pathway to the bathroom.

Megan quickly looked back at the sink and pretended to rinse her bottle out. And tried very hard not to smile as widely as she wanted to.

Jen joined her in the kitchen a few moments later.

Megan schooled her features into a less satisfied expression and turned to face her friend.

"Well," Jen said, her eyes wide. "I'm guessing you heard that." Megan nodded. "Don't think I've ever been shot down like that." Jen shook her head.

Megan reached out and patted her on the shoulder. "Sorry."

Jen shrugged. "Win some, lose some." She chuckled. "Maybe it's for the best—might have got a bit awkward me seeing her while she's living with you. Kind of a 'don't shit where you eat' situation, eh?"

Megan winced internally. Yeah, exactly. So how bad would it be if she allowed her attraction for Lena to get carried away? Definitely not a good idea. "Probably," she said. "Want another beer?"

Jen shook her head. "Nah, I think I'll take off. I could do with a long night's sleep—got to do a double tomorrow coz we're short-staffed."

"Ugh, on a Sunday?"

"I know, boring. Anyway, I'll catch you sometime during the week, yeah?"

"Sure. Take it easy."

"You too." Jen smirked. "Don't let the Ice Woman wind you up."

Of course, Lena would choose that exact moment to exit the bathroom. She stopped short at Jen's words, then glared at her before striding off to her room.

"Shit," Jen mouthed.

Megan shook her head. "Thanks a lot," she murmured.

"Sorry, I—"

Megan waved her off. "Get out of here, before you make it worse." She smiled to take the sting out of her words, but the smile felt awfully false. God, what a mess.

Lena lay staring at the ceiling, trying with all her might to tamp down her anger and get to sleep. It was impossible. That...woman. How dare she? Just because Lena had said no to a date with her did not make Lena the 'Ice Woman'. The arrogance of her. Lena had been sorely tempted to tell her exactly what she thought of her with her oh-so-seductive moves and cocky attitude. Sure, Jen was attractive—Lena wasn't stupid. Or blind. But the arrogance that came with it was such a turn off. Lena had always been attracted to someone with a quiet confidence, nothing overt. Chris had had that: she knew she was attractive but didn't flaunt it. She knew she was good at her job but didn't brag about it. Megan had that same quality, and it made Lena's stomach do a tiny little flip at the thought.

She blinked in the darkness. Where had that come from?

Groaning, she rolled over and pressed her face into her pillow. No, no, no. She could not be thinking about Megan that way. That was very much all kinds of wrong.

The tap on her door was quiet—if she'd been asleep it probably wouldn't have stirred her.

"Lena?" Megan's voice was equally quiet.

For a moment it was so tempting to ignore it. But Lena found herself reaching for the bedside lamp, then pushing the covers back. She padded across the room and inched open the door.

"Hi," Megan said, her eyes wide, and her arms wrapped round herself. "I'm sorry if I woke you."

Lena shook her head. "What do you want?" She tried to keep the bite out of her tone, but it was difficult.

Megan sighed audibly. "I wanted to apologise for what Jen said. It was out of line and—"

Lena opened the door slightly wider and held up a hand. "That's not your apology to make," she said, softening her tone in wonder at Megan's actions. How could she be this...nice all the time? "You are not responsible for what your friends think."

"I know," Megan said, "but, well, this is your home too now, and you shouldn't have to deal with that in your own home."

Lena was surprised at the smile her mouth formed. "Thank you. That's very...thoughtful of you."

"Well, that's all I wanted to say." Megan glanced away and back again. "Oh, and to tell you I have most of my family visiting tomorrow afternoon. Sorry, in all the rush over the last few days I forgot about it. They'll be here around two, and stay into the evening, I imagine."

Lena's good mood deflated. "Right. Okay. Well, I'll make myself scarce then." She made to shut the door, but Megan grabbed hold of it.

"Wait, please. I didn't mean that. You don't have to go anywhere. You can stay, if you wish? You've met Callum already, but you could meet everyone else, share all the food they'll bring. You know, hang out." Those pale blue eyes were pleading with her.

Lena shut her eyes momentarily, blocking out the distraction Megan's eyes always seemed to engender in her. How could she explain? That it was bad enough most of her routine had disappeared since Monday night and with it her sense of calm and control. That not being able to have her regular Saturday—breakfast with a book, groceries, cleaning, then more reading—had already freaked her out and caused her anxiety levels to rise even higher. Now she had to find somewhere else to go for the Sunday so that she didn't have to be surrounded by a flat full of strangers.

"I'll think about it," she said eventually, and gently shut the door, giving Megan just enough time to withdraw her hand as she did so.

CHAPTER 12

LENA CLOSED THE FORECAST SPREADSHEET and opened the quarterly review presentation from the September folder. The eighty-three slides in it were ugly, cumbersome, and cluttered with data that no one ever really looked at. No one had tasked her with redesigning the review, but she'd decided it was as good a job as any to keep her out of the flat for the day.

She couldn't do it. Staying home to meet Megan's family wasn't something she was ready for. She'd woken up determined to get a lid on her anxiety, and if she couldn't do that by maintaining some semblance of her pre-storm routine in Megan's flat, then she'd escape to work. Next weekend she'd visit Madhu and Jay, then maybe after that she would have a new routine mapped out that worked for her in her changed surroundings. She was almost there—shower times had been ironed out, as had evening meals, given that Megan worked most evenings until at least eight. That, at least, was some relief, as their paths rarely crossed except for later in the evening. Around that, Lena could almost pretend that things were normal. Except that they weren't, because she wasn't in her own bed surrounded by her own things, and she'd yet to receive the order of books to replace some of her lost collection.

Her phone rang, making her jump. Being in the too-quiet office on her own had her nerves on edge.

"Hey, Madhu," she said with some relief when she realised who her caller was.

"Hey, how are you?"

"I'm...okay." There was no real point in lying to her sister. "It's been a difficult week."

"I bet it has! Are you settled in at Megan's? I still think that is totally awesome that she offered you the room."

Lena smiled. That really was true. She ought to remember that amongst the turmoil. "Mostly. It's taking a bit of getting used to."

"Ah, I'm not surprised. I'm so proud of you for doing it though. It would have been an easy option to move into some short-term studio flat somewhere."

Would it? Lena wasn't so sure. That would have meant even more upheaval and surroundings that would have been less ideal. In comparison to where she was, and how lucky she'd been having someone like Megan willing to offer, her own space, however private, would probably have felt a lot worse. The more she thought about it, the luckier she felt. And the worse she felt for not making more of an effort with Megan.

"You still there, Lena?"

"Oh, sorry. Yes, I was just thinking."

"About?"

Lena's cheeks warmed with a gentle blush. "I-I think I've realised how lucky I am that Megan was there. That she is as nice as she is. And...well, I've not exactly been the nicest to her that I could have been."

"It's a habit you have, you know."

"What?"

Madhu sighed. "Don't shout at me, all right?"

Lena exhaled slowly, dreading what was coming. "Okay."

"Well, I know you have your issues with your OCD and your need for routine. But... Well, you're not very good at forgiving people either. You carry grudges. Megan did some things that upset you, and yes, before you say anything, I can totally see why you were upset. But it's not like she did any of them deliberately, is it?"

"No," Lena said in a small voice.

"Yet you carried on treating her in that same standoffish way even after she'd apologised and got everything fixed up. Seriously, the woman deserves a medal for still being kind enough to offer you a room after all that."

Lena's blush deepened and an awful sick feeling crept through her stomach. Madhu was right. She'd been entirely unforgiving of Megan, and continuing to give her the cold shoulder even when they were now living together was...mean.

"I'm an awful person," Lena whispered, tears pricking at her eyes.

"No!" Madhu exclaimed. "No, you're not, believe me," she pleaded. "You've just… Lena, you've got so bitter the past few years. First Mum and Dad, then Chris. I get it, I do, but…"

"What?"

"But I wish you could, I don't know, shake it all off. Forget it."

Lena's hackles rose. "Forget it? Forget what they said to me? Forget what Chris did to me?"

Madhu's sigh was long. "See, this is what I'm talking about." She paused. "Look, you know I am one hundred per cent behind you. And I know what our parents did was very upsetting. But, really, Lena, surely you weren't that surprised, were you? I mean, they're first generation. Of course they weren't going to jump up and down with joy at having a lesbian in the family."

"Oh, so that means I'm supposed to forgive them, does it?"

Madhu sounded exasperated. "No, of course not. What they said, Mum in particular, was horrible. It really was. I want you to find a way to get past it so that you can be happy. Carrying all this anger around doesn't seem to be doing you any good, that's all I'm saying."

Lena was silent for a few moments. It hurt to admit it, but Madhu was right. It was all so unjust, though. And Lena didn't think she deserved it. Once again the bile rose up and—

She took a deep breath. Here she went again, allowing it all to swamp her, to agitate her. Maybe Madhu was right. Maybe it was time to try to let go of the past so that she could find what she thought she did deserve: a little bit of happiness.

"This pasta is awesome, Mum." Megan grinned happily as she scooped up another large spoonful to dollop on her plate. Her mum's tuna pasta mix had always been a favourite, and she'd been delighted when a large dish of it had been one of the many items of food her mum had unpacked upon arrival.

Her mum grinned back. "I know how to keep my baby girl happy."

Megan glared at her. "I'm not a baby girl anymore, Mum."

Her parents both laughed.

"You'll always be our baby girl, Megs," her dad said. "Even when you're old and grey."

Her brothers laughed as she blushed. Being the only girl child had always been like this, and it hadn't changed now that she'd grown up into the only woman.

She was, however, grateful that no female stereotypes had been applied to her. Her mum had been content to watch Megan play with her brothers rather than force her love of cooking onto her only daughter.

Yet again, her mother had surpassed herself with the monthly family dinner. They rotated the get-together at a different home each time but with her mum insisting on doing most of the cooking. The feast laid out, buffet-style, on Megan's kitchen counters was enough to feed a small army. Megan knew she'd be contentedly munching on leftovers for the rest of the week, with any luck.

"So, where's your flatmate?" Jimmy asked, helping himself to a large serving of salad to go with his burger.

Megan swallowed a mouthful of pasta and washed it down with a gulp of juice. She glanced at her watch. "Well, she said she'd definitely be out until three. She went to work, I think." It was gone three thirty now, and Megan wondered if Lena really would return. She'd not seemed that keen when she left this morning, and Megan had the distinct impression she'd only been saying she would meet her family to appease Megan. She wasn't going to force Lena, but given how often Megan saw her family, she thought the sooner Lena met them and became familiar with them, the better. If Lena disagreed, so be it.

"How's it going with her?" her mum asked.

Megan shrugged, and put her fork down on her plate. "It's…okay. She pretty much keeps to herself. We hardly see each other."

Her mum nodded. "And what about getting the roof fixed? When is that going to be done?"

Megan shook her head. "No idea. She's still waiting for the insurance company to appoint a builder. Such a shame we couldn't get you to do it," she said, looking at Callum.

"True. But if they've got a list of approved firms it's going to be someone good—they wouldn't waste time with cowboys."

"Yeah, I guess."

The sound of a key turning in the lock sent all their heads swivelling in the direction of the front door. A warm spot bloomed in the middle of Megan's chest as she saw Lena push through the door with her briefcase in one hand and what looked like a cake box in the other.

When she realised so many pairs of eyes were on her, Lena stopped dead and blushed furiously. Megan leaped to her feet, only just catching her half-full plate before it slid off her lap onto the floor. Her dad sniggered and she glared at him before placing the plate on the coffee table.

"Hey, Lena. Welcome home." She offered an encouraging smile, hoping against hope that Lena was in one of her better moods. To her shock, Lena smiled just as warmly back.

"Hi, Megan. I-I bought this for you and your family." She held out the cake box. It was shaking slightly in her trembling hand. "I didn't know if you had dessert planned, and well, even if you have, you can never have too much cake, can you?"

Megan stared at her. Who was this new Lena standing in the doorway? She was...nice. Wow—who'd have thought that was possible?

"Oh, that's...that's lovely. Thanks." She took the box from Lena and laid it on the draining board, the only clear space in the kitchen thanks to her mum's overwhelming efforts with the food.

"Hi, Lena. I'm Rosie, Megan's mum." She rounded the sofa and held out her hand. "It's nice to meet you."

Lena dropped her briefcase quickly and shook the proffered hand.

Megan's dad was next. "Sean. Nice to meet you."

Within seconds Jimmy was following suit, and Callum waved from across the room. "Nice to see you again, Lena."

Lena smiled shyly.

Then Daniel walked hesitantly over, wiping his hand on his jeans. "Hi. Daniel."

Lena's smile widened a little, and Megan nearly laughed out loud as Daniel ducked his head, shoving his hands in his pockets and—wait, was that a *blush* from her brother?

"Would you like some food, Lena?" Megan's mum was already moving to the kitchen as she spoke over her shoulder.

"Um, I'm fine right now," Lena said quietly. "Maybe later." She turned to remove her coat and hung it on one of the hooks behind the door.

Megan watched Daniel watching Lena.

Uh-oh.

Lena turned back and caught Megan's eye. "I'm going to my room."

Megan knew her face dropped at the words, but she was delighted when Lena's eyes widened and she said, "I mean, just to change clothes. Then, if it's all right with you, I thought I would spend some time with you and your family."

Megan beamed. "Definitely all right," she said.

Lena's smile was almost as wide as her own felt, and that warm spot in Megan's chest burned even hotter.

Lena was trying. She really was. But some elements of the afternoon were far easier to deal with than others. On the plus side, Megan's mum, Rosie, was lovely. Chatty and welcoming, she had made Lena feel more at ease than she would have anticipated. Sean was a gentle giant with a delightful Irish lilt to his voice that Lena could have listened to for hours. Callum and Jimmy didn't say that much to her, but that was okay—they were embroiled in a discussion about motor racing that was going straight over her head.

The food was amazing, which was another plus, and Megan had whispered to her in the kitchen that all the leftovers would be staying with them, rather than being taken home by Rosie and Sean, which was even better.

There were two downsides to the day, neither of which she could do much about right now. Firstly, it was excruciatingly obvious that Daniel was rather enamoured of her. She had given him no encouragement, and while a very small part of her was flattered, mostly she squirmed under his puppy-eyed attention. It was not helped by the nudges Rosie and Sean kept sharing as they witnessed all of Daniel's attempts to talk to her. What was also strange, and she had no idea how to deal with, was Megan's scowling face every time Daniel monopolised Lena's attention.

The other downside was the mess. Megan's family were unbelievably untidy. Food and drink were spilled with no desire to clean it up. Empty plates were placed on the floor rather than being taken to the kitchen. Beer bottles, once devoid of their contents, were placed anywhere there was a space for them. The flat looked like a tornado had ripped through it, and Lena was squirming in her seat, itching to get up and start tidying it all away.

"So, Lena." Rosie's voice broke into her consternation. "Where are you from?"

Lena looked around, determined to meet Rosie's eye even though this conversation could take her into uncomfortable waters. "Bolton. Up north," she said, with a half-smile.

"I thought I could hear a bit of an accent."

Lena shrugged. "Yes, I never really had it that strong, so it's softened a bit since I moved to London."

"How long have you been down here?" Daniel asked, staring at her as intently as he had done all afternoon.

Lena totted it up in her head. "Nearly four years."

"You came down for work?" This was Rosie again.

"Er, yes." Why not? It was as good a reason as any. Not the truth, at all, but that wasn't going to be shared with the Palmer family today. If ever. She fidgeted slightly in her seat next to Megan on the sofa.

Megan caught her eye and lifted one eyebrow.

Lena smiled in a way she hoped would convey that all was good, even as her stomach clenched at the thought of more personal questions.

"Lena's an accountant. Works near Euston." That was Daniel again, and she cringed as she realised he was trying to show off the knowledge he had acquired before the rest of the family. Only she heard the faint snort that Megan emitted at that moment.

"Pays well, I bet," Sean said, and looked flummoxed when Rosie slapped his arm. "What?"

"Dad, I think that's a bit personal, don't you?" Megan said, standing up. "Hey, who wants some of that cake Lena bought?"

Lena could have hugged Megan at that moment—if ever she'd needed rescuing, it was then.

A chorus of "me" had them all laughing, and the strawberry gateau from Patisserie Valerie occupied everyone's attention for the next twenty minutes or so.

"Great cake," Sean said after practically licking his plate clean. "You can come again."

Lena smiled. "My pleasure," she said, and it truly was.

Rosie stood up then and headed for the kitchen. "I do wish you'd get a bloody dishwasher," she said to Megan as she rolled up her sleeves.

"Wait!" Lena leaped up from the sofa. Now was her chance. "Let me do that. You brought all the food, after all."

Rosie smiled at her. "Yes, but you've been working all day."

Lena reached her by the sink. "No, please. Rosie, let me. Honestly, it would make me very happy to do it."

"Let her, Mum. Trust me, she means what she says."

Lena turned to face her. The words had been warmly spoken, but she needed to check Megan's eyes, make sure nothing malicious had been meant by what she just said. Megan gazed back at her, with only a gentle understanding and warmth in her expression. The wave of happiness that washed over Lena in that moment seemed ridiculously out of proportion to what was happening, but she revelled in it.

Megan got it. And that felt very, very good.

CHAPTER 13

"YOUNG MAN!"

Dorothy's cry stopped Megan in her tracks as she walked out of her flat with her rubbish bag in her hand. She grinned. Someone else was on the end of Dorothy's wrath for a change.

"Huh?" a male voice said.

"This wall is part of my property. You will therefore take care when placing items against it. Is that clear?" Dorothy sounded royally pissed off, and Megan was again so very grateful she wasn't the one in the firing line.

Inching forward, she peeked over the bannister to see who today's unfortunate victim was. Ah, Sanjit. General labourer and dogsbody for the Patel brothers, whose firm had been—finally—granted the contract to fix Lena's flat. Poor Sanjit, who didn't seem like the brightest button in the box, had been running around like a headless chicken since the firm arrived two days ago, ferrying various supplies into the house and up the stairs. It looked like, in an attempt to save some time, especially time out of the persistently drizzling rain, he'd been using the walls in the hallway on the ground floor to stack things against and had presumably not been quiet about it.

And right now Sanjit was caught in the laser glare of the formidable Dorothy in full flow and looked about ready to take flight. Megan sighed and walked down the stairs.

"Hey, Sanjit," she said cheerfully. "Morning, Dorothy."

Dorothy huffed but muttered a "good morning" in return.

Sanjit looked mightily relieved at Megan's interruption. "All right?" he said, shuffling out of her way as she made it to the front door.

She smiled at him. "I've got a question about something outside. Do you mind?"

"No, course not." His entire face showed his gratitude at the rescue.

Behind them Dorothy tutted, and moments later her front door shut with a click.

"Shit," Sanjit muttered, running his hands over his cheeks. His hard hat sat crookedly on his head, and he looked almost like a kid playing dress up in the over-sized safety jacket and trousers. He turned quickly to Megan. "Sorry, what did you want to ask?"

Megan smiled at him. "Nothing, mate. I was just getting you out of danger."

He stared at her, then barked out a laugh. "Legend," he said.

"But seriously, Sanjit, do whatever you can not to piss her off, okay? No noise, no dirt, no swearing. Three simple rules."

He nodded vigorously. "Noise, dirt, swearing. Got it." He beamed at her, his crooked teeth seeming too big for his mouth. "Thanks."

"No worries." She smiled, deposited the rubbish in one of the wheelie bins, then went back into the house.

She carefully made her way back upstairs, making sure her feet didn't get caught in the copious dust sheets that had been laid all over the communal areas. It would be just like her to trip and fall flat on her face.

The Patels had brought a team of six men with them for the job, and she could hear many voices up in Lena's flat as she walked past the open doorway. They'd estimated it would take them six weeks to get the place habitable again, but that was weather-dependent. It was the middle of November now, over two weeks since the storm, and yet more rain had fallen in that time, making things worse on what was left of the roof. And with a cold December forecast, plus the Christmas holidays, the older Patel brother had been careful to warn Lena that the work could overrun the schedule.

Megan closed her front door behind her and walked back to the kitchen area to drink the rest of her tea. She was on a late shift today, with her first client at noon but her last one at nine that night, so she'd had a fairly lazy morning at home. She'd spent some time sorting out her desk and computer now all of that was moved into the living area.

As soon as the Patels had got on site, they'd agreed to move Lena's wardrobe and chest of drawers down to her room, and a big reshuffle had been required. It made Megan's living area less spacious than she'd planned, but it was only temporary so she couldn't grumble too much. And it made Lena's life far more comfortable in the spare room, and that helped *her* mood considerably, so Megan definitely couldn't grumble about that either.

Now that the spare room was clearly defined as Lena's space, she'd relaxed even more into her life in the shared flat. However, it still meant she spent more time in there alone than she did in the living area, and Megan was trying hard not to be offended by it. She had always had a fairly simple outlook on life, and as a consequence had struggled when dealing with people as complicated and complex as Lena.

It was the main reason things with Julie had gone tits up. Trying to understand all of Julie's moods and their swings had overwhelmed Megan in the end. Not that she thought Lena was as needy or moody as Julie. But she was certainly complex in her own way, and Megan would need a lot more time around her to see if she could understand her.

She cleaned her mug and left it to drain beside the sink. While she understood Lena was introverted, she didn't seem to want to spend *any* time with Megan. Did she not like Megan? Megan didn't think so. When they met, however briefly, as their days crossed, they chatted reasonably comfortably about what they were doing, the weather, the meals they might share. When they did share those meals, they seemed comfortable, if not overly chatty. Megan never got the impression Lena didn't want to be conversing, or sharing food, and yet, as soon as the meal or conversation was over, there Lena would be, practically sprinting back to her room and closing the door softly behind her.

Megan supposed she shouldn't complain—a lot of people who shared flats hated their flatmates getting in the way, leaving a mess, being obnoxious. Lena was none of those and yet Megan still couldn't help being disappointed at the complete oppositeness.

"So, if you don't mind me asking, how does it work, you being at the health club? Are you a full-time employee?"

Lena's question startled Megan. It was one of the longest and most personal questions she'd ever asked. They were sharing a rare evening meal together, and Lena had cooked up a delicious butternut squash and carrot soup that Megan couldn't get enough of. They'd been doing their usual, chatting about inconsequential things, when Lena's question had suddenly materialised.

Megan swallowed her mouthful of soup and put her spoon down.

"No, I'm a private contractor, self-employed. I basically pay a kind of rent to the club to be able to conduct my business on their premises. I could do shifts directly for them too, as a form of rent payment, but I choose not to. Kimberley, a friend of mine at the club, does it that way, spending half her week doing classes directly for them and half private clients. I brought some clients with me when I moved to that club and then got lots more from being there, so I can happily live off doing that."

"That sounds good, very independent."

Megan shrugged. "Yeah, it has positives and negatives. Obviously, I need to keep a good list of clients, otherwise suddenly I'm not making any money."

"But if you are good at what you do then presumably it's easier to keep that good list." Lena popped a small chunk of bread into her mouth, and Megan tried not to be mesmerised by the keen gaze Lena aimed her way as she chewed.

"Yeah, and I am. I mean," Megan hurried on when she saw Lena's eyebrows rise, "I'm not bragging or anything, but I am good at this. I've been doing it for ten years and I've got a good reputation."

"Good for you," Lena said, blushing slightly and turning back to her soup.

"I assume you're full-time employed in your job?"

Lena nodded, but kept her gaze averted. "Yes," she said, after swallowing her mouthful of bread. "I did contracting back in Bolton when I first qualified as an accountant, just to get some experience. Then I got a full-time job with a local council and after a few months realised I'd made a mistake. It was so depressing working there—we wasted so much time doing things twice because their processes and systems were so old-fashioned. And everything, from the computers to the kitchen equipment, was so second-rate. Which probably makes me sound like a snob." She laughed half-heartedly and finally turned to look at Megan.

Megan shook her head. "I don't think so. Working conditions are important. And if the work wasn't exciting you either, I can see why things like a chipped mug would annoy you." Megan hesitated a moment before adding, "Especially you."

She was thrilled when Lena laughed, loudly, her shoulders shaking. "Yes, especially me."

"So is that why you came to London? To get a better job? You said something like that when you met my family."

Suddenly Lena's face shut down, and her smile withered and disappeared. She let out a slow breath and pushed the tray containing her soup bowl and the remains of her bread roll off her lap and onto the coffee table.

"Sorry, did I say something wrong?" Megan asked, her own soup forgotten.

Lena shook her head and let out another breath. "No, it's…it's just very personal. And hard to talk about."

Megan held up her hands. "Then leave it, it's fine," she said, her tone gentle.

"I-I would like to tell you, actually."

Megan waited; Lena was obviously composing herself, and Megan dreaded what she was about to hear.

"As I'm sure you figured out already from my book collection—" Lena looked up at her and smiled thinly "—I'm gay. It took me a long time to be okay with that and do something about it. Being Indian, well, let's just say it's not the most welcoming community for someone who comes out. And my parents were—" her voice cracked slightly "—distinctly unwelcoming." She looked up at Megan then. "Hostile, nasty, those are other words that spring to mind."

"Did they kick you out?" Megan's question was whispered. The contrast between her own coming out and Lena's couldn't have been greater, and she was having trouble understanding how parents could do that to their child.

"Not directly. But they did give me an ultimatum: forget this horrid gay nonsense, settle down with a nice Indian boy of their choice, preferably, or else."

"And what was the 'or else'?"

Lena shrugged, and her mouth twisted slightly. "I don't know. I didn't hang around long enough to find out. I spent the next day updating my CV and contacting employment agencies down here. I knew if there was anywhere I could be comfortable, and have a good chance of a job, it was London. Plus, it was far enough away that my parents couldn't come knocking on the door to drag me home. I mean, Manchester was nearer, obviously, but distance away from them seemed like a good idea."

"Shit," Megan breathed. "I guess I thought, well, you know, in this day and age, that sort of stuff didn't happen anymore."

Lena laughed, but it was humourless. "You'd think so, wouldn't you?" Her voice had a bitter edge to it that tugged at Megan's guts. "Well, anyway," Lena continued, her tone a little softer, "I was lucky, I got a job pretty quickly. I had to do a lot of lying to both my work and my parents to get down to London for interviews, but I managed it. Quit the job at the council, and one Sunday when my parents were out visiting some relatives, my sister helped me pack up my stuff and drove me to the station."

"So I guess she's not like your parents then?"

Lena's smile was warm. "No, Madhu's great. She doesn't quite get the whole lesbian thing, but she loves me no matter what. Unlike my parents…"

"God, Lena, that's awful. I'm so sorry."

Lena shrugged. "As Madhu said, I should have realised they wouldn't be happy. I simply never factored in exactly how unhappy they would be."

"And have you been in contact with them since? You said you'd been here for four years, so…?"

Again Lena laughed that humourless laugh. "I tried to contact them, once. I phoned home a week later, to let them know I was safe, settled, and all that. You wouldn't believe the filth that came out of my mother's mouth."

"Shit," Megan breathed.

"For about a year after that there was nothing, but then about once a year since then, my mother has had some strange need to call me and try to talk some sense into me. Her words, not mine," Lena said, smiling bitterly. "Those are usually very short conversations—she simply cannot understand me, and feels that if I just went home I could be fixed."

"I can't get over the contrast between your story and mine. My mother's only concern when I told her I was gay was that I was going to cut all my hair off."

Lena's chuckle started softly, but soon progressed into a deep, throaty laugh, and rapidly transformed into a guffaw that had her holding her sides and her eyes shining.

"Oh, that's brilliant," she panted in between huge, heaving breaths, "I love it!"

Megan joined in the laughter but her heart was heavy. Poor Lena. No wonder she was as brittle as she was. How the hell did you ever cope with something like that?

Lena sunk into the hot water of the bath and sighed happily. The bubbles tickled her skin in a not unpleasant way, and the scent of them filled her nose. This was exactly what she needed after the evening's revelations. Those moments on the sofa over soup had taken her entirely out of her comfort zone and some time alone in the soothing embrace of a hot bath was the perfect way to reset.

Two weeks ago, she wouldn't have imagined ever telling Megan, someone she barely knew, her story. But actually, although the re-telling had been upsetting, it had felt okay to share it with her. And getting confirmation of Megan's own sexuality had felt good. More than good, she had to admit. This baffled her. Even though she'd had moments where she could acknowledge how attractive Megan was, and how all round nice she was, it was beyond ludicrous to think anything could ever happen between them. Megan was so…full of life, and Lena wasn't, not really.

Memories of that phone call with Madhu filtered into her brain, and Madhu's exhortations that Lena shake off the anger she was carrying around so that she could be a happier person. It wasn't easy, but she had at least made a start. Maybe, just maybe, if she kept it going, then someone like Megan would be interested. It wouldn't be Megan, obviously, as there was no way a woman like her would stay single for long and therefore still be available if and when Lena ever got into a position to even think about dating again.

Lena's eyes popped wide open. She had just made a massive assumption. Why did she automatically think Megan was single? Just because she hadn't mentioned a girlfriend, or had someone over to the flat who could possibly be a girlfriend, didn't mean she wasn't involved in some way with someone, somewhere. Lena had also made a second massive assumption: that Megan would even be interested in someone like Lena in the first place.

These thoughts made Lena squirm in the water, and her optimistic mood of only moments earlier burst like one of the soap bubbles in front of her.

She reached over the side of the bath for the book she had left on the floor. The box had arrived from Amazon that morning, taken in for her by the builders working on her flat. Only half a dozen new books, as that was all she could afford this month until her own insurance money came through for the loss of her belongings, but the sight of their pristine pages and glossy covers had thrilled her when she ripped off the brown tape holding the box together. She'd chosen two all-time favourites, needing the comfort of old friends such as these to take up what little shelf space she had in her temporary home. But she'd also gone for four recent releases by authors she knew well. Now was not the time to be trying new authors. She needed stability and reliability and—

She sighed.

All of that sounded so…boring.

But safe.

She sighed again and opened the book to page one.

The rapid tappity-tap knocking on the front door had Megan sitting bolt upright in alarm. It was nine thirty at night, and unless someone had got in through the locked main door downstairs, what on earth was Dorothy doing knocking on their door at this hour?

Megan trotted over to the door as quickly as she could, if only to put a stop to the incessant knocking. As she pulled open the door Dorothy's wide-eyed face came into view, her right hand raised in the action of knocking, the annoying sound of which had now been mercifully interrupted. She was breathing rather heavily, and her left hand was working knots in her cardigan where the two sides met over her rotund belly. She startled when she saw Megan, then her eyes narrowed into a squint.

"Where is Lena?" Her voice trembled, and Megan's concern shot even higher.

"What is it, Dorothy? Are you okay?"

Dorothy shuffled slightly, trying to look past Megan into the flat. "Is Lena not here?"

"She's in the bath, actually."

Dorothy's eyes widened again and her eyebrows made a beeline for her hairline.

"I mean, th-that's where she said she was going," Megan stammered, wondering how someone could reduce her to this quivering mess with one look. Dorothy was a master at it.

Dorothy snapped her attention back to look Megan fully in the face. "Well, be that as it may, you will have to do. Come on," she said, and turned swifter than Megan would have thought possible. She was three steps down the main staircase before Megan could gather herself enough to follow. Careful to put the front door on the latch so that she didn't lock herself out, she stumbled quickly down the stairs after Dorothy.

The older woman had come to a stop at the bottom of the staircase and the hand-wringing resumed, her glance flicking to her own front door and back to the descending Megan.

"Dorothy, please, what's going on?" Megan asked, as she hopped down the final step.

"A beast!" Dorothy's voice shook. "You will have to deal with it. As big as my hand and on the kitchen ceiling." She shuddered and grasped her cardigan even tighter.

"A...what?"

"A spider!" Dorothy hissed.

Megan back-tracked as fast as her feet would allow her. "Oh no, no fu...no way."

"What?" Dorothy screeched.

"No. No can do. Me and spiders, no. Sorry, Dorothy, you're on your own." Megan started to climb the stairs only to be brought to a shuddering halt by Dorothy's hand clamped on her forearm.

"But...but you *have* to, child!" Dorothy pleaded, her eyes watering. "I can't go back in there."

Megan prised Dorothy's hand from her arm gently and sighed. "Dorothy, I really can't. I'm sorry. I have a real fear of them, just like you."

"What am I going to do?" Dorothy whispered, her glance returning to her front door.

Megan sighed, wondering if she would regret this. "I take it Lena normally does this for you?"

Dorothy turned back to face her and nodded sharply.

"Well," Megan said, shrugging, "then how about I make you a cup of tea and we wait for Lena to finish her bath?"

When Lena exited the bathroom some twenty minutes later, the rapid transformation in her expression was comical, but Megan just about managed to hold back her laugh. Lena walked into the living area looking supremely serene, but as soon as her gaze landed on the inexplicable sight of Dorothy sitting on Megan's sofa with a cup of tea in her hand, Lena's face folded into a deep frown.

Megan was simply glad to see her, whatever mood she was in; making small talk with Dorothy for twenty minutes had been difficult, to say the least. Never mind the fact that they were both twitchy at the thought of the spider downstairs and where it might be wandering now in the time it had had on its own.

"Er, good evening, Dorothy," she said, pulling the two sides of her fluffy towelling robe closer together.

"Good evening, Lena," Dorothy replied, and Megan could swear her eyes were sparkling behind the thick lenses of her glasses.

Lena's gaze swivelled to Megan. She didn't speak, but she didn't have to—her face said it all. She wore what could only be described as a "what the fuck?" expression, even though Lena would never have couched it in those terms, given she didn't swear.

"Um, Lena," Megan began, her voice croaky with nerves under the intense glare of that look. "Dorothy seems to have a little issue that needs your attention."

"*Big* issue," Dorothy cut in, snippily. "There is nothing *little* about it, child."

"Of course. Yes." Megan cleared her throat. "Apparently there is a large spider on the ceiling of Dorothy's kitchen. As I'm also pretty terrified of them, I offered Dorothy…refuge, until you could go down and, you know, deal with it."

"Refuge," Dorothy murmured. "I like that."

"Thank you," Megan said out of the corner of her mouth, not daring to look away from Lena, hoping she was putting the right amount of pleading into her own eyes.

The snort of laughter that Lena emitted made both Megan and Dorothy jump. Dorothy just about held onto her tea, and tutted loudly. Lena ignored her.

"*You* are scared of spiders?" Lena asked, her hands moving to her hips, which in Megan's humble opinion—like the rest of Lena's body—looked even more deliciously curved in the big towelling robe she was wearing. Lena was looking Megan up and down, taking in the overall size of her, Megan presumed.

"Well, why shouldn't I be?" Megan said hotly. "Just because I'm the size I am has nothing to do with phobias like this, you know."

Lena's expression softened then, and she held her hands up. "You're right, I'm sorry." Her voice softened too as she said, "It's, well, you were so brave that day of the storm, when we wondered if it was burglars."

"You were," Dorothy concurred, nodding, and Megan's cheeks flushed.

"Seriously, I was shi…er, very frightened, actually. I hid it well," she finished, smiling as the other two women chuckled.

"All right," Lena said, sighing. "You two stay here and finish your tea. I'll deal with it." She looked down at her robe. "I'm not going down like this, however. I'll get into some clothes and then go down there. I'll shout up when the coast is clear."

"She's an angel," Dorothy said a few minutes later as Lena disappeared out the front door, now clad in her Hogwarts hoodie and a pair of pyjama pants.

"Yeah," Megan breathed, forgetting to filter herself, then squirming under the intense gaze Dorothy aimed her way.

"Are you like her?" Dorothy asked into the awkward silence.

Megan stared at her. "Like?"

"Lesbian," Dorothy whispered, her eyes darting right and left as if afraid to find someone had overheard her saying the word out loud.

"Yes, I am," Megan said, straightening her spine in anticipation of a battle.

Dorothy simply nodded. "Treat her right," she said quietly. "After that woman, she doesn't need any more unpleasantness."

Megan's cheeks burned. "I… We're—"

"All done!" Lena's voice called up the staircase outside the flat. "You can come down now, Dorothy."

Dorothy turned to Megan and patted her on the arm. "Thank you for the tea, child. And remember my words."

Before Megan could even think to respond, her neighbour from downstairs had shuffled out of the front door.

CHAPTER 14

"Hey, you!" Madhu pulled Lena into a big hug, or at least as best she could around her expansive bump.

"Madhu, you're huge! Are you sure you're okay to be travelling?"

"Well, thanks a lot," Madhu said, then smirked to let Lena know she was only teasing. "I'm fine. As long as I don't walk too far."

"Eight weeks to go, right?" Lena asked, and she took Madhu's arm to lead her away from the entrance to the platform where Madhu's train had just arrived at Euston.

"Yes. I can't decide if I want it to hurry up or never come at all."

"Madhu!"

Madhu waved a hand. "I don't mean I don't want the baby. I'm, you know, a bit scared of the whole giving-birth thing."

Lena grimaced. "So glad it's you, not me," she said.

"Thanks, sis, so supportive." Madhu laughed and pulled Lena into a hug again. "It is so good to see you."

Lena smiled against Madhu's lustrous black hair, holding her beloved sister as close as she dared. "Yes, it is. Now, we ought to get on the Tube and down to my place so that we can get that weight off your feet."

"I like your thinking," Madhu said, smiling.

Although it was the first Saturday in December, and the Christmas shoppers were already making their moves, the Tube south to Clapham wasn't horrendously busy. Madhu's very obvious bump got her a seat immediately, with Lena hovering protectively near her for the journey. Exiting the station at Clapham North, they turned round the corner towards Jackson Road, the cold wind cutting into their faces as they walked as quickly as Madhu's bulk would allow.

"Oh, that's better," Madhu said, sighing as she sat down on the sofa and kicked off her boots.

"Tea?"

"Definitely."

Lena made a pot—she'd rescued her own treasured teapot from the wreckage of her flat—and brought it over to the sofa on a tray complete with mugs and slices of lemon in a little dish.

"So how is the building work going?" Madhu asked after their first few sips of tea.

Lena sighed. "Slowly. They warned me the weather could get in the way, which it has, but it also seems they're not the fastest builders on the planet. Megan's often home in the mornings, and she says some days she doesn't hear a sound from up there, so I don't really understand what's going on."

"Worth checking with the landlord?"

The snort that Lena emitted was distinctly unladylike. "I doubt it. He's useless. And a complete miser. As long as he's getting insurance money to make up for my lack of rent he doesn't care." She pursed her lips. "But maybe I could call the insurance company themselves—after all, they're the ones who appointed the builders so it's in their interests that it doesn't overrun and cost more, surely."

Madhu nodded. "That sounds like the best plan then." She took hold of Lena's hand and squeezed it. "I'm so sorry you're going through this and that I couldn't help more with finding you somewhere to stay."

Lena smiled and waved her off. "Forget it, sis. This—" she gestured to the room around them "—has worked out fine, you know. I think I'm going to be okay."

Madhu beamed and squeezed Lena's hand again. "That is *so* good to hear."

"Anyway." Lena cleared her throat at the upwelling of emotion Madhu's obvious love brought on, suddenly desperate to change the subject. "I didn't know what you'd want to do for food later, so I did get some groceries first thing to cook for us, if you like. Or we can go out to the High Street where there's lots of places."

Madhu nodded slightly, as if accepting the change of topic. "Anywhere good?" Madhu asked over the rim of her mug.

Lena shrugged. "I... It's been a while since I ate out."

"Not since Chris, right?" Madhu's previous smiley face sunk into a frown. "Lena, that's months! Have you really stayed home every night and weekend since she left?"

Lena's blush was deep. When Madhu said it like that, it did sound pretty...pathetic. "I know how it sounds. I just, you know, couldn't face it. I was upset, at first, and then, well, it got too easy to stay home all the time. Safe," she finished quietly.

Madhu laid a warm hand on Lena's arm. "I get it," she said, her voice soft and full of tenderness. "I really do. But, don't you think that should start changing now? Or soon? I mean, you're not living on your own now, so you could at least ask your flatmate out one night, maybe?"

Lena stared at her sister, her mind churning. Could she? Not a date, obviously, and she'd have to make sure Megan knew that wasn't what Lena was thinking, because how embarrassing would it be if she thought Lena was asking her on a date and Megan said no as a result? But if she could avoid all of that it would be quite nice to go out for a meal. With Megan. Her eyes widened with a mix of excitement and fear at the prospect.

"What?" Madhu said, frowning.

"Er, nothing," Lena said quickly. "Just, you know, wondering if that would be possible because she works such different hours to me and—"

"Leelawati Shah, what are you not telling me?" Madhu's voice this time was firm and hard as steel.

"Nothing!"

Madhu arched one perfectly sculpted and pencilled eyebrow and said, "Really?"

Lena groaned and covered her face with her hands. From between her fingers, she said, "You know what, you're worse than Mum at this."

Madhu snorted, then laughed out loud. "I actually don't mind that. Which is bizarre." She shook her head. "This pregnancy has really screwed up my moral compass." She sighed dramatically. "Well, whatever. Spill."

Lena dropped her hands back into her lap. "I was thinking how I would ask Megan and not make it sound like I was asking her on a date, because I wouldn't be. I wouldn't want her to get the wrong idea and it make things awkward between us." She looked round at Madhu. "It's been nice, actually, the last couple of weeks. We've got on well, I think."

"That is so good to hear, sis." Madhu smiled. "But backtrack a step for me please. Why would Megan think it might be a date? She's straight, right? And she doesn't know you're a lesbian." This time both of Madhu's eyebrows rose and her eyes widened. "Hang on, is that what you're worried about, that she *does* know and she thinks you're going to jump—"

Lena was laughing, waving her hands trying to get Madhu to stop talking and eventually settled for putting her hand across Madhu's mouth to silence her.

"Stop!" Lena said. "Just stop. Wow, when you get a head start there's no stopping you." She took a deep breath, and removed her hand from Madhu's mouth, who looked sheepish. "I need to catch you up on some things. Megan is gay too, and she knows I am. Her friend, Jen, asked me out on a date—" Madhu squeaked "—and I declined. Too arrogant for me. Anyway, Megan also knows about me leaving home and why. Like I said, we've been getting on well, and, it, you know, seemed like the right time to tell her."

"Wow," mouthed Madhu, her eyes wide. Then she shook her head before saying, "Who are you and what have you done with my sister?"

Lena smiled and blushed, then squealed as Madhu pulled her into a fierce hug.

They ventured out to the High Street for food. Madhu insisted and Lena accepted it was as good a time as any to get reacquainted with her local area. They ended up at a wood-fired pizza restaurant.

"I know it's probably unhealthy but I really, really want one," Madhu said as she pushed through the front doors, a grinning Lena following close behind her. She couldn't remember the last time she'd had pizza and was feeling like an over-excited child as they sat down and opened the menus.

"Now," Madhu said, once they'd ordered, "I know you said it was okay for me to stay the night when we spoke last week, but are you sure? I have an open return, I can go back tonight if you'd prefer it."

"No," Lena said sharply. "It's totally fine, you staying. I won't have you doing all that travelling in one day. You'll have my bed and I'll be on the sofa. I already told Megan and she's working until nine tonight anyway so wasn't planning on doing anything at home. She said she'll come home straight from work and make sure she's used the bathroom et cetera before I'm ready to sleep."

"That's lovely of her. I hope I'm awake when she comes home so that I can thank her personally."

"Oh wow, that was such a good pizza." Madhu groaned as she sat down on the sofa, one hand rubbing her extended belly. "But I am completely stuffed now."

Lena chuckled. "Er, you did finish all the crusts on mine too, you know, so I don't know why you're so surprised at how full you feel."

"Whatever," Madhu said, smirking. "I'll be honest though, I might need to shut my eyes for a few minutes. Recharge." Her voice was already drifting, and Lena watched, overcome with tenderness, as her sister snuggled down into a semi-horizontal position on the large sofa, her head resting against the padded back, her eyes slowly closing. A few moments later, Madhu's breathing had deepened and Lena smiled. Her sister looked incredibly beautiful in this moment, and so peaceful. She pulled her phone out of her pocket and snapped a couple of photos to show Madhu later. Then she tip-toed to her room, pulled a blanket out of her wardrobe, and returned just as quietly to the living room to gently place the warm, fleecy blanket over her now deeply sleeping sister.

With that done, she crept back to her room and climbed into bed, tucking her legs under the duvet before reaching for her book.

Madhu's voice woke her, and she jerked her head up, realising it had dropped to her chest as she'd clearly fallen asleep reading at some point. Her neck ached, and she rubbed furiously at it to ease it before clambering out of the bed.

"You okay, sis?" she asked, as she walked into the living room. Madhu was walking slowly across the room towards the bathroom.

"Fine." Her sister waved over her shoulder. "Just shouldn't fall asleep on sofas. When I need to pee, it takes me forever to get upright and now my back is aching too." She disappeared into the bathroom and Lena pivoted back round to her bedroom. Somewhere in amongst her make-up and spare moisturisers she was pretty sure... Yep, there it was. Massage oil.

When she returned to the living room Madhu was filling the kettle. "I'm making myself at home, is that okay?"

Lena grinned. "Totally. Hey, look what I found—can I interest you in a back rub?"

Madhu glanced at the bottle in Lena's hand and beamed. "Leelawati Shah, I will love you forever if you do that for me."

"So," Madhu said a few minutes later as Lena's hands worked a gentle massage on Madhu's lower back. They were on Lena's bed, Madhu laying on her side, Lena kneeling beside her. It was awkward positioning for Lena, but Madhu's contented sighs told her it was worth it. "Tell me about this friend of Megan's who asked you out."

"Ugh, there really isn't that much to tell. She was the one that was with Megan that day she moved in. Jen's… Well, yes, I have to admit, she's very attractive. Taller than me, black, very cropped short hair. She sort of reminds me of that woman who was in *Orange Is the New Black*, you know the one I mean? Only Jen is taller."

Madhu turned her head slightly to stare at Lena over her shoulder. "Samira Wiley? Played Poussey?"

Lena nodded.

Madhu made a sort of whistling sound through her teeth. "Wow, and you turned her down? Even I think that woman's hot."

"Madhu!" Lena gasped.

"What? Is there some rule that says I can't appreciate a hot woman just because I'm straight?"

Lena gaped at her sister. "Er, no, I guess there isn't. It's… You've never said anything like that before."

Madhu shrugged. "Hey, I'm just feeling very comfortable about things now. You know, your sexuality, your life. I guess I would like to know that we can talk about stuff like this."

Lena didn't think she'd ever smiled so widely; it actually made her jaw ache. "Madhu, that's… Thank you."

Madhu smiled. "Shut up, or you'll make me cry. You know my hormones are all over the place."

Lena laughed and tapped Madhu lightly on her bare back. "All right. Well, anyway. Jen is very attractive, but she's also really full of herself. I can't stand that. And it's so weird because Megan isn't like that at all, and I wouldn't have thought she'd want to be friends with someone like that."

"There's more to Jen than that, I'm sure. And just because you don't like it, maybe Megan does."

Lena's shoulders dropped. Yes, maybe Megan did like that. Maybe she and Jen had been involved at some point. Somehow the thought made her feel a little nauseous.

"Hey, you okay?" Madhu asked, glancing round again.

Lena looked down and saw that her hands had stilled their massaging motion. "Oh, yes. Fine."

"Uh-huh," Madhu said, and turned back, but not before she'd given Lena another one of her penetrating stares.

It was a little before ten when Megan came home. Lena and Madhu were watching a film on Netflix, which Lena paused to make introductions.

"Hi, Megan. How was your day?"

Megan smiled, and Lena's stomach did that little flutter it had been doing every time she saw that smile recently. "It was good, thanks."

"So, Megan, this is Madhu, my sister."

Madhu made to get up, but Megan waved her back down again. "Don't get up, it's cool. Hi," she said, walking around to stand in front of Madhu and shake her hand.

"Nice to meet you," Madhu said, unsubtly giving her a once-over and making Lena blush to her roots.

"Have you two had a good day?" Megan asked. If she was bothered by Madhu's inspection, she didn't show it.

Lena nodded. "Yes, it's been really good. It's nice to have a whole weekend too, as we won't get to spend that much time together for a while soon."

Megan glanced at Madhu's belly. "How long now?"

"Eight weeks. I'm ready now though—hauling this around is getting pretty boring."

Megan laughed, her shoulders shaking. "Yeah, I remember Karen, my sister-in-law, saying the same thing in each of her pregnancies."

"Oh, that's something I meant to ask you," Lena said. "How come I didn't meet Karen and your nephews that time?"

"Oh, yeah. The boys had both been invited to some kid's birthday party that day, and Karen took them to that. She also said it probably wasn't a good idea having those two little buggers running around my small flat. If you think I'm clumsy, you should see the carnage those two can create."

"They must be bad, if you're saying that." Lena laughed.

Megan grinned at her. "I'm going to have a beer, you want one?"

Lena declined and watched as Megan strode off to the kitchen area.

"She seems really nice," Madhu whispered.

Lena turned to her sister and smiled. "Yes, she is. I'm very lucky, I really understand that now."

Madhu nodded, but there was a strange expression on her face, sort of thoughtful but more.

"You okay?" Lena asked.

Madhu glanced beyond Lena to where Megan was still busy in the kitchen. When she looked back at Lena, her face was even more serious. "Are you sure you're just friends?" she asked quietly.

Lena's eyes widened. "What?" she hissed.

Madhu shrugged, then smiled. "I'm just wondering. Because you look at her the way I looked at Jay when I first knew I was really interested in him."

CHAPTER 15

MEGAN COULDN'T PUT HER FINGER on what had changed, but something had. It had seemed to start shortly after Madhu's visit at the beginning of the month. Ever since then, Lena had withdrawn from Megan again, returning to her pattern of spending most of her time in her room, when in the two weeks leading up to Madhu's visit, Lena had really started to seem comfortable truly sharing Megan's flat. The one time Megan had dared to ask if Lena was okay, she'd simply nodded and said she was tired as it was very busy at work. But her eyes had flicked away as she'd said it, and Megan knew enough about body language to know it was a lie.

Placing the 8kg dumbbells back on their stand, she wracked her brains. Had she done something to upset Lena? Often it wouldn't take much, that was true, but she genuinely couldn't think of a single thing she'd done wrong. Any clumsiness that had occurred at home—and strangely, that had lessened since Lena was around—she'd cleared up without Lena being any the wiser, so it couldn't be that. Jen hadn't been round much when Lena was home, so it wasn't any discomfort from that situation, surely.

Settling herself onto the leg curl machine, she set the correct weight and began her slow reps. She had an hour between clients this afternoon and was making the most of it, not having had time for her own workout at all the previous day. It was the middle of December, and she was beyond busy. Many of her clients, most of them female, were cranking up their work ethic in advance of the Christmas binge they were all clearly anticipating. It was great money for her in the lead up to the holiday season, but her own body was feeling the lack of exercise.

As she settled into her rhythm, her mind drifted back to Lena. The other thing that was bothering her was that Lena hadn't mentioned any plans for the holiday season. She knew the only family Lena had was Madhu—well, at least family who would talk to her—but there had been no talk from Lena of perhaps travelling up to see her sister over Christmas. And Lena clearly had very few friends, as she was home most evenings and weekends when she wasn't working. Megan had started to formulate a plan to ask Lena to spend Christmas Day with Megan's family. They were all heading to Callum's place this year, as he'd finally finished the conservatory he'd been putting on the back of his house, and he and Karen now had just about enough room for the whole Palmer clan to descend for the day. Megan thought it might be fun for Lena to be surrounded by people that day, rather than stay home alone. Yes, obviously, Lena wasn't Christian and therefore didn't celebrate Christmas as a religious festival. But neither did the Palmer family—Aunty Jean excepted, and she wasn't invited to Callum's anyway—so it would simply be a fun day filled with food, games, and silly films on TV.

The trouble was, Lena had been so distant from her, she hadn't had the courage to broach the subject. The last thing she wanted was to upset Lena even more. The longer they spent together, albeit in fits and starts around their differing working hours, the more she liked Lena and the more she cared about her. She finished a curl, dropped the weights down, and sat back. Cared about Lena? Yes, actually, she supposed she did.

She inhaled deeply and thought back over the past few weeks, wondering when it had all shifted for her. They'd got into a lovely rhythm together at home, almost without it being spoken about. Lena would happily make meals for them, even if they couldn't eat them together—Megan had lost count of the number of evenings she'd arrived home from work to find something delicious in a Tupperware container in the fridge. Usually, she realised with a smile, with a cute Post-it note on it in Lena's meticulous handwriting, explaining exactly what it was and how long it needed to be reheated.

Megan, in return, did all their laundry, so that it was washed in the morning and close to being fully air dried when Lena got home from work. Lena had baulked at the concept at first, not happy with the idea of Megan handling her dirty clothes, especially her underwear. They'd soon worked out a scheme whereby Lena placed everything into one of those mesh wash bags, and so the whole thing got dumped in the machine as is, without Megan having to touch anything.

Megan chuckled at the memory of them discussing that situation, and Lena's blushing face as they'd done so. It was the first time she'd seen Lena blush as deep as she herself could. She moved over to the cross-trainer and programmed in a fifteen-minute hill climb. As her arms pumped the handle bars and her thighs strained slightly against the simulated hill climb, her brain sent her a multitude of images of her gorgeous flatmate. She closed her eyes momentarily and groaned inwardly. She knew what was happening, and she couldn't seem to stop it. It was hopeless—no one as serious, intelligent, complex, and challenging as Lena would be interested in a simple lump like herself. She needed to get past this crush and instead value the gentle friendship she'd found with Lena.

She would, however, ask her about Christmas, because that's what a friend would do, right?

"You want me to spend Christmas Day with your family?" Lena looked puzzled, and at the same time shocked, and it caused her face to scrunch up in a way so adorable it was all Megan could do to stop herself from cupping Lena's face in her hands. She shoved them in her pockets to resist the temptation.

"Well," Megan said, shrugging, wondering if she really had misjudged this after all, "I guess I assumed... Well, you haven't mentioned any plans, and I know the only person you'd see otherwise would be Madhu, and—"

Lena's confused face transformed instantly into one of anger, and Megan knew she'd said the wrong thing.

"I don't need your pity," Lena snapped. "I'm quite happy spending the day on my own. Unless you don't want me to be here that day either in which case I will make other plans." She crossed her arms over her chest and glared at Megan.

"Lena, no, that's not at all what I meant." She exhaled and pulled her hands from her pockets to run them through her hair, which she was wearing loose for the evening. Something indefinable flittered across Lena's face as she did so. "It wasn't that I thought you needed saving, or something. I thought it would nice for you to spend the day with a bunch of people who have a bit of a laugh, eat too much, and play silly games. I just—" she looked down and scuffed one foot against the floor "—wanted you to have some fun over Christmas, because I know how shitty your family, except Madhu of course, has been to you these last few years. And Dorothy said—"

"Wait!" Lena threw up a hand. "Dorothy said something?" Her eyes were wide in confusion.

Megan swallowed hard. She hadn't meant to let that slip. "Er, yeah. Um, she said something about some woman who'd treated you badly." When Lena said nothing, Megan continued, "I'm sorry if I've upset you. I didn't mean to. I, well, we've been getting on so well since you moved in, I guess I wanted to include you in some stuff. I-I'm sorry, forget I asked." Her shoulders slumped as she turned away from Lena's inscrutable face. Well, it had been worth a try. She only hoped it hadn't made anything worse between—

"Chris. Her name was Chris." Lena's voice was quiet behind her, and Megan took her time turning back round to face her so as not to spook her out of continuing to tell her story. Lena met her gaze and sighed. "We were together for nearly two years. She lived here for most of that. She...she cheated on me. I didn't find out until two months after it started."

"Oh, Lena. I'm so sorry."

Lena shrugged. "It was horrible, but it's over. She moved out back in April." She smiled wanly. "I knew Dorothy never liked her, but I didn't realise Dorothy knew so much about what was going on."

"Were you in love with her?" Megan moved to perch on the arm of the sofa and was pleased when Lena leaned in against the back of it not too far away.

"Who, Dorothy?" Lena asked with a smirk, and Megan laughed. Lena sighed again. "Yes, I was in love with Chris. Or at least I thought I was at the time. She was my first proper girlfriend. I'd had one, um, fling before her with a woman in Bolton. Kind of my coming out, I suppose. I think your first proper relationship always feels like 'the one', doesn't it? You think it can't possibly end."

"Yeah, I guess."

"Well, looking back I know it wasn't perfect. I think I was so caught up in being in a real relationship with a woman I didn't look too hard at all the things that were wrong."

"Yeah, been there."

"Yes?"

"Julie. We were together two years too. God, she was hard work. I had to walk away in the end but it took me a long time to get to that decision because, like you, I was all wrapped up in the newness of being in a 'proper'—" she made air quotes as she said it "—relationship. Amazing what you can convince yourself of if you try."

Lena smiled, and relaxed her arms. "Yes, that's true." She huffed out a breath. "If that offer of Christmas Day is still open, I'd... Well, I'd really like to accept."

Megan shot upright, her mouth dropping open in shock. "You would?"

Lena chuckled. "Yes, I really would."

"Cool." And there was that smile again, the one that made her jaw ache.

Having lived in the top-floor flat all the time she had been at number seven, Jackson Road, Lena had always had another flat as a buffer between herself and Dorothy's music, be that her organ-playing or anything she chose to play on her music system. Sometimes Lena had been vaguely aware of the noise, but it had never disturbed her.

On the morning of December 25, however, Lena discovered that living on the floor above Dorothy exposed a person to significantly higher levels of noise. At eight a.m. precisely, Lena catapulted upright in her bed as Johnny Mathis's voice boomed out below her, crooning—at a volume usually reserved for live concerts at the O2 Arena—the saccharine lyrics of "When a Child is Born". Upon stumbling into the living room, she bumped smack into Megan who was exiting her room at exactly the same moment. They rebounded off each other and just managed to steady themselves before they landed on their backsides.

"What the—?" Megan looked dishevelled and wild-eyed, and strangely alluring all at the same time. Lena blinked rapidly, her brain trying to process the multiple stimuli of the aural intrusion from below with the wonderful visual before her. Megan's T-shirt, which had "Resistance Is Futile" inscribed across it, was rumpled and had ridden up to reveal a glimpse of a pale, flat abdomen. Her shorts were loose but very short, and the big, muscly thighs they presented to Lena's sleep-deprived brain nearly had her short-circuiting. It was most definitely far too early on Christmas morning to be having such confusing thoughts as these.

"Dorothy," she managed to stammer out. "Music."

Megan glanced around then down at the floor. "Right. Okay." She pushed her hands through her messed up hair, and Lena only just bit back a small groan. This was starting to become a nuisance, this…crush, or whatever it was. She'd been successfully pushing it to the back of her mind for a while now, but—and perhaps it was because she'd been startled awake so rapidly—her normal resistance was indeed proving futile.

They each took turns making use of the bathroom and met back in the kitchen area.

"Well, I'm totally awake now," Megan said, rubbing her hands over her cheeks. "How about you?"

Lena nodded. "Coffee? Breakfast?"

Megan grinned. "Oh, yes."

They sat on the sofa and happily munched on scrambled eggs, hash browns, and grilled tomatoes, sipping at big mugs of hot coffee, all the while serenaded by Christmas songs and carols by such stellar artistes as Boney M, Dean Martin, and Andrea Bocelli.

"How do you know all the names?" Lena asked after Megan identified the version of "Ave Maria" as the one belonging to Michael Bublé.

Megan laughed. "Blame my mum. She loves all the crooners like Frank Sinatra, and anything from the eighties and nineties. I grew up listening to loads of this stuff."

"Do you think we should go and ask her to turn it down?" Lena asked, wincing as a particularly loud track started.

Megan looked aghast. "Argue with Dorothy on Christmas Day? Are you mad?"

Lena sighed. "Yes, I suppose you're right. I'd like to survive the morning to see your family."

"Great choice." Megan grinned. "So, are you finished eating?"

"Yes, thank you." Before Lena could say more, Megan stood and swept up their plates and cutlery, quickly returning them to the kitchen area. When she came back to the sofa, she stood in front of Lena, her feet shuffling, her hands tucked into the pockets of her shorts. Lena tried very hard not to stare at the thighs that now presented themselves at precisely her eye level and used all her willpower to raise her head and meet Megan's embarrassed-looking gaze.

"Now, don't be mad at me," Megan began, and Lena immediately went on alert. "But I … Well, it's Christmas, and that always means presents in my family, and I couldn't not get you anything. So I did. So is it okay if I give it to you now?"

Megan got her a gift? Lena didn't know what to make of that. She knew she resembled a goldfish as she gaped up at Megan, but no words would come.

"Er, well, I'll just give it to you anyway," Megan said, blushing deeply but scooting off towards her room before Lena could attempt to say anything. This was so embarrassing; she hadn't for one minute thought to get Megan anything. What kind of a friend was she?

Megan was back in less than a minute with a fairly large wrapped box in her hands. She placed it gingerly on the coffee table and stepped back, looking fearful.

Lena stood up, her mind now finally engaged.

"Megan, this is so lovely of you. I…I'm so embarrassed, I didn't even think to get you anything."

Megan shrugged, and smiled. "It's okay. It's not like we talked about it or—"

"It's not okay. You're…you're my friend, and we share a flat. I should have got you something." She felt terrible, and the next words tumbled out of her unfiltered as a result. "It's not much of an excuse, but I've got out of the habit of thinking of others." She swallowed back a lump that appeared in her throat. "Chris and I swapped gifts last year, obviously, but since she left I've… Well, I've been wallowing in a dark hole of self-pity, to be honest, and been very selfish as a result. So, I'm sorry."

"Oh, Lena," Megan said, stepping forward then halting abruptly. "It's okay, I understand. I really do. Look, what I've got you isn't anything spectacular, okay? It's just something I wanted you to have." She smiled and blushed again. "And at the risk of sounding very cheesy, it'll make me just as happy to have you with my family this afternoon than it would as if you'd got me a present."

Lena's own face flamed red and a warmth of a different kind swept over her body, starting from somewhere in the middle of her chest. She had to clear her throat before speaking. "That's a very nice thing to say. Thank you."

They stared at each other for a few moments. There was something there, in the air between them, that had Lena's toes tingling and her heart rate increasing.

"Well." Megan pulled her gaze away and gestured at the box. "Open it." Her voice was husky, and it caused those tingles to move from Lena's toes to every inch of her skin. She took a moment to compose herself before stepping forward and picking up the box. It didn't weigh much, and it wasn't particularly wrapped well, which made her smile. Ripping off the tape, then the paper, she gasped when she opened the flaps of the box.

Nestled in red tissue paper, their pristine white ears squished down on either side of their 'bodies', was a brand-new pair of floppy-eared bunny slippers.

"Oh, you didn't!" Lena squeaked, looking up at Megan, who was grinning widely.

"Yep. I did," Megan said. "I snuck up to the flat when the guys were clearing up all the debris and rescued the old pair. Then I worked out what size they were and got on the internet and—"

Lena's arms flinging around Megan's body cut off whatever else Megan was going to say. It was impulsive, and totally out of character, but in that moment Lena could not have done anything other than give Megan a great big hug. Dimly, lost in the heat of Megan's body, and the firmness of all that flesh pressed against her, she was aware of Megan's soft "oh", then Megan's arms wrapping around her shoulders and pulling her a little closer.

They fit.

Perfectly.

Lena's head was directly under Megan's chin, which rested gently on Lena's hair. Megan's arms could entirely circle Lena's shoulders, giving her a sense of safety she'd never quite known. Her own arms wrapped around Megan's waist, and the feel of the solid body encased in that circle had her head spinning. Where her ear pressed against Megan's chest, she could hear the rapid thump of Megan's heartbeat, and was sure her own was outpacing it by some measure.

Slowly, reluctantly, but knowing she had to before she did or said anything stupid, Lena started to pull back.

Megan's grip loosened slightly but not completely. She was staring at Lena, her face slightly flushed, her chest rising and falling rather rapidly.

"Thank you," Lena whispered. "That's the best present ever."

Megan nodded slowly, looking dazed, then said, "Lena, can I—"

The sound of Lena's phone trilling on the table beside them broke the trance. Lena stepped back as if she was suddenly electrified and moved quickly to retrieve the noisy instrument.

Madhu's name was on the caller display, and Lena didn't know whether to thank her sister or curse her.

CHAPTER 16

"LENA, ARE YOU NEARLY READY? Jimmy texted to say he's ten minutes away." Megan raised her voice so that it would carry through the door to Lena's room. It was funny, already she didn't think of it as the spare room anymore; it was most definitely Lena's room. She heard Lena's muffled affirmative and moved over to sit on the sofa to wait for her. Her knees jiggled as her feet tapped the floor, and her palms were already damp. She wiped them on her jeans.

What had happened between them this morning had had her head spinning ever since. Lena in her arms had felt so good she had wanted to pinch herself to see if she was dreaming. But it was simply the hug of a grateful friend, nothing more. Wasn't it? Or... There had been...*something* between them, and definitely the hint of a scowl on Lena's face when her sister's call interrupted whatever that was that they'd been sharing.

Megan shook her head. This was already turning out to be the most bizarre Christmas morning she could remember, thanks to Dorothy and the rude awakening. She guessed Dorothy had now gone out to lunch somewhere too, as all had been silent for at least thirty minutes. Resisting the urge to replay for the fiftieth time how good Lena had felt wrapped up against her, Megan stilled her feet and practiced some deep breathing exercises to calm her heart rate. She was actually glad they were going to spend the day with her family; right now she needed a buffer in the shape of the raucous Palmer clan between her and her escalating feelings for her flatmate.

Lena appeared eight minutes later, looking beautiful in a bright pink tunic-style patterned top and black jeans, her hair pinned back at the sides, and a hint of make-up on her eyes and cheeks.

"Wow, you look fantastic," Megan said, before she could censor herself. She blushed rich red when Lena turned to smile at her.

"Thanks," Lena said quietly, her gaze roaming Megan's body. "You look very nice too."

Megan's blush bloomed over her chest. Her outfit had been chosen with more care than she would normally take for a day with her family, and she knew impressing Lena had been in the back of her mind the minute she opened her wardrobe doors. The crisp white shirt was a favourite for special occasions, and the low-slung jeans, a deep, dark blue, had always been one of her favourite pairs. Finished off with her short brown boots and a matching brown belt, Megan had felt her confidence rise as she checked herself out in the mirror. Teased mercilessly her whole childhood and teenage years about her size, it took a lot for her to feel okay about her looks. But today, she did, and having Lena's validation was the cherry on top.

The door buzzer startled them both out of their mutual appreciation, and as Lena was nearest the door, she reached over to push the release button to let Jimmy in.

"I need to get my boots on and then I'm ready," she said, turning back to face Megan, although her gaze now darted everywhere else.

"No worries," Megan said, swapping places with Lena near the front door to let Jimmy in while Lena walked over to the sofa with her black boots in her hand. Megan forced herself not to look back at Lena while she waited for the sound of Jimmy's footsteps in the hallway outside.

"Hey, Megan," Jimmy said, pulling her into a tight hug as soon as she'd opened the door. She squirmed in his forceful hold. "Merry Christmas!"

"Put me down, you plank," she muttered, and Jimmy laughed and gave her one last almighty squeeze before releasing her. "And Merry Christmas to you too," she said, smiling.

"Hi, Lena."

"Hi," Lena said shyly, quickly returning her attention to her boots.

"Have you spoken to Mum or Karen yet today?" Jimmy asked Megan as she pulled on her jacket.

"No, why?"

Jimmy leaned against the door frame and laughed. "Karen's in a right panic. The main oven blew first thing this morning so she's been cooking the turkey at the neighbour's place, who'd given her a key when they went away for Christmas."

"No!"

"I know." He shook his head, still grinning widely. "She's says the place now stinks of roast turkey and she thinks they once mentioned being vegetarian. So, because she and Callum are at her parents for brunch tomorrow, Mum is hitting Tesco's the minute they open to buy about six cans of air freshener and is going to spend the morning there with all the windows open, spraying the whole house, until she and Dad head off to Aunty Jean's for lunch."

"She's bloody barking," Megan said, shaking her head. Then she became aware of a sound she'd never heard before, coming from the direction of the sofa.

Lena was giggling. Actual honest-to-goodness giggling, her shoulders shaking and her entire face shining with glee.

"You all right over there, Lena?" Megan asked, smirking. "My family amusing you, is it?"

Lena nodded, and took a couple of deep breaths before saying, "Oh, yes. Completely. Your family is…wonderful."

Megan saw the brief flinch in Lena's expression, despite her smile, and knew what it meant. She squared her shoulders. Lena Shah was about to have one of the best family days she'd ever had, if Megan Palmer had anything to do with it.

Lena had barely got in the front door of Callum's house before a projectile from something called a Nerf gun hit her square in the chest, which led to the offending toy being temporarily confiscated from the tearful shooter, Ben—or was it Jake?—and effusive apologies from his mother, Karen.

Lena did her best to wave off the apologies and act like the incident was just a little boy having some fun, but that missile, or whatever it was, had *hurt*. She caught Megan's concerned glance and made a supreme effort to plaster a smile on her face in return. Then she excused herself to the bathroom after shaking the entire family's hands. If nothing else, she needed two minutes to 'reset' and adjust to the noise level in the household.

Having been effectively kicked out of home four years previously, she had forgotten how loud a big family gathering could be. And no offence to the Palmers, but this wasn't exactly big. She could remember days back in her parents' house in Bolton when at least thirty people had crammed into their small living room and kitchen for a feast to celebrate either a birthday, or a holy day, or even India beating Pakistan at the cricket again. A jolt of something that felt like homesickness hit her stomach, and she pushed it back down.

No, they didn't deserve to be missed. She was determined to add some new family memories to her catalogue, even if they were from a family that wasn't her own. The Palmers had been nothing but welcoming to her, and she wasn't going to repay them by being maudlin.

She smiled as she dried her hands. Madhu would be proud of her.

As she left the bathroom, she glanced around at her surroundings. Callum and Karen lived in a typical three-bed ex-council house in Streatham. Extended out the back with a conservatory, the downstairs space was pretty substantial and definitely big enough for the Palmer family to fit in for a meal. She walked back into the living room. Yes, there was room—just. Although the only way they managed it was on two tables; the main table in the kitchen held the seven adults, and a small picnic-type table hosted the two young boys, Ben and Jake. Aged seven and five respectively, they were—as Megan had warned—right little buggers. Lena was breathless watching them race around the house before they all sat down for the meal. She'd always wondered if she'd want children herself; she wasn't particularly drawn to the idea, but neither had she written it off entirely.

Until today.

Megan sidled up to her with a cup of her favourite Earl Grey and whispered, "You okay?"

This time the smile that painted Lena's face was genuine. "Yes, thank you. I am."

Lena was seated between Rosie and Megan for the meal and opposite Daniel. While it was nice to chat to Rosie, the puppy-eyed looks Daniel was throwing her way as they ate were discomforting. She did her best to ignore him, without being too rude about it. If she'd learned anything from her time sharing Megan's flat, it was how to temper her natural reaction to snap and be short with people.

"So, how's the building work going?" Callum asked, as they all cleared their plates.

"Slow," Lena and Megan said at exactly the same time. Their eyes met and smiles spread across both their faces.

"I've spoken to the insurance company," Lena said. "They said they have no concerns. Although they did sympathise with my situation, there's nothing they can do about it because of that miser of a landlord we have."

Rosie tutted next to her. "I've got no time for people like that," she said, crossing her arms over her chest. "Why can't everyone just give everybody a fair go?"

Heads nodded all around the table.

"So," Sean said, his eyes glinting, "living with Lumpy proving difficult, is it?"

Lena blinked. Lumpy? She turned to Megan, who was doing a terrible job of trying to hide the scowl that now marred her features.

Turning back to Sean, Lena spoke through an anger that boiled up out of nowhere, fast. "Is that what you call your daughter?" Her tone was razor sharp, but she didn't care. How dare he?

A hand on her arm had her glancing in Megan's direction. Her flatmate was blushing and shaking her head slightly, but Lena had seen red and couldn't hold back. When she turned back to Sean, he was staring at her, but his eyes gave away how much her question had unsettled him.

"I-I've always called her that," he said. "We all have." He gestured round the table. Lena let her gaze briefly alight on five other adult faces all looking equally as uncomfortable as Sean's.

"That just makes it worse," Lena said, her hands gripping the edges of the table.

"Lena," Megan said quietly, "it's okay. Please."

"No, it's not!" Lena turned to stare at Megan. "Don't sit there and tell me it's okay to be called something so...horrible." When Megan said nothing, Lena continued, her tone softening, "Do you like it when they call you that?"

Megan closed her eyes briefly and swallowed. Then, opening her eyes again, she looked over at her father. "No, I don't." Her voice was a whisper, but the emotion in the words was evident for everyone to hear.

"Megan, love," Rosie said, reaching across Lena to touch her daughter's arm. "I-I'm sorry. I had no idea. I mean, like your dad said, we've just always called you it. You never said, and—"

"Actually, I did," Megan said, her voice stronger now. "Lots of times." She turned her gaze to her father. "You ignored it."

There was a painful silence. Dimly, in the back of her mind, Lena wondered if she'd ruined Christmas for the Palmer family. But hearing that awful nickname and seeing how much it hurt Megan, she couldn't have *not* said anything. She also realised this was the second time she'd come to Megan's defence from people laughing at her. She didn't know where this need to stand up for and protect Megan came from.

She did know, however, that it felt good doing it.

Sean cleared his throat and stood up. Carefully, he walked around the cramped room and touched Megan's shoulder, then motioned for her to stand. When she had done so, he pulled her into a gentle hug, shaking his head the whole time he held her.

"I'm so sorry, Megan," he said softly. "Please accept my apology."

Lena could see Megan's eyes glistening and she swallowed down the lump in her own throat. Within minutes, all the adults had taken turns to say sorry to Megan.

As Rosie, who was last to do so, pulled away, she clapped her hands together. "Right, let's have a bit of a breather before pudding, yes?"

Enthusiastic nods, and cheers from the two boys, greeted her suggestion, and everyone moved swiftly to finish clearing the tables. Touching Lena's arm as she stacked plates on the counter, Rosie twitched her head in the direction of the door that led out to the garden. Lena followed, her anxiety rising rapidly. Was Rosie about to tell her off?

Rosie shut the door behind them. It was a mild day, and the fresh air was a welcome respite from the warm, somewhat stuffy house.

"Thank you," Rosie said, placing a gentle hand on Lena's arm, and Lena let out a small "oh" of surprise. Rosie smiled weakly. "I feel like the worst mum in the world for not realising that name had been upsetting her all this time. But she never said anything to me..." She trailed off. "That's no excuse really, is it? I guess we all got carried away treating her like one of the boys. Her size has always made her seem so much like one of them, and she always seemed so thick-skinned, spending all her time roughing it with them too."

Lena didn't know what to say, or even if she was expected to say anything. She decided keeping quiet until she was asked a direct question was probably the safest option.

"Well, that's all I really wanted to say," Rosie said, inhaling deeply and smiling at Lena. "And don't worry, you haven't ruined anything." She smiled.

Lena gaped at her. How had she known? "Er, good. I-I didn't mean to snap, but—"

Rosie held up a hand. "Lena, it's fine. I'm grateful to you. Really."

Nodding, Lena smiled back weakly. "Okay."

The door opened behind them, and they both swivelled in its direction. Megan, looking determined, stood on the back step.

"I'll leave you to it," Rosie murmured, patting Lena's arm before pausing to give her daughter another brief hug, then walking back into the house.

Megan walked over to Lena. "You okay? Did she kick your arse?"

Lena laughed gently. "No, she didn't. And yes, I'm okay." She stared up at Megan and tried not to focus too hard on those eyes. "I'm sorry," she said quietly.

"No, don't be!" Megan took a step closer. "What you did in there, that was…amazing. Thank you."

"I… You're welcome." Lena was acutely aware of Megan's proximity; she could feel the heat from Megan's arm where it was nearly touching her own. This was getting out of control. She took a step back and forced a laugh. "At least I didn't ruin Christmas. Otherwise maybe your family would give *me* a nickname. The Grinch."

Megan threw back her head and laughed. "You've certainly earned yourself a place in Palmer history, I'll tell you that."

Lena grinned. There could be worse things to achieve in life.

CHAPTER 17

LEADING LENA BACK INTO THE house, Megan tried hard to tamp down the glow that had taken over her whole being at the course of events over the last twenty minutes. Lena calling out her entire family on her hated nickname had first stunned her, then pleased her in a way she couldn't define. She'd wanted to hug Lena but had been aware of Lena pulling back from the closeness of the moment they'd shared in the garden and decided not to push it.

They walked back into the kitchen to find Karen cutting slices out of a chocolate ice cream dessert.

"The boys," she said, waving her knife at the dessert. "They couldn't wait. If you don't want any now it's fine, I'll put it back in the freezer." Karen placed two hefty chunks of the treat onto some paper plates. "And if those two little arseholes throw up after this, I'll kill them."

Megan snorted and delighted in hearing Lena chuckling beside her. Megan's family could be a bit rough round the edges, so it was good to see Lena rolling with the punches.

"I'm going to use the bathroom," Lena said, and walked quickly out of the room.

"Everything okay, Megs?" Karen had paused in her slicing and was looking at Megan in concern. Her sister-in-law was usually brash and loud, her personality as big as her body, but every now and then she displayed a softer, more intuitive side.

"Yeah, all good. Don't worry."

"She's a nice girl. How long you two been seeing each other?"

Megan's eyes widened and her cheeks turned pink. "Oh! No, no, we're not together. She's just using my spare room, that's all."

Karen's eyebrows rose. "Oh. Okay." She turned back to the dessert and pushed the remaining chunk back into its box.

Megan should have let it go, she knew that. But she couldn't help asking, "What? Why did you think we were a couple?"

Karen turned back to her, smiling. "Nothing in particular. You just seem really…comfortable with each other. I assumed…"

"Oh."

Weird. First Dorothy, now Karen. What were they seeing? And was it really there?

When Lena returned from the bathroom, Megan had a hard time meeting her eye, as if what Karen had said had somehow been audible to Lena too.

"Want some tea?" she asked, reaching for the kettle. She knew from their time together that Lena usually wanted tea after a meal; it was becoming second nature to ask the question while automatically reaching for the kettle anyway.

"Please."

Megan turned back briefly to Lena, and it was her undoing. Lena was gazing across the kitchen at her with an expression so full of warmth and appreciation, it had Megan's breath catching in her throat. Which was swiftly followed by hacking coughs and splutters as she choked on her own oxygen intake. Lena was across the room like a shot, pounding on Megan's back before reaching for a glass and running tap water into it.

"Here," she said, passing the glass over, which Megan took hold of gratefully in a shaking hand. Her face was flushed, half from choking, half from embarrassment. She gulped down a few mouthfuls of the icy-cold water.

"Thanks," she sputtered, once she could trust her voice.

Lena smiled, and, inexplicably, returned her hand to the centre of Megan's back, rubbing comforting, firm circles while Megan breathed in deeply.

"Oh." Her mum's startled word came from the doorway. "Sorry, I didn't mean to interrupt."

Lena leaped back from Megan as if she'd been stung. Megan turned to face her mother, her cheeks flaring again. "You weren't. It's… I caught my breath, was choking."

Megan's mum glanced between the two of them, a strange little smile on her face. "Okay." She walked further into the room. "I was going to put the kettle on."

"Already done," Megan said quickly, turning back to the now-boiling kettle and pulling mugs out of the cupboard above it. "What does everyone want?"

When Megan turned back, Lena had left the room.

A few minutes later, Megan helped her mum take copious mugs of tea into the living room. Her two nephews were flaked out on the tatty old sofa that filled one side of the conservatory, empty dessert plates abandoned at their feet. Their eyes were glazed over as they stared, unseeing, at the small TV showing cartoons on the opposite side of the room.

In the main living room, the adults were also casually arrayed across the furniture. Her dad filled one armchair, Jimmy and Daniel were slouched on the floor in front of the window, and Karen, Callum, and Lena were on the sofa. Lena stood as soon as she saw Megan and her mum enter the room and helped hand out the mugs of tea before moving to sit on the floor at the end of the sofa, gesturing to Megan's mum that she should take her vacated seat on the sofa.

"Aw, thank you Lena. So kind," Megan's mum said, and sank into the space with an "oomph" of pleasure.

Megan glanced around the now crowded room, and determined the only free space was on the floor between Daniel and her dad, which put Daniel between her and Lena. Not quite able to fathom why that made her so edgy, she wedged herself into the small free space, and pulled her knees up before leaning back against the wall, surveying her family. There were two conversations already in full flow, involving everyone but Daniel. As she turned to open up a line of conversation with him, she saw that he'd already turned away from her and was chatting to Lena. Having lived with Lena for a few weeks now, it took Megan less than a minute to know that Lena was not exactly a willing participant in the conversation her brother had initiated. Berating herself for eavesdropping even as she did it, Megan tuned in to his words.

"...and so I was thinking, you know, if you were up for it, we could maybe go out one night, for a drink, or even for dinner. What do you think?"

127

Megan nearly choked again, a completely irrational anger burning bright within her. Although it wasn't quite anger. Something else...

"Um, Daniel, that's nice of you. But, no, thank you." Megan was impressed; Lena hadn't ripped her brother's head off in letting him down.

"Oh," Daniel said, blinking. "I mean, we could take it slow, it doesn't have to be real date, you know, if that's easier."

"Daniel," Lena said, her tone patient but firm, "I'm a lesbian."

Unfortunately for Lena—and Daniel—her words dropped into a now-silent room as, by sheer chance, the two other conversations that had occupied everyone else in the room came to a pause.

Daniel looked round, clearly wishing the ground would swallow him up whole, and clambered to his feet, muttering, "Right. Well. Okay. Great," before stumbling from the room to the kitchen.

Lena hung her head, shaking it slightly from side to side.

"Well," Megan's mum said, cheerfully. "That's cleared that up, at least."

It had been tempting to ask Jimmy to drive her home. The day had lurched from one embarrassment to another, and Lena's anxiety had ratcheted up as a result. But, strangely, at the same time she *was* enjoying herself. After outing herself to the entire Palmer family, seemingly breaking Daniel's heart in the process, Lena had spent a few quiet minutes in the garden, breathing deeply and talking herself down from the edge of a full-blown anxiety attack. She'd called her sister Madhu but only got voicemail, so when Megan had appeared, cautiously approaching and asking if she was okay, somehow, surprisingly, Lena had found herself being open and honest with Megan about what was happening.

"I'm okay," she'd said. "Well, now I am. I get...anxiety attacks, if I'm really upset or stressed by something."

"Oh. And I guess coming out to my family on Christmas Day kind of comes under that description, yes?" Megan's smile was wry, and Lena's chuckled response came naturally.

"Yes. Yes, it does." Lena shook her head. "I didn't know of any other way to get your brother to stop. I'm sorry if—"

Megan held up a hand. "Don't, he'll be fine. Yes, he's the quiet one, but he's done okay in the girlfriend department over the years. He'll soon move on, don't worry."

"Oh, okay. Good."

"So, um, these attacks. How do you deal with them? Is there anything I should know, in case, you know, you have one at home?" Megan was shuffling from foot to foot and looking adorable in her concern. Lena's heart started to thump in a way that had nothing to do with anxiety.

"Well, I've got used to dealing with them myself, over the years. There's some breathing techniques, and visualisation exercises I can use. I... It's nice of you to ask, but trust me, I can handle them. Nothing for you to worry about."

Megan nodded. "Fair enough. Well," she said, looking back at the house, "I'll leave you to it."

She turned to walk away, and Lena spoke before she'd really thought it through. "Megan." Her flatmate looked back over her shoulder, her eyebrows raised. "I-I'm having a lovely day," Lena said. It wasn't quite what she had wanted to say; she'd chickened out at the last moment. She'd wanted to thank Megan for caring, for checking up on her, for inviting her to spend the day with her family, and for not caring that Lena seemed to be putting her foot in it left, right, and centre. But the words had got stuck in her throat as something inside her knew she might reveal more than she intended.

Megan had smiled, nodded, and continued her path back into the house.

Now, Lena found herself roped into playing a game called Monopoly. She'd heard of it, of course, but had never actually played it. Apparently it was a firm favourite in the Palmer household, and an annual tradition over Christmas taken very seriously and containing its own potted history of famous victories and still-disputed "cheating" incidents.

Lena's playing piece was a little hat, and although still not entirely clear on the rules she was apparently suffused with beginner's luck, much to the ill-concealed dissatisfaction of her opponents. All except Megan, whose grin had begun about ten minutes ago and had only widened the more money Lena raked in for rents on her strategically placed hotels. The pile of pretend cash in front of Lena was growing and, although not one to gloat, she was thoroughly enjoying herself.

"How the—?" Sean tutted as he slapped down the last of his cash in Lena's direction. "That's me out," he growled, and for a moment Lena feared she'd made yet another Palmer faux pas, until she caught Sean's eye and he winked. "Lena, I can tell your accountancy training has done you well. You don't fancy doing my tax returns, do you?"

Lena laughed, scooping up Sean's cash and adding it to her pile. "Sorry," she said. "Not that kind of accountant."

"Damn, I was hoping you could find some way to get me some money back out of Her Majesty's government."

"Are you absolutely sure you haven't played this before?" Rosie asked a couple of minutes later as she handed over the last of her cash. "Megan, you've brought in a ringer."

Megan, laughing, raised both hands. "Swear to God, Mum, Lena has hidden talents I knew nothing about."

Rosie and Karen snorted. Lena smiled, a faint blush forming on her cheeks, as she caught Megan's eye and watched in amusement as Megan's eyes widened at the realisation of what she had said and how it could be misinterpreted.

Ten minutes later and it was all over—Lena had cleaned up and officially annihilated the Palmer clan in her first ever Monopoly game. Uncharacteristically, she basked in their praise, which seemed genuine rather than begrudging, and the warm glow that had stayed with her for most of the day reappeared tenfold at being made to feel so welcome.

She saw Megan catch Jimmy's eye and nod, then turn to Lena and say, "You okay if we head home now? Jimmy has to get up early to drive to his girlfriend's parents' house so I didn't want him having a late one today."

"Of course," Lena said, nodding, realising how tired she was now that home time was being mentioned. It had been an up-and-down day, and an emotional one in places. She glanced at her watch—it was only eight thirty, but she could easily crawl into bed right now. She'd coped though, more than coped and, given how far out of her normal the day had been, she was immensely proud of that.

After a protracted series of good-byes, coupled with a multitude of invites to be a part of future Palmer gatherings, finally Lena followed Megan and Jimmy out to his car.

It was a quiet drive back through the darkened streets of south London; this late on Christmas Day the traffic was light, and Jimmy had them home in less than twenty minutes. They didn't converse on the way back, all three of them seemingly content to watch the quiet world go by. When Jimmy pulled up in front of their building, he jumped out to say good-bye, pulling Megan into as big a hug as the one he had bestowed first thing that morning, and eliciting the same protesting groan from his sister as he did so.

To Lena's surprise, he also hugged her, albeit far more gently than his sister. "It was lovely to have you with us," he said, smiling as he let her go.

"It… I had a wonderful day," Lena stuttered. "Thank you very much for driving us."

Jimmy waved it off. "Laters." He got back in the car and sped off.

Megan let them into the house and, not knowing whether Dorothy was home or not, they crept up the communal staircase carefully to Megan's front door, trying hard not to giggle as they did so. After shutting the door to the flat behind them, Megan turned to Lena and said, "Tea?"

Lena shook her head. She was exhausted. "Thanks, but no. I think I'm going to go straight to bed."

Megan's face fell ever so slightly, but then she smiled. "Yeah, it was a long day given how early Johnny Mathis woke us up."

Lena grinned. "Indeed." She made to walk past Megan to the bathroom, but a gentle hand on her shoulder stopped her. When she turned slightly to face Megan, there was a nervous-looking smile on her flatmate's face.

"Are you okay?" Lena asked, bemused.

Megan visibly swallowed, and before Lena could react, Megan leaned forward and slightly to the side. Lena wasn't sure why she flinched; the unexpectedness of it, perhaps. Whatever it was, in flinching as Megan leaned, their heads bumped together and they both let out little "oomphs" of shock.

"Sorry!" Lena said, staring up at Megan.

Megan rubbed her forehead, blushing furiously. "No, it was me. Sorry." She snapped round and walked quickly off to her bedroom, leaving Lena in a daze near the kitchen.

What had just happened? Why was Megan leaning towards—

Oh.

Lena raised her eyes towards the ceiling and blinked slowly.

You. Complete. Idiot.

Before she could overthink it, she was walking, her footsteps measured and even. She knocked on Megan's door. When there was no answer, she knocked again, and said through the wood, "Megan, please. There's something I need to say."

Slowly the door opened, and an embarrassed-looking Megan peeked out from the small gap she'd allowed between them.

Lena smiled, putting as much warmth into it as possible, and gently pushed the door open further, noting with pleasure that Megan didn't resist.

"I never thanked you for making this such a lovely day for me," Lena said quietly, never letting her gaze drop from Megan's. "And again for my wonderful gift this morning. I still feel terrible for not getting you—"

Megan's face finally broke into a smile. "You did, actually," she said, just as quietly.

"I did?" Lena tilted her head, frowning.

Megan nodded, and pulled the door open even wider. "Yes. You did. You banished Lumpy."

"Oh. That." Lena's shoulders shook from her laughter. "Well, it was an unintended gift, but I'm glad you liked it."

"I really did," Megan replied, her hand twitching against the door frame.

Lena cleared her throat. "Well, that was what I wanted to say." And before she could chicken out, she pushed up on her toes, turned her head slightly, and carefully kissed Megan's cheek. The skin there was warm, and smooth, and Lena let her lips linger perhaps longer than was wise, but oh my, it felt good to do so. When eventually she pulled back, she didn't get very far; Megan's free hand took hold of her wrist to bring her motion to a halt. Lena looked up questioningly, Megan's face so close to her own that she feared she'd sink into those pale blue eyes and never resurface.

"I had a great day," Megan whispered, and she also turned her head and placed a kiss on Lena's cheek. Her lips were cool against Lena's skin, and they too lingered more than would be said to be usual in a kiss goodnight between flatmates. Lena's heart thumped against her ribs, and she only just held back a small moan.

Suddenly she was on shaky ground. There was danger up ahead, uncertainty, and the potential for embarrassment or even pain. She pulled back, smiling hesitantly but ensuring that her movement forced Megan to let go of her wrist.

"Goodnight," Lena said to the space between them, not daring to look up into Megan's eyes again, and she quickly turned and walked back towards the bathroom.

CHAPTER 18

Hi Lena, just so you know, I'm spending the day with Jen. Back sometime tonight. Have a good day

THE POST-IT NOTE WAS STUCK to the kettle, and its placement made Lena beam. Megan would know the first thing Lena did in the morning was make herself a cup of tea. And knowing Megan knew that, gave Lena a warm glow inside.

Although she was surprised at how early Megan was up and out, Lena had treated herself to a little lie-in this Boxing Day, given how early Dorothy had woken them the day before. So, at just after ten, Lena was only making her first cup of the day, completely out of routine and somehow not minding it at all.

She pondered that while the kettle boiled noisily beside her. She was feeling...relaxed. Calm. These were rare states of being for Lena Shah, and she knew an awful lot of that had to do with Megan, and whatever it was that was happening between them. The sweet kisses goodnight to finish off their eventful Christmas Day were still on replay in her mind's eye, but the nervous energy she'd taken to bed after that hint of intimacy seemed to have dissipated overnight. Now the thoughts didn't conjure up so much terror as excitement. Sure, she wasn't entirely sure what the kisses meant, and the fear of getting hurt still lurked in the background. But it felt lovely reaching that point with another woman, of gentle intimacy and connection, after she thought Chris had done an unfortunately good job of destroying that for her.

The kettle raucously completed its boil, and she made her tea on autopilot. She had a whole day ahead of her, home alone, and for once cleaning didn't factor into her plans at all. Instead, she had a book to finish, another to start, and some nicely cheesy movies to watch on TV. She popped two slices of bread in the toaster and pulled the jar of peanut butter down from the cupboard. She smiled as an image of Megan grimacing every time Lena ate the stuff popped into her brain.

Learning what each other liked or disliked had been one of the more fun elements of sharing Megan's flat. Somehow learning all those things from someone you weren't romantically involved with seemed...easier. There was no pressure to say the right thing, or worry what the other person thought of your tastes in music, TV, food. With no expectations of anything between them, it had been fun to exchange information.

As she munched her toast, Lena wondered about those expectations now, after the way they left things the night before. She didn't know about Megan, and could probably never second-guess her, but for herself, she wasn't sure her expectations were so low anymore. Or, at least, her hopes.

Megan swore as she heard the Tube train departing long before she was at the bottom of the escalator. The service was less regular on Boxing Day than a normal commuting day, and although that meant she'd probably only have to wait six minutes rather than two, those four minutes seemed precious right now.

She felt like shit. The cold, or flu, or whatever it was had ambushed her within the space of a couple of hours after lunch. One minute it had seemed she was fine—the next thing she'd been clutching at her throbbing head and struggling to breathe through her blocked-up nose. Jen had seen how bad it was getting and insisted they cut their day short so that Megan could get home to recuperate. Megan didn't argue.

Flopping onto a bench on the platform to wait for the next Tube, she wondered what kind of reception she'd get once she got back to the flat. The last thing she could deal with right now was any drama with Lena. Although, that wasn't entirely fair. Apart from the 'Lumpy' incident yesterday, and Lena outing herself to the Palmer family, she and Lena had shared some key, wonderful moments. The kiss goodnight, even though it was chaste and on the cheek, had left Megan tingling and unable to sleep for quite a while. The whole day had shown her some new sides to Lena, and she'd liked them. A lot. She could admit she'd found Lena physically attractive for a while, but her unpredictable, vicious tongue had made Megan wary of thinking beyond the physical appreciation. Now, however, after everything they'd shared on Christmas Day, her mind was starting to think about Lena in a way she'd tried very hard not to for some while now.

The Tube finally arrived to whisk her home. The weather was miserable when she left the station—the swirling wind coupled with drizzling rain only making her feel even more sorry for herself as she trudged back to her flat. She let herself in to the building, then quietly climbed the stairs, wiping away with her sleeve the rain that had dampened her face.

As she opened the front door, she was instantly assaulted by some delicious smells coming from the kitchen.

"Oh," Lena said, turning round sharply from her position in front of the cooker. "I thought you'd be back much later than this."

Megan pulled off her coat and hung it haphazardly on a hook. "Yeah," she said, her voice radically different due to her bunged-up nose. "I'm not well so we called it quits for the day."

"Oh, no." Lena walked quickly over and placed a deliciously cool hand on Megan's forehead. Megan leaned into the touch and tried not to moan.

Lena whipped her hand away, her eyes wide. "Oh, sorry. That…that was a bit presumptuous of me. Sorry."

Megan smiled weakly. "Oh, no need to apologise. It was very nice."

Lena smiled shyly. "Well, um, anyway, you're burning up. Have you taken anything?"

Megan shook her head and wearily walked over to the sofa. "Didn't have anything on me and neither did Jen." She slumped down onto the sofa, and rested her head back against the cushion.

"Right, wait there."

She could hear Lena walk into the bathroom and return a couple of minutes later. She pressed two paracetamol into Megan's left hand, a glass of water into her right. "Take two of these now, then again—" she glanced at her watch "—at nine thirty. Assuming you're still awake then, of course."

Megan grunted and threw the pills into her mouth, washing them down quickly with a mouthful of the refreshingly cold water. She gulped the rest of the glass down.

"Want some more?" Lena asked softly.

"I'll get it," Megan said, starting to rise, but a firm hand on her shoulder pressed her back into her seat.

"Let me," Lena said.

Megan gazed up at her. This was…nice. Being looked after. "Thank you," she whispered.

Lena smiled, then strode off to the kitchen.

"What are you cooking?" Megan asked as Lena returned with another full glass of water. "It smells amazing, even with a bunged-up nose."

Lena chuckled. "Just plain old curry. Sort of based on a rogan josh, with lots of vegetables. I haven't had time to make a proper curry in ages and realised that I could do it today." She paused, and tilted her head as she looked down at Megan. "Would you like some? It might do your sinuses good." She smiled.

Megan nodded. "If you don't mind sharing, I'd love some. Not a huge portion, I'm not massively hungry. But it does smell so good, I really want to try it."

"Okay." Lena smiled again. "So, it will be ready in about twenty minutes. Why don't you sit and relax there? Do you want a blanket or anything?"

"You know, I think I'd actually like to get out of these clothes." She bit back a groan as she realised how that might sound. "I mean, they feel kind of damp from the rain and probably from the fever I seem to be running."

Lena stepped back and motioned towards Megan's room. "Okay, you take care of that and I'll get back to the food."

Shuffling off to her room, Megan rolled her eyes at herself. She seemed to have a tendency these days to blurt out words that could be completely misconstrued. And usually around Lena. She shook her head. *Get a grip.*

After changing into warm sweatpants and a big, soft hoodie, she made her way back to her spot on the sofa. While Lena pottered around the kitchen, Megan pondered what she was in the mood to do while she waited for dinner. She knew there was no point in offering to help Lena; her flatmate had made it perfectly clear that Megan's only role was to look after herself. The care Lena was bestowing on her wasn't something she was used to, having been on her own for a while now. It was another new side to Lena—or actually, an extension of the side of her that had defended Megan only the day before. It seemed the festive season was revealing multiple aspects to Lena's personality that had until now been completely hidden. And all of them good.

The TV caught her eye, but immediately she discounted it. The noise would drive her nuts. There were no newspapers left on the coffee table—Lena's cleaning habits had taken care of those on Christmas Eve—and the only magazine left there was one she'd already read. Her gaze swept to the other side of the coffee table and alighted on a book placed face down on its surface.

"Is this what you're reading at the moment?" she asked, leaning forward to scoop it up. She turned it over to check out the cover.

"I finished that one this morning," Lena said, then blew on a spoonful of food before tasting it slowly. "Yes. Perfect." She looked up at Megan. "Ten more minutes. And you are welcome to read it, if you like."

Megan jolted. Read? A book? She hadn't read a book in… God, she couldn't actually remember when. She'd read quite a bit through school and in her late teens, but then got bored with reading tales of brave men—always men—who saved the world/solved the crime/defeated the terrorists. She glanced down again at the book in her hand. This didn't look anything like one of those books she used to read. For starters, the cover had a picture of two women on it, both in hospital scrubs.

"Is it a lesbian book?" she asked, her curiosity sparked.

"Yes. It's really good."

"Romance?"

"Well, yes, kind of." Megan glanced up; Lena looked embarrassed. "But it's more dramatic than that."

"And you really wouldn't mind me reading it?"

Lena looked down, one hand twirling unconsciously in her hair. When she looked back up, there was a resolute set to her face Megan had never seen before. "No, I don't mind. I-I'd like to ask that you don't turn the corners of the pages to mark where you are. I can lend you a bookmark for that. And, you know, just take care of it in general."

"Of course." Megan smiled inwardly. Right now, Lena looked incredibly cute, worrying about her book. Megan placed the book back on the table. "I'd really like to read it. I've never read a lesbian book before."

Lena's face was comical; for a moment, Megan worried her eyes were going to pop out of their sockets. "Never?" Lena squeaked.

Now Megan smiled outright. "No, never." She sighed, and sunk further down into the sofa cushions. Her entire body was aching now and if it wasn't for the promise of the curry she'd happily crawl into bed. "I'll start it tomorrow. Something tells me I won't be going to work."

I can't believe the girlfriend left her! Poor Anna...

Lena snorted. Rather loudly, it seemed, as a few heads turned her way. She blushed and ducked down at her desk.

The text from Megan had her grinning from ear-to-ear. Megan was clearly engrossed in the book if she'd got that far in the story. Lena's heart swelled with joy; the idea that Megan was enjoying a book Lena herself had loved gave her feelings she couldn't begin to name. Chris had always scoffed at Lena's reading habits—pointless chick-lit romances, she'd called them—and the amount of time Lena spent reading in general. Now, here was Megan not only reading one of Lena's books but so engaged with the story that she felt the need to reach out to Lena about how it had touched her.

Poor Megan. When Lena had got up that morning, a very sorry-looking Megan had stumbled from her room in search of her phone to call in sick. Lena had taken the phone from her and talked to someone called Alisha on Megan's behalf, then gently pushed Megan back to bed, made her a hot lemon and ginger tea, and written her instructions for re-heating some of the curry if she wanted it for her lunch. Megan had loved the curry the evening before, but she'd only managed a small portion before she had to give in and take herself off to bed.

It was…nice, looking after Megan. She was grateful for everything Lena did, thanking her profusely, but hadn't turned into someone demanding and self-centred with her sickness. Lena liked being there for her, making sure she was okay. Not mothering her, but…something else.

Caring for her.

She stared at the monitor in front of her, the Excel spreadsheet a blur before her unfocused gaze.

Yes, she cared for Megan. A great deal. Despite all the mood swings Lena had thrown at her since they'd first met, Megan had rarely reacted with anything in return but calm friendship and warmth. It felt uplifting and—she recognised—releasing, to start to return that state of being with another person.

With that in mind, she grabbed a piece of notepaper, her spreadsheet forgotten, and started writing out a shopping list for chicken soup.

When she got home late in the afternoon, Megan was dozing on the sofa. She looked even paler than usual, and her hair was slightly matted around the edges of her face. Lena quietly walked over to her and placed a hand on her forehead. Megan barely stirred. Her skin was hot, yes, but not as hot as when she had stumbled home the day before. Lena spotted the empty strip of paracetamol on the coffee table and nodded to herself. Good, her patient had followed instructions and taken her drugs when required.

After tip-toeing away from Megan, Lena unpacked the shopping, then walked to the bathroom. She grabbed a flannel from the cupboard and dampened it with cold water, and returned to the living area. Megan stirred as Lena perched on the edge of the sofa next to Megan's reclined body. Her eyes fluttered open.

"Oh, hey," she said huskily. "You're home." She blinked a few times. "How was your day?"

The urge to kiss Megan almost overwhelmed Lena. It was as if they were a couple, not flatmates. The thought, the image of it, seared Lena's brain and sent a hot flash of something deeper than pure desire rushing through her body. She took a deep breath, then said, "Fine. More importantly, how was yours?"

She reached out with the damp cloth and gently patted it against Megan's face, wiping carefully at her hairline, and down around her neck.

"Oh, God, that feels so good. Thank you."

Lena smiled and tried to tamp down the tremors that invaded her body at Megan's whispered words. She continued to wipe the cold cloth over Megan's face and neck.

"I've read and slept, mostly," Megan said. "Jen called at lunchtime to check on me." She stretched slightly and wriggled inside her blanket. "Offered to bring me stuff, but I said I was being very well looked after." Her gaze met Lena's. "And I am. Thank you for everything you're doing."

"My pleasure," Lena said quietly. "Have you eaten anything?"

Megan shrugged. "Not much. Just some toast. I know you left me curry, but I couldn't face it for some reason."

"That's okay, you can have that tomorrow. Tonight, it's chicken soup. Home-made, of course, which is the best." Lena stunned herself—never mind Megan, whose eyes went wide—by buffing her nails on her shirt at that last statement. The snort of laughter that Megan emitted had Lena laughing moments later too. "Was that too big-headed?" she asked, blushing slightly.

"Nope. Own it, I say. And," Megan said, placing a hand on Lena's arm, "chicken soup, home-made, sounds delicious."

Thirty minutes later, with everything simmering nicely in the big pan, Lena turned to see Megan with the book in her hands again.

"You're enjoying it then?" she asked.

Megan looked up, hooking a finger in her page. "It's brilliant! I wish I was well so I could read it faster."

Lena laughed in delight. "I'm so pleased."

"God," Megan said, "the things Anna's having to deal with. Suddenly taking on two kids who've lost their parents. I couldn't do it." She shook her head.

"Me neither."

"Do you ever want children?"

Lena shrugged. "I'm not sure. I'm really excited for Madhu and Jay having their baby, but the idea of having my own seems…daunting. But maybe that's more because I'm single. What about you?"

"I think I'd like to be a parent, but I don't want to give birth." She shuddered, and Lena chuckled. "I love looking after Callum's two whenever I babysit them. Although," she said, shaking her head, "I'm not such a big fan of theirs right now, as I'm pretty sure it's one of those little shits that gave me these germs."

Lena laughed. "Probably, unfortunately. I suppose I ought to be grateful that for whatever reason, I haven't got it too."

They ate the soup together, discussing the book and key moments in it that Megan had read thus far.

"I've never done this," Megan said, after they'd finished eating.

"What?"

"Discussed a book with someone."

"Oh."

"I like it."

"Me too."

They smiled shyly at each other.

CHAPTER 19

"WHAT DO YOU MEAN, THERE'S another delay?" Lena's voice rose to screech level.

Mr Patel raised his hands, palms outwards. "Miss Shah, the rafters are completely gone. We did hope we could replace the ones that came down in the storm, but it's impossible. As we suspected from the start, we need to take the whole roof off and replace it."

Lena closed her eyes for a moment. It wasn't Mr Patel's fault, but she had no one else to take her frustration out on. When she opened her eyes again, Mr Patel was staring at her, his eyes wide and his entire body braced as if for impact. Having been on the receiving end of two blistering attacks by Lena over the past few weeks, he was clearly prepared to face another. He was a tall, thin man, completely unlike the shape of any builder she'd ever seen before, but it had become rapidly clear that it was his brother who did the physical work, while this Mr Patel focused on project management. And making grovelling apologies to clients.

"How much time does it add to the project?" Lena asked, her voice sounding considerably calmer than she felt inside.

Mr Patel waggled his hands in that infuriating manner Lena had come to despise. "Two, maybe three weeks. It depends when we can get the timber..." His voice trailed off as Lena's eyebrows rose, and he took a step backwards.

It took the utmost effort to rein in her gut response to his words, and instead, through gritted teeth, she said, "Well, thank you for letting me know." She turned abruptly and walked out of the main front door, almost colliding with Sanjit who was stepping into the house with a large roll of tarpaulin on his shoulder.

"Morning," he said, smiling brightly and revealing his extraordinarily crooked teeth.

Lena tutted and strode off down the path to the front gate, her overnight bag gripped tightly in her left hand. As she stomped up the road, she tried to deepen her breathing, expanding her inhalations and taking her time on her exhalations. Her heart rate had risen to ridiculous levels at Mr Patel's news, and she knew there were two sides to her anxiety over the delay. Firstly, because it meant more time living in someone else's flat. And secondly, it meant more time being too close to Megan and all the confusing feelings that her proximity engendered.

It was now Saturday, December 30, and she was on her way to Madhu's for the New Year weekend. Lena was part sad, part glad to be putting some distance, even for three days, between herself and Megan. While everything they had shared from Christmas Day onwards had been some of the happiest times Lena could remember in the past year or so, her natural tendency to be pessimistic had nagged at her the past couple of days. Megan was on the mend, and Lena hadn't needed to look after her anymore. She missed having such a good reason to be so close to Megan, and at the same time, worried that she was letting herself feel things for Megan that weren't, or couldn't be, reciprocated.

She swiped her Oyster card at the barrier and trotted down the escalator to the platform. The indicator board informed her that she only had two minutes to wait for a train north to Euston, so she put her bag down by her feet and rolled her neck and shoulders a few times to ease out some of the tension that her chat with Mr Patel had only escalated further.

Lena couldn't wait to see Madhu. It had been weeks since her sister's visit to London, and although they had eventually talked—briefly—on the phone on Boxing Day, Lena was looking forward to hearing all about the progress of her sister's pregnancy and, she had to admit, to talking to her about what was or wasn't happening between Lena and Megan.

It wasn't clear at all what, if anything, was going on, and that was part of the trouble. Lena wasn't an expert in reading signals and knowing if a woman was interested in her or not, but even so, whatever this was that she was sharing with Megan was awfully confusing.

She sighed. The biggest problem, of course, was how scared she was of opening herself up to someone again. Of taking a risk with her heart. It was much safer to be single, to retreat into her books where everything always worked out and the women there always got their happy ever afters.

The Tube train whooshed into the platform, and she stepped aboard. She walked gingerly past a few people to one of the centre seats and placed her bag between her feet once she'd sat down. She immediately pulled her book out of her handbag; distraction therapy, she knew, but it was all she could handle right now.

"Shit, I forgot to get limes." Megan closed the fridge and stood up.

"No worries, I'll nick a few from the bar tonight. Carla won't notice." Jen smiled and patted Megan on the back. "Just chill."

"Cool. Thanks."

"No worries." Jen moved away and grabbed the kettle from its mooring. "Tea?"

"Yeah, why not. I could do with a break."

When Jen had made their mugs of tea, they slouched on the sofa with a music channel on the TV in the background.

"So, are you really fit enough for this tomorrow?" Jen asked after a moment.

Megan shrugged. "I'm good enough, I reckon. Still not one hundred per cent, but I've still got one more night of sleep to get more of it out of my system."

"Well, you know you don't have to go crazy—our crowd doesn't need you standing on ceremony, even if it is New Year's Eve."

"I know. Don't worry, I'll be careful. I don't want to miss my own party because I suddenly have a bloody relapse or something. So, what time did you say you can get away tomorrow?" Megan asked. She blew on her tea before daring to take a sip. It burned, as expected.

"I'm hoping eleven. I did a deal with Carla that I'd pull the lunchtime shift and do all the restocking through the afternoon if she let me go bang on, or even before, eleven. She managed to get her sister to agree to come in for a couple of hours to see them through the midnight rush."

"Cool."

"Yeah, but Carla knows she owes me so much for this year, and she knows I wouldn't ask lightly."

"It's awesome that you'll be at the party for midnight. I'd like to see the new year in with my bestie."

She and Jen shared a fist bump.

"So, Lena took off for the weekend, huh?" Jen's eyes twinkled over the top of her mug. "Still not up for one of your parties?"

Megan shook her head, sadness washing over her at Lena's absence. She'd left that morning, before Megan got up.

"Yep. I thought after how well Christmas Day went that this time she might be up for it. But then, I know she hasn't seen her sister in a while, so it makes sense she'd go up there for the long weekend."

"Yeah, true. Sooo, has anything more happened on the whole kissing-your-flatmate thing?" Jen smirked, then laughed outright as Megan blushed.

"You know, I wish I'd never told you that," Megan mumbled.

Jen snorted. "Yeah, big mistake." She flinched when Megan glared at her. "Okay, okay. Sorry. Look, you want to talk about it? Seriously, I mean."

Megan shrugged. "What's there to talk about? So we kissed each other on the cheek. Doesn't mean anything." She looked away, knowing that for her, at least, that last statement wasn't true. Especially after how…cared for Lena had made her feel these past few days.

"Hey," Jen said softly, her hand tugging on Megan's arm to pull her back round to face her. "Do you want it to?"

Megan stared at Jen. She had a distinct choice here in this moment. Laugh it off and keep it all a secret, or dare the truth and see what advice her friend could give her. While Jen passed herself off as a player, Megan knew underneath it all Jen wanted what she did: to meet that someone special to spend a lot of wonderful time with. When push came to shove, Jen would support her, and help her, and be there for her.

"I-I do," Megan replied, finally daring to meet Jen's eyes. "I really like her, Jen."

Jen smiled and nodded. "Yeah, I was starting to get that impression, but I didn't want to say anything outright in case I spooked you." She paused. "So what are you going to do about it?"

"I have no idea." Megan rubbed her face in frustration. "I mean, the kiss on Christmas Day was sweet, and the way she's taken care of me this week has been lovely. But it's not like I get any clear signals from her that she'd want more than being friends and flatmates."

Jen raised her eyebrows.

"Yeah, okay, I'm not giving her clear signals either," Megan said quietly.

"Why?"

"Because I'm scared." It was easier to admit than she would have thought.

"Of?"

"The usual." She huffed out a breath. "Thinking I'm not attractive enough for her. Thinking that someone as smart as her wouldn't be interested in someone like me."

Jen was shaking her head. "Megs, you're a gorgeous woman. If we weren't such lifelong friends, I'd do you."

"Ew." Megan grimaced then snorted with laughter when Jen looked affronted. "All right. Thanks, I think."

"Too right," Jen said, giving Megan her stink eye. "But seriously, you *are* gorgeous. Plus you're pretty smart too, and generous, and caring. You have a lot to offer someone. And I don't think Lena is out of your league, if that's what you're thinking. And I think she might be at least a bit interested. I've seen her look at you a couple of times that had me wondering if there was more than friendship on her mind."

"Really?" Megan's pulse jumped at the thought.

"Really. So, in my humble opinion, you need to just get on and ask her out."

Megan swallowed. "Ask her out?" she squeaked.

Jen nodded. "Yup. Ask. Her. Out." She lightly punched Megan in the arm. "You're a big, butch girl, you can handle it."

Megan buried her head in her hands.

"More?" Madhu asked, pushing the plate of chicken in Lena's direction.

"No, I'm full," Lena said, groaning as she eased backwards in her chair, sinking down slightly so that she was more horizontal than vertical.

"I'll take it," Jay said, his eyes sparkling as he grabbed the plate.

Madhu tutted but smiled and blew her husband a kiss.

Lena watched in contentment, as always loving seeing what a beautiful relationship her sister and Jay had, even though it was tinged with a hint of regret that she hadn't found that for herself.

"You okay?" Madhu asked. It was as if she had a sixth sense where Lena was concerned, always able to read her mind.

Lena smiled. "Mostly," she said. It was as honest as she could be; she'd done a deal with herself on the train journey up that she would try and be open with her sister. No more saying "fine" when she didn't mean it.

Madhu's eyebrows shot up. "Mostly? Not fine?" She grinned, and Lena laughed.

"I know I can't get away with that anymore. Not around you, anyway."

"You two want some sister time?" Jay asked. "Me and my friend the leftover chicken can easily get out of your way."

Lena patted his hand. "Finish your food in comfort. Then I'll take your wife away for some sister time."

He nodded and crammed another forkful of food in his mouth.

Ten minutes later, Lena and Madhu were comfy on the sofa while Jay could be heard in the kitchen, doing the dishes.

"Have you got everything you need for the baby's room?" Lena asked, matching Madhu's position with her feet propped up on the edge of the coffee table.

"Mostly. We need a cot, but Mum thinks one of our cousins may have one we could use."

"Well, let me know if that doesn't work out, and I'll buy you one as a present for the birth."

Madhu's eyes were wide. "You sure?"

Lena hugged her quickly. "Of course!"

"Thanks, because between you and me, the cousin she's talking about has questionable taste in a lot of things and I'm dreading what this cot might look like."

Lena laughed, and it felt good. She'd done quite a bit of laughing this week, mostly with Megan, and that had felt very good too. At that thought, her face fell.

"What?" Madhu asked, her hand resting on Lena's arm.

Lena sighed. It was now or never. Taking a deep breath, she related the full story of Christmas Day, including the cheek kisses that had ended it. She also outlined the whole looking-after-sick-Megan episode, and how much enjoyment she'd taken from sharing that book with Megan.

"Okay," Madhu said slowly, drawing out the two syllables. "Cheek kissing is nice. I can see that."

Lena nodded.

"But...?" Madhu prompted.

Lena blushed but plunged on. "But I think I want more," she whispered.

Madhu beamed. "At last! So, when are you going to ask her out?"

"What?" Lena squeaked. "Ask her—are you mad?"

Madhu tilted her head and frowned. "What do you mean? Oh, wait, are the rules different when it's two women? Does she have to ask you out because she's like the man in this relationship?"

Lena's eyes nearly crossed in her confusion. "What are you talking about? She's not 'the man'. She's a woman. Just like me." Her voice started to rise as anger at her sister's crass misreading of gender and identity twisted in her gut. Until she looked properly at Madhu and saw the twinkle in her eye and the smile forming at the corners of her mouth.

"Exactly," Madhu said quietly. "She's a woman, just like you. So why are you waiting for *her* to ask *you* out?"

Lena stared at her sister. "You..." She exhaled. "How come you're better at lesbian dating than I am?" she mumbled.

Madhu laughed. "Oh, Lena, I'm not. I just know you. Apart from when you came out to us all, you've always waited for things to happen. Waited for other people to do things that you really wanted. You told me you liked Chris the minute you met her but wouldn't ask her out, she had to ask you."

"That's not—" She stopped and thought about it. Actually, Madhu was right. She *had* always waited. Her first girlfriend in Bolton had asked Lena out, not the other way around. Chris had done it too. "I'm scared," she whispered. "Scared of being turned down."

Madhu's face softened into understanding. "I know, sister," Madhu said. "But trust me, from what I saw between you two when I visited, I don't think she'd turn you down."

"Really?"

Madhu grinned. "I never saw you with Chris, and I don't have any lesbian friends, but even so, I can recognise chemistry when I see it. And believe me, there was some smoking chemistry between you two."

"But she's so...gorgeous, and lovely, and outgoing. I mean, nothing like me. What would she see in me?"

"Oh, dear," Madhu said, shaking her head. "You really are delusional, aren't you? Leelawati, you are gorgeous and smart, and when you put your mind to it, very caring and thoughtful. You've been through a tough time this past year, and I know it's made you a bit scared and, well, bitter. But I know you are more than that and I reckon Megan can see that too, especially after you two have been living together these past few weeks."

She grinned. "And hey, you can't tell me that the bunny slippers were the gift of a casual friend. That took real thought and care, and shows she was really thinking about what would make you happy, yes?"

"That…that's true. But…"

Madhu raised one eyebrow, a feat that always astounded Lena even as it filled her with jealousy over the fact that she couldn't do it.

Lena crumpled under the intensity of her sister's gaze. A full confession was needed, clearly. "Well, one of the big issues with Chris and me was my, you know, need for routine and my cleaning habits and so on. I'm not the easiest person to be with, am I?" Even Lena knew her voice sounded pathetic but to Madhu's credit she didn't meet it with her usual sarcasm.

Instead, she took a deep breath and said, "But from a few things you've told me, once Megan got used to your little…quirks, she seemed okay with them, yes? Has living with her stopped you from following any of your routines?"

Lena thought for a moment. "You know, actually, it hasn't." She blinked. How had she not noticed that? Megan had accommodated Lena's needs reasonably quickly and with virtually no fuss. "She lets me be me."

Madhu nodded, her grin wide. "So, what's stopping you?"

Lena slumped back in the sofa. Could she do it? Could she actually be bold enough to ask Megan out on an actual date? Her stomach churned at the thought, but within the churning she recognised something else lying underneath.

Excitement.

CHAPTER 20

"Megan." Alisha's voice called out to her from the office as Megan walked by. She turned to her client, Geoffrey, and wished him a pleasant day, then walked into the office.

"Hey, Alisha."

Alisha smiled and stood up to meet Megan halfway across the room. "I wanted to share some news with you, before the grapevine got to work."

"Oh?" Megan stared at her; Alisha was practically glowing.

"I've been offered a new job. I'm leaving at the end of this week."

"Wow!"

Alisha nodded and grinned. "Indeed." She took a step nearer Megan, and a trickle of sweat immediately made its way down Megan's spine. "So, as we won't be working together anymore, I wondered if I could finally persuade you to go out with me."

"Wh-what?" Megan's ears were ringing and her palms were damp. Was Alisha serious? Had she been serious all this time, with the flirting and the looking?

Alisha chuckled. "No?" She stepped closer. "Are you sure?"

Her perfume filled Megan's nostrils. It was sexy, yes, but even so, nothing about Alisha or her obvious allure was actually that alluring.

"Er, sorry, I-I'm going to say no."

Alisha laughed and stepped back, trailing one long finger down Megan's bare forearm. "So sweet," she said. "I always assumed I was a little too much for you."

Megan gave her a sheepish grin, her cheeks flaming. "Um, yeah."

"You'll come to the leaving drinks though?" Alisha was all business now, walking backwards slowly to her desk, her smile wide but lacking its overt sensuality from moments earlier.

Megan nodded, relieved at the distance that now separated them. Breathing wasn't so difficult. "Yes, of course. When are they?"

"Thursday night. At the Red Lion."

Megan's face fell. Damn, that was the night she'd promised a drink with Jen.

"Problem?" Alisha asked.

Scratching the back of her neck, Megan said, "Well, would it be okay if I brought a friend? I'd promised her we'd go out that night too."

"Of course," Alisha replied. "The more the merrier." She curled her lips into a wicked smile. "Is she hot?"

The pub was packed when Megan strolled in a little after eight. Immediately she spotted Alisha by the bar, a glass of what looked like champagne held in her slender fingers. Alisha caught her eye, excused herself from the small group of people she'd been chatting to, and walked towards Megan.

"Very glad you came," she said, air-kissing Megan's right cheek. Despite everything, the nearness of Alisha still made Megan shiver. "What are you drinking?"

"Oh, you don't have to—"

"Let me," Alisha said, briefly touching Megan's bicep. "I'm buying everyone's first drink."

"Okay, that's cool. I'll have a beer, please."

"Of course. Be back—" Alisha's eyes narrowed and her gaze drifted over Megan's shoulder to something behind Megan. "Well," Alisha breathed, "what have we here?"

Megan turned to see Jen strutting across the room, as only Jen could do when she was up for a night of fun. She'd been delighted to receive an invite to Alisha's drinks, knowing she was finally going to lay eyes on the infamous "BDSM high-heels boss" that Megan had worked for all this time.

Jen's eyes were sparkling, and her trademark quirky grin was already decorating her face. She reached Megan and Alisha, gave Megan a quick fist bump in greeting, then turned her full attention to Alisha. Megan could have sworn there were sparks flying in the air between the two of them. Jen raised one hand and swept it over her cropped hair; Alisha's eyes tracked the movement and a sultry smile spread across her lips.

"Hello," she purred.

"Hey," Jen replied coolly.

Alisha took one step closer, but Jen didn't flinch. Megan was in awe of her friend right now, and, if she was honest, a little turned on by what was happening between Jen and Alisha.

"I'm Alisha. And you are?"

"Jen. Friend of Megan's." She tilted her head briefly in Megan's direction but didn't pull her gaze away from Alisha's.

Megan had never felt more like a spare part in her whole life.

Alisha licked her lips. "Can I buy you a drink, Jen, friend of Megan's?"

Jen smirked. "Sure. Lead the way."

As Alisha turned away and headed to the bar, Jen looked at Megan, her eyes wide. "BDSM high-heels boss?" she whispered.

Megan merely nodded, still in a daze at what she had witnessed.

Jen looked up at the ceiling, mouthed the words "thank you", then turned and was gone, striding purposefully after Alisha's swaying hips.

Megan exhaled loudly and pulled the neck of her T-shirt a few times in an effort to fan away some of the heat that had built up in her body over the last few minutes.

How did Jen do that? Her confidence was staggering. If only Megan could have even a tenth of that, she'd have asked Lena out by now. She'd been thinking about it all week, trying to build herself up to it. Of course, it hadn't been helped by the fact that Lena had had to put in some serious hours this week at work and Megan had hardly seen her. When she had, it was never a good time to ask something as huge as "Would you like to go out with me?"

She watched Jen and Alisha laughing and flirting so effortlessly, and something she hoped was resolve had her straightening her spine a little. There was no point wallowing in any more of this self-pity. If she wanted to be with Lena, wanted to see what it would be like to really get to know her and spend time with her, she had to pull her big-girl pants on and do something about it.

Lena was exhausted. Year-end always took its toll, but this one had been particularly hard going. Their head office had made even more stringent demands on when her regional area had to deliver their results, and as a result Lena and her colleagues had all worked crazy hours. The earliest she'd arrived home on any night was ten, and most nights not before eleven.

Which was why, against her own normal need for regulated routine, she was still curled up under her duvet at gone ten in the morning on the Sunday of the first weekend in January. She had worked for another six hours the day before, and if this was her only day off this week, she was making sure she made the most of the sleep time it offered. She rolled over, only the area above her nose outside the covers. It felt good being tucked up so snugly. Although, if she did any more of that, then breakfast would be very late, which would impact lunch, and of course, there'd been no time for cleaning yesterday and—

The covers were pushed back and she was on her feet, brain in overdrive. She only had today at home. What was she doing uselessly whiling it away under the duvet?

After showering and eating a quick breakfast of toast and jam, Lena rolled up her sleeves and began tidying the flat. There had been no sign of Megan since Lena had risen. Even though her bedroom door was shut, that didn't necessarily mean she was at home. As they'd passed so briefly in and out of each other's lives this week, Lena had lost track of Megan's timetable and had no idea if she was working today.

Briefly her mind spun back to the conversation with Madhu, and the almost-dare that Madhu had thrown at Lena to ask Megan out. She'd thought about it only a few times since the previous weekend; thankfully her busy week had at least stopped that idea careening around her brain too much. But now, in the quiet of the flat, as she methodically straightened cushions and began clearing the coffee table, the thought returned.

Could she do it? Could she ask Megan out and be prepared for the possibility of being turned down? Wouldn't things get awfully awkward between them if Megan did say no?

She frowned as she pulled together a few copies of the *Evening Standard* newspaper that had been strewn haphazardly on the coffee table. Some of these were days old; why couldn't Megan throw them—

A headline caught her eye and stopped all motion in her body.

DIAMOND DEALER ARRESTED IN DAWN RAID

Underneath the headline, in a deeply unflattering photo presumably taken at the time of her arrest, was Belinda.

Chris's girlfriend, the one who had stolen her from Lena.

Lena flopped down on the sofa with the paper clutched in her hand and rapidly read the short article. Belinda had been arrested Friday morning after a tip-off that she was handling smuggled diamonds. The details were sketchy but seemed to involve her returning to the country from Antwerp and trying to pass the diamonds off to UK Customs as synthetic crystals for adorning fashion items. She was being held in custody pending further investigations.

Lena knew it was wrong. She knew it was beneath her and somewhat immature, but she couldn't help it. The laugh started low in her chest and bubbled up and out of her mouth until she was crying with it, clutching at her sides as guffaw after guffaw escaped into the room.

Karma surely was a bitch, Chris.

It shouldn't feel this satisfying, but oh my goodness it did.

After composing herself, Lena continued to tidy up the living room, a huge smile on her face the entire time.

Later, after cleaning the bathroom to a satisfying shine, and wiping down all the kitchen surfaces with antibacterial spray, Lena relaxed on the sofa with a cup of Earl Grey and a book. Two hours of doing what she loved best and her equilibrium felt restored, her routine rescued as much as it could be, and everything felt set up right for the new week. She'd be less busy this week, and with a clean flat under her belt, calmness reigned.

She was engrossed in her book when the front door opened behind her an hour later.

"Hey," Megan said, tossing her keys onto the small, round table they kept by the front door for that purpose. "I feel like I haven't seen you in ages." She smiled as she walked over to where Lena was sitting on the sofa.

Lena tucked her thumb in her book, placed it across her lap, and returned the smile. It was good to see Megan. Really good.

"I know. Work has been super busy. Year end."

"I assumed. It's been crazy at the club too—it always is straight after Christmas. Everyone working off the excess food and alcohol."

Lena chuckled. "I can imagine." Then she glanced down at her own curves, the slight roll of her tummy over her jeans, and frowned. Did Megan think she was overweight? Megan herself was big and broad, but not fat. Lena had no idea what physical type Megan liked, but she doubted it was a woman like her with big hips and thighs...

"You okay?" Megan's soft voice came from somewhere close by, and it made Lena jump. She glanced up to find Megan standing in front of her, a glass of juice in one hand, the other hand hitched into her jeans pocket. She looked...sexy, and suddenly Lena's mouth went dry.

She nodded, which was about all she could manage in the face of the sight before her.

"Sure?" Megan tilted her head, a small frown marring her otherwise attractive features.

Breathe, Lena, breathe.

Her saliva glands started working again, and she unstuck her tongue from the roof of her mouth. "I'm good. I think I'm, you know, nice and relaxed for the first time this week. Oh, and," she giggled, "I read something in the paper that made me laugh."

"Oh yeah?" Megan took a seat next to Lena on the sofa. Their thighs almost touched, and Lena wondered what would happen if she dared to move her left leg one inch or so further to the left to bring it into contact with Megan's right leg.

I'll probably self-combust.

Lena cleared her throat. "Yes. Do you remember I told you about my ex, and how she cheated on me?"

Megan nodded and took a gulp of her drink, tipping her head back and exposing a tempting, long line of pale neck.

Lena forced her gaze away and continued with her story. "Well, the woman she went off with was some hot-shot diamond dealer in Hatton Garden."

Megan whistled through her teeth.

"Yes, except that the stupid woman got herself arrested for smuggling!"

Megan's eyes widened and she snorted out a laugh. "You're kidding? Oh, my God, talk about karma."

Lena smiled widely. "I know, that's what I thought. I kept thinking it was petty to laugh at it, but I couldn't help it."

Megan chuckled. "Nope, I'd be doing exactly the same, don't worry."

It comforted Lena that Megan felt the same way. Obviously Lena hoped Chris was okay—Lena wasn't that much of a bitch—but it did feel like the universe had handed Chris a lesson for her cheating, and Megan's response vindicated Lena's feelings.

She reached for her tea with her free hand just as Megan put her glass down, and their hands brushed slightly. Lena felt a jolt of excitement at the touch.

Was now a good time to be brave? Should she ask, get it over with?

"So, Lena, I kind of have something I'd like to ask you." Megan cleared her throat after those first words came out a little husky. "Do you mind me interrupting your reading?"

Lena put the book down on the sofa beside her after carefully notching the bookmark in between the pages. She hadn't finished the chapter, or even the scene, and although it made her twitch to leave it at that unfinished point, the determined look on Megan's face and the sheer warmth of her body so close by easily banished any reluctance. She turned to face Megan, doing her utmost to keep her breathing even and not look too directly into Megan's eyes.

Megan's face was slightly flushed, and she swallowed hard before speaking again.

"I-I hope this isn't going to be too weird, or make things difficult between us. But, I was wondering if…if maybe you'd like to go out one night."

Lena stared at her. Had she heard right? Had Megan just asked her out? She opened her mouth but no words would come.

"Oh," Megan said, her face crestfallen. "Well, can we forget I asked?" She jumped up quickly but crashed her knees into the coffee table, which knocked over her glass of juice and sent purple liquid splashing across the surface of the table. "Shit!"

"Megan, no, wait!" Lena stood up too, reaching out a hand to grab Megan by the bicep. The firmness of the muscle momentarily took her breath away, and she had to blink rapidly to remember to continue talking. "Yes! The answer's yes," she blurted out.

Megan slowly turned to her. Her long blonde hair was a little wild-looking, her face was flushed, and her eyes were wide, but to Lena she looked absolutely glorious. "You… Yes?"

Now it was Lena's turn to blush as she nodded slightly. "Yes."

"That's... Wow, that's cool." Megan was grinning so widely Lena feared she'd hurt her jaw.

"It is," Lena replied quietly. Then her gaze drifted to the mess on the table. "But can I please clean this up now?"

CHAPTER 21

SHE SAID YES. OH. MY. God.

Megan lay on her bed, her hands linked behind her head, and stared up at the ceiling. There was a grin on her face that might turn out to be permanent; it hadn't faded all evening since she'd finally found the courage to ask Lena out and Lena had said yes.

Best word in the world ever.

She shifted slightly on the pillow. Now, of course, the next problem was figuring out where to go. They'd agreed on Wednesday evening. Megan had an early shift that day so would be home by five, and Lena was fairly certain the worst of her year-end tasks would be done by then and that she'd be able to leave work on time at five thirty. Give Lena some time to freshen up and relax a bit, and that meant going out maybe at around seven thirty.

What kind of date would Lena like? It was obvious she was quite the romantic, if that book was any indication. So, dinner somewhere nice was probably the best bet, wasn't it? There were a few upmarket brasserie-style places along the High Street that probably wouldn't be that packed on a cold Wednesday night in January. And how much should she dress up? She wanted to treat Lena, wanted to make her feel special, so she really ought to go the whole hog. What about flowers? Too much?

She rolled over and grabbed her phone. Advice was needed, and it took her less than twenty seconds to scroll through her recent calls list for Jen's number.

At a little after six on Wednesday, Lena walked through the door of the flat. Megan smiled when she saw her; once again due to work conflicts they'd barely seen each other since Sunday. Lena looked a little tired, but she returned Megan's smile, albeit shyly.

"Hey," Megan said, shoving her shaking hands in her pockets. "How was your day?"

Lena shrugged out of her coat and hung it up. "It was okay. I think we're nearly done, thankfully."

"That's good."

Silence fell, and as they stared at each other Megan wondered if Lena felt it too, the change in atmosphere between them. Going on a date tonight altered their relationship. Even if they never went on another date again, by acknowledging there was an attraction, an interest between them, they were no longer simply flatmates.

Lena broke the tension. "I'm going to shower and get changed. I-I want to wear something nicer than this—" she gestured to her work suit "—for our d-date tonight."

Megan nodded and smiled in a way she hoped would come across as encouraging. "Me too. I mean, I've already showered, but I want to change into something nice too."

Lena smiled then, and bloody hell, how beautiful did she look when she did so. Megan's heart gave a little leap in her chest. She was going out with Lena tonight. Lena!

They met again in the living room around forty minutes later. Megan had lectured herself to remember to compliment Lena on what she was wearing, give her the flowers, help her into her coat—all the things she'd thought would make Lena realise how special she was. And she would do all those things in a minute, once she'd taken the time to appreciate the vision that stood before her.

Lena was wearing a simple pair of black dress trousers, pleated in the front with wide legs that flared slightly where the material met the tops of her ankle boots. The silky-looking shirt she wore was a vivid turquoise blue, shot through with random strands of silver thread that caught the light in multiple ways as Lena moved. It was fitted, not loose, and it showed off every amazing curve. The top two buttons were undone to reveal the most tantalising V of brown skin at Lena's chest. Her hair was pinned up in a fancy knot, and she wore simple gold hoop earrings as her only jewellery.

"You look stunning," Megan whispered.

Lena ducked her head, and Megan watched as a blush spread across her cheeks. She'd seen Lena blush many times before now, but this one tugged at something deep inside her, somewhere way down low.

"Thank you," Lena murmured, before raising her head again. "So do you."

Megan smiled. "Thanks." She'd stopped short of a full suit, but the charcoal grey trousers with the white shirt and open black waistcoat was one of her smarter outfits. She'd tied her hair back in a simple ponytail but left a couple of loose strands to frame her face. At Jen's suggestion, she'd touched her eyes up with some make-up—nothing too heavy, just some eye liner and mascara to bring out the blue.

She stepped forward and swept the small bunch of flowers up from the kitchen counter. "These are for you," she said, extending her arm to hold them out to Lena.

Lena stepped back rapidly. "Oh," she said, her eyes wide. "I-I'm sorry, I can't take them. I'm allergic to most flowers."

Megan's stomach dropped. *Shit.* She quickly pulled back her arm and placed the flowers back on the counter. "I'm sorry, I didn't—"

"No, don't! You didn't know." Lena smiled. "But I do appreciate the gesture."

They left the flat a couple of minutes later, Megan going ahead of Lena so that she could quickly deposit the flowers with a shocked Dorothy. After Megan explained the situation to their elderly neighbour, which she managed with only a few stutters and pauses, Dorothy gave Megan a beatific smile.

"Bless you, child. I hope you both have a lovely evening."

"Thanks," Megan said, shuffling on the spot. "We will."

The brasserie she'd chosen was cosy but not overly intimate. Megan wanted them to be able to talk without too many other people around, but at the same time she hadn't wanted to pick the most romantic place on the street for fear of putting too much pressure on both of them. They'd chatted a little about work on their way to the restaurant, and although it felt awkward in places, Megan was determined to put her nerves aside once they sat down. The table was small and covered with a simple white cloth. The smells coming from the kitchen area were mouth-watering, and there was a gentle hum of conversation around them from the few other patrons who'd braved this cold evening for a meal out.

Megan rubbed her hands together to bring some life back into them. "Can't believe I forgot my gloves," she said, with a rueful grin.

Lena smiled. "We could have gone back."

"Nah, it's fine. I'm a big girl."

Lena looked uncomfortable at the comment.

"Hey," Megan said softly, "I'm not bringing myself down saying that, if that's what you're thinking. This isn't the return of Lumpy." She smiled in relief when Lena rolled her eyes and offered a smile of her own.

"Okay. Point taken. I suppose I am still a bit...tender from that incident. I still feel guilty for snapping at your dad."

"Don't, honestly. He was totally cool with it, like he said."

Lena nodded slowly. "All right, I'll believe you."

They picked up their menus and perused them in silence for a while.

"What's grabbing you?" Megan asked, looking over the top of her menu at the gorgeous woman on the opposite side of the table. In the low light of the restaurant, Lena looked even more beautiful, if that was possible.

"The chicken, I think," Lena murmured, and she pulled her bottom lip between her teeth in a gesture she more than likely didn't intend to be sexy but which set off a tingling all over Megan's body anyway.

Megan cleared her throat. "Um, yeah, I looked at that. But I think I might have the lamb."

They placed their orders with the waitress and sipped from their water glasses. Megan had declined an alcoholic drink, wanting to keep her wits about her despite the additional relaxation the wine might have given her. But equally, Lena didn't drink at all, so Megan didn't feel right being the only one imbibing.

"So," Lena said. "How was your New Year party? I haven't even seen you long enough to ask about that."

Megan chuckled. "I know, it's been such a mad two weeks. Well, it was awesome, actually."

She filled in Lena on some of the details of the fun that was had, and in return Lena told her all about her trip home to visit Madhu.

When the food arrived, Megan saw Lena's gaze drift over the lamb dish.

"Would you like to try some?" Megan asked. "Before I get stuck in?"

Lena blushed. "Thank you, I'd love to."

Megan was transfixed by Lena's concentration as she sampled the dish. Lena was quite the foodie, and an excellent cook, and she clearly loved to learn about new flavour combinations. Watching her roll that mouthful of food around while she took in all its nuances was strangely erotic. Megan shifted in her chair.

"That's lovely," Lena said eventually, once she'd swallowed. "The meat is very tender and they've got the blend of Moroccan herbs and spices perfect."

Megan could only nod; she could listen to Lena talk about food all night.

Lena blinked a couple of times, her expression thoughtful. "Would you like to try the chicken?"

Megan nodded and smiled, reaching across to cut a morsel of the meat and pop it onto her fork and into her mouth. It was wonderful, and she moaned in appreciation. Lena blushed deeper.

They talked easily over their food and took their time eating. Passing on dessert at the end of the meal, they each ordered some mint tea. It was unspoken, but it seemed as if neither of them wanted the evening to end.

"Is this... It's been lovely, hasn't it?" Megan asked.

Lena smiled. "It has. Definitely."

"So, how would you feel about doing it again?"

"I would feel very positively about that." Lena's cheeky grin took Megan's breath away. Seeing Lena relax so much in front of her was intoxicating.

"You...you're such a different person than when you first moved in," Megan said. "Now that I know you better, I see so many fun parts of you."

Lena's fingers played with the collar of her shirt, and she smiled shyly. "I feel very relaxed around you. I know we didn't get off to the best of starts but now..." She looked away for a moment. "Now I feel comfortable around you. I...trust you. Trust you not to play me around."

"I wouldn't," Megan said fervently. "I really like spending time with you, laughing with you, talking with you. I-I'd really like to see what we could make of this."

Lena said nothing, but her smile and gentle nod told Megan everything she needed to know.

They finished their tea in silence, but it wasn't awkward. Small smiles and lingering looks made it an intense experience, and Megan had goose bumps up the length of both arms by the time the waitress placed the bill on the table in front of her. Megan had already made it clear to Lena when they'd planned the date that she was paying. She had done the asking, after all, and besides, she wanted to treat Lena. She checked the total, noted that it already included the tip, then reached into her coat for her wallet.

Which wasn't there.

She closed her eyes for a moment, then plunged both hands into each pocket to check again. Nope. Nothing. Even though she knew it was pointless, because she could feel they were empty, she checked the pockets on her trousers.

Nothing.

Oh, holy shit.

"Are you okay?" Lena asked, looking puzzled.

Megan dared to meet her gaze. "Er, well, no. Not really." She took a deep breath. "I left my wallet on the kitchen counter. After the fu—mix up with the flowers, I forgot to pick it up again." She hung her head in her hands. "I'm so sorry, Lena."

There was nothing but silence from across the table. When Megan raised her head again, Lena was glaring at her.

"I left my bag at home. You were so adamant about paying that I have nothing with me either," she said in tones so icy that Megan's stomach turned over the lamb she'd just ingested.

And it had all been going so well.

"Um, okay. God, I'm so sorry."

Lena folded her arms across her chest and exhaled loudly. "Right. Well, one of us will have to go home and get some money, won't we?"

"I'll go." Megan jumped up. "You stay here. Order some more tea, if you want. I'll explain to the waitress and be back as quick as I can, okay?"

Lena nodded, and Megan's insides churned even more. Trust her to fuck this up good and proper.

She found the waitress and told her what had happened. "I swear, I only live about ten minutes' walk away, so I'll be back in twenty, okay? My friend is staying so that you know this isn't some kind of scam. Please can you bring her another mint tea?"

The waitress frowned. "Let me check with my manager."

Megan groaned. *Come on, people, the longer this goes on the more Lena is going to stew.* The manager appeared, and Megan told her sorry tale all over again. Thankfully he agreed to her plan, and soon she was half walking, half trotting up the High Street back to their flat.

The wallet was exactly where she'd left it, looking benign and innocent—how dare it—and she snatched it up before jogging back down the communal stairs and remembering at the last second not to slam the door on her way out. The last thing she needed to top this evening off was a rant from Dorothy.

When she rushed back into the restaurant, more than a few heads turned in her direction. As she looked at their table and Lena, her insides turned to jelly. Lena looked embarrassed, and she wouldn't meet Megan's eyes. A spark of annoyance flared in Megan—it wasn't like she'd done this on purpose. It was an innocent mistake, and Lena needed to accept that sooner rather than later.

Megan waved at the waitress and handed over her credit card. "Please," she begged, "as quick as you can."

The waitress nodded, then gestured Megan over to the card machine where it sat on a counter.

"Look," she said, her voice low, "I think you ought to know, your friend had something that looked like an anxiety attack while you were out. She seems better now, but she was quite upset for a little while."

"Oh, God." Megan glanced back at Lena, whose hands were twisting her napkin into a ball. "Damn. Thanks for telling me."

"No worries." The waitress peeled off Megan's receipt and handed it and the card over. "Sorry to have been so suspicious earlier. We've had a few people leave without paying by using the 'lost wallet' excuse so we're a little jumpy."

"No, it's cool, I get it. Thanks again."

Megan turned, took a deep breath and walked over to their table. Lena was standing and already pulling on her coat.

"Done?" she asked through gritted teeth.

"Yes," Megan said. "Look, it's not like I did this deliberately—"

"I know." Lena's tone was curt, then she exhaled. "Can we please just go?" Her words were so plaintive they tugged at Megan's heart.

She led Lena out of the restaurant to the cold street. "Are you okay? The waitress said—"

"I'm fine. Please, can we go home?" Lena sounded on the verge of tears, and Megan longed to be able to wave a magic wand and have the last half hour never happen.

They walked home in silence, their pace quick, both of them with heads down against the cold, hands shoved in pockets. Lena pushed open the front gate, and Megan's heart sank again. Busy putting her rubbish in one of the wheelie bins was Dorothy. She looked up as Lena and Megan walked up the path.

"Ah, good evening," she said pleasantly. "How was your meal?"

In a voice that quivered, Lena said, "Hi, Dorothy," then carried on walking past her. "We had a lovely time, thank you." She stepped into the house.

Dorothy's eyes blinked comically behind her large spectacles, then she turned her attention to Megan, her eyebrows raised in question.

"It... We..." Megan sighed. "I screwed up, Dorothy."

Dorothy motioned for Megan to follow her back into the house. She shut the door behind them just in time to hear a thump. They looked up to see Lena on her hands and knees halfway up the staircase. It became rapidly apparent that in her rush to get back up to the flat—and away from Megan, presumably—she'd caught her boot in the dust sheets covering the stairs and had tripped forwards.

"Argh!" she cried, hauling herself upright again. Then she burst into tears. She didn't look back as she climbed up the rest of the stairs.

"Oh, dear," Dorothy said.

"I know," Megan replied sadly.

"What happened, child?"

Bizarrely, it didn't feel odd telling Dorothy. She gave her the shortened version, feeling that Dorothy probably didn't need to know too many details about the date aspect of the evening. But when she recounted the part about leaving her wallet behind, and Lena's upset state as a result, Dorothy simply patted her arm.

"She will come around, don't you worry. Lena doesn't do well with embarrassment."

"I didn't realise you two knew each other that well."

Dorothy shrugged. "We are not close, that is true. But when that woman hurt Lena the way she did, there were some fearful rows that spilled out into the hallway. I heard some things, enough to know what Chris had done and how it made Lena feel."

Megan stared at the older woman in amazement. "You're full of surprises, Dorothy, you know?"

Dorothy smiled warmly. "Let her be, child. For a while. All will be well, trust me." And with that, she patted Megan's arm again, and walked back to her own flat.

CHAPTER 22

LENA PACED THE LIVING ROOM floor in front of the TV, her mind churning.

Her embarrassment at falling apart in the restaurant, then tripping up the stairs in front of Dorothy, had drained her by the time she'd yanked her coat and boots off and walked through to her bedroom. When she'd sat down on the edge of the bed, her gaze had fallen on the floppy-eared bunny slippers, and suddenly the only image that played in her mind was of Megan looking hurt and upset as Lena brushed her away once they could finally leave the restaurant.

Lena wiped at her teary eyes and took a few deep breaths. Megan had paid for the meal, and Lena hadn't even had the courtesy to thank her. Megan had made a simple mistake in forgetting her wallet, and Lena had treated her appallingly. She knew why. Every memory of being teased and bullied at school for being so different, for being embarrassed by her peers all through her school years, had risen up in those relatively few minutes where a few patrons of the restaurant had noticed her panic attack.

Lena hated being stared at, pointed at, and made fun of. All her life she'd suffered at the cruel tongues of people who couldn't accept her OCD tendencies for what they were—simply a part of Lena's personality that hurt no one and made her feel comforted in her world. To sit all alone, feeling embarrassed about the situation, wondering just how long she'd be there, stuck out like a sore thumb, until Megan returned, had brought on all her old fears of being the item of ridicule. It cut even deeper after that wonderful evening they'd shared.

All those people, looking on as she'd gripped the table and rocked in her chair. The waitress attempting to come over and talk to her before Lena had waved her off. All of them, staring. All those faces with their eyes wide and—

She raised her head as sudden, blinding understanding jumped into the front of her brain.

They hadn't been staring at her in amusement or about to mock her.

They'd been staring in concern.

She rolled that thought around her mind for a few moments. She hadn't been laughed at or ridiculed. Everyone who had noticed what was going on was only worried for her. They probably weren't even aware of the fact that Megan had left. All they could see was a young woman in distress and they had...cared.

She shook her head; she could see it now, but was it too late to fix the damage she'd done to her and Megan's fledgling relationship? Right up until the wallet incident, and Lena's overreaction to it, the evening had been something special. Megan had been attentive, and funny, and displayed a level of intelligence that Lena had always thought was lurking below her rough exterior. The food had been delicious, and as they'd sipped their tea at the end of the meal, Lena's chest had swelled with happiness. Finally something was going right, something was setting her world on fire in all the right ways.

And then she'd been a complete...bitch—her mind stumbled on the word, but she knew it was the appropriate one—to Megan and ruined it all.

She groaned. She needed to apologise to Megan, and fast.

Head down, she stared at her slippers once more and her heart tugged as she remembered Megan giving them to her on Christmas morning. She stopped pacing, and stared at the front door, willing Megan to walk through it so that she could put this right.

She startled when the door opened a moment later, then winced as Megan stopped dead in the doorway, her face, as always, an open book. Her expression was a painful mix of confusion, fear, and hurt.

Lena pressed her hands together and took a deep breath. "Megan, I am so sorry," she said.

Megan's eyebrows shot up, and her eyes widened. She shut the door behind her without taking her eyes off Lena.

When Megan didn't reply, Lena swallowed and said, "Please, could we sit down so that I can explain?"

There was a slight hesitation before Megan said, "Sure." She shrugged out of her jacket, kicked off her boots, and walked over to the sofa.

They perched on an end each, and Lena's hands held tightly on to her knees as she said, "I had no right to get so angry with you about the wallet. I-I was embarrassed. I thought everyone in the restaurant would notice and make fun of us. Fun of me. I've realised that of course that wasn't true. I..."

She swallowed. It was going to be hard to talk about this with Megan, but she knew she had to if they had any chance of seeing what they could become. "I was picked on and bullied at school for being different, with all my little routines and habits. When I was young, maybe up to about ten years old, none of it hurt. But as I got older, I got more sensitive to it." She looked down at her hands. "If I feel exposed, or that people might be about to make fun of me, sometimes I can have a form of panic attack. That happened while you were out and made the whole situation worse. When you came back, all I wanted to do was get home, get away from that place and all those people I thought were staring at me." She looked up again and met Megan's eyes. "I was so rude to you, and I'm sorry. It's...it's something I know I need to work on, and I'm very sorry that I let it ruin our evening."

Megan smiled, gently, and Lena couldn't believe the rush of relief that swept over her at the sight.

"It's okay," Megan said. "I understand. I won't lie, it did hurt how you flew off the handle at me, but I can see why that situation brought back so much pain for you. I'm sorry you ever had to go through that, and I'm sorry I accidentally did that to you."

"And that's why I'm so disappointed in myself—it was totally an accident on your part, but all my old fears took over and in my knee-jerk reaction to the situation, I was so horrible to you."

"It's okay," Megan repeated. "Really. As long as you are okay, and we're still talking, then it's okay."

"Oh, I am, and we are!" Lena enthused. "Definitely."

Megan shrugged. "Then good." She stood up. "Okay, I'm off to bed."

It wasn't cold, as such, but it did seem like a brush-off all the same. Was Megan more hurt than she was letting on? Or had she already decided Lena wasn't worth any more of her energy? That last thought twisted Lena's insides, and galvanised her into bold and unprecedented action. She stood too, and before Megan could walk away, Lena grabbed her arm to hold her back.

"Megan," she said softly. When Megan met her gaze, Lena said, "I-I was wondering. Would you, maybe, like to go out again? Perhaps this weekend?"

Megan's face registered her shock, but in the next moment her mouth split into a big smile. "You...you'd really like to do that?"

Lena nodded shyly. "Yes, I would. If you would. I had a wonderful time with you tonight, and I'd really like to see you again. Well, on a date, I mean. Because I see you every day, really, but—"

"That would be awesome," Megan cut in, grinning.

Lena's stomach clenched, but in a good way. "Yes?"

"Yes," Megan whispered, nodding.

There was an exquisite moment of tension between them. Lena was very aware of her hand still holding onto Megan's forearm, of how the white cotton felt beneath her fingers, and of the strength that was apparent in Megan's flesh beneath the fabric. Their gazes locked, and without any thought for whether it was right or wrong or what the consequences might be, Lena leaned forward, pushed up on her toes, and kissed Megan.

Clearly taken by surprise, Megan froze, so for a moment it was all Lena kissing Megan—their noses bumped, and their lips didn't quite coordinate, and there was something strange about kissing an unresponsive mouth that was in danger of making Lena freak out. Just as she was about to panic about how messy this kiss was and what a disaster it was turning out to be, Megan came out of her stupor and—blissfully, sensuously, deliciously— her lips lined themselves up with Lena's, and opened slightly, and the kiss transformed into something that Lena didn't think she'd ever quite experienced. It was slow, and gentle, and yet deeply passionate all at the same time.

She moaned and let herself sink into it, her hand now clutching tightly at Megan's arm, her body thrilling as Megan's other arm snaked around Lena's waist and pulled her in a little closer. Megan's mouth on hers was all sorts of lovely and seemed to sum up everything she liked about Megan— warm, attentive, sexy.

Megan released her slowly, her lips lingering to kiss and nip lightly at Lena's bottom lip before she lifted her head away and stared at Lena.

"Wow," Megan whispered.

Lena could only nod; words were something she remembered being able to use in the past but not here and now.

Megan cleared her throat. "So, um, I think I'm going to say goodnight now, okay?" Her voice was husky, and Lena melted at the sound.

"Yes. Goodnight." It was all she could manage. Her mind and body were stuck in a delicious haze that might very well last until morning.

Megan smiled, leaned down to give her the briefest of kisses again, then turned and headed to her room.

Lena walked to the bathroom slowly, locked the door, and stood in front of the mirrored cabinet. Had that really just happened? Had she, Lena Shah, kissed Megan Palmer? She touched her fingers to her lips, and a huge smile spread across her face.

Oh, yes. She had.

The warmth that pervaded Megan's body at the sight of Lena walking, bleary-eyed, towards the bathroom the next morning meant her smile threatened to dislocate her jaw. At six in the morning it was way too early for Lena to be up—this was, however, Megan's usual start on an early shift, as her first client came in at seven before they started whatever their day job was. Lena's normal weekday seven a.m. start hadn't changed once in the time they'd been living together, so it was amusing and confusing to see her at this early hour.

Lena didn't even seem to be aware that Megan was quietly watching her from the kitchen area as she wandered by. When Megan cleared her throat to gently let Lena know she was there, Lena jumped and her eyes went wide.

"Oh, sorry," Megan said sheepishly. "I just wanted to let you know I was here."

Lena's startled expression instantly melted into a warm smile, and Megan shifted slightly on the spot. When Lena smiled at her like that, she pretty much forgot her own name.

"Morning," Lena murmured, her hands twisting at her pyjama top. It was Megan's favourite of Lena's, the lilac plaid looking amazing against the colour of her skin.

"You're up early," Megan said.

Lena shrugged, and her smile turned wry. "I haven't slept that well all night. Something on my mind, I suppose."

To Megan's astonishment, Lena winked. The sight of it sent a shockwave of something powerful pirouetting down Megan's body from her brain to somewhere much further south. Megan nodded. "Uh-huh, I think I know what you mean."

Lena blushed then, good and red, and motioned to the bathroom behind her. "I need to…"

"Sure, carry on."

Megan watched her walk off to the bathroom, her heart pounding behind her ribs. Six a.m. was way too early to be in a mild state of desire for a woman she'd only shared her first kiss with the night before. But, bloody hell, what a kiss it had been. All the more special because it had come out of nowhere, on the back of being made to feel so useless with the wallet incident. After the apology from Lena, then that kiss, all of that was forgotten, and all Megan could think about was (a) kissing Lena again and (b) spending a lot more time with her—hopefully kissing her a lot more.

She snapped herself out of her reverie and turned back to the lunch she'd been preparing. By the time she'd finished that, Lena was exiting the bathroom. Not sure if or how to approach Lena, Megan decided to wait. Lena made her think of a deer, someone you shouldn't approach too fast or too boldly in case they skittered away. So she was doubly pleased when Lena walked over to where Megan rested against the counter, eased her arms around Megan's waist, and tilted her head up expectantly.

Oh, yeah.

Megan dipped her head and savoured those incredibly soft lips once more. The kiss wasn't long, and their tongues barely brushed before Lena pulled gently away.

"Have a good day," Lena said, and with that she was off, strolling back to her room, presumably to finish her sleep before her alarm went off at precisely seven a.m.

Megan was left behind in the kitchen wondering if her legs would ever work again.

Lena awoke with a jerk as her alarm trilled beside her. She grabbed her phone, hit the snooze icon, and flopped back against the pillows. That had definitely not been the best sleep of her life. She groaned and rolled over onto her stomach. Waking at six and needing the bathroom had been the final straw after lurid dreams and thoughts had churned her brain over all through the night.

Her eyes popped open as the memory of what happened at about five past six that morning slammed into her consciousness.

Oh my. She'd kissed Megan again. And she herself had initiated it. Again.

She squirmed, a grin breaking out on her face. It had felt *really* good. Both the kiss itself and the boldness of her action in strolling up to Megan to do it. Megan had looked stunned, and Lena didn't think she'd ever had that effect on anyone. Well, except maybe her parents when she'd come out to them, but that was a whole different breed of stunned, and not one she ever wished to repeat.

She rolled back onto her back, and flung her arms above her head. Kissing Megan at six o'clock in the morning. She snorted. Madhu would be so proud of her.

With that in mind, she grabbed her phone again, switched off the alarm, and opened her messaging app.

Morning. Hope you are okay. I kissed Megan!!!

She suspected Madhu was still fast asleep, and she chuckled to herself as she imagined her sister's reaction to reading the message when she did finally wake. Madhu probably wouldn't believe her. Lena's behaviour and even the fact that she was messaging about it was so out of character for her. She would have fun telling Madhu all about the date—she'd even confess to how badly she'd treated Megan and how she'd worked out the source of her anger and dealt with it all so quickly. She fervently hoped Madhu would be proud of that too.

She'd been at work for about an hour when her phone beeped with Madhu's response to her message.

Tell. Me. Everything.

The office was quiet but it was still no place for that kind of discussion. She messaged Madhu back to say she'd call her in a few minutes, then quickly finished the report she was working on, e-mailed it off to her manager, and walked away from her desk with her phone clutched in her hand. Her company didn't particularly frown on personal calls during work time, but it was best to be discreet about it. The main kitchen was empty, and she pulled a chair up to the window that looked out over a desolate courtyard four floors below.

"How? When? What was it like?" Madhu skipped any form of greeting and got straight to the point.

Lena laughed. "Last night, after our first date. She took me to dinner." Lena filled Madhu in on the restaurant events, but before Madhu could get started with her admonishment, Lena cut in. "No, I dealt with it. Straight away. Well, about ten minutes after we got home. I worked out why it made me act the way I did, explained to her, apologised, and then, well, then I kissed her."

Madhu squealed. "Oh, Lena, this is good on so many levels!"

"I know," Lena said, smiling to herself.

"So how was the kiss?"

Lena cringed at the personal nature of the question but answered anyway. "It was…hot," she whispered.

Madhu yelped, then said, "You know, I am so proud of you for getting on top of things so quickly. I mean, obviously it would have been better that it didn't happen at all, but at least you know what the trigger was, and maybe that means it won't happen again?"

Lena pondered that idea for a moment. "Actually, perhaps you're right. I hope nothing like that sets me off in the future, but if it does, hopefully I'll recognise it straight away and it'll be okay." A yawn suddenly overtook Lena. "Oh, sorry."

"Was it a late one then?"

Lena laughed sheepishly. "No, I-I couldn't stop thinking about her after I went to bed, and then my dreams were very strange all night. I feel like rubbish, actually."

Madhu howled with laughter. "And this is before you've stayed up all night having sex," she said, snorting.

"Madhu!" Lena exclaimed, a deep blush speeding across her cheeks. "I can't believe you."

"Oh, Lena," Madhu said, chuckling softly. "Get over yourself."

Lena was reading on the sofa when Megan got home at four that afternoon, and Megan did a double-take when she saw her stretched out under a blanket.

"Hey, everything okay? How come you're home so early?"

She walked over to the sofa and looked down at Lena, who looked very sorry for herself.

"Well, it's a bit embarrassing, but I had to come home because I was too tired."

Megan chuckled.

"Don't laugh at me," Lena said, but her tone was light and a dazzling smile painted her face. "It's your fault."

Megan laughed louder. "Hey, I'm more than willing to take the blame."

"It's so stupid, but I also think it was a bit of a catch-up from the previous two weeks at work, which have been intense. My manager was pretty good about it—she laughed, and said she understood. Everything I was working on can wait until tomorrow."

"But it is just tiredness? You're not ill?"

Lena shook her head and reached out a hand. Megan took it without thinking, then marvelled at how good it felt to be so natural about holding Lena's hand in hers. "No, really, I'm fine. I'm chilling out with my book, and then I thought I might make us some pasta for dinner." Her eyes widened. "Oh, wait, I've assumed you're home for the evening, but maybe you have plans?"

She made to pull her hand back, but Megan held on tight. "No, no plans as such. I did promise my mum we'd have a big catch-up on the phone, but apart from that, I'm all yours." Now it was her eyes widening as she realised how that might sound. "I mean, as in, I'm—"

Lena snorted, and Megan stopped talking, blushing furiously. "I knew what you meant," Lena said, laughing softly. "Don't worry." Then her expression turned serious. "I... Well, actually, I did want to talk to you about that."

"About?"

Lena coughed and looked away. "Um, us. And what we are, or…might be. About the fact that we're dating but we share a flat. And, you know, physical stuff. Between us, I mean."

"Oh. Um, okay." Megan let go of Lena's hand and walked around the sofa to perch on the edge next to Lena's reclined body. "Well, I am happy to date and see where this leads." She shrugged. "I know we share a flat, but we don't get to see each other that much. And we know the sharing is only temporary too, so for me, that's not really a big issue. Does it worry you?" *Please don't let her want to put a halt on things until she's moved out.*

Lena sighed. "A little, I guess. I think you know I value my own time and space. A lot."

Megan smirked and nodded.

Lena chuckled. "But you're right, we don't actually cross paths that often so I'm sure we can manage this while I'm still using your spare room. But, I'll be honest, I'll feel more comfortable about this once I'm back in my own flat."

Relief swept over Megan. "I can understand that." She smiled as something prodded at her mind. "So, am I to take it that if you're looking ahead like that, you are also happy to carry on dating and see where we end up?"

Lena smiled shyly. "I am."

"Cool." Megan's grin was wide. "And while we're talking about…us, I want to get it out there that I want us to be exclusive while we date. I believe in monogamy."

Lena nodded. "Me too," she murmured.

"Okay, good." Megan smiled gently. "So, okay, as for physical, what exactly do you mean?"

Lena was silent for long moments, and Megan waited, not clear what was coming but knowing she had to be patient. Eventually, Lena turned back to her, her hands fiddling with the book held between them.

"It's just, I don't want to rush into anything. This is very new, between us, whatever it is. I know some people would jump right into things, but I'm not like that. I mean, I've loved our kisses—" Megan gave an enthusiastic nod, which made Lena smile "—but I'm the sort of person who needs to take…other stuff a little slower. I suppose I'm telling you to see if you are okay with that."

Megan shifted in her seat. "I," she began, daring to reach out a hand and gently run her fingertips down the softness of Lena's cheek, "am very okay with that. I'm not a rusher, either, all right?"

Lena's relief was palpable. "Oh, okay. Good."

Megan traced her fingertips across the fullness of Lena's lips. "Would it be okay to have another one of those kisses though?" she asked quietly, and smiled at the small moan that escaped Lena's throat. Without actually waiting for an answer—the moan told her everything she needed to know— she leaned down and met Lena's lips with her own.

Once again she lost herself in softness, and heat, and pure unadulterated pleasure. When Lena's lips parted a few moments later, Megan carefully let her tongue play across Lena's, and the action elicited a groan from each of them. They kissed more deeply, Lena's book falling to the floor moments before she reached up to wind her fingers into Megan's ponytail, pulling Megan that little bit closer.

After a couple of minutes, Megan's back began to protest at the position she was holding, and she pulled away reluctantly.

"That was...exactly what I wanted," she said, staring into Lena's eyes. "Kissing you is amazing."

Lena smiled shyly. "Thank you. I quite like it too."

Then she chuckled as Megan arched one eyebrow and said, "'Quite like'. Really. Gee, now I feel special." Megan kept her tone light and teasing, hoping Lena would understand her humour.

To her delight, Lena waggled her hand back and forth and said, "Well, you know, I can't have you getting big-headed about these things."

Megan roared with laughter.

CHAPTER 23

SATURDAY WAS POSSIBLY THE SLOWEST day Megan had ever experienced in her entire life. Her mind was nowhere near her job; instead it was focused on a beautiful woman back in Clapham whom Megan was going to be spending at least four hours with later that day.

After their scorching kiss and flirty fun on Thursday evening, they'd settled in for pasta, and Megan had held her promised call with her mum. She hadn't mentioned the turn of events with Lena, feeling the need to keep it close to her chest for now. When she'd returned to the living room, Lena was practically asleep on the sofa, so they'd shared a brief kiss goodnight and gone their separate ways.

Friday they'd not seen each other at all—Megan was on a late shift, and by the time she got back Lena had left her a sweet note to say she'd had to go to bed early.

I really wanted to stay up and see you, but I couldn't keep my eyes open. Sorry!

The words had been followed by a smiley face and a small line of neat crosses to represent kisses. Megan had beamed the whole way to bed.

Now, she had one more client appointment to get through before her day could end, and it was all she could do not to sprint the poor woman through all her exercises. Finally, with the last stretch out completed, she bade her good-bye and practically ran to the changing room to grab her gear.

She got home around four thirty. Lena was nowhere to be seen as she opened the door, but the flat was sparkling clean and held the aroma of something freshly baked. Was that possible? Megan dumped her bags near the door and strode across to the kitchen area. Oh my God, it was. Laid out on a cooling rack were roughly two dozen sinfully tempting chocolate chip cookies. It would be rude to take one, wouldn't it? Without asking? She glanced around.

"Lena?" she called. Silence. Just when she thought she was alone in the flat and was reaching for a cookie—

"Yes?" Lena appeared from her bedroom, her hair looking a little wild, her hands rubbing her eyes. "Sorry," she said through a yawn, "I was having a nap." She stopped and stared at Megan, her gaze drifting down to the tray of cookies and back up to Megan's face. Lena grinned. "What do you think you're doing, Ms Palmer?"

Megan chuckled and backed slowly away from the cookie tray. She held up her hands. "Come on, you can't blame a woman for trying. They smell soooo good, Lena."

Lena laughed, and Megan revelled in the sound of it for a moment. Knowing that she could laugh like that, and because of something they were sharing, still caused her wonder. Who would have thought that grumpy woman she'd met back in September would be standing here now in her kitchen, laughing over Megan's attempt to steal a freshly baked cookie? She shook her head.

"What?" Lena asked, tilting her head.

Instead of answering, Megan walked around the counter to where Lena stood, bent her head, and dropped the softest of kisses on Lena's lips.

Lena stared at her as she straightened up afterwards. "W-what was that for?"

Megan shrugged. "Just...because. Because I'm happy. Because what's happening between us, now, after everything that went before, is making me happy."

Lena let out a soft "oh", and before Megan could draw breath, Lena's hands were on the lapels of her jacket, pulling her down roughly where Lena's lips seared hers with a hard kiss.

"Whoa," Megan mumbled as Lena released her. "That was..." She trailed off, having no idea what to say. Lena was continuing to surprise her in the most incredible ways. For a brief moment, she wondered if she could handle it, the rollercoaster that was Lena. Then she cast all doubt aside as Lena smiled up at her, her eyes shining. Yeah, she could handle it.

"The cookies," Lena said, "are for later. For the cinema."

"Really?"

Lena nodded, then shuffled on the spot. She raised her eyes to the ceiling for a moment, then looked back at Megan. "I have this thing about cinema food. I-I think it's all a big rip-off and not very good anyway. So I always make a treat to take instead. And, you know, extras for the next day."

Megan's heart lurched. Could this woman be any more surprising, and adorable, all in one go?

"You're amazing," she breathed, and leaned down for another scorching kiss. Lena's arms snaked around her neck, and Megan placed her own hands on Lena's hips, gently pulling her in but careful not to take things too far. Lena wanted time, and Megan would respect that.

When they came up for air a few minutes later, they were both breathing heavily and smiling.

"So, er, I need to get showered and changed," Megan said, her voice croaky. "How much time do I have?"

Lena cleared her own throat, her brown eyes blinking rapidly; Megan secretly delighted in the effect she could have on this woman she once thought of as uptight and icy.

"The film starts at six, and it probably only takes about ten minutes to walk there, doesn't it?" Megan nodded. "Okay, so plenty of time for both of us to use the bathroom and get ready."

"Great."

"Are you sure you're still okay about my film choice?" Lena's teeth immediately worried at her bottom lip after she'd asked the question, and Megan used every ounce of strength she had not to pull Lena back into her arms.

While *Hidden Figures* would probably not have made Megan's top ten must-see movies of the year—NASA, maths, seriously?—Lena had been so excited to see it, Megan couldn't say no.

"Definitely. I'm really curious to see what it's like."

"Okay." Lena smiled shyly. "Well, you go and get ready and I'll have a cup of tea."

Megan grinned. "Of course you will," she said, and Lena laughed.

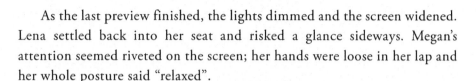

As the last preview finished, the lights dimmed and the screen widened. Lena settled back into her seat and risked a glance sideways. Megan's attention seemed riveted on the screen; her hands were loose in her lap and her whole posture said "relaxed".

Which was more than Lena could say about herself. Her reasons for being far from relaxed were twofold: one, she'd chosen a film she was sure was out of Megan's normal watching arena, if her DVD collection was anything to go by, and Lena was worried Megan was simply being polite when she said she was looking forward to it. And two, Lena really, *really* wanted to hold Megan's hand while they watched but had no idea how Megan felt about public displays of affection.

That she was even considering holding Megan's hand in public was testament to the journey she had undertaken since Christmas. It seemed every minute more she spent with Megan, the more she gained in confidence in herself. Megan had a way of making Lena feel special, no matter what they were doing. She listened to what Lena had to say. She didn't scoff at any of Lena's habits or routines. She kissed Lena like she really meant it.

Lena shivered at that last thought. Honestly, kissing Megan was spectacular. Lena's first kiss with a woman had not been that good, but it had at least told her she was finally kissing the right gender. She'd enjoyed kissing Chris in the early part of their relationship, but then Chris's kisses had become almost too hard, too bruising, too demanding.

Kissing Megan was just how she'd always imagined kissing a woman would be, both for the physical aspects of it, as well as all the extra emotional elements the kisses engendered. Feelings stirred deep in Lena's soul when Megan's lips were on hers. Never mind what feelings those lips elicited in certain areas of Lena's anatomy...

Lost in her reverie, she nearly gasped aloud as Megan's left hand gently clasped Lena's right and entwined their figures. Lena whipped her head round to meet Megan's gaze as the opening credits rolled on the screen before them.

"Is this okay?" Megan whispered, raising their joined hands slightly.

"Perfect," Lena whispered back, her heart swelling.

"Oh my God," Megan gushed as they left the cinema a couple of hours later. "That film was incredible!"

"Wasn't it? Wow," Lena breathed.

Their hands were still clasped tightly together, and Lena didn't want to mention it to Megan in case she pulled away. It had been a wonderful evening so far—holding hands throughout the movie, occasionally looking at each other at key moments in the story, and both wiping at their eyes at a couple of the more emotional scenes it contained. Lena felt like she was walking on air as they strolled back up Clapham High Street to the Mexican restaurant she had booked for a quick supper after the film.

"Thanks so much for suggesting it. You were right, it wasn't what I would normally have tagged to go and see, but wow, it was awesome."

"I am so glad you enjoyed it," Lena said, smiling widely.

Megan nodded. "I really did. But now," she said with a grin, "I have to confess, I'm starving!"

Lena laughed. "Me too!"

Their table wasn't quite ready when they arrived, which the old Lena would have thrown a small fit over, but the new version of herself rolled her shoulders, accepted the apologies from the waitress, and gently pulled Megan over to the side of the entrance so that they could wait away from the door. The waitress handed them menus to peruse while they waited, so by the time their table was ready they could order straight away.

"You okay if I have a beer?" Megan asked.

"Of course," Lena said. "Please don't ever think you can't drink around me. I really don't mind."

"Thank you." Megan smiled. "I wasn't sure if you not drinking meant you had an aversion to alcohol or something."

Lena shook her head. "No, purely upbringing. I know a lot of young British Indians who drink, but even after I left home I didn't feel the need to experiment in the same way a lot of my peers did."

"Such a contrast," Megan said, leaning back in her chair. "I've been drinking since I was fourteen. And my dad gave me my first drink."

Lena's mouth opened in a shocked "O". Megan shrugged.

"Hey, in south London, in a working-class suburb, that's usual. And it seems to go one of two ways. Either starting that early sends you down a very bad path or, if you're brought up by my parents, you understand that it's only for social occasions, and standing around on a corner with your mates drinking cheap lager from Tesco's late on a Saturday night really isn't what it's about at all."

Lena wondered if she should ask, then plunged ahead anyway. "And now? I mean, you have a lot of parties, and…"

Megan smiled. "I do, but actually I only have a couple of beers at those, maybe some tequila shots if I'm feeling particularly in the mood. I actually prefer being the host, looking after my guests, making sure everyone's got what they need. I've only had two hangovers this past year." She smirked. "Mind you, they were big ones."

"You didn't mind me asking?"

"Not at all. This is what dates are about, isn't it? Getting to know each other, ask all the important questions."

Lena frowned. Did she dare admit it? She took a deep breath. "Well, actually, these two dates with you are the first proper dates I've been on."

Megan stopped her beer bottle on its way to her mouth. "What?"

The blush heated Lena's cheeks. "Well, I did go on a date, of sorts, with Chris. We met at an accounting seminar, but…" Oh dear, now she'd started she really couldn't back out. "Um, well, I went home with her that night, and then… Well, then we were seeing each other and very soon after she moved into the flat with me."

Megan's shocked face softened, and she reached a hand across the table. "No wonder you want to take things slow this time," she said gently.

Lena nodded, not trusting her voice right now. Megan had just said the most perfect thing—rather than express shock at Lena being…easy, she'd offered understanding and support. Lena had thought Megan was special before now, but now she *knew* it.

"So," Megan said, drawing the word out, "you tired?"

They were standing in the living room, having arrived home a couple of minutes before. The flat was warm, the night was still relatively early, before ten, and Megan didn't want to say goodnight. The date had been spectacularly good. From the movie, holding hands, eating some great food, and getting to know each other more—all of it had added up to leave Megan glowing from the inside out.

Lena gazed up at Megan, her eyes looking an even deeper shade of brown in the soft light of the lamps that they'd switched on around the room after peeling off all their outerwear. She blinked slowly a couple of times, and Megan was mesmerised by her long eyelashes as they closed and opened. Lena's eyes were Megan's Kryptonite; if she stared too long into them, the entire world disappeared.

"I-I don't mind staying up a little longer," Lena said quietly. "M-maybe I'll make some tea."

She turned quickly and moved away towards the kitchen. Megan was tempted to follow her, but the nervous energy emanating from Lena made her walk in the other direction, to the sofa. She sat down, leaving plenty of room for Lena to sit and keep her distance, if that was what she needed. Megan hadn't meant anything too...forward by asking her question, but she had the distinct impression Lena thought she did. She waited patiently on the sofa until Lena eventually returned, a mug of what smelled like camomile tea in her hand, which she carefully placed on the coffee table before sitting down pretty much as far from Megan as she could and still actually be on the sofa together.

Megan held back a smile, then said softly, "I didn't mean anything by it, you know."

Lena looked at her, wide-eyed.

"I just didn't want the evening to end," Megan continued, reaching out a hand and placing it on the empty sofa space between them. "I told you before, I am happy to take things slow, and I meant it."

Lena looked down at Megan's hand, then back up at Megan's face. She inhaled deeply, then shuffled nearer to Megan and took her hand.

"I'm sorry," she whispered. "You're being incredibly patient with me. I appreciate it."

Megan shrugged and smiled. "I happen to think you're worth it."

Lena's blush wasn't surprising, but her lunge across the sofa was. When her lips landed on Megan's, full of warmth and lush softness, Megan moaned deep in her throat and slowly wrapped her arms around Lena's shoulders to pull her closer. Their position was awkward, side-on to each other, but they coped admirably. Lena's full curves snuggled up to Megan's body and moulded themselves into her.

When Lena's tongue pushed tentatively into Megan's mouth, she opened up, hungrily, greedily, and they sank into the kiss as if their lives depended on it. Lena's hands clutched at Megan's shirt where it was tucked into her jeans, her fingers gently kneading and sending delicious thrills through the whole lower half of Megan's body. Megan ran one hand slowly up and down Lena's back as the other drifted into Lena's hair and wrapped thick strands of it between her fingers. Lena groaned and Megan repeated the action, all the while letting her tongue stroke at Lena's. It was tempting to try to devour Lena, but she held back, keeping the kisses passionate yet still tender.

Lena pulled her mouth away from Megan's but only so that she could then plant a line of open-mouthed kisses all along Megan's jaw and down her neck. The collar of Megan's shirt impeded her slightly; she used her nose to push it away, and the wet warmth of her mouth on Megan's skin sent shivers to all the good places on Megan's body. She arched her neck, giving Lena better access, and Lena chuckled against her skin.

"Good?" she whispered.

"Oh…yeah."

Lena continued, swapping sides and this time moving upwards to nip and lick under Megan's ear.

Alarm bells of the sweetest kind started clamouring in Megan's body. She eased herself away from Lena, who looked up at her, confused.

"Ah, sorry, but…um, if we're to take things slow, that's an area you really need to stay away from for now."

Lena's frown transformed into a slow smile. "Okay," she murmured. "Noted." Then she returned her mouth to Megan's lips and they were off again into the world of incredible kissing.

When they came back to Earth, some fifteen minutes later, Megan's chest was heaving for breath and Lena's hair was in wild disarray around her shoulders. She looked stunning, and holy crap, so sexy, and Megan willed herself to pull back, to let go of Lena's body, and to shuffle back a little.

"I-I think we should stop," she said, panting slightly. "I… God, that was…"

"Uh-huh," Lena said, nodding slowly, her eyes shining.

Megan stood up carefully, aware in no uncertain terms of the ache between her legs, and knowing she had definitely called a halt at the right time. She had only so much patience, after all…

"I had a fantastic evening, Lena."

Lena smiled up at her, running her fingers through her hair to straighten it. "Me too. I'll…I'll see you in the morning."

"You will," Megan said softly. "Goodnight."

CHAPTER 24

LENA COULD HEAR THE RAISED voices before she'd even opened the door to let herself out of the flat. Dorothy and one of the Patels, by the sounds of it, and her theory was confirmed a minute later once she'd locked up and started down the main staircase.

Dorothy was standing in the hallway, her arms folded across her formidable chest, which was never a good sign. Tall, thin Mr Patel was a few paces away, hard hat in hand, a clipboard tucked under his arm.

"...and I am getting very tired of all this mess, Mr Patel," Dorothy was saying. "I assume your people will be cleaning our carpet once you are finished, hm?"

"Yes, yes, of course, Dorothy—"

"It is Mrs Patterson to you, Mr Patel," Dorothy snapped.

Poor man, Lena thought, as she descended the stairs. Dorothy looked up at her approach.

"More delay!" she exclaimed as Lena stepped off the last stair. Dorothy pointed at Mr Patel. "He is telling me it is at least another two weeks until all this...this *mess* is finished." She pressed her palms together in prayer position. "Lord tell me, when will it end?" she wailed dramatically.

"Middle of February, at the latest," Mr Patel chimed in.

"That long?" Lena asked, aghast. She had been told end of January only two weeks ago. Now they'd extended it another two weeks beyond that?

Mr Patel dipped his head. "I am very sorry. We encountered many problems with the roof. It has not been an easy job. And I have two men who are off sick at the moment so I am short of staff." He gazed at Lena. "I am truly sorry."

Dorothy huffed loudly and opened her mouth to speak, but Lena jumped in. "Mr Patel, I'm sure you are doing everything you can. Thank you for the update."

Taking it for the dismissal it was, Mr Patel quickly climbed the stairs. Turning to Dorothy, who looked less than pleased with Lena's intervention, Lena took a deep breath before saying, "I really don't think it is his fault, Dorothy. Rebuilding a roof in the middle of winter can't be an easy job."

Dorothy stared at her, tilting her head slightly, a frown creasing her brow. "What has happened to you?"

Lena looked down at herself, then ran her hands over her face, thinking perhaps that she'd obtained some injury or left part of her breakfast stuck to her features.

"Not physically, child," Dorothy said, in a biting tone. "I mean, in your demeanour. You seem—" Suddenly she stopped, and an enormous smile broke out on her face. "It is her, isn't it? Megan."

Lena's mouth dropped open and a deep blush covered her cheeks. "Wh-what?"

Dorothy chuckled. "Good," she murmured, turning away. "Very good." She shut the door to her flat behind her, leaving Lena stunned and bemused in the empty hallway.

When she finally gathered herself and remembered she was supposed to be going to work, she pulled open the front door and walked out into the cold day. Side-stepping the piles of building supplies on either side of the pathway that led to the street, she pondered what Mr Patel had said. Another three to four weeks was yet another long stretch of time for her to be living in Megan's flat, away from her own home, away from her own furniture and belongings. And imposing on Megan's space. While she was sure Megan wouldn't call it that, Lena was still very much aware of how Megan's plans to have a big place to call her own had rapidly changed with her offer to give Lena a room. And now that they were dating, it made her even more edgy about sharing the flat.

She'd rushed into living with Chris and was sure it had contributed to the problems they had with their relationship. If they'd only taken more time to get to know each other, they probably would have realised much sooner how unsuited they really were. But Lena had become swept up by Chris's attentions, and her vastly more superior experience of actually being a lesbian, so falling into Chris's arms, then her bed, had been far too easy for Lena. Although she and Megan hadn't slept together yet, they were already living together, even if it was temporarily. And it scared Lena as much as if they'd done it the other way round.

She walked up the road, hunched down in her coat against the biting wind that cut into her from, it seemed, all angles.

This new...relationship with Megan was exciting, and definitely felt different from what she had shared with Chris. Megan made Lena feel positive, attractive, and fun. All things she never would have described herself as when she was with Chris. Lena didn't want to ruin this before it even got started, hence the nerves over mixing their living arrangement, which was purely business, with their burgeoning relationship, which was all about pleasure.

She crossed the main road and walked into the Tube station. Oh yes, pleasure indeed. Their kissing session on Saturday night had left Lena turned on, that was for certain. She'd gone to bed soon after and lay awake in the dark for quite a while, reliving some of the best highlights before realising that doing so would mean she would never get any sleep. When they'd interacted on Sunday it was fun and lighter, and Lena was thankful; the seriousness of the passion between them on Saturday wasn't something she was sure she could match in the cold light of day, but Megan didn't seek it either, and that felt okay.

They'd made a meal together once Megan got back from work late in the afternoon, with Megan being chef's assistant and good-humouredly following all of Lena's instructions to chop this, stir that. After eating, they'd simply snuggled on the sofa watching a film, and Lena had experienced a contentment level that kept a smile on her face the whole evening.

The Tube train arrived and she wedged herself in between the various suited men and women wrapped up in voluminous coats and scarves.

Today was Wednesday, hump day, and—as a true sign of how things had changed for Lena these past few months—she couldn't summon any enthusiasm for her work, nor could she wait for the weekend to arrive. She and Megan would only cross paths briefly all week due to Megan's work pattern, so they had already planned to spend as much of the coming weekend together. Simply the thought of it sent tingles down to Lena's toes and back again.

Yes, what she and Megan had started was wonderful in many ways, and not something Lena wanted to either disappear or screw up. The quicker she got back into her own flat, the better. Then they could really see what they had while still having their own space to breathe in whenever they needed it.

Madhu's had her baby!!! A girl, called Sunaina. Can you call me when you get this?

Megan found the text from Lena once she broke for lunch at two. It had been a crazy Thursday morning of non-stop private coaching sessions with some of her more demanding clients. While the money they brought in was worth it, sometimes she wondered if the attitude that came with it was. However, Lena's message put a big smile on her face for the first time that day, and she strolled out of the health club into the weak winter sunshine that played across the small courtyard near the entrance, hitting the callback icon as she did so. She wasn't sure if Lena would be able to answer in the middle of her working day, but—

"Hey! You got my message?" Lena's voice bubbled with her excitement at Madhu's news.

"I did. That's fantastic news." Megan spotted an empty bench off to the side of the courtyard and walked over to it. The wood of the seat was cold on her backside, but she'd suffer it for Lena and her excitement.

"I know! Jay called me around noon. He'd messaged me early on to say they'd gone in around five that morning. I thought it would be hours, but my sister, typical over-achiever that she is, only spent six hours in labour!"

"I bet she's pleased about that," Megan said, laughing.

"Yes. I know I would be." Lena paused, and Megan could hear her breaths coming in pants. "I can't believe it, I'm an aunty!" She squealed, and Megan's heart turned over. God, this woman...

"Congratulations. It's wonderful. So, when will you go up and see them?"

"Yes, see, that's the thing." Lena's voice was suddenly much more subdued. "Of course, with work, the only time I can go is at the weekend."

"I know," Megan said softly. "But you have to go. Just because we had plans doesn't matter. You and I can spend time together any time, but it's not every day you get to go and see your new niece, is it?"

"Thank you," Lena whispered. "Megan, you're...you're an amazing person."

Megan sucked in a breath. Those worlds were even more special coming from Lena. "Thank you." She paused. "So are you."

There was a short silence, then the sound of Lena clearing her throat. "Okay, well, I need to get back. I have some train tickets to book."

"Yes, you do. So, I'll see you this evening, after you get back from that seminar?"

Lena groaned. "Oh yes, the seminar. Not really what I want to spend my time on today, but I know I have to." She inhaled. "Okay, I will see you when I get home. Probably about nine thirty."

"Okay, babe."

Megan sat bolt upright on the bench. The term of endearment had slipped out without thinking. Would Lena hate it? Would she—

"That was very nice." Lena's soft voice almost seemed to caress Megan's ear.

"O-okay," Megan stuttered.

"Bye," Lena whispered.

"Oh, Madhu, she's *gorgeous*!" Lena looked down at the perfect little baby she held carefully in her arms, and her eyes pricked with tears. "Hello, Sunaina, I'm your aunty Lena."

The baby blinked once then closed her eyes and slipped easily back into slumber.

"She seems comfortable with you. That's good, chief babysitter," Madhu said, smiling when Lena's eyes went wide. "Relax, not yet. Trust me, I don't need to be going anywhere in a hurry without her." Madhu shifted slightly on the sofa and winced.

"Still sore?"

"Like you wouldn't believe." Madhu reached for her tea and sipped at it, gazing at Lena over the top of the mug and smiling.

Jay walked into the room from the kitchen. "Need anything?" he said, shuffling from foot to foot. "Food? More tea? A blanket?"

Madhu rolled her eyes and reached out a hand towards her husband. "Jay, stop it. You're giving me palpitations." She smiled as he took her hand.

"I'm fine, honestly. I love how much you're doing to help, I really do. But please try and relax."

He blinked behind his thick-framed glasses and ran a hand through his mop of black hair. "Okay," he said. "Okay, I can do that."

"Here," Lena said, shifting to one side of the sofa. "Come and sit next to me while I drool over your daughter."

Jay laughed and sat down, staring at his child as he did so. "Isn't she beautiful?" Lena moved the baby in her arms so she could reach out one hand and grasp his shoulder. "She really is," she said. "I'm so happy for both of you."

"Thank you," Jay and Madhu said simultaneously.

"And thank you," Lena said, "for making sure I could have this amount of time with you. I didn't want to cause any problems between you and them."

Madhu held up a hand. "There is no problem. Mum was here all of Friday and this morning. She comes back tomorrow afternoon with Dad, and she knew I meant it when I told her to stay away while you were here. Trust me, I don't think she wants to see you anyway, harsh as that sounds, so it didn't take much persuasion."

Lena shook her head. "Do you think they'll ever accept me as I am?" she asked, gazing back down at the baby. Something about watching Sunaina sleep had an incredibly calming effect on Lena and enabled her to have this conversation with Madhu without her temperature rising as it would have done in the past.

"I don't know," Madhu said quietly.

"I think they might, in the long term," Jay contributed, and the two sisters turned to look at him. He shrugged. "I see something in your mum's face when your name comes up. Anger, yes, but..." He shrugged again. "I don't know, maybe I'm imagining it, but I think there's regret there too."

"Maybe," Madhu said. "And maybe I can't see that because I'm still so mad at her about it myself."

"True," Jay said. Then he stood, leaned over Madhu where she sat in the small armchair, and kissed her tenderly on the lips. "I'm going to start on dinner," he said, and without waiting for an answer, he walked off to the kitchen.

"I am so glad I married for love," Madhu said quietly. "Imagine who I might have got if I'd let Mum have her way with all those setups with second cousins and sons of aunties."

Lena shuddered, and Sunaina stirred in her arms. Lena made shushing sounds and watched, enraptured, as Sunaina settled right back down again. "Yeah," she said, meeting Madhu's eyes. "I know exactly what you mean."

Madhu's eyes widened. "Oh, yes! Ugh, poor you having to suffer all of that when you knew you didn't even want a man, never mind an arranged meeting with one."

Lena chuckled, and her sister joined her, and soon they were laughing hard but trying not to make any sound to disturb the baby.

"Poor Mum," Madhu said, eventually, wiping at her eyes. "Absolutely clueless."

"Oh, wow," Madhu breathed, staring at Lena across their breakfast the next morning. Jay was upstairs feeding Sunaina with some breast milk Madhu had pumped earlier, giving the two sisters some quiet time. "This is all sounding pretty serious, Lena."

Lena smiled, and ducked her head. "Yes, I know. It's a little scary."

She'd just updated Madhu on how things were developing between Megan and herself, to the accompaniment of much squealing and gasping from her younger sister.

"Scary how? Being involved with someone again?"

"Yes, essentially. I'm not sure I've fully recovered from Chris."

"Okay, I get that. But Megan's nothing like her, from the sounds of it. And when I met her she seemed lovely."

"Oh, she is," Lena gushed. "I... Well, it's more about me, really. About being able to trust people."

Madhu nodded. "Okay, that I can understand. But Lena, don't let your fear take over, you know? Remember I talked about this before Christmas? I love this new version of you since then. The effect this thing with Megan is having on you. Even if you and Megan don't work out, and I don't think that's anything you need to worry about, actually, even taking a chance again seems to have done you so much good."

Lena couldn't help but agree. "That is all true. I know. Some habits are very hard to break," she said sheepishly.

"Of course they are. Doesn't mean you shouldn't try, though." Madhu grinned.

Later, on the train back to London, as she scrolled through the many photos she'd taken of Sunaina, Lena's thoughts turned to Megan, whom she would see in a couple of hours. Spending that wonderful time with Madhu and the baby had filled her heart with such joy, she couldn't wait to share some of that feeling with her...girlfriend.

Was that what Megan was now? They'd said they were dating, and that they were doing so exclusively while they got to know each other. But the kissing, and the snuggling, and that new term of endearment that Megan had let slip the other day, all of it added up to Lena *wanting* to call Megan her girlfriend. Wanting to name what was happening because it felt so important. Did Megan feel the same? Lena dared to presume she did, if her being called "babe" was anything to go by.

The smile crept across her face in sync with the delightful shivers that trembled across her body. She couldn't wait to see Megan again. To tell her all about her weekend and show her the photos of the baby. To hear all about Megan's Saturday night hanging out with Jen at the bar where Jen worked.

She couldn't wait to hold Megan, and kiss her. She shivered again.

Oh my.

The thought of Megan's lips had her shifting in her seat, and heat rising up from her chest.

Her legs jiggled rapidly. Why wasn't this train going any faster?

CHAPTER 25

MEGAN WAS SLOUCHED LENGTHWAYS ON the sofa, flicking through TV channels with the remote, when the front door opened behind her. She popped her head up over the back of the sofa and smiled at Lena, who was beaming at her while unwrapping herself from her heavy coat and scarf.

"You look happy," Megan said, hitting the mute button before throwing it onto the sofa.

Lena nodded vigorously and bent to remove her boots. "I am. My niece is adorable. And Madhu and Jay are so happy, and so…everything." She straightened, and her face was flushed with excitement. It was a good look on her, Megan noted to herself, then swallowed hard as she realised where her thought process was leading. *Down girl.*

Lena walked towards the sofa, and Megan took another look at her. There was a kind of determination in Lena's expression Megan had never seen before. She somehow stood taller than usual, and her entire being seemed to almost glow with some hidden energy. Megan swallowed again, unable to take her eyes of this version of Lena.

"Y-you okay?" Megan asked, her voice croaky, her stomach tightening in a deeply pleasant way.

"Uh-huh," Lena murmured, and before Megan could wonder at what this change in demeanour meant, Lena knelt on the sofa, one knee either side of one of Megan's outstretched legs. In the next moment, giving Megan only that short time to suck in a deep breath, Lena dipped towards Megan, her hands landing on Megan's shoulders, her lips curved in a soft smile. She kept her eyes open, staring at Megan as she planted a soft, brief kiss on Megan's lips.

Megan lay rigid beneath Lena, only a couple of inches of air between their bodies. Her arms were desperate to encircle Lena; her hands were aching to touch her. The sizzle between them was practically visible, and while she had entertained thoughts of when Lena might be ready to take their relationship further, now that it seemed to be happening, she couldn't seem to move. Lena was in total control in the moment, and it turned Megan on more than she would have thought possible.

"Hi," Lena whispered against Megan's mouth.

Megan nodded, words failing her. Lena smiled and kissed her again, longer this time, and firmer. Megan's lips awoke and moved against Lena's, and she opened her mouth readily when Lena's tongue demanded that she did so. Moments later, she groaned as Lena descended fully on top of her, pressing against her from knee to chest. Jesus, she felt so good against Megan—the softness, the weight, the shape of her. Megan lifted her arms, finally remembering how they worked, and wrapped them around Lena's torso. Lena sighed into Megan's mouth, and Megan pulled her closer, deepening the kiss.

Lena's hands moved, one upwards to caress Megan's neck, one downwards to—oh, God. Lena's hand wrapped tentatively around Megan's breast. She was wearing a hoodie over a t-shirt, but even so Lena's touch, shocking in its unexpectedness, seemed to burn her skin.

"Lena," she gasped, in between deep strokes of Lena's tongue inside her mouth.

"Yes?" Lena was nibbling at her neck now, her mouth moving to that danger zone below Megan's ear. The area Megan had warned her she needed to stay away from if she wanted them to go slow.

"Lena, what—"

"I want this," Lena whispered, moving so that she could meet Megan's eyes.

"Are you sure?"

Lena nodded and waited. Megan blinked, her brain catching up to what Lena intended. Then she lunged upwards, devouring Lena's mouth like she'd wanted to all this time since their first kiss. Lena moaned and squirmed on top of her, her hand going crazy at Megan's breast.

"Bedroom," Megan murmured, reaching round to still Lena's hand. "Please."

Lena said nothing but moved sideways and worked her way up off Megan's body. Once she stood by the side of the sofa, she reached out a hand, a shy smile on her face. Megan took the hand gently and let Lena pull her up.

They didn't speak as they walked to Megan's room; it was unspoken but both knew a sofa bed was not ideal for lovemaking. As they entered the room, Megan let go of Lena's hand and walked to the side of the bed. She switched on the lamp on the table beside it.

"Enough?" she asked, and Lena nodded. Lena's gaze darted round the room, and her hands twisted together in front of her. Megan inhaled slowly. "Second thoughts? It's okay to change your mind."

Lena finally met her gaze. "I'm...a little nervous. It's been a while, and—" she breathed in deeply "—I'm never comfortable getting naked with someone for the first time."

"Okay," Megan said softly, walking slowly over to Lena. "Thank you for telling me." She reached out a hand and stroked a loose strand of hair away from Lena's face. "We can take this as slow as you want. Nothing actually has to happen tonight, you know. We could just kiss and cuddle in bed."

Lena let out a soft snort. "No," she said, and smiled. "Believe me, I want more than that."

A spike of desire shot through Megan's body at the words, and she moaned.

Lena's eyes widened, then she was on the move. Her hands went to Megan's hoodie, unzipped it and pulled it back from Megan's shoulders. In a blur of movement, she then removed Megan's T-shirt and unhooked her bra, her mouth kissing and licking at Megan's neck the whole time.

Megan stood mute, her skin tingling and breaking out into goose bumps all over at the intensity of Lena's kisses and touches. So much for slow.

When Lena's hands cupped her bare breasts and squeezed, she gasped and pulled Lena's head up for a deep kiss. She reached for the buttons on Lena's shirt as she kissed her, but after a few moments of fumbling, none of them would open. How the hell did you get her out of this thing? She stopped kissing Lena long enough to look down and see that the tiny buttons were hidden behind an extra layer of fabric. Eventually, she finally got the first two open, but the third defeated her. She groaned in embarrassment.

"Is there any way we can take this off over your head?" she asked, not quite meeting Lena's eyes. Trust her to not even be able to undress Lena properly.

"I think so," Lena said, pulling the shirt up. It just about squeezed over her chin and nose, and finally she got it over her head and flung it to the floor.

Megan gazed down at Lena, her full breasts encased in black satin, the tops of them overspilling the cups. So much for her hands to play with. She licked her very dry lips and reached out to stroke the soft skin where the swells of Lena's breasts met the rest of her chest. Lena's soft moan only stoked Megan's desire higher, and suddenly she had to see them. She reached behind Lena, and while Lena returned her own hands to Megan's breasts, pinching her nipples slightly, her breathing quickening with each touch, Megan took hold of the clasp of Lena's bra.

Over the years, Megan had divested a number of women of their bras in moments such as this. Up until this point, she'd never met a bra that defeated her. The worst she'd ever done was two goes at one she hadn't realised was front-fastening until the woman in question sniggered at her fumbling around the back and finally pointed her in the right direction.

But Lena's bra appeared to have a fastening designed by the people who built Fort Knox. There was something…odd…about the…hooks that didn't seem to…work…the…same—

"Er, Lena? How…um, how does this open?" She hated asking, but this was getting ridiculous.

Lena's fingers stilled their ministrations on Megan's nipples, and her mouth pulled back from Megan's neck long enough to murmur, "Four hooks. Do them one by one."

Right. Okay. Megan returned to her task. Within moments she had three of the four hooks unlocked, but the fourth was playing hard to get. She tried a different position with her thumb but forgot how much more give there was in the back strap with three hooks undone, and the next thing she knew, the entire strap snapped back against Lena's skin with a loud slap.

"Ouch!" Lena gasped, her hands flying to her back.

"Oh, God, Lena I'm so sorry," Megan said, mortified.

Lena looked up at her, and Megan could see the effort it took her to calm her expression, and smile—although not widely—before saying, "It's okay. It surprised me, that's all."

"I'm sorry," Megan said. "Maybe you'd better get that last hook."

Lena did so, and the bra joined the growing pile of clothes at their feet. Megan gazed in unabashed appreciation at the wealth of breast now on display. Lena's body was exactly what Megan dreamed about: soft, curvy, no bony bits sticking out anywhere. Lena was definitely not a size ten, and Megan couldn't have been happier as she stared at Lena. She'd never been good at verbalising stuff like that, so she did the next best thing and leaned down to lavish attention on the skin before her. She kissed Lena's breasts, swirling her lips around each nipple, and revelling in Lena's gasps and moans above her.

Lena's hands were at her shoulders, pushing gently, and Megan got the hint. She walked carefully backwards, aware that the bed was somewhere close behind her, and—

With a loud oomph from both of them, Megan collapsed backwards onto the bed with Lena falling on top of her a millisecond later. Their breasts bounced painfully together and they both grimaced, clutching at their own flesh, Lena balanced precariously on Megan's torso as she did so.

"Oh, God, sorry!" Megan said. "The bed was nearer than I realised."

Lena smiled, but Megan could see a tightness around her eyes that hadn't been there earlier. This was not going well and clearly not helping Lena relax into the moment. Sighing inwardly, Megan wrapped her arms around Lena carefully and pulled her close for a kiss.

"Are they sore?" she asked, trying to inject a playfulness into her tone and nodding down towards Lena's breasts. "Shall I kiss them better?"

Thankfully, Lena played along. "Mm, I think you should."

Megan grinned and shimmied her way down the bed a little to bring her in line with the big brown nipples that made her mouth water. Taking one gently between her lips, she kissed it, then laved it with her tongue, feeling it harden as she did so. Lena squirmed and moaned, so Megan repeated the action on the other nipple. "Better?" she murmured.

"Oh, yes," Lena breathed.

Megan continued her first aid, delighting in the movements Lena's body made in response and the sounds that escaped her throat. She moved her hands down to Lena's trousers, located the side-fastening zip, and—thankfully—eased it down without a hitch. Lena leaned on one arm to help Megan push the trousers over her hips, and she was aware of Lena kicking them off when they reached her ankles. As Lena lay back down on top of Megan, the damp warmth between Lena's legs heated the skin of her thigh, and her breath hitched.

"Oh, Lena," she whispered, her hand already on the move, her fingers seeking the source of that warmth, that wetness. Her hand swept over the swell of Lena's belly, and she felt her pull it in as she passed, and wondered why Lena felt the need. Then her thoughts focused elsewhere as she brushed her fingertips over the cotton of Lena's underwear.

Lena groaned loudly, pushing her hips further into the touch.

"Yes?" Megan said, stroking softly back and forth, feeling Lena's clit swelling beneath the cloth as she did so.

"Um, yes, but..." Lena's voice was quiet and small.

"What?" Megan said, trying to meet Lena's eyes, but Lena wouldn't let her.

"Um, well, I'm...I'm still wearing my socks. Could I... Please can we move so I can take them off?"

Megan smiled. "Of course." She removed her hand from between Lena's legs and stayed motionless while Lena sat up, turned away, and peeled off her socks.

"Sorry," Lena mumbled.

"What for?"

Lena waved a vague hand. "For interrupting...things." She looked towards the ceiling, then back over her shoulder at Megan who was still sprawled on the bed beside her. "It's not exactly romantic, is it? Stopping to take your socks off in the middle of things."

Megan chuckled and reached for Lena. When Lena didn't move, Megan sat up. "Lena, it's fine. Come on, it's funny. And sex is allowed to be fun, okay?" Somehow, deep down, looking at Lena right now, Megan knew Lena had never been told that, never experienced it. Had Lena always expected everything to be perfect? Like movie sex, or romantic book sex? Or had her partners given her that expectation?

"Sorry," Lena said again, looking forlorn, and she crossed her arms protectively over her breasts. Megan wasn't stupid; everything about Lena's posture and voice told her Lena was having major second thoughts.

Carefully, Megan extended one arm and placed a hand on Lena's warm back. She bit back a moan at the feel of that soft skin beneath her fingers. "Do you want to stop?"

"Yes. No." Lena shook her head. "I'm sorry," she whispered.

"It's okay," Megan whispered in return. "Can you tell me what's wrong? Was it because I was clumsy again?"

"No!" Lena said quickly. "Well, maybe a little bit. Sorry, it's not your fault, it really isn't." She inhaled deeply and finally turned to look at Megan. "This is mostly about me. About how rubbish I am at all this."

Before Megan could stop her, Lena stood, then bent down to gather her clothes, which she clutched against her naked torso.

"I'm really sorry, Megan. I think I need a bit more time."

There was nothing Megan could say. She couldn't—wouldn't want to—force Lena to stay, to try to pick up where they left off. It was clear Lena didn't even want to talk about it right now, and forcing her into that wouldn't solve anything either. So Megan did the only thing she could. She smiled as genuinely as possible, gave Lena a quick squeeze of her hand, and watched her walk out of the room.

Megan flopped back on the bed, arms above her head, her bare torso cooling rapidly now that she was alone in the room. She gazed up at the ceiling, tracking back through every action from the kissing on the sofa onwards that had led them to this point. While Megan had found their stumbling and fumbling amusing, and endearing, clearly Lena had not.

Dorothy's words, after their first date ended badly, came back to her. *"Lena doesn't do well with embarrassment."*

Was that what it was this time too? Embarrassment over all the silly things that had gone wrong as they got naked? Even though Megan didn't particularly think they were wrong, as such. Just funny, and—she'd thought—ways that helped ease the nerves in what could have been a tense situation. They'd seemed to have the opposite effect on Lena.

Megan sighed. If Lena wanted perfect sex every time, they were in a heap of trouble.

CHAPTER 26

LENA TRIED HARD TO CONCENTRATE on her spreadsheet but failed dismally. Memories of the night before, and the cringe-inducing events that had led to her fleeing Megan's room, wouldn't let her go. She stood up from her desk and walked with determination to the kitchen to make some tea. Anything to try to distract herself. But, of course, as she waited for the kettle to boil, her mind returned to the scene of last night's crime.

She had wanted Megan so much, from the minute she got home. Seeing her so happy to see Lena, feeling so flushed herself with the joy of the weekend, and how good it felt to come home to Megan—all of it had triggered something in her that had lain dormant for a long time. Actual desire. Not the vague, fantasy-type desire that reading her books engendered, desire for an as-yet faceless woman who would sweep Lena off her feet and ride off into the sunset with her. No, actual, real desire for a real, living woman who looked at Lena in ways that made her melt.

So what had gone so wrong in the bedroom? Where had that desire gone? Because it had, snuffed out like a candle once she'd realised she was still wearing her socks while Megan stroked between her legs. She squirmed slightly as her clit quietly reminded her how wonderful those touches had been.

She poured the hot water onto the tea bag and stirred slowly. Megan's touches *had* been wonderful. Feeling Megan's skin against her own, hearing the sounds she made as they moved together, had heated Lena's blood and had her aching for more. And yet…the bra snapping, and the bumping into each other on the bed, had immediately stirred up embarrassment. Megan staring at her when she was naked had been hard to take too; Lena hadn't been able to tell if Megan found her body exciting or disappointing.

She'd almost squirmed under the attention, her instinct to flee building in strength by the second, but then Megan had touched her and she'd thought she'd be okay.

However, as hard as Lena had tried to tamp it down, the sock incident had exacerbated her stress, and suddenly her discomfort was all she had been able to focus on. Which she knew now was stupid—Megan hadn't laughed at her, nor had Megan been overcome with embarrassment. She'd even tried to explain to Lena how it was just fun, and sex was allowed to be fun. But it was as if a wall came down, somewhere inside Lena, and Megan's words couldn't get through it.

Maybe she should have stayed. Maybe she should have let Megan touch her again, see if they could rekindle what had started on the sofa. She closed her eyes, remembering being pressed against Megan. Oh, how she wanted to feel that again. She truly did.

She sighed. This was all down to her, she knew that. Megan wouldn't try to force anything. If Lena wanted this, she needed to go after it. And she needed to find a way to stop her old fear of embarrassment ruining everything.

A new fear gripped her and churned her stomach. What if Megan had had enough? What if Lena's issues were too much for her to think she was worth it? They hadn't crossed paths at all earlier that morning—Megan was on a late start, and even though she could have got up around the same time as Lena, to say hi, as she often had in the past few weeks they'd been dating, she hadn't done so today. Did that mean she didn't want to see Lena? Or was she trying to be nice and give Lena some space?

Lena wrung her hands and paced the small kitchen. She was caught between a rock and a hard place. She needed time to sort herself out, to be able to commit to a physical relationship with the woman she was attracted to. More than attracted to—Lena knew she was falling for Megan. Maybe that was part of her problem; fear of falling. And, while dealing with all of that, she had to do so in a way that meant Megan didn't give up on her.

She stopped pacing and leaned against the counter. This was all so... messy. And Lena didn't do mess. What happened to her neat, ordered little life? The life she'd had before that stupid roof caved in and literally turned her world upside down?

That boring life, a little voice—sounding suspiciously like Madhu—said in the back of her mind. *That boring, lonely, predictable life that had you friendless, loveless, and dreaming of more.*

I know, Lena thought, but it was *safe.*

When she got home that night, Megan had left her a note, and as Lena read the words, relief flooded through her.

Hi Lena. I hope you had a good day. Sorry we won't see each other tonight, I'm pretty sure I'll be back after you've gone to bed. But maybe tomorrow evening? Could we have dinner together? xx

Okay, this was good. Megan hadn't given up on her. Not yet.

Megan felt as if she were walking on eggshells this week. And for a big woman like herself, that was no mean feat. She and Lena had only seen each other on Tuesday evening, eating a simple supper at home that they'd prepared together. It had been okay, but Lena had seemed reluctant to talk about what happened on Sunday, and Megan didn't want to push. It was frustrating, but they had at least had a sensual—and long—kiss goodnight that had calmed Megan's nerves a little. She was worried Lena was pulling away, giving up before they'd even got started.

On Thursday night, Megan hung out with Jen at the bar.

"So, how's things going with Alisha?" Megan asked as she sipped a cold pint of pale ale.

Jen's eyes glazed over and a big smile split her face. "So good. So, *so* good."

"Wow."

"Tell me about it." Jen nodded. "And I ain't just talking about the sex, you know. Which is hot. With a capital H."

"Jesus. TMI, Jen."

Jen snorted and disappeared for a minute or two to serve a customer. When she returned, she leaned on the bar and stared at Megan.

"Something's wrong, isn't it?"

Megan looked away from her intense gaze and took another gulp of her beer. Which nearly choked her because her throat was suddenly so tight from an upwelling of emotion mixed with frustration.

"Come on, Megs. Talk to me."

When she looked back at Jen, she was throwing her the puppy eyes, that look she had perfected over the years when she really wanted something from Megan. Usually it was something far more mundane than Megan opening up her heart and spilling out all its secrets.

Megan took a deep breath, then spilled. In between a slow stream of customers needing drinks, she told Jen everything, from the first date to the aborted intimacy on Sunday night.

"Whoa," Jen breathed. "I had no idea it had been such hard work."

"See," Megan said, "until Sunday, it wasn't that much hard work. Yeah, I know, to you she seems high maintenance. But to me, she's just Lena. Someone who has a certain way of thinking, and I don't know, somehow I get that and I can work with it. But Sunday..."

"Are you sure she's worth all this?"

"Yes," Megan said automatically, and realised in the next moment it was absolutely true. Lena was. Apart from what happened on Sunday, they fit so well together—Lena never demanded more of Megan than she was capable of giving in terms of her time, not like Julie had done. Lena cared for Megan in ways she'd not experienced yet in a relationship, but none of it felt smothering. And Lena looked at Megan like she was the best thing since sliced bread, and every time she did, a thrill ran through Megan's body that left her breathless and wanting. And, of course, she kissed like a total dream...

"Yes," she said again. "She is."

Jen shrugged. "Then maybe you need to tell her that. Make it clear. Not like laying down the law, but just to emphasise it." She paused, fiddling with a bar mat. "I know you, you don't do much talking in relationships, and maybe with her, that's what she needs to hear, you know?"

Megan stared at her friend. Sometimes Jen could be as rough as sandpaper. Other times, like now, she had the smoothness and clarity of a diamond.

"Thanks, Jen," Megan said quietly. "You're a legend."

Jen buffed her nails on her T-shirt. "I know."

On Friday evening, Lena pushed open the main front door and came face to face with Dorothy, who was vacuuming the carpeted area in front of her own flat. She had pushed back the dust sheets, it seemed, to get at what was underneath. Dorothy spotted her and used her foot to switch off the vacuum cleaner, before meeting Lena's eyes and smiling at her.

"Hello, child," she said. "You are just in time. Why don't you run upstairs and see what that nice Mr Patel has for you."

"What?" Lena was trying to process what Dorothy had said when one of the older woman's surprisingly strong hands gripped her forearm and turned Lena around in the directions of the staircase.

"Up. Go on."

"O-okay," Lena stuttered, and her feet moved of their own accord, up the stairs, following the bend round to the front door of her flat, where Mr Patel stood with a beaming smile on his face.

"Lena, good afternoon," he said. "Please, follow me. I have a proposal for you."

"Er…what?"

Mr Patel chuckled. "Trust me, Lena. Come." He turned and walked up Lena's stairs, and once again she followed on autopilot. When they reached the top of the stairs, Mr Patel turned back to her.

"As you can see," he said, spreading his arms wide, "we are mostly done. We managed to bring in some extra men from a job elsewhere that had to be delayed. And I knew how keen you were to have this finished, so…" He shrugged. "Here we are."

Lena looked around, her heart rate increasing as she took in what she saw. The ceiling was back in one piece. The skylight was back where it belonged, and new carpet had been laid throughout the living area. She couldn't quite see all the kitchen area, but she could at least tell from this vantage point that the counter had been replaced and looked immaculate.

"Oh," she breathed, her jaw aching as her smile widened. "Oh, Mr Patel."

He nodded, his smile revealing all his teeth. "Yes, yes," he said. "Now, the insurance company came this afternoon, and they have declared the flat fit to live in again." He gestured towards the kitchen. "We have switched all the services back on, and everything appears to be in working order.

Now, what is left is the painting of the walls. The ceiling we did before the carpet was laid. It seemed sensible." He chuckled, and Lena gave him a weak smile, her brain not quite caught up with all the information he was imparting. "We have just the walls in here to do. Two days' work, maximum." He looked at Lena, tilting his head slightly. "If you like, if you are comfortable with this, I am proposing that we could help you move back in here tomorrow, and we will simply work around your furniture as we paint on Monday and Tuesday. By Wednesday, we will be done."

"Seriously?" Lena blurted. "I can move back in?" It was too much to hope for. Just when she really needed some space around her to figure out what she was doing with life—and, mostly, with Megan—Mr Patel was handing it to her on a plate.

"As long as you are okay with us still coming in during the day while you are at work. I promise we will cover all of your furniture and the new carpet very carefully to avoid any issues with paint spilling." He stared at her. "Well?"

"Yes!" Lena practically shouted. "Yes. Thank you!"

With hindsight, choosing a pizza place on a Friday night wasn't the best idea Lena had ever had. She'd just been thinking of somewhere quick, and local, where she and Megan wouldn't have to stand on ceremony for what was sure to be an awkward date. If it still counted as a date. The noise level in the restaurant was ridiculous and made conversation all but impossible.

"Sorry," Lena said, for about the fifth time, as they neared the end of their pizzas.

Megan smiled, but to Lena's eyes it looked forced. "Like I said, it's no problem. Look, we'll be finished soon and then we can get home and relax a bit."

Lena's stomach knotted. She still hadn't told Megan about Mr Patel's news. It had all happened in such a rush, and within minutes of Mr Patel leaving, locking up Lena's flat behind him, Megan had come home and they'd got changed ready for their date. She knew Megan could tell Lena was distracted, as she gave half-hearted answers to any question Megan asked. The trouble was, she couldn't think of a way to tell Megan she was moving out the next morning without it sounding like she wanted to get away from Megan. Which she did, but not for the reasons Megan might presume.

Okay, so honesty was going to have to be the best policy. Only, not here, she thought, glancing around at their loud surroundings.

"Shall we go?" she blurted out.

Megan stared at her, but wiped her mouth with her napkin, threw it across her nearly-finished pizza, and nodded. "Sure," she said, waving over the waiter. "Can we get the bill, please?"

They walked back in silence. Lena's pizza was not sitting well in her tense stomach but as they turned up Jackson Road, she thought she had the words rehearsed in her head. By the time they'd settled on the sofa, she was about as ready as she thought she'd ever be.

"Lena," Megan began, but Lena held up a hand.

"Do you mind if I say something first?" she asked politely.

Megan shook her head, but her shoulders tensed and she shuffled a couple of inches back further in her seat.

Lena swallowed. "So, um, I have some news. I haven't had a chance to tell you because it all happened in a rush this evening." Lena thought she was probably talking too fast, so took a deep breath and tried to slow down. "Mr Patel was waiting for me when I got home from work."

"Oh?" Megan's eyebrows crept up.

"Yes. It's good news. The flat, my flat, has been declared fit to live in again. It's not quite finished yet, but close enough. So Mr Patel and his team have offered to move me back in there tomorrow. And I, um, I accepted." Megan opened her mouth to speak, but Lena plunged on. "I know this might seem quick, and after what happened on Sunday night you might construe this as me, well, running away. I promise you that isn't it. I really appreciate you letting me live here all this time. And I know that through that, you and I have become...close."

She paused for breath. "But as I said on Sunday, I think I need some more time, to get used to being in a relationship again, to being...intimate with someone again. And I truly think that being back in my own space will help me do that. So, although it's a little sudden, and we didn't think this would happen for a couple more weeks, it's, well, that's it really."

It hadn't come out quite how she'd planned in her head, but it sounded okay. To herself, at least. She waited, watching Megan for her reaction.

Megan exhaled slowly and leaned back against the sofa properly. Her gaze drifted away from Lena, but Lena waited, as patiently as she could, for Megan's thought process to run its course.

After a couple of tense minutes, Megan returned her gaze to Lena's face, meeting her eyes and taking a moment to keep the contact. Lena tried not to squirm.

"Okay," Megan said, her voice soft. "Okay. I-I'm pleased for you. I know sharing my space has sometimes been difficult for you. And yes—" she held up a hand when Lena made to interrupt "—I know that is not anything I have done. I accept that. As much as I am trying to accept what you said about not running away…"

She leaned forward suddenly and took Lena's hand. The touch sent a shiver coursing through Lena's arm. "Please promise me you won't shut me out, Lena. I…care about you. I really want us to continue dating and see what we can make of us. I'm…ugh, I'm rubbish at saying these kinds of things."

Megan looked at the ceiling then back down again. "But I really like you, Lena. You're gorgeous, and funny, and kind of cute with all your little habits and the ways you like things done. You're an amazing cook, and I've loved sharing your books with you, and talking to you about, well, everything. I think we've had a lot of fun, and I don't want that to end." She squeezed Lena's hand a tad tighter. "So please, if you feel the same way, at all, please don't shut me out. Okay?"

With Lena's heart pounding beneath her ribs and her throat tight with emotion, she nodded. "Okay," she whispered. She wrapped her other hand over Megan's and enclosed it. "And yes, I d-do feel the same way. About all of that."

Megan smiled tentatively, and exhaled loudly. "Well, all right then." Then, slowly, carefully, she leaned in to Lena and kissed her, the barest touches of lips. She pulled back an inch and looked into Lena's eyes. Lena could barely breathe for the sensuality of the moment. She too leaned in and returned the kiss, firmer and longer, and trembled when Megan's tongue brushed against hers. They kissed for some minutes; slowly, tenderly, not touching, just kissing. When they pulled back finally, and Megan rested her forehead against Lena's, she breathed in the scent of Megan, of her shampoo, her face cream, and a hint of perfume that, in her worry about sharing Mr Patel's news, she hadn't noticed earlier.

"So," Megan said, sitting up slowly, smiling. "Let me know when I can take you out again. You know where I live—just knock on the door."

She grinned, and Lena chuckled.

CHAPTER 27

LENA STOOD NEAR THE KITCHEN of her flat, hands on hips, and surveyed her domain. Her face ached from smiling. Everything was back where it should be. Well, nearly everything—she'd need to buy a new sofa, and also a bookcase and the books to fill it, but she knew that would take some time. She had the insurance money, but it hadn't made sense to go shopping until she knew when she was moving back in. For now, two large cushions borrowed from Megan would do for sitting on to read, or to watch the new TV that would be arriving later that week, and she could at least sleep in her own bed, in her own bedroom.

The move had gone well. Mr Patel's men had clearly been under the strictest of instructions to be *very* careful with Lena's things; sometimes it paid to have a reputation. She'd now re-hung all her clothes, cleaned the bathroom—obviously—and sorted out the kitchen. It was three in the afternoon, and she was ready for some tea before thinking about what to cook for the evening.

She shifted slightly, a small frown creasing her forehead. While everything looked sorted and she was pleased to be back, something felt… off. Not quite right. It was quiet, and there was no other presence in the flat. She was on her own. She closed her eyes for a moment as an image of Megan, smiling at her from a position on the sofa they had shared for the past three months, flashed across the front of her mind. The image warmed her. Settled her.

She wondered how Megan was doing. Lena knew she was working all day and she had disappeared around nine that morning, briefly wishing Lena a good move and waving good-bye, but there'd been no hug, no kiss. Maybe—

Stop! Stop always thinking the worst!

She could almost imagine Madhu standing in front of her, waving her finger in Lena's face. The thought made her smile, and she inhaled a deep breath before letting it out again. She shook out her hands and rolled her shoulders a few times. *Come on, you can do this. Think about all the good things you and Megan have shared. Don't focus on the things that went awry. Megan isn't, so you shouldn't be either. You can do this relationship…thing, you know you can. Okay, so the first time didn't go so great. Doesn't mean this next one will fail too.*

The internal pep talk did her good, bringing back a sense of calm. She walked into the kitchen, admiring yet again her gleaming new countertop, filled the kettle and switched it on. As she began pouring the steaming water into her mug, her door buzzer sounded.

Puzzled, she walked over to lift the handset for the intercom. "Hello?"

"Leelawati, this is your father." His voice was unmistakeable, and the sound of it sent a shockwave through Lena's body. The room actually swam before her eyes. She leaned against the nearest wall for support, and sucked in a huge lungful of much-needed oxygen.

"W-what?"

"Leelawati." Her mother's voice this time, strident and piercing even over the less-than-perfect intercom line. "Open the door."

Hands trembling, Lena replaced the handset and pressed the button that would release the main front door.

Like a condemned prisoner being led to their fate, Lena walked slowly down the narrow staircase to her own front door, unlocked it, then opened it. She waited, palms damp, as she heard the heavy tread of her parents' footsteps ascending ever nearer. She was trying to breathe evenly, but it was proving difficult. Why were they here? *How* had they managed to get here? Why was she shaking like a leaf?

Her father appeared first, her mother two steps behind him. They hadn't seemed to age much in the four years since she'd last seen them. Her father's hair maybe had a little more grey at the temples, but that was all. He was wearing one of his suits, perfectly tied tie, crisp white shirt. Her mother wore a sari, as always. This one was a deep blue with gold highlights. Over it she wore a thick navy-blue coat, and she was peeling a pair of woollen gloves off her hands as she ascended the stairs.

"Leelawati," her father said, tone solemn.

"Father." The word sounded strange, not only because her voice was slightly strangled, but because it had been so long since she'd actually been able to address him.

"Well?" Her mother's eyes were narrowed, her mouth set in a thin line that she opened only enough to force her words out. "Will we go in?"

"Um, yes, of course," Lena stuttered, stepping aside so that they could pass. She trembled as she closed the door behind her, watching the backs of her parents as they climbed the stairs to invade her home. Dimly, somewhere deep inside herself, she wanted to be angry at the intrusion, but for now, fear overrode everything. Fear of what they might say, and how it might be said. Fear of where their relationship would be once they had said it. Although, she rationalised as she followed them up the stairs, wherever they ended up after this visit probably couldn't be worse than where they were before her parents turned up on her doorstep.

"I-I was just making tea," Lena said. "Would you like some?" If nothing else, her mother had brought her up with impeccable manners, no matter the occasion. One never lost face by forgetting manners.

Her parents stood in the living area, their eyes taking in their surroundings, deep frowns marring both their faces.

"Yes," her mother said crisply.

"Where do we sit?" her father asked, looking perplexed.

Lena almost laughed, but knew it would be a mistake to let it out. "I only have those two cushions. Otherwise you will need to stand."

Her mother tutted loudly. "So," she said, "it is as bad as we thought. She cannot even afford furniture."

Lena's father shook his head. "Leelawati," he said, and never in her life had she heard her name expressed as such a disappointment. Her heart lurched.

"Wait, that's not true," Lena retorted. "I have only just moved back in. There was a storm. The roof came down, and I had to move out." She was talking quickly, determined to get her side of the story in before her mother had a chance to let loose any more sarcasm. "I have the insurance money now and I can replace the sofa very soon."

"And this is precisely why we are here," her father said, turning a stern gaze onto Lena. "When your sister told us that your flat had been destroyed and that you were homeless, we knew it was time."

Wait, what? *Madhu* had told them about the storm? What the—

"What do you mean, time?" Lena asked, folding her arms across her chest.

"Time to make you finally see sense!" her mother snapped. She walked closer to Lena, who barely resisted the urge to take a step back. "You have made bad choices in your life, Leelawati, and this is the price you are paying."

Now the anger started to come through, and it was like hot acid churning in her stomach. "What on Earth are you talking about?" She glared at her mother, who glared back. "I am—"

"Your life is a mess, Leelawati! You make that silly announcement about being a les...one of *those* women, you leave your home, where you were perfectly well looked after—" Lena snorted, and her mother's face scrunched even deeper into its frown "—and a perfectly good job at the council." Her voice rose in volume. "You had plenty of opportunities to meet the right man and make a proper life for yourself, a decent life. And now look at you," she said, gesticulating with her hands at the half-furnished room. "You cannot even offer your own parents a seat."

Her mouth pulled into a sneer. "You were homeless, begging off the favours of strangers, when you could easily have come home and given up all this...this *nonsense*. You have no...partner, and your job cannot be paying well if this tiny place is all you can afford to rent."

Each word stuck like a dart in Lena's mind and in her heart. She knew her mother was aiming to hurt, but that didn't lessen the pain. Lena wanted to refute her mother's wildly untrue statements, but as she gathered herself to respond, her father stepped forward.

"Leelawati," he said, somewhat gentler than her mother. "We only want what is best for you. We always have."

Lena did laugh this time. "Oh, Dad. No, you don't. You want what is best for *you*, what you think a daughter should be. You don't want me to be me, and *that* is what would be best for me."

Her mother gasped. "Always so selfish. Always." She glared at Lena. "How can you stand there, knowing what you have done? You have disgraced our name, brought shame on us for long enough."

Ah, now they came to the crux of it. Lena had wondered if that's where this was going. For one brief moment, in her mother's earlier tirade, she had dared to hope the rant came from genuine concern for Lena's wellbeing.

Now she knew the truth. There had clearly been talk, and if there was one thing Lena's mother wouldn't tolerate, it was being the subject of gossip. Oh, she could dish it out, definitely. But she hated being on the receiving end.

"You don't care about me at all," Lena said quietly. "This—" she waved a hand between herself and her mother "—is all about you and your position in our community, isn't it?"

"Leelawati, don't speak to your mother that way," her father interjected, but his stern words and tone couldn't scare her anymore.

"In my home I will speak to her any way I like," Lena snapped. She stared at the pair of them as they stared back. They looked at her as if she were an exotic animal in a zoo, a creature they had never seen before.

Her mother's eyes narrowed to hard flints. "This is your last chance, Leelawati. Come home, to where you belong, and save yourself. Regain some respectability. Get—"

"No." Lena announced the word, clearly and loudly.

"Leelawati," her father pleaded, for the first time looking genuinely concerned that his eldest daughter was slipping away from him.

"No, Father. I-I can't."

"Then we have wasted our time," her mother spat, and turned on her heel and headed for the stairs.

Lena's father gave her one last, beseeching look. Although it pained her to do so, she shook her head. His shoulders slumped, but he too turned away and followed his wife to the stairs. Lena walked slowly after her parents, a few steps behind. They let themselves out of her front door and stepped into the communal hallway.

Her mother turned back, one last time, and for the briefest of moments, so brief Lena almost thought she imagined it, her mother's hard expression dropped away, and her eyes reflected something...else. Pain? Love? Lena couldn't tell, but whatever it was, it wasn't anger. Then the moment passed, the wall came down, and the hardness was back with a vengeance.

"Good-bye." The word had a hard finality to it that wrenched at Lena's insides.

"Mum...please," she said, tears pricking at her eyes. Her mother turned her back and headed down the main staircase.

Lena turned to her father, who lingered at the top of the stairs. "Dad?" Tears streamed down Lena's face. The reality of her parents' departure was fully sinking in. This could well be the last time she ever saw them.

Her father's eyes were glistening. He raised one arm and made to reach for Lena, but then dropped it in the next moment as his wife issued an imperious, "Come!" from a few steps below.

He turned and lumbered down the steps to meet his wife at the bottom. Neither of her parents looked back up at her as they pulled open the main front door and left the building. The door closing behind them sounded awfully loud in the empty hallway.

CHAPTER 28

MEGAN PLACED A LATTE AND a scone in front of her mum.

"Oh, lovely," she said.

Megan put her own drink down and flopped into the armchair opposite her. They were in the Starbucks near where Megan worked. She was on an hour's break between clients and her mum had texted to say she was in town, shopping. Arranging this little meeting had taken no effort at all.

"So, what have you bought?" Megan asked, pointing at the three bags at her mum's feet.

She grinned and rattled off an impressive list of purchases—all for herself. "Your dad gave me some cash, told me to go get something new for the holiday next month." She beamed. "I was not going to say no to that."

Megan chuckled. "Definitely not." She sipped her cappuccino. "How's everyone?"

"Everyone is good," Rosie said, lifting her latte to her lips. "But worried about you," she offered after she took a sip of her drink.

"Worried? What about?" Megan was baffled.

"Well, no one's seen or heard from you since Christmas, pretty much. I mean, you and I have talked a couple of times, but even then..." She pursed her lips. "You've been different. Too quiet. Like there's something you're not telling me." Leaning forward, her face scrunching into a frown, her mum asked, "Megs, are you in some kind of trouble?"

"No! God, no, Mum. I'm not in trouble." Megan sat back. She thought she'd done a pretty good job of hiding all that had been going on with Lena so that she didn't have to face her mum's scrutiny, but it seemed in doing that she'd only acted in a way that freaked her out.

Maybe now was a good time to share, especially with Lena moving out that morning. It had given Megan an ache deep in her chest, waving good-bye to Lena, fighting the urge to kiss her because she didn't want to put any pressure on her. Knowing when she got home her place would be all her own again. And not liking that idea one bit.

She took a deep breath. "So, okay. There has been something going on. I didn't want to tell you before, until I knew how serious it was. And now, well, I guess it's serious. At least, I think it is."

"For crying out loud, Megs, spit it out!"

Megan blushed. "Sorry. Okay, well, here it is… I'm dating Lena."

Her mum's mouth dropped open.

Over the next half an hour, Megan told her mum everything. Some of it not in that much detail—this was her mum, after all—but enough for her mum to understand why Megan felt the way she did about Lena, and why she was now worried that Lena was going to disappear on her.

"Are you in love with her?" her mum asked bluntly, once Megan had finished her tale.

Megan nearly choked on her coffee. "Um, God. I don't know. Not quite. But I guess I could see me getting there sometime soon."

Her mum sat back, one finger rubbing slowly up and down her own chin, a clear sign she was deep in thought.

Megan let her be, knowing her mum was gathering what she wanted to say, and how to say it.

"She's a lovely woman," her mum said eventually.

"But…?" Megan prompted, knowing there was one there.

"But…I'm worried she's another Julie. And look where that got you." When Megan made to speak, her mum held up a hand. "I've listened to you talk about Lena and tell me how things have developed between you, and all I've heard is how hard you've worked to make something of this, and how little she has worked in return. I worry that you're repeating your old mistake, always giving, giving, giving, and not getting anything back."

Her mum leaned forward and placed a warm hand on Megan's knee. "You have a heart of gold, love, and that really shouldn't be something to criticise, but I'm scared you're being walked over, quite frankly."

Megan blinked a couple of times. "You think people walk over me? That I let them?" Her tone was harsher than she'd intended, but her mum's words had stung.

"Oh, Megs, love. I didn't mean to upset you. But, well, yes. Sometimes I do think you're too kind for your own good, and people take advantage of it. And, sometimes, you can't see that."

Honesty had always been the best policy in the Palmer household, for as long as Megan could remember. But this level of honesty was a little hard to take, even when she knew her mum meant well.

"Megan?" Her mum's voice held concern.

Megan waved a hand vaguely in the air. "I'm…okay. A bit hurt by what you said, but I guess I understand why you said it." She blew out a breath. "The thing is, even though I have worked hard with Lena, since Christmas it's really felt more even between us. And she's changed, so much—really come out of her shell. The more she does that, the easier it gets." She stared intently at her mum, trying by sheer willpower to get her to understand.

"Okay, but how long do you wait for her to catch you up? You say you're worried she'll retreat from you, now that she's moved out." She shrugged. "If she does, how long do you give her before you're the one doing all the work again? Before you're the one who has to walk away because she's not giving anything back?"

Megan slumped back in her chair. She didn't have any answers to those questions, and that niggled at her.

There was a small patch on the bedroom ceiling, just above the door to the small en-suite bathroom, where it looked like the builder's paint roller had scuffed. It wasn't a big patch, and it presumably only showed from a certain angle—like this one, lying flat on your back gazing around the room. But now that Lena had spotted it, she couldn't take her eyes off it, and it was annoying her.

Or, rather, she was annoyed already and the patch only made her annoyance run deeper.

Her parents had left an hour ago. When she had climbed back up into the living area of her empty flat, she had simply turned left into the bedroom and flopped onto the bed. Her energy was depleted, both physically and emotionally. Repeated snatches of her mother's diatribe rattled through her brain. As did images of her father looking so disappointed in her.

The words and pictures carved through her like knives, and although she tried to use her anger at their impromptu visit and harsh words to shield her, it was no good. Her defences were down, and the tears that fell from her eyes onto the duvet below took a while to ease.

Now all she had the energy for was to lie staring at her ceiling. She felt battered, and bruised, and...unsure. Her mother's vitriol was, on the one hand, just that—poison intended to hurt, which it had. But... She hated the way her brain kept going back to key words and phrases, and wondering if there was a kernel of truth in them.

She *had* been homeless and she *had* had to accept the comfort and help of relative strangers to get her a place to stay. If she hadn't left the bosom of her family, she would have had a much wider pool of resources to call on. But then, if she followed that line of thought back to its origin, she never would have needed them anyway, because she wouldn't be living in London and renting this tiny—she'd preferred to call it cute up until now—flat with a dodgy roof. And she wouldn't be living free, as herself, able to pursue a future that would make her truly happy.

While her mother had suggested she was partnerless, that bit wasn't entirely true either, was it? She and Megan hadn't given themselves a label, like girlfriends, or partners. But they'd been on a few dates, and they'd nearly slept together so they weren't exactly nothing to each other, were they?

She shook her head against the pillow. Damn her mother for planting all these seeds of doubt. Lena had already been feeling confused and fearful about everything, especially regarding Megan, with that dreadful attempt at sex the week before and Lena's own inability to shake that off and move on. She'd wanted to focus on the feelings that led to that intimacy and pursue those, even if she wasn't ready to be so intimate again. Now all she had careening around her head were even more questions and fears. She could do with talking to Madhu, but she was too mad at her for not warning Lena about letting out whatever she'd told their parents that had sent them down to London in the first place. She'd call her later, when she'd calmed down, and let Madhu tell her side of the story.

She managed a weak smile—it was bound to be a good one, knowing Madhu.

When Megan had first moved out of home, her mum had been adamant that she get a landline wherever she lived, with a proper answerphone, not simply a service.

"If your mobile runs out of battery, or you lose it, I want to know you can still get in contact with us. I also want to know I can leave a message for you and a little red light will tell you it's there," her mum had said, handing over the box containing the machine.

The same machine had been used everywhere Megan had lived since that time. She rarely had messages on it, in fact, as her family—her mum included—always used her mobile.

So when she walked into her flat a little after six in the evening—her *empty* flat, she noted with a sigh—the flashing red light on the answering machine was the first thing she noticed. She peeled off her coat and scarf, kicked off her sneakers, and walked across the room to where the machine sat on the TV stand.

She hit play and her eyes widened as the message boomed out into the room.

> *"Leelawati Shah, stop ignoring me! I know you said to only use this number in emergencies, but if this isn't one, I don't know what is. Call me. Please."*

Megan stared at the machine, trying to figure out who had called when the phone itself rang, loudly, nearly parting her from her skin as she jumped at least six inches in the air. Grabbing the handset, she managed to squeak a "hello" as she rubbed her chest, trying to calm her pounding heart.

"Lena?"

"No, this is Megan. Lena—"

"Is she there? Tell her I'm not hanging up until she speaks to me. She can't hide forever."

"Wait, is this Madhu?"

"Oh. Yes. Sorry, Megan." Madhu sounded sheepish and chuckled. "Sorry, is my sister there? I can't believe she won't return my calls."

"Um, Madhu, I'm guessing you haven't spoken to her since yesterday?"

"No, why?"

"She doesn't live here anymore." The words, said out loud, caused a strange jolt in Megan's stomach, and it was deeply unpleasant.

"What?" Madhu's voice went up an octave.

"She moved back to her own flat this morning. It was all a bit of a last-minute thing with the builders. I guess she didn't get a chance to tell you."

"No, she didn't. Oh, no, does that mean she had to deal with them on her own?"

"Who, the builders?"

"No, our parents!"

"What?" Megan's head hurt. This conversation was getting weirder by the minute.

"Oh, this is bad. This is *so* bad."

"Madhu," Megan said, with all the patience she could muster, which wasn't much, "what the hell are you talking about?"

Madhu groaned. "Ugh, this is a nightmare." She took a deep breath. "Okay, this morning my parents came around to see the baby, have breakfast and so on."

"Oh, yeah, how is the baby?"

"Fine, but seriously, Megan, focus."

"Sorry."

"So, they turned up way earlier than I was expecting. Sunaina hadn't slept well, I'd been up three times in the night to feed her or cuddle her, so I was knackered. Then my mother starts in on me, five minutes after she's walked in, criticising every way I'm raising my child already. Anyway, I'm still not really sure how it happened, but at some point she said something like 'I can't believe my only daughter already has her first child'."

"What the—?"

"Yeah, I know, right? Well, I blame the tiredness but I saw red, and the next thing I know, I'm going hard at her about how she's got *two* daughters, and if she would ever bother to be a real mother to Lena she'd know she's been through a really hard time lately and a bit of family love and support wouldn't have gone amiss, and on and on about the roof and living with you and all of it."

"Oh."

"Yes. The next thing I know, she's demanding Lena's address from me. Stupid, tired me gave it to her, thinking that Mum meant to write to her or something, you know? Then she stands up, grabs my dad's arm and says, 'We have to go to London and get her home before she makes complete fools out of us. Now'."

"Oh, shit." Megan ran her free hand through her hair. "So they turned up here today? To talk to Lena?"

"Yep. I tried to stop them, but when my mother gets started on one of her missions there isn't a person or army on earth that can stop her. I tried to phone Lena, but her mobile kept going to voicemail. So, I left a message hoping that would warn her, but she hasn't returned any of my calls."

"You…you don't think they hurt her, do you?" Megan's heart was racing again. If those people had laid one hand on—

"No, nothing like that. Well, not physically anyway." Madhu exhaled. "But trust me, my mother's words can hurt worse than a punch or kick. No, I'm worried they've messed with her fragile emotions. She…she told me how things were going with you two, but also how unsure and scared she was, even though she's so into you."

"S-she is?" The jolt that hit Megan's stomach this time was much more pleasant a sensation.

Madhu laughed softly. "Oh, yeah. She'll have been rubbish at telling you, but yeah, she is totally gone on you. And I'm worried my mother will have stormed in there, told Lena what a failure she is, and that will only have added more fuel to Lena's internal doubts." She paused, then said, "Do you like Lena as much as she likes you?"

"Yes, I do," Megan replied quietly. "I've… Well, I've been having trouble convincing her of some things. I was really worried when she rushed to move back to her place that she might start pulling away from me."

"Oh, she will, no doubt about that. But honestly, Megan, if you can keep trying with her, I think she'll finally think she's someone that someone else thinks is worth it. If that makes sense."

Megan chuckled. "Yeah, I got it." She huffed out a breath. "She's a little bit of hard work, though, you know."

Madhu guffawed. "Oh, yeah, tell me about it! But," she said, sobering quickly, "she's also an incredibly warm and sweet person under that rough exterior. She's had a few emotional setbacks the last few years, that have changed her a bit. But in the past few weeks I've seen the old Lena returning, and I think that's all down to you. So, if you can stick with her, please do. I haven't seen her this happy in ages."

Megan exhaled slowly. Madhu's words were a balm to the unsettled feelings she'd been having since that coffee break with her mum earlier. Hearing how much Lena had obviously talked about her with her sister also felt good.

"Okay," Madhu said, clearing her throat. "Back to the latest crisis. I'm guessing you haven't seen Lena today then? Or at least since my parents probably shocked the life out of her?"

"No, I'd only just got in when you called. I'd played your first message when you rang again. Hey, random question—who is Leelawati?"

"That's Lena's birth name," Madhu said, laughing. "She hates it, changed it to Lena when she was a teenager. Only Mum and Dad would never call her it, only me and her co-workers, because they didn't know any different. I always use her full name when I'm mad at her."

Megan laughed. "Yeah, I've got a few choice names for my brothers when needs be."

"Megan," Madhu asked, suddenly back to serious, "what are we going to do?"

"Want me to find her and try to talk to her? See how she is, see if I can get her to call you?"

"Please, if you wouldn't mind. That would be wonderful. I don't know what else to do. I can't come to London, not with the baby."

"No, I understand. Let me see what I can do first before we think about something that drastic, okay?"

"Thank you, Megan. You're amazing. Lena's a lucky woman."

Megan blushed.

CHAPTER 29

"LENA!" THE CALL OF HER name followed the rapid knocking on her front door. The voice was unmistakably Megan's, and Lena's insides turned to mush. And not in a good way. She wasn't ready to talk to her yet. Not while still feeling so raw from her parents' visit.

"Lena, if you're in there, please let me know you're okay at least."

More knocking, harder this time.

Lena knew she could simply stay still and make Megan think she wasn't home. But the guilt that flooded her had her cringing, then rolling over and sitting up. The bedroom was dark, the sun having set long ago. She tapped the touch lamp next to her bed onto its lowest setting, blinking as her eyes adjusted to the new light level.

"Lena!"

Inhaling a deep breath, Lena walked out of the bedroom and down the stairs. She inched open the door and saw Megan's face peering at her through the gap.

"Oh, thank God," Megan said. "We've been worried sick."

"Sorry," Lena whispered, chastised. It hadn't occurred to her that people would be looking for her. Wait, who was—?

"Who's we?" she asked, more bluntly than was probably wise in the circumstances, but the simmering anger at Madhu's actions hadn't taken much to resurface.

"Your sister. Me," Megan snapped back.

Lena recoiled. Megan had never talked to her like that.

Megan sighed and ran both hands through her hair. Lena watched them travel through the blonde strands and briefly wondered if she'd ever be able to push her own fingers through that hair again.

"Sorry, I didn't mean to jump down your throat. But, Lena, when we knew your parents had been here, well, of course we were worried. And—" she rushed on, before Lena could say anything in response "—Madhu's left you lots of messages and you haven't returned any. She was frantic."

"Oh." Messages? Actually, come to think of it, Lena hadn't seen her mobile all day. Oh, wait… She placed a hand over her eyes, not daring to look at Megan as she said, "I've just remembered, I left it on charge in your spare room this morning and forgot to bring it up here with me when I'd finished the move."

Megan let out a sound that was a mix of exasperation and humour. "Oh, Lena. That's the sort of stupid thing *I* would do."

Lena offered a wan smile.

"Are you really okay?" Megan asked softly, tilting her head.

Lena nodded, but she knew it wasn't convincing. "I-I will be." She stared at Megan. "So, wait, how have you spoken to Madhu?"

"She rang the landline just as I got home. She's so worried about what your parents said or did." Megan paused, her face softening further. "And so am I."

Lena closed her eyes briefly. She was tired, and emotional, and all she needed was some alone time.

"It wasn't fun, let's put it that way," she said. "I-I need to be by myself for a while. Think some things through."

"Lena, please don't think you have to do this alone," Megan pleaded. "I want to be here for you. To support you."

Megan's words made Lena tremble, but was it from desire or fear? She couldn't tell.

"I-I know you do. And that's…lovely to know. But I can't, not right now. Maybe tomorrow."

Megan stared at her, her eyes narrowed slightly. "Well. Okay. Um, I'll see you tomorrow then, yes?"

Lena nodded weakly. "Goodnight," she said, desperate now to close the door and hide, shed some more tears, and do a lot more thinking.

"Wait, let me get your phone!" Megan called through the diminishing opening between the door and the frame.

Lena halted the door's progress. "Oh, yes. Okay. Thank you."

Megan's footsteps retreated down the hallway to her flat, and a minute later she was back, passing Lena's phone and its charger through the gap.

"Call your sister," she said gently before she would let Lena take hold of the phone.

Lena met her gaze, and for one moment she wanted to throw herself into Megan's arms, shut the world away, and pretend that nothing else existed except the two of them, curled up together. She resisted that urge, but did lean up to kiss Megan briefly on the lips.

Taking the phone from Megan as she pulled back, she whispered, "I will," and closed the door.

Sunday morning was one of those gorgeous, sunny winter days, with a bright blue sky, no clouds, and a crispness that would nip at your nose if you ventured out into it.

Megan wasn't venturing anywhere. After a fairly sleepless night, she was up early making some scrambled eggs for breakfast. Something told her she needed the fortification, fuel for dealing with Lena today. Megan had woken up determined to make it clear to Lena that shutting her out of stuff like this was not what building a relationship was about.

She knew Lena had taken an emotional knock yesterday, and although she didn't want to push her too hard, she did want to get a few things clear between them. She hated that Lena had had to go through all the drama with her parents alone. But equally she hated the fact that Lena had spent the evening alone too, possibly talking herself back into her quiet, lonely life. Lena deserved so much more than that.

Megan had promised Madhu she wouldn't give up, but her own mother's words were also playing on her mind. How long did she try to convince Lena before she had to give her up as a lost cause?

One more time. She knew she had to try once more, or she'd always be asking herself "what if?". But then, maybe, if Lena didn't respond, that would be it.

Suitably fed, she glanced at the kitchen clock. A little after eight. Probably a bit too early, but she would now keep an ear out for sounds from above so that she could make her move.

She didn't have to wait long. Only fifteen minutes later, she heard the squeak of floorboards above her ceiling and took a deep breath before heading out to the hallway.

She knocked twice on the door, fairly hard.

"Megan?" Lena's voice came from behind the door a few moments later.

"Yes. Please, can I come in?"

Lena opened the door a crack, not much further than she had last night.

"Hi," she said. She looked tired; there were dark circles under her eyes, and her hair was a mess. It was worrying and adorable in equal measures.

"How are you? You look tired."

Lena shrugged. "I didn't sleep well." She tilted her head slightly. "You look tired too."

She seemed puzzled. Did it not occur to her that Megan would have had an equally bad night?

"Yes, I am. I didn't sleep well either." Maybe she *did* need to spell it out. "I was worried about you. About how you were feeling, how you were doing."

"Oh." Lena's eyes widened.

Megan breathed out an exasperated sigh. "Lena, can we please talk? Inside?"

Lena seemed to flinch slightly, and Megan cursed her own impatience. At the same time, exasperation at Lena's reticence heated her blood. Megan rarely lost her temper with people, rarely even raised her voice. But standing in front of Lena now, feeling that whatever they'd started to share was slipping away, was infuriating her beyond anything she'd ever known.

"Look, Lena," Megan said firmly. "I...care about you. A lot. I hate seeing you like this, and I want to be able to help you through this difficult time. However, I don't want to push you away, so I'm trying really hard to find the right balance here."

Lena stared up at her. "I-I'm not trying to be difficult, I promise. I'm so tired. This week has been hard for me, and yesterday was the final straw."

Clearly Lena wasn't going to let her into the flat, but equally she wasn't closing the door, so Megan pushed on.

"Okay, I get that. Maybe one day you'll tell me what they said, but know this, Lena." Megan pulled herself up straighter, and the words that came to her spilled out in a rush. "From all that Madhu told me last night, you must know that everything they said, every hurtful thing they threw at you, is shit, yes? Just utter shit. Please don't be swayed by what they said. You are a wonderful person, Lena, no matter what they said."

Tears welled in Lena's eyes, and she raised a hand to her face to wipe at them. "It's hard for me to believe that."

Her words were spoken so softly Megan almost didn't catch them. When she registered what Lena had said, her heart almost came to a stop. "Oh, Lena…" she breathed. "What can I do to help you get past this? To see how amazing you are?"

Lena blinked rapidly, and her hands were white-knuckled where they gripped the door. "I don't know," she said, shaking her head. "Please, can you leave me alone, for a while? I just need some time."

"How long do you need? How long do I wait, Lena?" Megan regretted it the moment the words burst out from her mouth.

Lena recoiled, her eyes wide.

"God, sorry," Megan said, trying to convey with her tone how deeply her regret went. "Lena, I'm so sorry. I don't mean to push you so hard, but I'm scared." That was surprisingly easy to admit. "I'm scared I'm going to lose you. I seem to be the only one fighting for this. For us. And I honestly don't know how much longer I should."

Lena reached out a hand, placing it on Megan's arm. It was a cool touch, but Megan relished it anyway.

"I'm sorry," Lena said quietly. "All I can say is, just give me some time." She stared at Megan for a few moments, then pushed the door closed.

Megan didn't stop her. She knew there was no point.

Lena didn't think she'd ever been so miserable in her life. And the worst of it was, it was mostly her own fault. She knew that, deep down, but she still couldn't seem to snap herself out of her downward spiral to do anything about it.

Megan.

She had pleaded, cajoled, almost threatened, and still something inside Lena held her back. Life was easier, wasn't it, when you were on your own? When another person's feelings and needs didn't have to be considered?

Despite how wonderful that person was, and how they made Lena feel. Despite how lonely being on your own could often feel.

She was sitting on the two floor cushions—Megan's cushions, she reminded herself, wallowing in even that small connection. She had her back wedged against the radiator under the window, her knees drawn up and her arms wrapped around them, making herself as small as she felt inside.

Everything her parents had said to her the day before had hit an enormous nerve. And even though Megan was right, that what they said was shit, all her worst insecurities about herself had come flooding back. She'd tried so hard, all morning, to focus on Megan's words instead, but they felt elusive, their true depth just out of reach.

She picked up her tea and took a sip. At some point she ought to think about putting something more than tea inside her, but the thought of getting up from her warm, cosy nest to make food was not appealing. She felt safe, down here on the floor, tucked into the corner, the warmth of the radiator infusing her body. Her phone buzzed beside her; another message from Madhu. Lena had texted her a while ago, checking in, telling Madhu she was okay but would call later.

Well at least you're ok. Don't leave it too long please. Worried xx

She read the message then tossed the phone back on the cushion beside her. Part of her brain acknowledged how good it felt to be cared about, by both her sister and her girlfr—Megan. But still, the biggest part of her was too tired to face up to it all. It was far easier to wallow, and hide away.

The knock on her door made her groan. Surely Megan wasn't going to try again? Yes, she understood Megan was worried but this was getting ridiculous. And she couldn't even pretend not to be here, because Megan would know she hadn't left her flat.

Tutting, she hauled herself up off the cushions and stomped down the stairs to the door. Flinging it open, she said, "Yes?" in her grumpiest tone possible, only to gasp as she realised it was Dorothy outside her flat, not Megan.

Dorothy arched one eyebrow, and glared down her nose at Lena over her glasses. "Good afternoon, Lena," she said, her tone dripping with sarcasm. "Am I disturbing you?"

"No." Lena shook her head vigorously. "Sorry. What can I do for you?"

"Well, there is something I require your help with, if you have a moment?"

"Of course." Given how rude Lena had been to her, she would agree to anything right now to avoid incurring the worst of Dorothy's wrath. "Down in your flat?"

Dorothy nodded.

"Is it a spider?"

"Not this time, no. But there is something that is concerning me."

Thinking that sounded rather cryptic, Lena could only nod, grab her keys, and follow Dorothy downstairs to her flat.

Dorothy led her through into her living room, which was a relatively small room at the front of her flat, overlooking the front garden. It contained a small, dark green fabric sofa, and a wooden coffee table, but what dominated the room was the organ with which Dorothy regularly tormented the other residents of number seven Jackson Road. It was only the second time Lena had been in the room, and she felt as if she were about to have an audience with the Queen when Dorothy gestured to the sofa and said, primly, "Please sit."

Lena did as she was told, perching on the edge of the sofa, staring as Dorothy slowly paced the floor before her.

"You had two visitors yesterday," Dorothy began, and Lena couldn't have been more shocked at that opening statement if Dorothy had announced she was the next woman in space.

"I... What?"

"They buzzed my flat first, clearly unsure which flat you lived in. When they explained who they were, I told them which buzzer to use. I knew you had moved back in yesterday, hence sending them to your own flat rather than Megan's."

"Oh. Okay." Where on Earth was this going?

"I should like to apologise."

Lena stared at Dorothy, who waited, presumably for Lena to say something. *Say something!*

"Um, thank you. But...what for?"

"I fear letting those...people into this house may have been a considerable error on my part, Lord forgive me." She closed her eyes momentarily.

Lena's mouth was open like a goldfish; she literally had no idea what to say.

Dorothy moved, suddenly, making Lena startle. In the next moment, her neighbour was perched alongside her on the sofa, hands wringing together in her lap.

"Lena, as you know, I believe in the words of the Lord. I also believe in the goodness in people, but I am also aware that some harbour ill feelings in their hearts." She cleared her throat. "Misguided feelings, borne of fear and ignorance. I have struggled with many of the teachings I was brought up to believe in. These past few years I have come to my own understanding with the Lord, and it works fine for both of us." She blinked a few times. "Some may disagree with me. That is their prerogative." She turned slightly on the sofa, and gazed at Lena. "Your parents caused you some hurt yesterday, yes?"

Lena nodded dumbly.

Dorothy sighed. "As I feared." She paused, and Lena felt no need to fill the silence of this surreal moment. "Do you not care for Megan?"

What the—?

"Dorothy, that's... Well, it's private." Lena's cheeks were flaming.

"Child, I heard most of your conversation this morning. Lord forgive me for eavesdropping, but I was on my way to church. I opened my door and I heard...what you were talking about."

Lena shook her head and made to stand. Helping Dorothy with spiders was one thing, but this was too personal. She couldn't begin to confide in Dorothy, of all people.

Dorothy's hand quickly shot out and held Lena's wrist. "Wait, child. Please." She gazed up at Lena, her deep brown eyes wide and guileless.

Lena sat down, unable to fight those eyes.

"Lena, fear is a part of life. It is how you face that fear that is the important lesson to learn. I, as you know, am scared of spiders. I could perhaps teach myself to deal with them, to...kill them, maybe, but never catch them. I could not do what you do, get that close."

She shuddered, and Lena felt it all the way through her body as she realised Dorothy still had a hold of her wrist.

"But I learned that it is easier to ask the help of someone who *can* do that," Dorothy continued. "I don't want to kill one of God's creatures, and nor, thankfully, do you. When I find one, I know that I do not have to remain in fear for long. I can rely on you to assist me, to remove the source of my fear."

She stared intensely at Lena. "There is no shame in finding someone to help you face your fears. To help you deal with them. Especially when that someone is more than willing to do so, because they care about you, and about your wellbeing."

Lena swallowed down a sudden lump in her throat.

"Megan cares for you, child," Dorothy said softly. "I have seen it first-hand. And I believe you care for her too. When there is that much care between two people, it seems to me it would be a shame to allow fear to stop that care before it can become...love."

She moved her fingers from Lena's wrist to hold her hand, gently. "Megan is a good person. A very good person. If you care for her as much as I think you do, let her help you. Let her love you."

The tears were warm on Lena's cheeks and salty on her lips as they tracked down her face.

"I'm so scared, Dorothy," she sniffled. "I like her, very much. More than like." She dipped her head and heard Dorothy's gentle chuckle.

"Is that so hard to admit?"

Lena looked up and smiled weakly. "To you, yes."

Dorothy laughed and squeezed Lena's hand again. "Then why don't you tell *her*, and let her care for you the way she wishes to?"

"Is it that simple?" Lena asked, bewildered. Could it be? Forget everything that had gone before and simply tell Megan how she felt, how much she wanted her, and wanted to be with her?

Dorothy nodded sagely. "Sometimes in life, Lena, yes, it is that simple. I have a spider, I knock on your door. You need Megan to love you, you knock on her door."

CHAPTER 30

MEGAN IDLY FLICKED THROUGH THE TV channels.

Old film. *Click.*

Rugby. *Click.*

Nature documentary. *Click.*

Even older film.

Nothing caught her attention for more than a nanosecond. Huffing out a breath she flicked the TV off and threw the remote onto the coffee table. The back snapped off in protest and the two batteries ejected themselves, lemming-like, and rolled onto the rug beneath.

Typical. She made to retrieve them but gave up before she'd moved more than an inch. *Fuck 'em.*

She closed her eyes and slouched back on the sofa, one foot on the floor, the other tapping against the sofa's arm rest farthest away from her body.

The day had been a total balls up. She should never have gone down to Lena's so early. She should have left Lena a decent amount of time to wake up, to pull her thoughts together. Instead Megan had blundered into Lena's Sunday morning like a bull in a china shop, and the carnage was just as spectacular. She'd heard Lena leaving her flat a while ago, presumably taking herself away, as far away as possible, from Megan and the pressure Megan put her under.

Stupid. Why, oh why, couldn't you have waited?

She knew why—because while Lena's fear made her retreat, Megan's made her want to grab tight onto what she thought was slipping away.

Briefly, she contemplated ringing Jen, or her mum, to talk through what had happened but with a grunt she realised if she did that, she'd probably get a whole load of "I told you so" from either or both of them. She couldn't face that. Not yet.

She sat up. This was pathetic. She couldn't throw a whole day away on this. Maybe she'd go out too. Take a walk, if nothing else. It was still a gorgeous day out there, with a good couple of hours' daylight left. With a start, she realised she'd been wallowing on the sofa for about three hours, with only trips to the bathroom and endless cups of tea to break the monotony. Her stomach rumbled, and suddenly food sounded like a cracking idea. Maybe a nice, fat, juicy burger from that place near the Tube station.

The knock on her door wasn't loud, but as the flat was silent she heard it anyway. Her stomach went into free fall. Every instinct she possessed told her Lena was on the other side of the door, even though her rational brain told her Lena was still out, as she hadn't heard her come back. Commanding her heart to slow its racing and her breathing to even out, Megan slowly stood up, straightened her clothes and her hair, and headed for the door, ready to meet her fate.

There was another gentle knock, just as she reached it. She pulled it open, and there Lena was, looking slightly puffy-eyed, one hand still raised at the end of her knocking action, the other twisting in the hem of her favourite Hogwarts hoodie. Her expression was a mix of fearful and... something else. Hopeful, maybe?

"Hi," Lena croaked.

"Hey," Megan said softly, determined not to blow this, whatever this moment was. However frustrated and out of control of things she had been feeling all day.

"I-I would like to talk to you," Lena said. She gestured to the flat behind Megan. "Could I come in?"

"Of course," Megan said quickly. "Please." She stepped aside and motioned Lena in, catching the scent of her shampoo as she passed; coconut and lime, one of the scents she hadn't realised she'd got so used to—and missed—until it was no longer part of her daily stimulation.

Closing the door behind her, Megan watched as Lena walked over to the sofa. When she reached it, she turned round and seemed surprised that Megan hadn't followed her.

"Can we?" Lena pointed to the sofa.

Megan sat down on the opposite end from Lena, giving her space. Her heart thudded as Lena shuffled nearer, close enough that their thighs were almost touching. She could feel the warmth emanating from Lena's body, and she ached to reach out, to pull her in. It took everything she had to wait, to see what Lena had to say.

"I'm sorry," Lena whispered, meeting Megan's gaze and smiling weakly. "I'm so sorry for taking myself away from you."

"It's—"

Lena held up a hand. "Don't say it's okay, because it really isn't." She sighed. "I was so wrapped up in my dark place, I couldn't see what it was doing to you or Madhu. I think I've spent so long protecting myself from other people who didn't care if they hurt me, I've completely forgotten how to actually behave around people who *do* care about me."

She slowly, achingly slowly, reached out a hand and placed it over one of Megan's. "And around people who I care about. Greatly," she whispered.

Megan couldn't breathe. Lena's words skidded around her brain for a few moments before she actually got hold of them and forced them to a stop so that she could take them in.

"Lena," she said on an exhalation. "You mean…?"

Lena smiled, tentatively. "If you'll have me back, yes. Please." She gripped Megan's hand tighter. "I'm not easy, I know that. I promise I will work on that. I promise I won't shut you out again."

She inched closer, and now their thighs were touching and the heat of that connection seared through Megan's body.

"I promise to be as much for you as you have been for me. As I hope you will continue to be. I know what we've shared is still something we're working out, but Megan, I really, *really* want it."

Megan smiled and reached out for Lena, inching her hands around Lena's waist.

Lena let out a tiny gasp, and her own hands found their way to Megan's thighs.

"Thank you," Megan said softly. "For saying all of that. I'm…I'm so glad you want this, that you want to make it work."

"I do," Lena said, gazing into Megan's eyes, her brown eyes wide and shining. "You don't have to fight for it on your own anymore. Believe me." She placed extra emphasis on the last two words, her tone beseeching.

The dark cloud that had followed Megan around all morning drifted away as if it had never had substance. She smiled and leaned in, because there was nothing else to say. Lena had said it all, and now they just needed to…be.

She placed a soft kiss on Lena's left cheek, then one on her right. A gentle one went on Lena's chin, and a small trail of them down her jaw to her neck, and back up again. Lena's breath hitched, and her hands gripped at Megan's thighs.

"Megan," she breathed.

Megan pulled back to look at her. "Okay? Should I stop—"

"Oh, no," Lena murmured. "Never stop."

And that was all Megan needed. She pressed forward, her lips meeting Lena's, trying to rein in her hunger but moaning as Lena's mouth opened up beneath hers. Lena's tongue pressed into Megan's mouth, Lena's own hunger sending a deep wave of arousal flushing through Megan's body. Megan pulled Lena as close as she could, wrapping her arms around her. Lena moaned into Megan's mouth at the contact, and her hands moved to Megan's hips, gripping at the waistband of Megan's sweatpants. When Lena's fingertips dipped inside the back of the pants and started to stroke the soft skin at the base of Megan's spine, she gasped, her arousal spiking, and twisted away from the kiss, panting.

"Lena, if you do that, I don't know what I'll do… God."

Lena smiled, her eyes bright. "Maybe I want you to…do," she whispered. Her teeth nibbled at her bottom lip, her nerves about saying something so bold clear to see. The throb that started between Megan's legs at that boldness sent heat pouring through her.

"Only if you're sure. We can take it slow, and—"

Lena pressed a finger against Megan's lips. "Slow, yes, but I am definitely sure." She pulled out of Megan's arms, took a deep breath, and reached for Megan's hand.

Megan smiled, her heart thudding. She allowed herself to be pulled up, and let Lena lead her to the bedroom. Lena seemed to want to control this, and Megan was only too happy to oblige.

The room was bathed in the gentle, late afternoon sun. Megan realised with some embarrassment that the bed was in total disarray from her fitful night but when she attempted to apologise, Lena simply smiled and stepped forwards, placing her hands on Megan's body, below her breasts. The heat from her hands was delicious, and images of that heat covering her breasts set off more throbbing between Megan's legs. Lena's thumbs moved in small circles against Megan's T-shirt as she gazed up at her, an enigmatic smile on her face.

"Somehow," she murmured, "you seem more nervous than me."

Megan exhaled and chuckled. "Yeah, I am. I don't want to mess this up."

Lena raised one hand to cup Megan's cheek. "You won't," she said. "Trust me."

She raised up on her toes and kissed Megan, greedily, devouring Megan's mouth and turning her knees to jelly.

Megan crushed Lena to her, running her hands up Lena's spine and back down to the curves of her ass. Every sweep over those curves elicited a soft moan from Lena, and even hungrier kisses. Then, deliciously, Lena's hands crept inside Megan's T-shirt, first roaming over her back, then boldly moving round to her abdomen, and up, and oh *God*, Lena's hands cupped Megan's breasts through the soft fabric of her sports bra, and Megan gasped against Lena's mouth.

This was intoxicating. The unexpected boldness, the complete turn-around of events between them in these past few hours, all of it added up to a heady mix. Megan was floating on a cloud of desire and delight, Lena's gentle yet firm ministrations on her breasts making her nipples ache for more direct attention—as well as other parts of her body.

Lena's mouth was hot against Megan's neck and throat, her hands now strong against Megan's breasts, her fingertips pulling at Megan's nipples through the cloth.

"I want to touch you," Lena said, tipping her head back to meet Megan's gaze. Lena's face was flushed, her eyes dark, her breathing ragged. "Can we—?" She moved her hands to pull at Megan's T-shirt.

"Oh, yeah." Megan grabbed the hem of her shirt, yanking it over her head at lightning speed. Her sports bra followed moments later, and she heard Lena's appreciative moan as her breasts were revealed. Lena lunged forward, taking a nipple between her lips and sucking gently, then using her teeth to tease it into rock hardness.

Megan gasped, gazing down at the beautiful woman who was working such magic with her mouth.

This new Lena, the bold, take charge one, was *hot*.

Lena's hands moved to the waistband of Megan's sweatpants and tugged them downwards. Megan stumbled slightly as she tried to extricate her feet from them and quickly looked up to make sure Lena wasn't struggling with the clumsiness of the moment. The smile that Lena sent her way caused Megan's heart to jump in her chest. Lena's hands gently gripped Megan's hips.

"Here," she said. "In case you fall."

At that moment, Megan knew they were going to be okay. Whatever demons had tortured Lena these past few days appeared to have been banished. A fresh wave of warmth for this woman washed over Megan, and she smiled widely.

"Thanks. We know how clumsy I can be." She grinned, and Lena laughed before giving Megan a gentle push in the middle of her chest. It wasn't strong enough to topple Megan but she did it anyway, knowing that was how playfully Lena had intended the move. She allowed herself to fall back on the bed, arms wide, legs slightly parted. She ached as Lena's gaze raked over her naked body.

"You're gorgeous," Lena whispered.

"You are," Megan replied. She motioned with her hands. "Please, can I see you? You are so beautiful, I can't wait to look at you again."

Lena blushed, but she also didn't hesitate. Her hands moved to her sweatshirt, hauling it over her head and dropping it to the floor beside her. Her plain white cotton bra was slowly unsnapped from behind and shyly passed down her arms to join the sweatshirt. Her breasts looked amazing in the soft light; round and heavy, her nipples already tight buds that made Megan's mouth water.

"Oh, God," Megan managed to squeeze out through her tightened throat. She wanted this woman so badly.

Lena smiled, her blush fading, and reached for her pyjama bottoms. As she slowly pushed them downwards, Megan's breath caught in her throat; Lena wasn't wearing any underwear either, and the trimmed patch of dark hair between her legs was already glistening with evidence of how turned on Lena was right now. Megan licked her lips involuntarily and startled as the action drew a long groan from the naked Lena.

"Come here," Megan said, opening her arms, and Lena moved instantly, pressing her entire length against Megan. The touch made her shiver, everywhere. Eagerly she sought Lena's mouth; Lena mirrored the action in the same moment, and their teeth clashed noisily.

Instead of pulling away, as she might have done the week before, Lena giggled and simply readjusted the position of her mouth.

Megan smiled against her lips, happiness welling up from deep within. Then she gasped as Lena's hands went on the move.

First, they swept up to Megan's breasts again—squeezing, pinching, pulling. Every touch made Megan wetter, made her breathing quicken, and ripped moan after moan from her throat. Those same hands moved down, over Megan's torso, caressing her thighs, one hand then dipping between Megan's legs and dragging slowly, *so* slowly through the wetness it found there.

Megan arched up against Lena, moaning her name, and Lena repeated the gesture. With each brush of her fingers against Megan's clit, Megan pressed her head even further back into the bed, her hands clutching at Lena's back.

"Lena, please," she begged, her body on fire.

Lena obliged without hesitation. She slipped one finger inside Megan, slow but deep, and Megan's eyes rolled back in her head at the exquisite sensation of Lena pressing into her.

"Yes," she breathed, and writhed in Lena's arms as Lena began a perfect rhythm, long, slow strokes that filled Megan just the way she liked it.

Lena kissed her throat, then her lips. Megan tried hard to maintain the kiss but Lena's palm was now pressing on her clit with every thrust she made inside Megan, and she had to tear her mouth away to breathe, and groan, and gasp.

"Look at me," Lena said, her voice strained. "Megan, please look at me."

With the greatest of difficulty, Megan forced her eyes open and found Lena gazing down at her, her hand never once stopping its rhythm.

"I want this," Lena breathed. "I want you."

"Oh, *God*. Lena." Megan stared into Lena's eyes, the deep brown depths of them, and something let loose in her. Moments later, her climax thundered through her. Her hips rose up off the bed, her hands clutching at Lena's shoulders.

"Oh, yes," Lena hissed, pressing even deeper. "So beautiful, Megan. *So* beautiful."

There were tears in Lena's eyes, but she was smiling and Megan understood. Lena slowed her hand's movement, bringing Megan gently down as she relaxed her body back into the bed.

"Lena," Megan said, her eyes wide in wonder. "That was…incredible."

Lena nodded and placed gentle kisses in a random pattern over Megan's face and neck. She shifted position slightly, and searing-hot wetness scalded Megan's thigh.

"Oh, Lena," Megan whispered. "You are so wet."

Lena nodded, her cheeks only pinking slightly. "That's you," she said softly. "What you do to me."

"Well, in that case," Megan said, smirking, "I think it's only fair I do something about that, don't you?"

Lena laughed, then gasped as Megan ran her hands down Lena's back and dipped boldly into that pool of delicious wetness with the fingertips of both hands. She gently stroked back and forth, as far as she could reach, loving the noises Lena made as she did so.

"I think you should lay down," she whispered, gently nudging Lena to one side. "And let me touch you."

Lena gazed at her and nodded before rolling carefully off Megan and laying on her back beside her. Her hands twitched at the sheets, but she held Megan's gaze as Megan leaned up on one arm and looked down at her.

"You are so gorgeous," Megan said, letting one finger trace a meandering pathway down between Lena's breasts, then over to one nipple, where she let it play back and forth over the top of the hardened peak.

"Oh," was all Lena seemed to be able to manage, and Megan smiled.

Then, unable to resist any longer, she dipped her head and wrapped her lips around that nipple. It felt glorious, hard and responsive under her lips. She cupped the breast with both hands, revelling in the abundance of flesh for her to hold, to press, to knead. Lena came alive under her, her body moving restlessly, her fingers loosening their hold on the sheets to reach up and touch whatever part of Megan she could find.

Megan moved, carefully swinging one leg at a time over Lena to place herself between Lena's thighs. She kissed her way down Lena's warm, soft body, over her rounded belly, until her nose rubbed into the damp hair between Lena's legs.

She lifted her head. "Can I?" she asked up the landscape of Lena's body.

Lena met her gaze and nodded once, groaning as she did so. Megan couldn't wait; she opened her mouth and let her tongue travel a slow path through Lena's wetness. Lena's tortured groan was all the encouragement she needed, and she feasted.

She licked, and tasted, and held Lena's thighs tight as Lena's orgasm crashed over her, her breathy cries loud in the quiet room.

"Please," Lena gasped, "come here." She tugged gently on Megan's hair, who placed one last kiss on Lena's centre before crawling up the bed to press her body flush against Lena's. Lena held her close, kissing her shoulders, her neck, her face. Finally, she gazed up at Megan, her smile lighting up her entire face. "That was…amazing. *You* are amazing."

Megan shook her head. "Nope. That's you. I don't know what happened today, but I am so glad it did."

Lena chuckled, and closed her eyes momentarily. "Dorothy happened," she said, and snorted as Megan gaped at her.

"W-what?"

Lena pulled Megan close. "I'll tell you about it tomorrow." She kissed Megan slowly, lingeringly. "Right now, I want to do some more of this," she whispered, kissing Megan deeply again.

When she could finally breathe, Megan stared down at the woman in her arms. "Whatever you say. Kiss me like that and you can have anything you want."

Lena raised her eyebrows and smiled mischievously. "Anything?" she asked, almost purring.

"Oh, yeah," Megan said, and groaned as Lena's lips found hers again, kissing her senseless.

CHAPTER 31

"LENA. LENA!"

Lena could hear her name being called, but there was no way she wanted to leave the warm, snuggly place she was buried in. It was peaceful in here, and safe, and she felt marvellous.

"Lena, we overslept. It's nine o'clock!"

Lena's eyes finally opened, against her will, to find a concerned-looking Megan staring down at her. Lena's mind caught up with events and her thoughts spun through the situation—it was Monday morning, so she was already supposed to be at work by now. Okay, that could be a problem. However, it wasn't month end, and if her hazy memory served her correctly, her calendar wasn't exactly full of meetings for the day ahead. So, here she was, wrapped up with Megan after a wonderful night of getting to know each other physically, and she should be panicking about the late hour. Yet, somehow, she wasn't.

She had a twinge of anxiety about calling her manager to say she would be late or—the thought came to her unbidden—maybe she wouldn't even go in at all. She smiled. Was she, Lena Shah, seriously contemplating playing truant from her job for a day? She'd never done that in her life. Even when she'd been job hunting in London she'd only ever taken a couple of hours off work from the council at the end of a day, feigning a doctor's appointment. And each time she'd done it her stomach had been tied in knots for hours.

The thought of doing it now excited her rather than stressed her, and her smile widened.

"Really?" she asked, wriggling under the duvet, acutely aware of Megan's naked body pressed against hers and revelling in the multiple sensations that body elicited in her own. She gazed up into the pale blue of Megan's eyes, smiling at the panic they contained. "What shift are you working today?"

Megan stared at her, mouth agape. "Er, start at, um, noon," she stuttered.

"Well." Lena reached for Megan, pulling her even closer. "Why don't you come here and kiss me good morning, then I will have a think about what excuse I will use to call in sick."

Her confident tone stunned even herself, and she laughed as Megan snorted and shook her head.

"Okay, who are you and what have you done with my girlfriend?"

Lena laughed louder, then sobered and stared deeply into Megan's eyes. "Megan, right now, the last thing I care about is my job." She stroked a fingertip down Megan's cheek. "Right now, this is the most important thing to me, and I want to stay right here, wrapped up in you this morning. I will tell work I suddenly had to move back into my place, which is not a complete lie. They'll be okay, I've done lots of overtime recently."

The justifications came surprisingly easy, and the release she found from letting go of even one day of work and routine and commitment was overwhelming.

Megan nodded slowly. "Yeah, I suppose that's true." She paused, and a gentle blush covered her cheeks. "This is the most important thing to you right now?"

Lena smiled and pecked a brief kiss on Megan's lips. "Yes. Absolutely. Let's just say, thanks to Dorothy, I had an epiphany yesterday. And this—" she said quietly, as she motioned between them, their naked bodies wrapped up under Megan's duvet "—is the result."

Megan chuckled. "Okay, so I am now officially a fan of epiphanies."

"Good." Lena kissed her again. "Now, I hate to be practical, but I do need to go to the bathroom and phone the office. But then," she said, daring to run her tongue up the length of Megan's neck, "I am all yours."

"Oh. My. God." Megan groaned and flopped back on the bed. "I think you might actually kill me."

Lena laughed and couldn't remember if she'd ever laughed so freely, naked in bed with someone. She crawled out from under the covers, ignoring Megan's protests and playfully slapping her hands away as they quested after Lena's skin.

The flat was cold, but Lena didn't bother with a robe or even a T-shirt. She walked stark naked across the living area and into the bathroom. As she washed her hands afterwards, she smiled at herself in the mirror above the sink. She looked…sated. Glowing.

Happy.

It felt amazing.

"Hurry up!" Megan's shouted words made her snort with laughter.

"All right," she called as she exited the bathroom. "Are you always this impatient?"

"You bet!"

She called the office, and not surprisingly her manager was absolutely fine about her absence. They moved one meeting, and Lena agreed to dial in to another in the afternoon, but otherwise her manager expressed happiness in Lena's news that she'd got her flat back and signed off with a cheery "see you tomorrow".

Lena took a deep breath and checked in with herself. While telling the little white lie to her manager had caused her some discomfort, she could acknowledge that in the grand scheme of things, it wasn't the end of the world. Then she looked down at her naked body and took a moment to remember Megan's worship of her the night before.

Megan had made her feel wanted in ways she'd only dreamed of. For someone who didn't think she was very good at expressing her feelings verbally, Megan had outdone herself during the night. Words like beautiful, and sexy, and gorgeous, had been showered on Lena until she glowed from them alone, regardless of how Megan touched her. And oh, how Megan had touched her…

Tingling with the memories, and keen to repeat them, Lena strolled back into the bedroom, comfortable in her nudity, especially under the extremely attentive gaze of her girlfriend. Megan's gaze roamed her body, and she shifted slightly in the bed as Lena approached.

Girlfriend. That had such a good ring to it. It was a label she was happy to repeat on a loop in her brain as she crawled back into the bed to greet Megan with a deep kiss. This, she knew, was the start of something that could last.

Megan had never once tried to change Lena; she had accepted Lena for who she was, with all her quirks and foibles. Instead, she had quietly, without judgment, seen in Lena the scared person that simply needed some encouragement to let go, and open up, and...be.

In return, Lena accepted she had offered less, so far, in their fledgling relationship, but at the same time she also knew that what she had offered, Megan had wanted and been grateful for. Care without smothering. Time spent together without being joined at the hip. Things that Julie had done to Megan and which would never have occurred to Lena to inflict on a partner.

So far, they had given each other exactly what they needed, with—she admitted wryly—a few bumps in the road along the way. She knew they may not have seen the last of those, but everything that had happened the last two days had taught Lena many things. Not least of which was how much she wanted—no, *needed*—Megan in her life.

She gazed down at Megan, holding her girlfriend's amorous hands at bay for a moment. "If I haven't said it before," she started, nervous but excited about what she was about to say, "you are very special to me, Megan."

Megan seemed to melt at her words. For all her apparent confidence, her sheer physical presence, she appeared to possess about the same level of self-doubt as Lena did. It was something Lena needed to remember—that they were virtually equal in this, in their own ways. They both had issues with how others perceived them, and they both had tender sore spots over past relationships. One night of incredible sex didn't fix all of that, but it certainly had been a rather lovely start.

"And you are to me," Megan whispered in reply. "I'm so happy right now, so excited about what we have."

"Mm," Lena murmured, nuzzling into Megan's soft neck, an area that was rapidly becoming one of her favourite places. "Me too."

"Lena." Megan's voice was tight.

"Yes?"

"Touch me. *Please.*"

"Anything you want." Lena smiled against her girlfriend's warm, soft skin. She shifted so that she could lay on top of Megan, and the bunched sheets twisted around her knees. "But first, I need to do something about these sheets. It will only take a minute."

Megan laughed.

ABOUT A.L. BROOKS

A.L. Brooks currently resides in London, although over the years she has lived in places as far afield as Aberdeen and Australia. She works 9–5 in corporate financial systems and spends many a lunchtime in the gym attempting to achieve some semblance of those firm abs she likes to write about so much. And then promptly negates all that with a couple of glasses of red wine and half a slab of dark chocolate in the evenings. When not writing she likes doing a bit of Latin dancing, cooking, travelling both at home and abroad, reading lots of other writers' lesfic, and listening to mellow jazz.

CONNECT WITH A.L. BROOKS
Website: www.albrookswriter.com
Facebook: www.facebook.com/albrookswriter
E-Mail: albrookswriter@gmail.com

OTHER BOOKS FROM
YLVA PUBLISHING

www.ylva-publishing.com

MILES APART

A.L. Brooks

ISBN: 978-3-95533-866-4
Length: 240 pages (85,000 words)

Which mistakes are irredeemable? Would you fight to save a five-year relationship after your lover has had a drunken one-night stand? Alex is torn by this question. Then, on a business trip to Canada, she discovers she's drawn to another woman, shattering everything she thought she knew about herself. A lesbian romance that asks the interesting questions, not the easy ones.

JUST MY LUCK

Andrea Bramhall

ISBN: 978-3-95533-702-5
Length: 306 pages (80,500 words)

Genna Collins works a dead end job, loves her family, her girlfriend, and her friends. When she wins the biggest Euromillions jackpot on record, everything changes...and not always for the best. What if money really can't buy you happiness?

A WORK IN PROGRESS
L.T. Smith

ISBN: 978-3-95533-850-3
Length: 121 pages (37,000 words)

Writer Brynn Morgan has been in love with her best friend and muse, Gillian Parker forever. She's the only one who can fill the emptiness in Brynn's life, ease the ache in her chest, and get her writing juices flowing again. The problem is Gillian is straight. And she's more focused on enlisting Brynn to see whether her doctor fiancé is a cheat. No matter what Brynn turns up, what should she tell Gillian?

This UK rom-com, part of the Window Shopping Collection, proves that the path to true love has more than a few bumps in it.

WHO'D HAVE THOUGHT
G Benson

ISBN: 978-3-95533-874-9
Length: 339 pages (122,000 words)

When Hayden Pérez stumbles across an offer to marry Samantha Thomson—a cold, rude, and complicated neurosurgeon—for $200,000, what's a cash-strapped ER nurse to do? Sure, Hayden has to convince everyone around them they're madly in love, but it's only for a year, right? What could possibly go wrong?

Up on the Roof
© 2018 by A.L. Brooks

ISBN: 978-3-95533-988-3

Also available as e-book.

Published by Ylva Publishing, legal entity of Ylva Verlag, e.Kfr.

Ylva Verlag, e.Kfr.
Owner: Astrid Ohletz
Am Kirschgarten 2
65830 Kriftel
Germany

www.ylva-publishing.com

First edition: 2018

Credits
Edited by Lee Winter and Amanda Jean
Proofread by Paulette Callen
Cover Design and Print Layout by Streetlight Graphics